BLACK SEA TWILIGHT

Also by Domnica Radulescu

Train to Trieste

Black Sea Twilight

Domnica Radulescu

For Peggy,
Hoping you'll enjoy the twilight.
Domnica Radulescu
04-15-2010

Doubleday

LONDON • TORONTO • SYDNEY • AUCKLAND • JOHANNESBURG

TRANSWORLD PUBLISHERS
61–63 Uxbridge Road, London W5 5SA
A Random House Group Company
www.rbooks.co.uk

First published in Great Britain
in 2010 by Doubleday
an imprint of Transworld Publishers

A CIP catalogue record for this book is available from the British Library.

ISBN 9780385614283

Addresses for Random House Group Ltd companies outside the UK can be found at: www.randomhouse.co.uk
The Random House Group Ltd Reg. No. 954009

The Random House Group Limited supports the Forest Stewardship Council (FSC), the leading international forest-certification organization. All our titles that are printed on Greenpeace-approved FSC-certified paper carry the FSC logo. Our paper procurement policy can be found at www.rbooks.co.uk/environment

Typeset in 11/15pt New Baskerville by
Kestrel Data, Exeter, Devon.

Printed and bound in Great Britain by
Clays Ltd, Bungay, Suffolk.

2 4 6 8 10 9 7 5 3 1

For all women artists, known and unknown.

'I hope the exit is joyous and I
hope never to return.'

Frida Kahlo

How I Painted My First Fish

'Jump, Nora! Jump!'

'No, Gigi, I won't. Never!'

The sea is a blue mirror sprinkled with millions of diamonds in the morning sun as he pushes me and I fly through the air. I cut through the liquid silver mercilessly and with precision. Like a blade. I go deep, past glossy fish, translucent jellyfish twirling in their tutus, confused crabs and green, slimy algae, keeping my eyes open to see everything and to see him come down to meet me. He appears right in front of me, his reddish curls sticking up in the current, his eyes bulging at me in the water, his cheeks swollen from holding the air in. I must look just as funny. He wraps his arms around me and we go up, up, holding our breath one more second, then gulp for air, screaming and splashing in the blue-green water.

'Ninety seconds,' he says. 'Better than yesterday!'

I have known Gigi for as long as I have known myself. We do this almost every day in the summer, learning how to hold our breath longer and how to become stronger under water. Only the days of bad storms, when his father's boat is docked, keep us from the sea. I hate diving, but I love swimming under water and watching the green insides of the sea. Gigi has to push me, as that's the only way to get me to jump. We pretend we are having a fight, and then he asks me to dive. I say no and he pushes me, but he always comes down after me the next second. It's a special ritual we have created over the years, a little drama to make us feel adventurous.

In the dining room at our house there's a lacquered cupboard where my mother keeps all our family portraits, from our dead ancestors to the youngest members. Here I am in this photograph with a white face and dark long plaits down my back. No, correction! That's how I imagine myself sometimes, based on a reproduction of a mosaic I saw of Dido, Queen and founder of Carthage. In reality, I have a round swarthy face, curly brown hair like the people on my mother's side and green eyes like no one else in my family. Gigi says they are the colour of the sea, that exact hue of green, like the seawater deep down. When I spend time with Gigi at the beach in the summer, the way we have done summer after summer since the age of six, I forget about my imperfection. My mother calls it 'unevenness', though once she called me a cripple, which made my father furious. When my father's sister, Tudoriţa, married Doru, the architect whose right arm had been cut off in a railway accident when he was fourteen, my mother said: 'That's all we needed in our family: another cripple.' I was only ten then, and my father was furious because he knew she meant the other 'cripple' was me; he picked me up, swung me in the air and yelled at my mother: 'She is no cripple, woman, she is the star of all stars! Don't you ever dare call her that!' She never did, though she still mentions my 'unevenness' once in a while, as if somehow my birth defect was my own fault or some punishment I deserved.

My family is noisy, turbulent and violent. It is unpredictable and tormented, and I often wish to escape it. We blame it on the Communists and on 'all the tragedies our people have suffered' but I think we would be the same even if we lived under the Sun King. We have secrets and relatives that we talk about only in whispers. Like my twin brother Valentin, who doesn't live with us in Mangalia but with my mother's sister Raluca, in Bucharest, because he is some kind of piano prodigy and needs to be in the capital to get proper piano tuition. Raluca wanted very much to bring up Valentin because of the tragedy she had suffered, and she kept pushing my parents to let him live with her in Bucharest. First it was for a few months, then the few months became years, and soon enough it was the eighties and we both turned fifteen. I have only seen my brother a total of five times since we were very little: the times he and Aunt Raluca came to the seaside for the summer holidays. And because my mother never got used to Valentin living away from her and she resents her sister for 'stealing' her son, she always mentions his name in a whisper, as if he were a saint whose name we should not take in vain and use any time and in any way we felt like.

Gigi, who is already sixteen, has dreams of becoming a naval officer and a captain like his father, Luca. He imagines himself sailing our seas on his father's cargo ship and transporting iron ore from port to port. Nobody knows where iron ore is shipped from and to, but our city of Mangalia is proud to be Romania's largest naval base and Gigi is proud of his father's prominent role in the port. During the short breaks from working on the cargo ship, Luca usually takes a small fishing boat out to sea in the middle of the day, letting us dive and swim under water while he throws out the big fishing nets to catch carp and sturgeon and very small fish called *guvizi* and *hamsii*. As they are Turkish, Gigi and his family live in the area behind the Post Office, where the little stucco houses with vegetable gardens, small vineyards and red beaten earth stretch out like a different kind of town. Once in a while Gigi and his family go to the service in the mosque on Fridays, but he says it's no big deal. What makes them Turkish, he says, is the food they eat and the language he speaks at home, mostly with his father. My mother, on the other hand, makes a big deal about us being Christians, though we hardly ever go to the Orthodox church in town, except for Christmas, Easter and a wedding or funeral. She refers to all the people of Turkish origin in town simply as 'the Turks', and Gigi as 'the Turk', hardly ever calling him by his real name.

My father says it doesn't matter what religion or God the people in our town believe in because in our country Marx and Lenin and President Ceauşescu are the only gods. We might as well be governed by the Huns or the Visigoths. My mother gets furious and tells him to shut up and not just blurt out whatever silly stuff comes into his head. She is angry for three reasons: first because he blasphemes, second because he could get into trouble if he makes fun of our president and the Marxist leaders, and third because she is always angry.

My mother is afraid that someone in our family will be arrested and killed. Her father disappeared soon after the war, when the new Communist leaders in Romania were 'weeding out' dangerous influences. He had laughed out loud in a town meeting when one of the new Comrades said that everybody would have to give up their property for the common good, and my grandfather said: 'That'll be the day!' He resisted the nationalization of his property with fierce determination. He kept a loaded gun in his study and used to say he would fire at anyone who tried to take away his land. That's what my mother tells us. But he never got to use his gun because they took him away while he was having dinner one night with the family. My mother is always agitated at dinnertime because she remembers how they took her father away. She was only ten. She is also sad because she misses my brother most at dinnertime, when 'we should all be together, not spread all over the country'. She usually eats her supper by herself after we have all finished, and she stares at the weeping willow in front of our kitchen window. Sometimes she gets annoyed at the willow for being so sad and weepy and says she will cut it down one of these days.

Before I could even talk I scribbled and drew and painted on all the white surfaces around me. I couldn't stand plain white surfaces. I want to be a painter more than anything and to fill white surfaces with my own ideas. Gigi says if I'm serious about my art I'll have to study at the art school in Bucharest after high school. But I don't know about that. Our city, Mangalia, is older than Bucharest and was founded by the Ancient Greeks. They gave the sea the name it has today: *Pontus Euxinus*, the Black Sea. They left two stone columns on the beach as marks of their passage. The Greek stone columns are the only white surfaces I respect and that I have never scribbled on. The idea of living away from the seashore doesn't seem terribly appealing to me. I don't know where I would find all my ideas for paintings.

The Romanian painters of the Balchik school in the days of Queen Marie came to the sea in the twenties and thirties in order to soak up the light and the blues of these shores and then spill all that back in oils and watercolours. In the living room, above the cupboard with the pictures of our family, we have a painting by one of the Balchik artists: a corner of the shore, a golden beach shaped like a horseshoe, a bluish-mauve splash of water and sky, white and yellowish houses layered on a green hilly area. Romanians including my father whisper nostalgically about that inter-war period and that part of our shoreline, while in the same breath they curse the Bulgarians who 'stole it from us' and the Russians who facilitated the 'theft'. I care about the blues and yellows in the painting much more than about the politics and I try to imagine the delicate cameo-like Queen Marie in one of her lacy dresses walking along the horseshoe beach flooded in light. She wanted her heart to be buried in Balchik when she died and indeed it was placed in the Stella Maris or Star of the Sea Chapel in a castle in her beloved holiday town. In 1940 it was moved to a castle in Northern Transylvania. People say that in the sixties the Communists broke its case with a crowbar and stole the heart from the Transylvanian castle that is said to have also belonged to Count Dracula. Nobody knows where the heart of Queen Marie of Romania is now. I imagine it in a golden box inside one of the ochre-coloured houses in our painting of the Balchik shore.

On some days I imagine people as fish. Today I dreamed of my brother like a fish dressed in a tuxedo and with his tiny, sad face the way it was on the day he and Aunt Raluca took the train back to Bucharest many summers ago: his face was stuck to the carriage window and his lips were glued to the glass like the mouth of a fish inside a fishbowl. He was crying and waving at me from inside the compartment. I thought of a painting of just one rainbow-coloured fish with human eyes and long eyelashes like a girl, rocking in a lacy cradle in the middle of the emerald sea, surrounded by orange corals, algae and shells.

I draw only geometrical flowers and shells, because that's what we did in school for a whole year in art class. Then the following year, when we moved to a higher class, we had to draw our leader, Nicolae Ceaușescu, from a model the teacher gave us. She said he should be our highest inspiration. Or the map of our country with the leader in the centre, like the heart of our country. *Like our leader was the beating heart of our country*, the teacher repeated. I didn't want to draw the leader or the map of our country, so I drew lots of geometrical coloured flowers and said I drew them in honour of the leader, because I wasn't yet good enough to attempt to draw the leader. My father laughed so hard when I told him that, and said I was cunning like a ferret. My mother said we would all get in trouble one day if we joked about things like that.

I want to make my first real painting today on the beach at dusk. I go first to Gigi's house on the other side of town. I want to tell him that tonight I will finally paint the images in my head. I take short cuts I know through people's gardens, stop to pick green grapes from the miniature vineyards in that part of town, and a handful of plums from somebody else's tiny orchard. Marița, the Gypsy woman who used to tell me stories about Turkish princesses when I was little, happens to be walking by and she winks at me and tells me, laughing, not to get up to any mischief. I reach the bazaar, where men with boxy hats and women in skirts like overlapping rainbows sell sesame desserts, the Turkish drink made of barley called *braga*, wooden spoons and pumpkin seeds, round pottery with traditional motifs, colourful porcelain birds which when filled with water sing like real birds, seashell jewellery, lacquered seashells and Turkish *lokum* or *rahat*. I steal a couple of *lokum* pieces on my way through the bazaar and keep running with my mouth full.

I get to the back alleys where there is no pavement, just red beaten earth and thistles. I hurry straight to Gigi's yellowish house with its patch of corn, the three sunflowers and its big apricot tree in the front. Gigi is sitting on the steps eating tiny fried fish, *guvizi*, that are tied on a string. His father, in his white and navy uniform, is standing on the front porch smoking his pipe. Through the open door I see Gigi's mother at the dining-room table in the middle of their tiny house, drawing something and eating pumpkin seeds. She is a geography teacher and can draw the most beautiful maps of different countries, just from memory. I make a sign to Gigi to get up because I have to talk to him. I want to tell him in secret of my plan to paint on the beach this afternoon. His father winks at me and blows the smoke in my direction. His mother lifts her head from her papers and waves. Gigi smells of fried *guvizi* and algae; his tangled red hair is shining in the sun.

'Gigi, I'm going to the beach this afternoon,' I say quickly. 'I'm going to paint something, an idea I had today . . . I want you to meet me there after I do it. I want you to be the first one to see my painting.'

'Finally, here is my artist siren. Finally she's got her inspiration,' he says, smiling. 'Can't I come and watch you paint?'

'No, no, you can't. You know that I don't like anyone to watch me paint, or I won't ever paint anything . . . ever again.' My voice is raised and I feel my face flush.

'I'm not just anyone, you know,' he says, ignoring my flare-up. 'Don't worry. You know I'm just kidding. By what time will Miss Michelangelo be done with her masterpiece?' He grins and swallows another silver *guvid* whole from the whitish string.

'Come at sunset, you know, just a little before it gets dark,' I say and start running in the direction of my house.

I want everything to be perfect. I want my real painting career to start today, this afternoon at dusk. I decide I've had enough of the geometrical flowers and shapes! It's time I started painting the images in my head, even if they are weird. I take the same route home and even pass by all the traders I teased and stole from only a little while ago, that's how wicked I feel. They all think I'm crazy anyway and once I heard Lili, the one who sells lacquered seashell jewellery and shells, tell another woman in the bazaar that I was 'not right in the head' and generally not normal, what with the smaller breast and arm and 'all that'. I didn't know what 'all that' meant, what else was wrong with me. When I told my father what Lili had said, he yelled that he was going to wring the woman's neck like a chicken, and my mother said it was a very good example to give to his child, to be so violent. 'Don't we already have enough tragedies in our family?' she asked. My father said: 'What tragedies?' Why was she always exaggerating about the tragedies in our family? he wondered. My mother should just go and stare at her weeping willow for a while, he concluded. My parents always argue and wound each other like that. It's like living on a battlefield all the time.

I arrive at my house panting, sneak in through the back door and try to get to the pantry unseen and unheard, to fetch the easel that my father bought me when I turned fourteen. I tiptoe like a thief through the room that serves both as living room and dining room, and I see my mother with her back turned sitting at the sewing machine in the little sitting room next door.

I take a quick look at the painting of the Balchik shore, the blues mixed in with whites and yellows, the light in the painting. It should have been me who painted that.

A seagull shrieks in its rushed flight towards the beach, and when I get to the kitchen it is all flooded with afternoon light, like under orange honey. I open the door to the pantry and see my easel in a corner, behind the huge jars of pickled cabbage and bottles of Turkish *braga*, dusty and covered in spiders' webs. The easel still has the first white sheet of paper on it from the time my father prepared it for me, thinking I would paint something right away. But I didn't want to, because my head was filled with severe geometrical flowers.

Instead of coming out through the house with the easel and paints, I decide to jump out through the pantry window, which gives on to the side of the house facing the beach. I open the window and pick up the easel, breathing in all the dust, and put it outside with a thump, after which I jump too. I feel I am an adventurer, a painter like Van Gogh or Gauguin, about whom I had read in the art history book that I found in the art classroom. The art history teacher told us these were unstable, bourgeois reactionary artists, that we shouldn't waste our time looking at their pornographic art. I didn't understand why paintings of sunflowers in bloom and crooked chairs were reactionary and pornographic. I don't want to cut my ear off or abuse my body like Van Gogh did, but I think that sometimes great artists have some infirmity. I have uneven arms and breasts. Maybe it's a sign I'm meant to be an artist.

I race on to the warm sand, take off my sandals and carry my easel in my arms like a baby. There are only a few families left on the beach, it's still early in the season and the loud Bucharest tourists haven't started their holidays yet. A little girl with black hair falling in waves is running around in circles and throwing herself on the sand with peals of laughter. I set up my easel at the edge of the beach, next to the dunes which are covered in thistles and prickly plants, so I have the full view of the sea and also of the black-haired girl running in circles. I decide I'll model the fish face after the girl; it will be a wild, fantastical painting, something to really scare my mother and make her go on about how I am crazy like the people on my father's side.

I set all my tempera tubes on the edge of the easel, take the little brown porcelain cup I stole from the kitchen and pour some water from my thermos into it. My heart is beating wildly, like when I am about to jump into the sea and I know Gigi is going to push me. I stick my brush into the water and then into the colour green. I want to start with green, the green seawater deep down where Gigi and I meet after we have both dived in. The girl is shrieking and laughing and running in circles on the sand, and the sea is turning violet the way it always does at sunset, on calm bright days. Only it's a different violet every day. Today it is violet with dark and bright streaks. Something in the way the sun hits the little girl's dark waves of hair produces a short circuit in my brain. I have been in a similar scene before. It was long ago, and my brother Valentin was here too. His dark hair, which used to be long like that of a girl, was touched by the afternoon sun. My mother and Aunt Raluca were both on the beach with us and my mother held Valentin up in the air like a trophy. She had tears running down her face. Raluca also had tears on her face. Only Valentin was laughing and squealing joyously. I don't know what I was doing. I don't see myself in this memory though I know I was there. I want to make the face of the fish like a cross between this girl's face and that of Valentin.

I paint the sea from the inside and my hand is moving freely over the page, as if it had a mind of its own, filling the white with shades of green, watery, translucent. For the first time I use both my hands to paint the sea, because my hands are different in size, and somehow I get a different effect from each of them.

I discover one advantage of having a birth defect. But when I am about to start working on the face of the fish I had been imagining all day, I see instead the face of the leader as it looked on the pictures that our art teacher always made us use as a model during our art classes. The image is like a fly that keeps buzzing around me and I can't get rid of it; it keeps coming back, again and again. I see the rosy skin on the face of the leader, like that of a pig, pink and smooth, like the skin of pigs I've seen in the countryside, in the peasants' yards in the Danube town where my mother's family comes from. The blue eyes, of a blue so fake that you wonder what the artist who made those portraits was trying to convey. Then the lips curl into a perfect smile, the grey hair is shaped in perfect waves, the pig skin and the fake blue eyes. Furiously I start painting my fish in all the colours that are *not* the colours of the portrait of the leader: dark red and orange and green, no pastels, no curls and no waves. But somehow I can't get away from the expression of the leader staring at me against the pink background of the portrait, pig-rosy skin against pig-rosy background. I make my fish of triangles and corners and semicircles, like the geometrical flowers I used to draw. I can't get away from them either. I make my fish with red eyes, and an angular face and long black eyelashes over the red eyes, a silvery body, long and pointy. I take quick turns with each hand, indulging in the eerie asymmetry of the portrait. No smile on the face of the fish, just bloody eyes and curly eyelashes. I paint corals and algae and other small grey fish swimming around the fantastical fish.

The girl running in circles has left the beach and I can't remember her face. The beach is empty and I have a hollow feeling in my heart. A feeling like the sound of the inside of a shell; people are fooled into thinking they hear the sea when they put a shell to their ear, but it's just air going through the cavities of the shell, nothing else. The sea looks uselessly beautiful in the sunset, just before dark. My fish looks like a heartless shell, like the empty box from where Queen Marie's heart was stolen. Communists are thieves of hearts and of imagination.

'Have you been hallucinating?' Gigi touches my shoulder gently and buries his face in my hair.

I push him away. 'Don't laugh at it, I know it's awful!' I say, resigned.

He says it's not at all awful. 'In fact, it's quite spectacular,' he says, 'but why did you make the fish look like Ceauşescu?' he asks. 'The lips, the smile, can't you see, it's like his smile? Is he your highest inspiration?' Gigi says, quoting my former teacher. He touches the curly lips, which indeed came out curly. I tried to make no curls, no smiles, no waves, just angles and triangles. Somehow the lips still came out curly just like in the generic smile of the leader's portrait. I take Gigi's hand, put the brush between his fingers and move his hand into black paint, then make him move it over the mouth of the fish, round and round with black paint. A big hole, an endless scream! A fish screaming a deep, mute scream from a black mouth in the middle of the green waters at the bottom of the sea!

I start laughing so hard that I can't keep my balance with Gigi leaning on me as I pull his hand and make him paint the black circle of the fish's mouth. We both fall in the sand, the easel collapsing on top of us. The painting falls face down and when I pick it up there is sand stuck on to the entire page. I want to crumple the wretched painting, to tear it up and destroy it on this day that was supposed to be so special. But Gigi stops me, holds me by both wrists until I calm down and tells me to keep the painting, it will be funny to look at it when I am older and a famous artist.

The waves are making delicate splashes against the shore. The sea usually becomes a bit restless at sunset, before it quiets down for the night. The sun is a dark red ball before it goes down and its last reflections turn into wild purples shimmering one more time over the rippling surface of the water, before the waves greedily swallow them in a few hungry gulps. I am slowly passing my hand over the painting, my right hand, the smaller one, which feels just the right size as it rests over the grainy paper with the fantastical fish and its black silent scream.

The Storm before Carnival Nights

For two and a half months in the summer, at the height of the tourist season, most of the rooms in our house are rented out to people from Bucharest who spend their holidays at the beach and want to experience a little bit of rural life, with a back yard and vines hanging above their heads. My mother and Aunt Tudoriţa cook for them from morning till night because that's the deal, they all get a room and two meals a day. They come in from the beach after many hours of baking in the sun, red like lobsters, dragging their tents and lilos, speaking loudly as if somebody among them is deaf, and their children always whining and throwing themselves down on the cement in our back yard in a temper tantrum. They sit at the tables laid out in the yard and ask my mother: 'What good things have you prepared for us today, Mrs Rodica?' And my mother promptly answers: 'It's your favourite today, Mrs Ramona: stuffed peppers and cabbage salad,' or: 'Today I made your special dish, Mr Dinu: fried carp, baked potatoes and plum cake.' My mother always cooks everybody's favourites except mine.

My parents and I crowd into the one room at the back where it's hotter and stuffier, because the tourists are all lodged in the front rooms that look out on the sea. I spend a lot of the day at

Gigi's house. His family don't rent out their house, mostly because none of the Bucharest tourists want to live so far away from the beach and also because his mother hates cooking and doesn't like having strangers in the house all the time. My mother is so busy from morning till night that she doesn't have a moment to nag me the way she usually does. Just once in a while she tells me not to spend all day long 'with that Turk of yours' and not to 'get in trouble like you always do, shaming your parents', after which she goes back to peeling endives or skinning a chicken. Food is harder to find every year, so my mother and Tudoriţa now stand in line from five in the morning to get the food for the tourists' meals at the *alimentara*, the grocery store in the centre, or in the market; they even get chickens from the Turks in Gigi's neighbourhood. And luckily, around here there is always fish. So the Bucharest crowds come to the seashore hoping to eat better and then to go back as dark from the sun as the darkest Gypsies, with strings of seashells around their necks that they buy from Lili, the Turkish woman who sells jewellery in the bazaar.

My mother hates the work she does during the rest of the year so much that she is happier spending her summers cooking from morning till night for the spoiled Bucharest people. At least she is freer, she says, and in her own house rather than cooped up in that God-awful office at the school. And we earn a lot of money from the tourists, which my mother says is 'for a hard day'. I also think she is happy to avoid the suppertimes with us, with the sad weeping willow waving its lanky braids in front of our window and her dwelling on how her father was picked up by the Communists from the dinner table and then killed in prison. She works in the same high school where Gigi's mother teaches geography, only in the school director's office, and she is responsible for the professional development of the teachers. She keeps files of their activities and teaching hours, and occasionally holds meetings in which she has to talk to them about the newest Party guidelines, or she has to organize and keep track of their hours of civic duties, such as doing volunteer work that is in fact obligatory unpaid work for the cooperatives or factories in the surrounding area.

Mama wanted to be a concert pianist like her mother had been before the war. We have a picture of my grandmother standing in front of a grand piano, wearing a sumptuous black taffeta evening gown, a long string of pearls and an orchid in her hair. She is looking slightly sideways with almost a smile, her right hand touching the piano and her left hand casually brushing the string of pearls. Next to this picture on the lacquered pine cupboard in the dining room, because everything in our house is lacquered, there is the only picture we have of my grandfather, the one who was taken away and tortured to death because he had said 'that'll be the day' and resisted the nationalization of his land. He was a landowner before the war, in the region of Tulcea, near the Danube Delta, and loved his land more than anything. Even more than his children, they say. He is known to have once said: 'Your children come from your own loins, but land comes from God's own loins.' In this picture he is standing on his land, which stretched for acres and acres, in front of a crooked bare tree in the middle of an empty field, with a fedora on his head, a white shirt with the sleeves rolled up, and breeches. He has a dark bushy moustache and a fierce look in his eyes. My mother always says he used to work his land right next to his peasants, from sunrise to sunset every day, and that's how much he loved his land, before 'it was all over for him'. That's the highest form of criticism that my mother ever dares to utter of the Communists who tortured and killed him the way they did lots of other landowners after 1945. She says it's best to keep your mouth shut, times have changed and there is nothing you can do about it but try to survive the best you can. My mother also says that with all the people we have in our house every summer, she wouldn't be surprised if our house was bugged, and she always says it in almost inaudible whispers, moving her hands in pantomime fashion to explain.

Once when I was looking for an old bathing suit early one morning before going to the beach to meet Gigi, I caught my mother touching the keys of the old piano hidden in the basement as if they were living creatures and one long tear on the side of her nose was hanging there ready to fall. I tiptoed out because I did not want her to know that I had seen her in that melancholy state. Then she would have started screaming at me, that didn't I have anything better to do with my time than sneak into the basement. That day I dived and swam in my underwear and Gigi said I should wear that all the time. I didn't tell him about my mother stroking the piano keys and crying in the basement with a huge tear at the tip of her nose, mostly because then every time I complained about how mean my mother was with me, Gigi would have told me to give her a break, it was life that had made her that way, she'd had a hard life and she was bitter, that was all.

When we are bored in the summer, Gigi and I go to the market place in bare feet, dressed in old and raggedy clothes, and pretend we are beggars. We cross ourselves over and over again, saying: '*Doamne ajută, Doamne ajută, daţi-ne şi noua ceva să mĭncăm*', God bless, God bless, please give us something to eat. The tourists who don't know us give us money when they see us looking so sad and poor, but the women in the market shake their fingers at us threateningly. We sometimes stop and pretend we want to buy *lokum*, and we put some in our mouths and run away. I hear the women scream at me that they'll tell my mother what a thief I am. They say: 'Just look at her, will you? That's Sandu and Rodica's daughter: the worst-behaved child in the whole town. She's a bad influence on that nice Turkish boy, too.'

We stop by Mariţa's corner and try to attract tourists to buy her stuff by buying some ourselves with the money we got from begging. Mariţa and her daughter Gabi sell everything: beach balls with coloured stripes, sesame sweets and corn on the cob, little coloured pretend-watches for girls, porcelain singing birds, roasted sunflower seeds, pumice stone for women's feet. When I was little Mariţa would tell me the story of the Turkish princess Esma, daughter of Sultan Selim II, who had the mosque in our town built in 1525 as a sign of gratitude to Allah for having secured her safe passage to this faraway part of the world.

Next week the preparations will begin for Zilele Marinei, the Navy celebrations, when all the ships and boats in the port line up on the horizon and hang strings of lights from their masts and let off fireworks. That's when Luca takes out his big ship and lights it all up for people to see and admire from the shore. The band plays every night on the pier with the lighthouse, and the whole *faleza*, the high beach walk, looks like a fairy tale, with lights and rows of fragrant petunias. The Bucharest women wear their gauzy dresses made from *panza topita*, burnt cotton, as they stroll on the arms of their husbands or boyfriends up and down the *faleza*. Gigi and I want to go to the discotheque at the big Ziemens Hotel where all the foreign tourists stay. I don't want to tell my mother I'm going to the discotheque because she'll never let me, and she'll scream for a whole week about how I'll get into trouble for life and never be admitted to the university if I go to a place filled with foreigners. We are not allowed to speak to foreigners because the Party is afraid that if we did, we might find out that in other countries there is more freedom than in ours and we might be tempted to run away. As if we didn't know that already. My father, who has to work very late every night checking all the restaurants in town because he is the epidemiologist responsible for local hygiene and sanitation, doesn't care where I go, and tells my mother to take a break from her howling; at least for a few days during the Navy holidays it would be nice to have some peace in the house.

Since my creepy experience with the fish painting at the beginning of the summer, Gigi and I have been together almost every single minute of the day, running around town and the bazaar, hanging out near the casino to listen to the orchestra and thinking up all sorts of new pranks that are getting the women traders red with anger. We make fun of the Bucharest tourists in their fancy clothes and we go around the market stealing little objects. During the day we get better at holding our breath under water. Sometimes we take the mini train that goes to all the modern resorts along the shore, the ones with the names of the planets, Venus and Saturn, Neptune and Jupiter, and we get on and off the train without paying, jumping out into the street with a shriek when we see the ticket collector get on. I haven't had any more painting ideas. It's as if a hole like the black mouth of my fantastical fish had installed itself inside my head. One day I told Gigi that I wanted to become a sanitation and hygiene expert like my father and forget about being an artist. 'It's too hard being an artist in our country,' I said. 'Better to do something practical, with no political implications.' He looked at me mockingly, crossed himself like the superstitious Christians in town and said in a plaintive voice: '*Doamne fereste*', God help us! That's all he said. Maybe the Navy celebrations next week, which Gigi and I like to call the 'carnival nights', will give me new painting ideas. I'm thinking of a painting that captures light in the middle of the night, and the special blackness of the sea under the moon.

Gigi's father is busy from morning till night on his ship, preparing for the Navy days. He asks his friend Mr Bekta, who is also Turkish, and who pilots the tourist ship that goes out to sea and up to the Danube Delta on cruises, to show us his ship. Luca cannot take us on the ship that he pilots as it's a big cargo vessel. There are always two guards with rifles standing on the pier in front of it, when it's at anchor in the port. But Mr Bekta is happy to show us the cruise ship and even lets us wander around on board. We take advantage of all the activity in preparation for the next cruise to roam all over the ship and explore its most secret nooks and crannies, the tiny spaces where the sailors sleep during the voyage all the way to the old city of Babadag and into the Delta, the pilot's cabin with its important logbooks, the large control panel with illuminated buttons, the dining room with the long wooden table in the middle where the crew eat together when they are at sea. Gigi is happiest when he is on a ship, imagining himself in his father's shoes, giving orders to the sailors, operating the complicated piloting system, wearing the white and navy uniform with the white cap.

When his father takes the fishing boat out of the port, we go back to our diving exercises and our ritual of having a fight so he can push me into the water. We have got so good at swimming that now we can cover the two kilometres to the shore in less than half an hour, when the sea is smooth and clear like today. We get to the shore slightly tired and I throw myself on to the sand right where the waves break. The mushy, warm surface of sand under my back feels comforting after the strain of swimming two kilometres in thirty minutes. Gigi runs over to the bushes at the edge of the beach, to the secret place where we always hide our clothes before we go into the water. As I look at Gigi walking towards me against the white columns, and admire his taut and freckled body, I notice the unusually dark clouds that are gathering behind him from the west. A storm on the eve of the Navy holidays is the last thing we want, it will ruin everything. We haven't had a storm for the Navy celebrations since I was ten and my mother locked all the outside doors and hid the keys, for fear I would run to the beach to watch.

'Look at those clouds, Gigi. Do you think we'll have a storm?' I ask, hoping he will say they are cumulus, good weather clouds.

He doesn't even turn to look. 'I know, I saw that. There is a big storm coming. No Navy days for us this year,' he says, resigned.

'No, no, no, there will be no storm, stop calling for bad things and jinxing the weather,' I yell childishly, as I pull on the Levi's that Gigi's father got for me from Yafsin, an Arab man in town, who got them from another Arab man in the port of Constanţa. I put on my burnt-cotton white shirt and throw the wet bathing suit at him in annoyance at his bad weather warning. In one move he turns fully towards me, trying to grab me, but I slip away and run off along the beach. Gigi is a better swimmer but I can run faster; that's one thing I do better than him. And painting, if I ever paint again! I run in the direction of the lighthouse at the end of the pier and feel light like a seagull at sunrise emerging from the waves. I could run for ever and be chased by Gigi. I laugh and run. The beam from the lighthouse is just beginning to flicker, showing the ships at sea the way to the port; dusk is falling and laying its thin greyish veils all over the water. I slow down because of the laughter and Gigi catches up with me, grabs me and we both fall into the delicate foam where the waves crash against the sand.

Now the sky is black and the waves are getting bigger. We start to run up the spiral stone steps that lead from the beach to the *faleza* and the street, and I already feel large, heavy drops of rain falling quicker and denser by the second. Gigi takes my hand and we run to find shelter in the hallway of the hotel up the street, the Scala Hotel, at the opposite end from the villas where the Party leaders take their holidays. We reach the awning of the hotel and watch the storm in fascination the way we have done so many times, except that now I'm a little less fascinated than usual because the first day of the Navy holiday will be spoiled. The waves are getting higher and the sea has changed to its angry dark green, with streaks of glassy, lighter green where the water is churning its insides before a big wave rises again. From where we are, I see a blonde woman who must be a foreign tourist from a Nordic country, because nobody in our town is so blonde, running on the sand like she is going to a party, and enter the sea happily, as if it was a sunny day with no waves. Silently I point her out to Gigi.

'Look at that crazy woman, what is she thinking? Has she had enough of life?' Gigi says to me, laughing. The *salvamar*, the lifeguard, has tied up his boat on the shore quite a while ago and is whistling and making desperate signs to her to come back. The black flag forbidding swimming is whipping in the wind, which has become quite wild. At first the woman seems to be handling the waves quite well, and we think she's just going to stay near the shore playing in the water. The rain is pouring vengefully and driving in sideways gusts to where we shelter under the hotel awning. I like to play in the waves with Gigi when there is no rain and thunder, but no native would ever go swimming in this kind of weather. We know better. We know how cruel and irrepressible our sea can be in a storm like this one. No wonder the Greeks called it the Black Sea, the Inhospitable Sea, furious, dark and voraciously hungry.

'Gigi, she's going to die, we have to do something,' I say, grabbing Gigi's hand.

I feel Gigi's pride swell up inside him as he thrusts out his freckled chest. Other tourists are gathering at the hotel door to watch the Nordic woman drown herself in the churning waters.

'I'll go,' Gigi says, releasing my hand, and he starts in the direction of the beach. I hold him back and say: 'I'm coming with you. I'm just as good a swimmer, you know.'

At first Gigi tries to stop me but he knows he can't. He knows there is no stopping me when I set my mind to something. We run back to the beach holding hands. The rain is hitting us mercilessly, the waves are rising higher and one of them pushes the woman under. We can't see her any longer. Then her head comes out again for seconds at a time. We fly down the stone steps, take a short cut through the thistles and the bushes, and find ourselves on the wet sand, the wind hitting us full force in our faces. The *salvamar* is still standing and waving on the beach. It's a boy in town we know, whose father works on Luca's ship. We ask him to give us the two life jackets he has. He knows we are better swimmers than he is. At first he hesitates, while the rain whips us with fury and the woman's head bobs between the waves like a miniature yellow buoy. We put on the two heavy life jackets and rush to the water. This is my first big adventure ever. I see us two: Gigi and me, holding hands, as wet as we'll ever be, rushing into the merciless waves, two small silhouettes against foamy, dark green waters, and a sky all in dark oils, thick, impenetrable.

We move through the dark green oils of the sea, violent waves on top of violent waves, and the sand is running quickly from under our feet, and we are just two specks of flesh in an immensity of foaming green. Gigi reaches the woman first and pulls her above the water, trying to make her keep her head up. She seems unconscious, and her head is bobbing back and forth. Then Gigi is hit on the head by an enormous wave. I manage to get to him; he has come back to the surface but he looks dizzy and is making signs to me to help him hold the woman. We both grab her and do our best to keep her head above the water, by wrapping her arms around our necks. Lightning slices across the black skies and Gigi and I know how dangerous this is, that we could be struck any moment and turned to ashes right in the middle of the roaring sea. Another huge wave hits us from the back, wickedly, mercilessly. I am sucked into it, shoved against the bottom with its scratchy surface, then I'm churned this way and that inside the belly of the brine. I remember what Gigi taught me, always to keep my mouth shut under the water no matter what. *No matter what, bite your gums, your tongue, clench your teeth, just don't open your mouth,* he had said. I am still holding on to the woman, I'm grabbing her arm, she feels like a rag, maybe she's already dead. Another wave and we roll at the very bottom of the sea. I feel her body on top of me. I wonder what Gigi is doing. I don't feel his closeness any more. This time I don't know how I'll get back up to the surface, but somehow I do, probably it's the life jacket that's keeping me afloat. For a second I want to let go of the woman, let her die and save myself. Why in the world did I have to jump in and act so brave? Now I'll never become a painter. I'll just end up a bloated corpse on the shore. I feel Gigi pull me up by the hair. I feel the woman's body slam into mine again. I find myself at the surface. I gulp for air, shake my head from Gigi's grip, and try to make a huge leap towards the shore. We are almost there. Another great wave rises up behind us, and Gigi yells at me: 'Go with it, go under, don't resist it!' I do as he says and now we are holding the woman by her arms again, the wave is above us, I go with it, I keep my eyes open and my mouth shut. Furious green algae and clouds of little shells and sand, whitish foam, green, boiling water all around me. My eyes sting but I never close them. I don't remember the last leap to the shore or how exactly we got there.

But here I am lying on the wet sand, rain pouring over me. Next to me is the woman we pulled out of the water and Gigi is on top of her, performing mouth-to-mouth resuscitation. I see I'm still holding on to her arm as if trying to pull her after me. Her flesh is soft and white, not brown and firm like mine. Someone has called an ambulance because I hear the siren in the distance. Gigi keeps blowing air into the woman's mouth and it looks too similar to how it would be if he were kissing her. I'm so weak I can't move. An idea pops into my head at the sight of Gigi performing mouth-to-mouth: I've never kissed Gigi, and he's never been so close to my mouth as he is now to the mouth of this other woman. A man who looks like a paramedic comes over to me and pushes into my chest with his fists, then turns me over with my face to the sand as if I were a doll. I want to say I'm fine, I'm not drowned like the woman that Gigi keeps kissing, but I can't. No words come out of my mouth. He turns me on to my side. The woman jolts and sends a huge jet of green vomit into the air. Gigi looks happy and says: 'She's alive, we did it, we saved her.' I don't know why Gigi is so happy about this unknown and reckless foreign woman, and doesn't even ask how *I* am doing. I'm happy that she's alive too, but not quite like Gigi. I manage to whisper in his direction: 'Who is she?' That's all I can say. 'Who is she?' Then more men and women in white coats and with large black umbrellas and stretchers arrive on the beach. I remember that someone needs to call my parents, but I can't say a word. 'Somebody please call my parents,' I finally whisper, 'Rodica and Sandu Teodoru.' The doctors and nurses put me on the stretcher as if they haven't heard a thing, and I'm thinking that my mother will really kill me this time. She will never understand why I was swimming in the sea in the middle of the biggest storm of the season.

Carnival Nights

There is no trace of the storm the next day. The sea is sparkling and swaying languidly ahead of us as if nothing had happened the day before. We will have our carnival nights after all. We were discharged from the hospital the same evening, and it was my father who picked us up since he happened to be in the cafeteria in the centre when the ambulances brought us in from the beach. A fellow doctor had told him he saw his daughter on the beach during the storm, as she was being pulled out of the water. My father was awfully angry when he picked us up from the hospital. I had never seen him like that. His lips were pursed and he wasn't saying a word. I begged him not to tell my mother what had happened, and he was still quiet. I knew he wouldn't tell, and that he would protect me from my mother's rage, because he didn't like her fits of anger and her saying she was going to kill me with her own hands any more than I did. But I was sad to see him so upset and quiet. He just said: 'Why fool around with life like that?' That's all he said and he turned away from me.

The woman's name is Anushka Pomorowska and she is a Polish émigré living in France. We find her on the beach the next morning. We communicate in the little French we both know and with lots of gestures. She wanted to die, *she didn't care*, she tells us. Her boyfriend had died in a motorcycle accident in Paris and she wanted to die too. Life didn't matter to her any more, she said. She didn't know what to do, how to die, she just knew she didn't want to live any longer. So she looked at the map and the first place her eyes alighted on, that was where she chose to go. Her eyes happened to fall on the Black Sea in Romania. She thought she'd leave it to chance to choose her place of death. But it's not all chance, she tells us with a smile. She tells us that our city of Mangalia is at the exact same latitude on the map as the French city of Nice on the Riviera. She pronounces Mangalia in a sing-song manner with the accent on the last syllable, not on the second like it's supposed to be pronounced. Gigi is enraptured by her story and pronunciation and watches her without blinking. I think it's stupid to want to die like that in a storm on an unknown shore. And to pick your place to die on someone else's shore, in someone else's country! Why couldn't she die in France? Why couldn't she throw herself in the Seine, for instance? Or go to Nice in a storm and drown on *that* beach?

Her body is white and perfect, evenly built, and her blonde hair is falling in smooth waves on her shoulders. Next to her, my limbs and breasts seem even more unbalanced than usual, my right breast too small, my left one too big, and my mane of brown hair is flying in all directions like a witch's hair. She has small blue eyes that squint in the sun, which makes her face look childish. I find myself slightly drawn to her too as she tells her story of tragic love and suicide wishes while blinking and squinting her blue eyes and scrunching up her little white doll-face. Judging by what she tells us of her life, that she is a student at the Sorbonne, and about her complicated love story, she must be about twenty, though she looks barely older than Gigi and me. She suddenly embraces and kisses us on both cheeks and says: '*Merci, merci beaucoup, vous m'avez sauvé la vie.*' I take it she is thanking us for saving her life. I don't know why she should be grateful if all she wanted to do was die and she took the trouble to come to this forsaken corner of the Balkans to do it. It must be that she didn't really want to die, she just wanted a diversion. She needed some attention and adventure in an 'exotic' place. And divine providence threw her in our lap. During Navy days, when Gigi and I had planned to go dancing at the disco and to the party on the cruise ship.

I won't let Anushka spoil our fun with her suicide story. Gigi and I will still go to all the festivities tonight, and to the disco at the foreign tourists' hotel. Now that we have spent all morning with a Polish refugee living in France, how bad can it be to be seen dancing next to Algerian or Madagascan students? I suddenly take Gigi by the hand and drag him into the water, to get away from Anushka. Because Gigi is all kindness and sweetness he goes along with me, but also resists a bit and asks if it's all right to leave Anushka alone on the beach like that.

'She's much better off alone and on the shore than she would have been if we hadn't rushed into the sea like fools to save her,' I tell Gigi as we plunge into the cool silky waters.

He's already swimming under water and I can't see his face, so I can't know what he's thinking. We swim fast, past the buoys and the lifeguards' boats, towards the horizon and the long line of ships. From where I am in the water I can see Anushka sitting on the beach embracing her knees and staring at us, her blonde hair flying in the wind. For some unknown reason my heart aches at the sight of her. I'm starting to think of Gigi in a way I have not thought of him before. Anushka's presence suddenly awakens me to something new, a bittersweet feeling, a heartache, an irritating longing. Gigi has been my playmate and swimming companion for ever, another part of me. With the French woman between us he appears to me in a new light. I want to turn into a magic human fish and live with him under water, not ever come back out, just keep gliding in the liquid emerald of this mad sea for ever, among the red coral.

When we get back to the shore, Anushka is gone and I feel great relief together with a renewed fondness towards her. In her absence I can afford to think of her with more kindness and even feel a little bit sorry for her, the way Gigi does: her dead motorcyclist boyfriend, her desperate flight to an arbitrary point on the map, her desire to die and her reckless rush into the stormy sea, then our rushing after her which almost cost us our lives. I stop feeling sorry for her and start being angry again when I think that Gigi and I nearly died because of the whim of a depressed foreign student. My mother would have been right to kill me if she found out. I twist and turn this nagging thought in my mind until I know I have to make a painting of it. I haven't had the urge to paint since the grotesque fish painting earlier this summer. And now it comes to me not with joy and lightness the way it did the last time, but with rage and sadness. Maybe it's a sign I really am an artist. All the artists I admire are heartbroken, depressed and raging mad. After tonight I'll paint something about Anushka and her exasperating story.

In the evening Gigi comes to pick me up to go to the Navy celebrations that start at dusk. The city is swarming with tourists and the line of ships on the horizon is starting to flicker: a myriad of lights strewn along the masts and decks. I hold Gigi's hand in a tight grip like I haven't done before. Gigi is wearing a perfectly ironed and starched white shirt that suits his tanned face and reddish curls beautifully. I am wearing a bright yellow burnt-cotton dress that is loose around the breasts and gathers around the waist, then flares out at the bottom. It hides all of my unevenness and makes me look slender and womanly at the same time. I know the yellow of the dress brings out the green of my eyes. I walk confidently with a little bit of a hip sway and let the skirts swirl this way and that. My hair is down over my shoulders and I put a seashell barrette in it to keep it from falling into my eyes and to make a contrast with the brown of my hair. I also put a red taffeta belt around my waist and I feel as bright and colourful as one of Van Gogh's sunflowers. I see men turn their heads to look at me, and Gigi seems very proud to be walking next to me tonight.

We hear the band play festive melancholy songs at the casino across from the beach, the petunias along the beach walk fill the air with heavily sweet fragrances and by now the ships that stretch across the horizon are shining in the night like strings of stars sending golden bridges across the sea. We enter the discotheque with its hallucinating strobe lights as the DJ is playing the Pink Floyd song 'Another Brick In The Wall'. The air is sultry and smoke-filled and Gigi and I start dancing, twirling and holding each other. Then there is my favourite song, 'I Will Survive'. The foreign students have all the fun in this country, they get all the best music, and they can buy Toblerone chocolate with foreign currency in the little stores that we are forbidden to go into. As we glide slowly on the dance floor I see Anushka across the room, dancing with an Arab student. She has certainly got over her death wish and dead boyfriend pretty fast. I am now putting up some resistance to Gigi's movements, trying to keep him from turning round and seeing her. I remember Gigi's mouth-to-mouth resuscitation on Anushka only yesterday, like a desperate kiss for life. I have never kissed Gigi, I hadn't really thought of it until I saw his mouth glued to Anushka's mouth. I just assumed that Gigi belonged to me, that he was my eternal companion. But that was our childhood, and now Gigi is waking up to manhood. And where have I been? Something new and raw is starting: a bitter yearning, a nagging feeling that I have overlooked something, that I have missed a chance and let something slip. Anushka's white flesh is glowing under the disco lights and I see Gigi's eyes sparkle when he finally notices her. A sudden smile lights up his entire face.

Through my half-open eyes I still see Anushka hanging on to the neck of the tall Arab, moving slowly in the rhythm of the song and smiling dreamily. She is wearing a silky bright red dress that makes her blonde hair look even lighter. 'Oh, look who's there, let's go and say hello,' says Gigi. Before I know it, he is dragging me towards Anushka and her dance partner. She sees us right away, throws her head back, laughing, and moves towards us. She kisses us on both cheeks the way she had done on the beach this morning, introduces us to her new friend, Afsan, and when a new LP starts with my favourite Queen song she takes Gigi by the hand and dances with him with more animation and sexy moves than I had thought her capable of, judging by her doll-face and melancholy manner this morning. I am left with Afsan, who takes my hand and starts twirling me round the dance floor. I have no desire to dance with the unknown foreign student while Gigi and Anushka seem to be having so much fun.

My yellow dress suddenly seems too yellow and peasant-like next to Anushka's slinky red dress, probably from Paris, my hair too unruly and wild, and my body feels just like my mother had called it before: a cripple's body. I want to cry in the middle of the dance floor or run away from Afsan's grip, but instead I go on dancing, pretending I'm enjoying myself, with a fake grin stretched across my face. I summon my next painting inside my head and focus on it under the ridiculously fast strobe lights: Anushka's face the way it looked when she was almost drowning in the stormy sea yesterday, bloated, her eyes closed, looming big, bigger than a human face amid the fierce waves, half human half fish, a mythic creature, an omen of misfortune. Anushka, with her white skin and blonde hair, is bringing misery and doom into our lives. I convince myself that, if I paint that image, I will cast aside whatever misfortunes may loom ahead of us, like an exorcism. I open my eyes and Gigi and Anushka are still dancing as if I have fallen off the face of the earth. Gigi is smiling his charmer's smile. He is dancing with slick rhythmic moves, twirling Anushka this way and that on the dance floor. Gigi is a good dancer, I think, and my heart feels as if a long thin knife just like my mother's fish knife has pierced the centre of it and then been pulled out, leaving the hole in my heart to bleed.

Yet I am fascinated by Anushka and her smooth way of moving, her grace, and the flood of silky blonde hair falling down her back. I want to do something shameless myself, something crazy to break the spell. I leave Afsan in the middle of the floor and rush towards Gigi and Anushka, break in between them and start dancing with both of them. Anushka is taking it all with good humour, smiling and swaying, she even takes my hand and swings me round, but I see that Gigi is slightly embarrassed and uneasy. I take him in my arms and whisper to him in his ear that I don't feel too well, 'please let's go away'. Anushka keeps dancing, the lights are maddening. I hate this discotheque. I ask Gigi one more time to please leave the disco, and he takes my hand, turns to Anushka and tells her we have to go, as if he were apologizing. Once outside in the fresh salty air, I start running with Gigi down the steps from the hotel to the street and towards the beach walk where people are gathering and the Navy celebrations are taking place.

'I thought you were not feeling well and ready to faint just a minute ago,' Gigi says.

'Yes, I was, it was the heat and the smoke. I couldn't stand it, I felt sick. But I'm fine now in the fresh air,' I hear myself saying and for the first time since I've known Gigi I know I am not telling him the truth. I know that it wasn't the heat and the smoke at all, but Anushka and the sadness that her presence next to Gigi causes me. I start seeing Gigi in a whole new light. I watch his moves, his nonchalant manner of swaying his shoulders a little as he strolls down the crowded beach walk, self-confident, oblivious to my sadness.

Later that evening Gigi suggests we go to the party on the cruise ship. Indeed, Luca waits for us at the end of the pier, with a rescue boat to take us to the cruise ship. We push our way through the crowds to get to it. The waves are hitting the rocks at the bottom of the pier with a steady beat and their sound is mixed up with the band's sentimental songs. We step into the boat, which sways violently for a few seconds before we steady ourselves and sit on the little wooden benches. Luca tells me I look so pretty and that yellow suits me very well. He is rowing the boat with assurance. Here in this little boat moving softly towards the lit ships in the distance, Anushka seems unreal, like the memory of a strange dream.

We climb on board via a rope ladder hanging by the side of the ship and my yellow dress swells in the evening breeze, showing off my legs and thighs and cooling my heated body. Gigi is climbing right below me and he looks up under my skirt just as the wind blows through it and lifts it. 'This is the best picture in the world,' he says, laughing, and I feel strangely elated by his comment.

There is an orchestra on the ship too, playing 'The Blue Danube', the classic Navy celebration song. Lots of men in uniform and women in fancy, flowing summer dresses are standing around and talking, but most are waltzing to the romantic music. Some men in black suits stand against the ship's rails, smoking and staring at everybody. They must be the secret police. Luca slaps his son on the back and tells him to be good, and he gently takes my hand and kisses it as if I were a grown woman. Then he disappears into the crowd of elegantly dressed loud men and women.

Gigi and I walk around the ship, inspecting it and admiring the beautiful decorations. The larger-than-life portrait of the leader is swaying in the wind, hanging from the mast like a bad omen. He is flying like that on every one of these ships, like an enormous bat. All the tempera paint that the artists must have used for those God-awful portraits! We walk up and down the stairs, enter the various rooms which we had visited only during the daytime and that have a mysterious air at night. We enter a room that seems set up for another private party: plush velvet chairs around a table set with candles, and a little radio that is playing Romanian pop music, a tango or something old-fashioned like that. We pretend to dance the tango. We make dramatic, exaggerated moves like we've seen Fred Astaire and Ginger Rogers do in a movie. Gigi tries kissing me and I push him away. I ask him about Anushka and his dancing and flirting with her. He smiles peevishly and asks: 'What flirting?' I am left speechless, I feel clumsy. I hate the 'Blue Danube' waltz. Gigi suddenly seems a different person, as if a new creature was emerging from under his old skin. His freckled face with the snub nose and brown eyes is glowing with confidence and a mischievous smile. Why didn't I let him kiss me when he wanted to? The mouth-to-mouth resuscitation kiss blooms painfully in my memory again. That's why. I wish it had been me who had almost drowned, who had almost committed suicide, and who had been saved by Gigi through prolonged mouth-to-mouth resuscitation on the rain-drenched beach. Now it's too late. Nothing has even started and it's already too late. Our childhood memories are too heavy; we are like two old people already, with too many memories to make it new and exciting any more. Anushka, on the other hand, is fresh and white-skinned and French.

My Second Sea Painting

The celebrations are over and the city has quietened down. I am left with an unpleasant feeling and a heart as heavy as Luca's cargo ship. Something feels misplaced, and there is a knot in my throat as if I have swallowed something the wrong way. For a couple of days after the Navy celebrations Gigi and I don't even see each other, until he comes to take me to the beach for a swim one bright morning. He looks fresh and joyous and acts as if everything was exactly the same as before. We haven't seen Anushka since the evening at the disco on the first carnival night and we believe she must have left the city. We never mention her any more, as if she had never existed, although we both know she did.

Until one day when we see her walking by the sea in a silky blue beach dress, with her blonde hair blowing in the morning breeze. We are just getting ready to start one of our swimming sessions and there she is. Gigi looks surprised and happy to see her, as if he couldn't help it. As if her presence brightens his day. As if I wasn't enough to brighten his day and make him happy. My heart sinks, all the colours turn to black, my paintings are melting and my body feels grotesquely uneven. I get mean, wicked thoughts: *We should have let her drown. Why did I have to draw Gigi's attention to the drowning woman? A few more minutes and she would have been dead.* Maybe it's true what Lili in the bazaar says about me, that I'm 'not quite right in the head, and all that'. Otherwise I wouldn't be having such black thoughts just because my childhood friend has looked at another woman.

Gigi reaches Anushka before I do and before I can hear what they are saying. She kisses him on both cheeks and smiles. He smiles back, and their bodies are almost touching. Or so it seems. She throws her head back, laughing, the way she did in the disco. What could he have said that was so funny? My pain is a hot liquid burning in my every vein. Yet I'm curious, I'm fascinated, I want to see how far he will go. I intentionally move slowly on the hot late-August sand, to be able to watch more of this tormenting sight and see where it will take us all. To see what painting will come out of it. One of the Gypsy women in town comes along with boiled corn on the cob and blocks my view of them for a second. I imagine they kissed in the moment she passed in front of me. I call to her and buy corn on the cob though I have no desire to eat. I don't want to show Gigi any part of my torment. I take the corn cob and start gnawing at it like a starved rodent and simultaneously begin to leave the beach, wanting to see if he notices, if he calls out to me. Sure enough, after I take two steps I hear Gigi calling: 'Hey, Nora, what are you doing? Aren't we swimming?'

I don't know what to say. I must be hallucinating about Gigi and Anushka.

'Sure, let me finish this corn,' I say and hear the tremble in my voice and the fake tone. This is harder than drawing geometrical shapes in school when you are asked to draw the portrait of the leader. The game of pretending you are happy and indifferent about something that makes you miserable is harder than anything I've done before.

Anushka comes over to me and kisses me on both cheeks too,

just like she did with Gigi. *Just like she kissed Gigi*, I think. *There is nothing wrong with it.*

'Anushka is going to swim with us to the boat,' Gigi announces cheerfully.

The painting of Anushka that I had planned rushes back to me, only darker. All my revenge is in my bloody, imaginary paintings. Anushka's bloated white face like a deity of death and misfortune, rising above the dark waves, the black Black Sea where I heard that Medea cut her brother Absyrtus to pieces and threw him in the water when she was fleeing from her father with her beloved Jason. Jason was a liar who used Medea to get his hands on the silly golden fleece, brought her to his kingdom and then married someone else when he got tired of her. I grow dizzy from my thoughts and my mouth is dry. I say to Gigi almost in a whisper: 'Oh, I'm glad, and then we can show her the boat.'

The rest of the day is blurry and in the centre of it is always the image of Gigi and Anushka together. Like a human compound. Gigi and Anushka are swimming behind me, because Gigi is all politeness and purposefully slows down so that Anushka won't be left behind. Anushka's white, even arms move softly through the water, her blonde hair spreading around her like a golden web. Gigi's beloved freckled body is getting too close to Anushka. I feel so little, my body so obviously uneven, and my brown curls coil like strings of snakes about my head. My mother was right to warn me about Gigi. My mother knows, having suffered tragedies in her life, and being sad as a weeping willow, and not having been the pianist she once wanted to be. Sad people have good instincts. I should listen to my mother more. My thoughts become more tangled as the day goes by, an interminably long day, stretching like snaky elastic, one sticky minute after another. But I don't want to let Gigi see anything so I smile and pretend I'm happy and I laugh, and speak loudly. I mix French with English when speaking to Anushka. I want to show Gigi how I can get along with a foreigner, for that's all

Anushka is: an insolent, crazy foreigner who took the trouble to come all the way to our city of Mangalia in order to kill herself. So she says. But I don't believe her. I've heard of foreign women who come to our coast just to find themselves a man when they are lonely. Whatever happened to all the French men?

Through the pretence games and the swimming and eating fried *guvizi* on the boat, Anushka's French chirping scratches my brains: '*Oh c'est formidable*', '*c'est chouette*', '*oh, comme c'est drôle*', '*ah, mais dis donc, c'est si beau*'. For a twenty-year-old at the Sorbonne she doesn't have much of a vocabulary. I can understand every irritating word of it. And why does she have to exclaim all the time? But Gigi seems charmed by every syllable and comma. I stare in fascination at his eyes as they rest on the cleavage between her white, even breasts, as they stare in wonderment at the small, squinting blue eyes, or at the curve of her tiny lips as she produces her French exclamations. And Gigi's attempts at French sound ridiculous. For the first time I find Gigi irritating, exasperating.

Throughout this long, long day in which the sun has forgotten to set, I occasionally become choked by tears and cannot speak. In order to hide it I start laughing. I swim or walk ahead of them, pretending not to care. I won't let anyone see me cry. I think of Doru, Tudoriţa's husband with the missing arm. They say he didn't cry at all when the train cut off his arm that foggy morning and all that was left were shreds of bloody flesh. And there he is, travelling all over Europe building beautiful modern houses for rich people. The least I can do is to stand here on this God-forsaken Black Sea shore watching Gigi fall in love with a French woman and not cry. When I get home at night I'm more exhausted than if I'd swum fifty kilometres. My head is burning and I feel a need to be close to my mother. I stay with her in the kitchen and help her clean up after the last tourists have finished eating and gone to their rooms.

'What's this? Miss Artist has remembered she has a home, has she?' says my mother in her usual sour way. This time I ignore her sourness because I need her so badly.

'Mama, I'm not feeling well tonight. I have a bad headache,' I say, and finally all the tears I kept inside me all day long at the beach and in the sea and on the boat squirt out of me like a fountain.

My mother swishes her wet cloth over the outdoor dining table again and looks at me over her glasses, the way she often does to see if I am telling the truth about something. I see she has two new long wrinkles crossing her forehead, yet her tanned face, dotted with beads of sweat from cooking all day in a small kitchen in forty-degree heat, is majestic and handsome. I look straight at her through my tears, hoping that for once she'll be sweet and say something kind to me. But before she can open her mouth I hear myself say: 'Mama, can I sleep with you tonight, please?'

She scrutinizes me a little more, and miracle of all miracles, I see something that might resemble the beginning of a smile in the corner of her mouth.

'You've come to miss your old mama, hein?' she says, and she pinches my cheek. For my mother, pinching my cheek is an effusive show of affection. I know she means yes, that I can sleep with her tonight. Somehow, for now, that seems like the most immediate solution to all my problems.

My mother tells my father he has to sleep on the sofa because 'Nora needs to sleep with me tonight'. She almost sounds proud of her motherly concern.

My father opens his eyes wide as if he can't believe his ears, but tired as he is after his long day of running around town and along the whole seashore and making reports and studying the spread of various strains of dysentery, he decides to keep quiet and just goes to lie on the sofa. I watch my mother get ready for bed, wipe her face with a washcloth, take off her shoes, undo her hair and let it down, sit on the bed and massage the back of her neck. She looks tired and worn out, not just by the non-stop cooking and caring for a bunch of capricious tourists but by life in general. I wish things had been different between my mother and me. I wish I could talk to my mother and tell her about my problems with Gigi and Anushka. But I know that the second I said anything, the sentence 'I warned you about that Turk of yours, didn't I?' would fly out of her mouth like a poisoned arrow. For the moment I am content with what I have. I cuddle next to my mother and my tears stop, my body relaxes. It was a very long time ago that my mother kept me close to her in the afternoon when we took a nap. Although I never slept, I lay unmoving, regulated my breathing as if I were sleeping, just to prolong that time of closeness. My mother even passes the back of her hand over my face, as if wiping my tears, then turns over and in less than a minute she is asleep. My father is already snoring and the steady sound of the waves comes into the room. Tonight they have a sluggish beat, hushing and rustling and then leaving a second of silence in between. There are still people walking about outside and laughing.

Just as I am about to fall asleep, it seems to me I hear Gigi's voice in the street. And then Anushka's voice. Her laughter. Maybe I'm dreaming. I must be mistaken. I try to go to sleep, but there they are again: Gigi's unmistakable clear syllables, a little bit high-pitched but smooth, Anushka's chirping French, her childish laugh. Sounds of hurried steps. Certainly theirs. Now I'm fully awake and there is no sleeping for me tonight. Not ever. I can't quite make out what they are saying. I almost catch it, but not really, maybe '*dis donc*' and the word 'Paris' once or twice, maybe she is just telling him about Paris; then the word *capitaine* from Gigi, maybe he is telling her how he wants to become a ship's captain, then more laughter, then the steps are moving further away and there is silence again. And the beat of the waves. Gigi is walking with Anushka late at night in the street, passing my house. And then what? By the direction of their steps it seemed they were going towards her hotel. Their steps are moving in the direction of the *faleza*, close to the sea. They are talking about Paris late at night, without me, and heading towards her hotel. And then what? That must be their final destination, the Scala Hotel, her hotel. I want to get up and run after them. I want to call out to them in the night to tell them to wait for me, that I'm coming too. I want to walk on the *faleza* too. My parents are both sleeping and their steady breathing measures the seconds that go by in the night. They measure the time since they brought me into the world: an imperfect, weird child with fish paintings in her head. I don't want to move in case I wake my mother. I lie unmoving next to her. I've almost stopped breathing. Anushka's and Gigi's voices are ringing in my head over and over again, sometimes in low sneaky whispers, sometimes unbearably shrill. Paris, Paris, Paris, where women wear slinky dresses that cling to their bodies and smoke thick, smelly cigarettes called Gitanes, where women change their mind ten times a day to be more feminine and gasp and say things like '*oh, mais dis donc*', just like their pointy heels on those Parisian pavements: tic, toc, tic, toc, '*dis-donc, dis-donc*'.

The idea for my next fish painting comes to me. Right in the eye of the storm, the head of Anushka rises above the waters like a huge human buoy, bobbing this way and that above the boiling sea. There will be black and dark green oils in this painting, squirming and coiling waves and Anushka's whitish-pink face rising above them. But in fact Anushka's face is my own. I am the one drowning while Gigi and a blonde girl are trying to save me. They are pulling me by the hair and trying to wrap my arms around their necks. But I want only Gigi to save me, not the blonde girl. On the beach, the old Gypsy Mariţa is waiting for me with corn on the cob. She is waving to me from the shore, holding a corn cob in her hand. I have to get to Mariţa, if only I can get to Mariţa and her barrel of corn then everything will be fine. Gigi and the blonde girl are moving away from me and letting me drown. My head is not Anushka's head after all. I need to be saved, to get to Mariţa. In the basement of our house Gigi and Anushka are making love on my grandmother's grand piano. Anushka is riding on the piano and Gigi is holding her and thrusting into her. Then they are resting on the ivory keys and eating *guvizi*. I am screaming: '*Nu, nu, nu pe pian*', no, no, not on the piano. Gigi is smiling at me and telling me he can do that with Anushka because she is a real woman, not an imperfect girl like me. He says I missed my chance. I could have done that with him, exactly like that, the way he did it with Anushka. Anushka is the real thing, he says, and grabs her and starts all over again.

It is dawn and my parents are sitting beside me, putting cold compresses on my head. My father says I have forty-one degrees of fever. He says prolonged fever is dangerous to the brain. He asks if I can see or hear him. He appears to me in a fog. I tell him I can hear him fine. My mother is stroking my face; she hasn't done that in ages. I want to have a forty-one-degree fever for ever. My father takes my temperature and says with a serious face: 'It's not going down.' He takes out his syringe and gives me an injection. How convenient to have a father who's a doctor. You can be treated at home. You can die at home.

My mother makes me drink chilled camomile tea. And then another tea. A whole day passes with teas and syrups and injections. I need to paint my fish painting before it leaves my mind. I ask my father to bring me my easel and he says I'm not well enough to paint. I say I've never been in a better state to paint. I drift back to sleep and dream that Mariţa is showering me with sea jewellery and making me drink Turkish *braga*. The Turkish sweets are the best. Gigi is Turkish. Gigi loves Anushka, I love Gigi. It's a merry-go-round like the one on the pier for the Navy days. I go to the mosque and ask the Turkish women to help me get Gigi back and break Anushka's spell. They say it doesn't matter; because I'm not a Muslim, Gigi will never be mine. They offer me *baklava* instead. I don't want *baklava*, I want Gigi. They speak Turkish and they turn into cats. Black, glossy Muslim cats. I am going to tell Gigi that the mosque is full of black cats.

Now I'm awake and Tudoriţa is on the bed next to me too. Soon the whole neighbourhood will be here. She is nursing her baby. She also strokes my forehead and my face and smells of baby milk. She talks to me sweetly and asks me what's wrong and she says: 'Come, little Nora, come, my sweetie, wake up, say something to Aunt Tudoriţa.'

Her presence makes me feel better. I like seeing her naked breast and the baby's mouth suckling it. Tudoriţa has symmetrical breasts and arms. Everybody but me has symmetrical breasts and arms. My father said my breasts will even out when I nurse my own baby. Yes, my breasts, all right. But how about my arms? When will my arms even out? And how about my silly walk when I pull a little to the side as if my longer arm is too heavy for me and I am dragging it along?

'How about that?' I asked my father.

He didn't answer.

'How about that, Daddy, how about my arms? When will my arms even out?'

'Just think of your uncle Doru, he doesn't have an arm at all,' said my mother. 'You are lucky.'

'Yes, you're lucky,' repeated my father.

I'm a lucky girl, I guess.

My fever goes down by evening and my mind is clearer, though I feel weak. Around suppertime, I hear Gigi's voice at the door asking for me. He asks my mother if I'm all right, if he can see me. Gigi's voice is like cool honey. Suddenly I don't feel so weak any more and I want to get out of bed but I'm so dizzy that I fall back. My father pushes me back into bed. Gigi appears at the door. His round brown eyes are wide open with surprise.

'Hello, Mr Teodoru,' he says politely. My mother comes in behind him and invites him to sit down on the sofa. How come now that I've been raving mad with fever everybody is being so nice to Gigi?

'I think I got sunstroke on the beach yesterday, too much sun, and then the fish on the boat . . . it made me sick,' I say, trying to sound as neutral and peaceful as possible.

'I can't believe you got sunstroke,' Gigi says. 'I should have been more careful, I shouldn't have said we should go to the boat and spend so much time in that blasted sun.'

'What's done is done,' says my father, closing up his doctor's kit. 'You kids have had quite an adventurous summer, haven't you?' He winks at Gigi. He means the almost-drowning adventure. My mother is staring at us, becoming her stern, edgy self again. My father realizes his blunder and tries to repair it. 'I mean with all the storms this summer, and the Navy days and all the tourists in town, and now this . . .'

'Mama, can I have some more tea?' I call suddenly, trying to distract my mother, although I feel I will burst if I have one more cup of tea.

'Yes, I'll bring you your tea,' my mother says and goes away, wiping her hands on her apron.

I know Gigi is trying to talk to me but he feels inhibited because of my father's presence. My father understands, picks up his medical kit and leaves the room.

'I must be getting myself back to work now,' he says. 'You kids be good. No swimming for you today, Madame la Princesse.' Sometimes my father teasingly calls me Madame la Princesse, but now the sound of French irritates me because it reminds me of Anushka.

'I wanted to drop by last night to ask you out. I passed by your house but it was all dark. I was going to the port to take some food to my father and ran into Anushka on the way. We talked about you,' Gigi says cheerfully.

If he only knew that I almost died because of that stroll he and Anushka took past my house last night . . . But he will never know,

I must never tell Gigi about these snaky feelings that torment me. Gigi's eyes are sparkling with something new, a smile of confidence, a thread of mischief. I don't believe he wanted to ask me out, I don't believe he talked about me with Anushka. But what I do believe tears me to shreds. I know what I'll do. Suddenly it came to me in a vision just as I was coming out of my delirium at dawn.

'Yes, I went to bed early,' I say with matter-of-fact ease. 'I started feeling bad around seven or so and then it got worse.'

My mother comes into the room with another cup of chilled camomile tea. She thinks it's the cure to everything because of its calming properties. She looks Gigi up and down and speaks to him with no kindness, as if talking to a delinquent.

'So what are you up to today, hmm?'

Gigi doesn't blink at the harsh tone because he knows my mother and he always excuses her 'because of her hard life'. He answers politely: 'I'm going to spend some time with my father on the ship this evening, Mrs Teodoru, to help him clean out his cabin . . .'

'Well, goodbye then,' my mother says suddenly. 'Nora needs to rest now because she's had a fever all night and all day.' Last night I would have died of happiness to hear my mother talk so protectively about me, but now she irritates me again as she does nine times out of ten, every day of my life.

Gigi gets up and says his polite goodbyes to my mother and me, winks at me behind my mother's back and moves softly out of the room. His smell of algae and fish lingers in the room for a while. I sleep well tonight with no dreams.

I am calm the next morning. The fever took away my craziness. Fever cleans you of all your toxins, I always hear Tudoriţa say. She knows, being a nurse and dealing with feverish patients every day. I know my mother is in the kitchen again, getting back to her day's cooking which she is already behind with, because of my sudden sickness. I get up slowly after she leaves. I put on my white cotton shirt and my jeans, because I feel boyish and strong when I wear them. I tiptoe out of the room and out of the house. The salty morning air wakes me up. Autumn is coming soon, I think as I pick a little grape from our hanging vine and taste it. I walk determinedly towards Anushka's hotel at the end of the *faleza.* The petunias along the walk are still sprinkled with the morning dew. Their smell gives me a jolt of new energy. As does the sea this morning, stretching out in its greenish-violet, oily, lazy way.

I reach the awning of the hotel, the same awning under which Gigi and I stood that evening in the storm and saw the blonde woman being tossed this way and that by the wild waves. I walk in with confidence. We can't just walk into a hotel like that if we are not a guest, and we are not allowed to go to foreigners' rooms, but the receptionist recognizes me as Dr Sandu's daughter and lets me go in. Everybody is scared of my father because they know he gives them their hygiene ratings. I get to Anushka's room and wait a little before knocking to review in my mind the speech I made up yesterday afternoon. Anushka is crying with little hiccups, softly, monotonously. Then I knock three times. There is a moment of silence, probably the moment in which she pulls herself together.

Then I hear a cheerful: '*Qui est là?*'

I gather my courage, set my arms akimbo, and say in an equally cheerful voice: '*C'est moi,* Nora Teodoru.' As if Anushka could have known several Noras this summer in Mangalia. I hear a shuffle of shoes, Anushka's nose being blown, and then she opens the door. Her eyes are red. Her face looks even more childlike. She is wearing jeans and a red and white striped shirt. Somehow everything she puts on looks good and sexy on her. Whereas me . . . But I don't let my confidence diminish.

She kisses me on both cheeks as she always does and says: '*Tu es très belle aujourd'hui, Nora.*' I never know whether Anushka's compliments to me are for real or out of pity because of my bodily imperfection. I caught her looking at my breasts and arms the day we undressed at the beach and then I saw her quickly turn her face away when she realized I had seen her look.

I don't respond to her compliment with anything other than a grateful smile, and I pull her out on to the balcony because I know that foreigners' rooms are bugged. She is surprised but follows me obediently. There, in half-whispers, I tell her in a medley of French, English, Romanian and gestures that I know how sad she is because of her boyfriend's death. That Gigi and I saved her life and although she wanted to die, life is not that bad. That she has the Sorbonne classes and all her beautiful Parisian dresses and her French and Polish friends to live for. That my lousy provincial high school is tapestried with portraits of Ceauşescu and that I can't learn the skills I need in order to become a real artist. And that Gigi means a lot to me, that's all. She should get out of our lives. As I am talking to her I realize that, ironically, it is because of the drowning episode and the damned mouth-to-mouth resuscitation, because of Gigi's flirting and attentions to Anushka, that for the first time I give voice to feelings I didn't know I had. They are clear-sounding words that in turn make my blood boil and my heart pound. I am surprised by it all. 'Gigi is a boy and like all boys he is weak when it comes to beautiful women,' I say to Anushka. She should leave today, right away! Now! She looks at me and touches my curls. She tells me I have beautiful hair. What does my hair have to do with anything I've just said? She is just buying time so she can hurt me afterwards.

But to my surprise Anushka says: '*Ah bon, très bien, je pars cet après-midi.*' Just like that. There is a train to Bucharest in the afternoon and then a flight to Paris that night, she says. I'm surprised she knows the train and plane timetables so well. Then I find out she's been meaning to leave every day, but some kind of inertia would keep her for one more day, make her think she would feel better and less sad if she stayed another day. *Yes, right, thinking how to seduce my Gigi*, I think. She thanks me for pushing her to leave. '*Non . . . vraiment, merci,*' she says and embraces me. Then she tells me that I am strong and I know what I want, that she would like to be like me. That's the first time I ever hear anyone say they want to be like me, and it's almost funny because for so much of the time I want to be like so many other people except myself.

I think it's a misunderstanding, but she repeats: '*Vraiment, je voudrais être comme toi, Nora!*'

Maybe Anushka is not a witch, but just confused. There is something pathetic about her, something that makes you feel both sorry for her and angry with her. She starts packing feverishly. She hums a French song while she packs. God, you get to be sophisticated when you don't live under a stupid leader like ours. You learn to do whatever you feel like at any hour of the day. Even spin the globe and go wherever your finger happens to land on it and choose an exotic place to commit suicide. From the mound of clothes she crams into her suitcase, which contains more items of clothing than all the women in our family own put together, a yellow-orangey scarf has fallen on to the floor. It has the colour of Van Gogh's sunflowers. It must be silk because it shimmers and catches the light like a watery surface. I have never seen a fabric as beautiful as this one. I fix my mind on the scarf, think that if I don't mention it, since it has fallen almost under the bed, she might forget it. Then I'll come back and tell the receptionist I left my scarf in Miss Pomorowska's room, can I please go back and get it. But then I feel ashamed of my thought, so I lean over, pick it up and hand it to her.

I say: 'Here, you dropped this . . . it's a beautiful scarf.' Anushka takes it and throws it unthinkingly in the suitcase. Nothing seems special when you have so much.

After a second, Anushka removes the scarf from the suitcase and hands it to me, saying: 'You can have it.'

I blush terribly, as if she could have guessed my thought of two minutes ago and I say: '*Oh non, non merci, merci beaucoup!*'

She takes it and wraps it around my head loosely in one swing of her arm. Everything comes so easily to Anushka. '*Tu es très belle,*' she says. I love the feel of the orange silk around my neck, my face, and its soft texture makes me feel light as a feather. I want the scarf so badly. I don't say anything. I just touch my head wrapped in this textile masterpiece and smile as a thank-you to Anushka. Then I actually get up from the bed and kiss her on both cheeks the way she has been doing with Gigi and me all along. She takes my hand in hers, looks into my eyes and tells me that if I ever, ever want to come to Paris, because she knows how much I want to become an artist, if I ever decide to come to Paris, to call her, that she'll help me. She'll always be grateful to me and Gigi for saving her life. Having tried to commit suicide in the Black Sea turned out to be the best thing she'd ever done, she says, and produces one of her girlish giggles, throwing her head back. She turns to the bag lying on the bed, takes out her little notebook and tears out a small sheet of paper. She writes her full name, address and telephone number on it. Her address sounds like a line of poetry: 27 Rue Lecourbe, Appartement 10, Paris. She folds the paper, opens my palm and places it inside, then carefully closes my palm over it. I feel like I am part of a secret ritual. My palm is suddenly a flower unfolding at dawn and folding back into itself at dusk. I keep my fist closed tight, like nobody in the world could ever take the paper away from me.

When I come out of the spell of this moment, I thank Anushka but I also laugh at the idea of me just 'deciding' to go to Paris, as if that were really a possibility, as if one could just decide to go to Paris to study when one lives in this country, and could simply take the train to Bucharest, hop on the plane to Paris and then study art with French artists. Nevertheless, I keep my fist closed tight over the piece of paper with Anushka's address and phone number.

Then Anushka says: '*Au revoir, bonne chance . . .*' and adds: '*Dis au revoir à Gigi de ma part.*' I feel the sharp sting in my heart at the sound of his name in her mouth. But then I look at her face and it seems to me I understand Anushka a little better now. Almost as if we could have been friends. Too late though because she'll be gone in a few hours.

I'm getting ready to leave. I see Anushka is almost done with her chaotic packing. I want to make sure she catches the train back to Bucharest. We stand in the middle of the room looking at each other. I see tears in Anushka's eyes and for some awkward reason I feel tears welling up in my own. Anushka embraces me. She holds me for a few seconds and repeats her invitation to Paris. She whispers '*merci*' one more time. I don't say anything and leave the room in a rush, wanting to escape the tears and this sour taste of something final and sad.

When I'm out in the street I look up and see Anushka at the hotel window looking at me, waving. I run towards my house and feel the light silkiness of the orangey scarf around my face, caressing me like a feather. I believe I am in love with Gigi.

When I get home, I go directly to the pantry and take out my easel. This time I don't want to go to the beach to paint. I want to stay in my own garden, in the exact place where if I look very attentively through the grapevine and the geraniums, and the bushes and the trees, there is one tiny blue shimmering glimpse of the sea. My mother is in the midst of her cooking and won't bother me. I sit on a little stool that I bring out from inside and neatly line up all my tempera tubes in front of me. Now I start at a very different point from the last time. I begin with yellow, Anushka's yellow hair. I want to capture all the fury and pain I felt during those days, the ache of hearing Gigi and Anushka's voices in the night, as if they were lovers, as if they were going towards her hotel, as if I didn't exist.

Ever since Mariţa told me the story of a Turkish princess called Esma in the market on a hot summer afternoon, I have often thought Esma was living through me and that's why I've always had this obsession with painting. Mariţa said that 'Esma used to possess the magic skill of creating images on a canvas with colours and shapes.' She came to our part of the world on a black steed at the crack of dawn, wearing a soldier's helmet. She was carrying with her a painting based on a dream she had had and which had been the inspiration for her journey. Mariţa's way of describing Esma's talent for painting and turning her dreams into real images opened up a magic well of desire inside me: to create the world, *my* world, on canvas with colours and shapes. My hands have always been restless.

Now, on this summer afternoon of so many important realizations, I wanted to make Anushka's face frightening and strange, the way I had seen it in my dream. But something else comes out of my brush: her face as she was this afternoon in the hotel room when she gave me the orange scarf: soft, sweet, her eyes slightly rimmed with red from the tears. She is emerging from the stormy dark green waters like a benevolent goddess, not like the evil one I had imagined. My paintings have a mind of their own, and they always come out different from what I set my mind to do. I am brushing one layer of yellow tempera on top of another, making it as bright as I can. It becomes luminous and translucent like a river of gold. I move across the page with quick and sure strokes. As I am painting I speak softly to Esma, whispering to her. I feel awake and dreaming at the same time, my right hand is gliding on the paper softly, my left hand, the larger one, spreading the paint with quick moves. Anushka's face is appearing clear and bright, wide-eyed from inside the storm, like a sun in the middle of the vicious waves. My painting is growing on the page like a living creature.

Anushka is on the train to Bucharest right now, and I feel peaceful as I touch the feathery yellow scarf around my face. Anushka must be nearing the capital right now and I have finished my painting of her.

My Brother's Arrival

Towards the end of the summer, my mother announces at dinner: 'Your brother is coming to live with us.' I'm startled and choke on the piece of bread I have just swallowed. The last time I saw my brother was when we were ten and he came with Aunt Raluca to spend part of his summer holiday by the sea. Raluca had mud treatments every day while Valentin spent several hours a day playing the piano in the basement, and then going to the beach with my mother and me. Those were the rare times my mother went to the beach and endured the sun and the sand, which she had never much cared for. She satisfied every one of Valentin's whims and he had many. If he wanted to eat Turkish *halvah* she ran around the Turkish neighbourhood trying to get him the best and freshest brand. One day he asked if we had a swing in our yard and that very day my mother called a carpenter she knew in town and begged him to install an old wooden swing that she had found in the pile of junk in our basement. She sat next to Valentin while he practised at the piano, quite still, in utter adoration. She stroked his hair and squeezed him to her chest any chance she got. I watched with a mixture of fascination and jealousy my mother's fulsome shows of affection towards my brother. Mostly, though, I benefited as well from my brother's visit because my mother softened her wild temper a little, and since Valentin always wanted to play with me, she took me along on each of the outings she organized.

When Valentin wanted to take a boat trip, my mother left her tourists in the care of Tudoriţa and took us both early in the morning to the port for the three-hour cruise out to sea. That day my mother actually dressed us like twins, both in sailor's clothes: navy blue and white shirts, navy trousers for Valentin and navy skirt for me, and a white and blue cotton beret for each of us. My mother, usually so morose and so reluctant to talk about anything personal with anybody, now showed off her son to anyone who stopped in the street and greeted us. As soon as so-and-so said: 'Good morning, Mrs Teodoru, how are you?' my mother would immediately say: 'Oh, I'm taking the children for a boat trip. This is my son Valentin, he lives in Bucharest with my sister for part of the time . . . to study the piano, he is a music prodigy.' Valentin invariably blushed and cast his eyes to the pavement or to his white and navy shoes and refused to talk to anyone who addressed him. 'He is shy, musicians are usually shy,' my mother would offer as an excuse. I remember that on that particular morning, after the third time Valentin had done his shy act on the beach walk towards the port, I secretly pinched his arm as hard as I could. He didn't say a word, just lifted his eyes at me with a pleading look. He was not only shy but pale and sickly-looking and after a day at the beach his face went bright red. His hair was dark and lank, sort of like my father's except that Aunt Raluca insisted it should grow longer than was customary for boys. I sometimes teased him and told him he looked like a girl. Did he want to wear one of my dresses? I would ask.

On the boat, we sat on the top deck right near the edge, to have the best view of the sea. Valentin was sitting between my mother and me. My mother put her arm around both of us when the boat began to move. 'Isn't this nice, children?' she asked with a smile. And her face was both radiant and sad. The ship slid out of the port towards the horizon. It was a perfect summer day, not one single cloud in the sky, a sea as smooth and shiny as a silver mirror and white seagulls circling around the boat, shrieking vigorously. I took my brother's hand. It felt fragile and moist. He squeezed my hand and I remember feeling a flood of affection for him then, for his small frame, his white face turned red from the sun, his thin legs with the bony knees. My mother looked at us and her eyes were full of tears. A pop song about a crazy heart by one of our most popular singers, Corina Chiriac, started playing through the loudspeakers and the ship moved forward, leaving behind the long stretch of beaches filled with coloured umbrellas. It felt like a perfect moment, though sadness and joy both seemed to be oozing through it. Something was not perfect, and that was our bizarre living arrangements and the prospect of the imminent separation at the end of the holidays. I didn't understand why this piano tuition was so important and why my brother had to live all alone with that serious, sad-looking aunt of ours when his real family all lived here by the sea. For all the talk about how he was a genius and a prodigy, my brother looked sad and unhealthy. But for the duration of that boat trip he was happy. He held my hand until we arrived back in the port and my mother concluded the trip by saying: 'That was nice, wasn't it? We'll go again.' We never did go again. When we got off the boat, Aunt Raluca was waiting for us, waving as if we couldn't see her right in front of us. She was coming from her mud treatments and smelled weird. Raluca held out her hand to Valentin, but instead he took our mother's hand. Raluca smiled a fake smile, pretended she didn't care, and then asked how the trip was.

My mother says that Raluca is very ill, that she is dying and cannot take care of Valentin any longer. So he will come to live with us, 'where he belongs'. Doru, who lives part of the time in Bucharest, will look after Raluca for a while, and then my mother will go and stay with her till the end. It was only after that last summer with Valentin that my mother told me about Raluca's tragedy. She said she had received the call in the evening and her sister was screaming and announcing the worst, the unbearable: her child, Gabriel, had fallen from the balcony and died. The bedroom balcony, she said, as if it mattered which balcony. But she repeated that it was the bedroom balcony. My father got up immediately and took the night train to Bucharest to find out what had happened. My mother stayed with my brother and me and did not want to go to Bucharest to be with her sister. She was afraid to let go of us even for a few hours. We were only three years old, Valentin and I. She kept us close to her and took us into her bed at night for months after that. She kept having dreams of the two of us falling in an endless dark tunnel. We had slipped out of her arms, just like that. After Gabriel's death my father brought Aunt Raluca to live here with us because she kept trying to kill herself. The first thing she did when she came was to go to the kitchen and slice her wrists with the fish knife. My father had to sew her up and bandage her. He gave her intravenous tranquillizers and she slept for a long time. Then her eyes fell on Valentin. She stared at him for a long time, watched him walk round the room and fall on his face, suck his thumb, pull my curls, grab at my mother's skirt. Raluca wouldn't take her eyes off him, not one of his gestures escaped her. She sat on the sofa in our living room for hours and did nothing but watch Valentin. He was a curious little boy and he started going to her and pulling at her long, lank hair. He chirped at her in his own language, and once he bit her thumb. She smiled. She picked him up and put him on her knee. He sat quietly in her lap as if wanting to soothe her. One day my mother grabbed Raluca, dragged her outside and asked her to go to the beach. The sisters walked along the beach in the wind for hours, yelling at each other. They spilled out all the venom from their childhood, all the recriminations for their life choices and misfortunes. How Raluca had the piano lessons although it was my mother who was passionate about music. Raluca ended up a botanist. They both felt short-changed by life. It turned out that they both hated their father and had never admitted it. My grandfather and his mania about land! But then when he was killed by the Communists they made him into a hero, a martyr. And what about my grandmother? No wonder she had cheated on him. She was a concert pianist, admired and loved by everyone, playing for high society even during the war, in her black taffeta gown and her long string of pearls. What was she doing with a peasant who had become a big landowner? Then they felt sorry for their father again. He had gritted his teeth and worked himself to death to offer their mother a luxurious life, until the day he was taken away. Only to be tortured and killed afterwards. If it hadn't been for the war, for the Fascists who profited from the worst instincts of the Romanian people, for the Russians who came and ravaged everything, for the Communists who settled in for ever, maybe things would have been different, they might have had a chance at something better. They fell on to the sand, crying, sobbing and tearing at their hair. Raluca asked if she could have Valentin with her in Bucharest once in a while. Wouldn't it be of help to Rodica if she shared in his upbringing and exposed him to the culture in Bucharest? He seemed such an unusual child. My mother said he was fine where he was, growing up by the sea, and it wouldn't be good to separate him from his twin sister. But then when she saw Raluca's deathly pallor, she said, well, all right, maybe sometimes, for a week or two. So Raluca first took him for two weeks, during which she said she was going to show him round the city, take him to a concert or two and maybe to the circus. Mama thought that would be good for Valentin and went along with the plan, packing his little things in a suitcase for two weeks. She took them both to the station and when she saw her boy waving from the train window as Raluca held him up, she had a bad feeling that he was slipping away from her, that she was losing him. Mama told me this story that very afternoon after Valentin's return to Bucharest, soon after our special boat trip out to sea. Throughout the story she had globes of tears in her eyes, which never fell down her cheeks, just filled her eyes and made them particularly shiny. That was one of the few times in my life I felt sorry for my mother. But it was for a very short time that I experienced that feeling, because no sooner had she finished her story than she blurted out, as if she was sorry for her few moments of warmth and gentleness, that I wasn't good enough in school, how I had to stop my scribbling on walls and tablecloths. And why couldn't I be more like my brother? I remember hating not only my mother that afternoon but my brother as well. After he had taken all the space for himself while we were sharing our mother's womb, and pushed me so that I came out with this lopsided body, now my mother was blaming me for everything that was not Valentin. She made me feel guilty even for the air I breathed in that wretched house at number nine filled with the ridiculously shiny lacquered furniture.

'Aren't you happy?' my mother asks after giving me the news of Valentin's imminent arrival and his new living arrangements. I don't really feel I'm bursting with joy, but rather confused and angry. I'm sorry for Raluca to be dying while still pretty young, but since I know her so little I'm not terribly sorry either. When my brother left five years ago after his last summer holiday at the beach, I locked up that part of my heart. I cried at the station until my eyes were blurry, and my mother had to drag me from the platform after the train was gone because I still wouldn't budge. She said that he would be back the following summer, but for various reasons he never came. She would usually take a short trip to Bucharest in the spring to see her son and carry an entire suitcase of food just for him. She would come back filled with news of my brother and talk only of his piano success and how he was top of his class. She would look at me to make sure I realized that I was *not* top of my class. With exams for the music school and getting ready for one recital after another, he was always too busy and Raluca never seemed to find the time to travel to Mangalia any more. I stopped thinking of him. I locked up the room with the memories of my twin and sometimes, when a new kid came to our school, I never even mentioned him. What was I going to say: 'I have a brother but he is too clever to live here in Mangalia with all of us, so he lives with his aunt in Bucharest and drowns in piano lessons from morning till night'?

And now Valentin is coming to live with us, and according to my mother I have to give up my room because 'he needs peace of mind to concentrate on his music'. 'I need my peace of mind too so I can concentrate on my painting,' I tell my mother. My mother asks wickedly: 'What painting?' I feel such rage that I turn the bowl of soup upside down all over the freshly ironed white tablecloth and stand up. The tablecloth becomes a yucky green. My father stands up as well and tells me to calm down. That makes me even angrier. I have a sour feeling that I don't belong in this family, that my parents have lied to me, they have made bad choices in our living arrangements, have gone along with things they shouldn't have. They never cared for my painting talent while always extolling my brother's musical genius.

I don't hear anything of what the two of them have to say any more. They look like the characters from the silent movies I watch sometimes when we get our foreign TV programmes on Saturday: Laurel and Hardy or Charlie Chaplin, moving their lips and going this way and that, only nothing is heard. Just a big subtitle once in a while announcing across the entire screen: 'I think we are in trouble!' or 'See that man over there? He's after us.' Or 'Run!' Just that one single word on the screen: 'Run!'

I stand up in front of my parents and I hear myself telling them: 'I don't trust you any longer. You have lied to me my whole life. I don't love you. I don't care if my brother Valentin is coming to live with us. You have always loved him more than you have loved me.'

I get up from the peach-upholstered chair at the head of the lacquered table and I leave the room. I open the front door with the lacquered surface and the metal number 9 stuck to it and I go out into the street. I run down the street towards the centre of town. I pass by the casino in the corner, the *alimentara*, the grocery store in the square, I pass by the mosque with its three golden crescent moons and its walls lit for evening prayer, I pass by the big square with the huge Communist mural of the man and the woman walking or flying in a trance, holding a baby towards the sun, with the hammer and sickle at the top. In our country parents give away their children to the common good, to the sun, to the future, we make babies for the Communist future. I keep running and I don't stop. Nobody can keep up with me. A funny thought comes to me as I run: I thought I had problems because Gigi was staring at Anushka's cleavage, when all the time my whole life is one huge problem! From even before my birth, when I was in my mama's womb and Valentin was squishing into my body to get all the air and all the space so that I came out uneven. I run in meandering lines through the city. I pass through the little bazaar, hoping to see Mariţa, but I don't stop. I am the fastest runner in this wretched town. Mariţa is not there. I keep running towards the end of the town where the Gypsy camp is. I go through the Turkish district and through all their back yards. I jump over fences, I push through the vines.

I am running through the sunflower field now, it's so dark out here and there is not a soul in sight. I keep running towards the line of smoke in the distance. The Gypsies are burning leaves. There is music in the Gypsy camp, someone is playing the accordion and someone else is playing the harmonica. The fire of leaves is burning high tonight. The Gypsies are warming up around it, and some of the younger women are inside the tents with their babies. They keep their babies close to their hearts like their most precious possessions. The Gypsies know me and they let me pass. A young girl with enormous black plaits shows me Mariţa's tent. It is only inside Mariţa's tent that I stop.

She doesn't ask anything, because Mariţa always knows what to do on every occasion. First she gives me water in a stone jug. I drink the water. I catch my breath. Mariţa doesn't ask anything because she knows I will tell her everything once I am ready. I pour it all out to her between cries and hiccups and swear words addressed to my parents. She just says: 'Shush, my turtle dove,' and she rocks me at her breast. She smells of dried plums and pipe smoke.

I tell Mariţa that my mother destroyed our lives, that she destroyed my life, and that she should never have accepted that crazy arrangement for Valentin to grow up away from his family. That she has never cared about my art classes, but everybody had to make such sacrifices for Valentin's piano lessons. My mother has been a crazy viper my entire childhood because she missed her son so much and all she saw in me was the son she had lost who was growing up in her sister's house instead of under her eyes. And my ugly imperfection reminded her every second of what she was missing.

Mariţa sits motionless. 'Life is about learning to endure the pain, my turtle dove. Your mother didn't destroy your life, so how is your life destroyed, hein?' Mariţa asks and I see she is getting all worked up the way she sometimes does. 'So you had it a little bit harder, your mama wasn't all sugar and honey with you, so what? It taught you to be tough. So one of your sides is a little off? Big deal. You are still one of the most beautiful girls around. It would have been impossible for Valentin to find a piano tutor in this small town of ours, and Raluca needed to care for another child after her loss. Sometimes people need to make sacrifices, it's what life is all about . . .' I'm sick of hearing about all our tragedies and sacrifices, how about my feelings and my talents, and my growing up neglected and hated by my own mother? 'Do you want me to show you all the maimed children we've got here in the camp, from all the stupid accidents our people get into because we are always desperate and hungry and running away from someone?' asks Mariţa.

I sit and pout stubbornly on Mariţa's bed. I don't want to see any maimed children from Mariţa's camp right now.

'Your parents worked for you all day long, your mama cooking herself to death in the summer for them tourists, your tata running himself to death on his medical assignments so you can live in one of the most beautiful houses in town. Only Party people have better houses than your folk. And look at you: a healthy, beautiful girl who can paint all sorts of wonders on a sheet of paper just like that. And Miss Nora is all misery and tragedy. Didn't you learn anything from the stories I told you when you was little? I don't ever want to hear you talk like that about your parents. You can sleep here tonight and in the morning I'm taking you home and tomorrow you are going to greet your brother and get reacquainted with him and love him. And you're going to be kind to your mama, she's been through enough hard times in her life.'

The smell of burnt leaves and the sound of Gypsies playing and singing and the day's upsets are finally making me sleepy. Mariţa crouches on the earth floor of her tent and says some kind of prayer in her language. She is rolling beads in her hand; her voice is low and melodic. I'm drifting into sleep and Mariţa lies next to me after her prayer. I feel safe next to her full body. Little gusts of cool September air are coming in through the flaps of the tent. The Gypsy songs are getting softer, like a dream. Valentin, what a funny name, like a tango step with a stumble! I dream of us at age ten on the boat, holding hands and looking out at the shiny blue sea, my mother's arm curled around us and white seagulls shrieking above our heads. That was a happy day.

A Box Full of Surprises

It is my Uncle Doru who brings my brother Valentin to our house, from Bucharest. He took care of the practical things for Valentin's departure and made sure Aunt Raluca was well looked after in the hospital. He sweeps in like a hurricane as always, speaking and laughing in a thunderous voice and smelling of foreign cologne, with the empty sleeve of his right arm elegantly tucked inside his coat pocket, his left hand hugging people and a cigarette hanging in the corner of his mouth. I am always in awe whenever Uncle Doru enters the room and I expect something extraordinary to happen, for the weather to change suddenly or for my mother to become sweet and kind. Aunt Tudoriţa, who is always slightly sad in the absence of her husband, is now circling around him like a frantic hen and smiling continuously. I am sitting on one of the peach-upholstered chairs in the corner of the living room and staring madly at the door, waiting for my brother to make his appearance. I am dying to see how he has grown, how he compares to the ten-year-old boy whose fragile little hand I held for the three hours of that magical boat ride with our mother. I am wearing my Levi jeans, the white cotton shirt and the yellow silk scarf from Anushka around my neck. Its soft texture makes me feel calmer, more in control, as if Anushka's spell was on me.

'He is getting his stuff out of the car, the rascal,' says Uncle Doru. He is the only member of our family who has a car and who can drive, although he has only one arm. *Uncle Doru is a force of nature*, I think, staring at him in fascination, trying to distract myself and calm my wild impatience.

My mother is very quiet and sits on a chair at the other end of the room, her hands in her lap, staring at her fingernails. My father is standing by the door, looking casual and calm, but I know that he is just as nervous from the way he keeps sniffing as if he has a cold. My mother has made *galusţe cu prune*, plum dumplings, and *pateuri cu branza*, little salty cheese pastries, and put on the table a big jug of Turkish *braga*. There is a short moment of complete silence, in which we all seem confused, and then my father opens the door wide.

He is tall and lanky and has dark hair falling over his forehead. A taller, more mature version of the ten-year-old I remember. My heart is beating so fast that for a second my vision gets blurry. Then I stare at him again as he is standing in the doorway, with a suitcase and a clutch of bags, looking confused and disoriented. I burst out laughing and he looks at me. He smiles too and when he smiles the door to that secret room in my memory opens up. I remember the small boy he was, always a little fragile, a little whiny, a little dreamy, yet somehow utterly sweet. I remember the flood of affection I felt for him when we held hands on the boat going out into the sparkling summer sea and how badly I wished he would stay so we could play together and talk about everything and share secrets. How inconsolably I cried on the station platform and then the little click and crack sound with which I locked up the secret room of my psyche with my brother in it. Uncle Doru takes the stuff out of his hands and throws it on the floor with a loud thud. My father is directing him towards one of the chairs, the peach-upholstered chairs around our lacquered dining-room table, and gently makes him sit down. I am surprised to notice again how much Valentin looks like my father and how he bears no resemblance to either me or my mother. Our mother. We are twins but not identical twins, that's why.

I can see that Mama is unable to articulate any sounds except for little squeaking noises from her throat which she is covering with a pretend cough. Tudoriţa is going around Valentin, offering him plum dumplings.

'No, no, I am not hungry. Maybe later,' are the first words that my brother utters. His voice surprises me like everything else about him. It must be changing because it is low and deep but then it breaks and squeaks in places. Gigi's voice has already broken, I think. Gigi is already a man.

The air in the room is warm glue. We are stuck, our breathing is gooey, our silence is sticky, I am desperately playing with my yellow-orange silk scarf and my hands are moist with perspiration.

'Do you want to go to the beach for a swim?' I yell suddenly, remembering that taking someone to the sea when they have just arrived after a long trip has always been a good way to escape the unease of the first moments. The sea is the solution to everything around here.

Valentin seems relieved and immediately answers yes, he would very much like to go to the sea. His voice breaks again in a little squeak at the end of the sentence and I burst out laughing again. He says he hardly remembers the sea. What a messed-up family we ended up in, this would never have happened if we'd had half-normal parents, and if Valentin and I had both grown up with the sea around the corner, smelling and breathing it every day, swimming in it, running by it and drinking it all in. And we wouldn't all be sitting here like a family of confused morons swimming in gluey air. Maybe we are all cursed because my grandfather loved his land more than his own children. What kind of madness was that anyway to love your land more than your children – and all that crap about God's loins! Maybe we are cursed for other reasons I don't know. Maybe every corner of this house is boiling with sickening secrets of dead children, murders, suicides, maimed creatures and a lot of cursed land that isn't even ours any more as since the war it all belongs to the State. I notice that my parents and even Uncle Doru, who is always so in control of everything, seem relieved by my initiative.

On the beach Valentin is ill at ease at first. He walks slowly on the sand, and doesn't even look up at the sea. I nudge him and show it to him, make him look.

'I know, I feel it, I had forgotten how beautiful it was. I sometimes dream of it. The way it was that day on the boat.'

He is walking towards the water as if in a trance and his long black trousers are getting all sandy at the bottom. He doesn't mind. He is walking into the water and doesn't care that his trousers are getting wet. There is something in his lost and oldish manner that makes me feel sorry for him. Normally Gigi and I would laugh until our sides cracked when we saw what we called the 'Moldovan bumpkins' come to the sea for the first time and walk in with their clothes on. I draw his attention to the fact that he is going into the water with his trousers on; would he like me to run home quickly and bring him an old pair of trunks of my father's?

He looks at me, surprised, as if woken up from a dream and says: 'Oh no, don't worry. I'll just take these off.' And he takes off his black trousers and remains in his underwear, a pair of worn-out yellowish boxer shorts. His legs are scrawny and he looks like an overgrown child standing in his underwear with his ankles in the water. The sea is at its most ravishing this afternoon: lazy and milky, with little nervous ripples at the edges, a smooth silvery surface with rosy streaks from the setting sun. I ask him if he is cold, if he needs anything. He doesn't answer and he keeps staring at the expanse of water around him. He takes off his white shirt, a man's shirt with cuffs, and throws it on the beach. He crouches in the water as if it were a bath. That's when I start laughing wholeheartedly. He looks at me and smiles too. It is when he smiles that I recognize again something in him, a familiarity from far away . . . I see that he has a beautiful face. During the times we spent together when we were very little and then our two-month vacation at ten years old, I wasn't thinking of his physical beauty but just cared about the idea of a twin brother and a playmate and about holding his thin, fragile hands or, at times, pinching or teasing him when he irritated me. He has delicate and precise features, a thin nose, high cheekbones, a high forehead, and I become aware with some surprise that we share a feature: green shimmering eyes. I take off my white shirt and jeans since I almost always wear a bathing suit under my clothes in the summer. I don't get that itchy nervousness I usually get when I am in my bathing suit in front of someone I am meeting for the first time. I didn't use to care about that furtive look people always cast at my body and then the quick way in which they would avert their eyes and the fake smile they would put on as if they hadn't seen anything. I didn't think of that when we were just children playing in the sand, but I do now, because my uneven body has become a constant obsession and with the growth of my womanly features my unevenness has become more obvious. The comparison with Anushka's perfectly chiselled body made it more of an obsession. Valentin looks straight at me shamelessly and smiles. I like his bold look, he is entitled to it. We held and faced and squished each other for nine months in our mama's belly and then fought for her breast and for her attention until we were separated.

I don't want to make him feel clumsier than he must already feel, so I crouch next to him in the water. He starts swimming with long elegant breaststrokes. I imitate him and ask him where he learned how to swim so well. I don't remember him being such a good swimmer five years ago. I don't want to show off my fast swimming. He says at the swimming pool in Floreasca Park, near the State Circus. I have never been to the State Circus. Every word and bit of information that comes out of his mouth makes me think of the world he has grown up in, a world completely unknown to me. I imagine him as a little child going to the State Circus with Aunt Raluca, who apparently 'raised him like he was her own child', and staring in amazement at the ballerina in a shiny red costume hanging from the trapeze by her teeth. I am dying to ask him about the State Circus but I am afraid he will think I am childish and provincial. I compliment him on his swimming. There is so much to find out about each other.

'It's been a long time, Sister, hm?' he says abruptly.

'It certainly has,' I answer, trying to sound cool. 'Was it fun growing up in Bucharest?'

'Fun isn't quite the word, I would say interesting,' he says pedantically.

'Are you very sad?' I ask, curious. He nods yes, and doesn't say another word. I feel almost envious of Valentin that he is sad for the approaching death of the woman he considers almost his mother, because it means she was a good mother to him and he will miss her. I never missed my mother, not even when she was gone for a week to her relatives in Tulcea for her great-aunt's funeral. I felt relieved when my mother was absent. I miss missing my mother the way Valentin will miss Aunt Raluca when she dies.

'I will go to Bucharest to visit her at the hospital every Sunday until the end,' he says with determination.

I find out more about his and Raluca's life in Bucharest. She is a botanist who has worked at the Institute for Biological Research her entire adult life. They lived in a little two-room apartment in one of the new buildings put up by the State, the *blocuri* near Floreasca Park. He has studied piano since the age of five. He knows the story of our concert pianist grandmother.

Actually he has heard that story many times from Aunt Raluca, he says almost with irony. In the winter he and Raluca went ice skating in Floreasca Park near the State Circus. So much in his life seems to rotate around that park and that circus.

I realize we have swum far out into the sea and it is getting dark. I turn round and let him follow me back to the shore. We return in silence and get to the beach just when the sun is squeezing out its last rays from behind the hotels and villas. The sea is now enclosing itself in a greyish-mauve shroud and only one small fishing boat can be seen out on the horizon, the Navy days now long gone. The lighthouse at the end of the pier is rotating its determined rays.

'I didn't know it was so beautiful,' says Valentin again as he is putting on his black trousers over the wet underwear. 'All my childhood memories from here seem like a faraway dream.'

When we get back to the house, a big festive meal is laid out on the lacquered dining-room table. Everybody sitting round the table is speaking in whispers as if they were at someone's wake. Only Doru laughs his enormous laugh once in a while and breaks the whispering. I see that Valentin looks amazed at the sight of the food: *saramură de crap*, baked carp in tomatoes and onions, *salată de varză*, cabbage salad, *ardei copţi*, roasted peppers, *salată de vinete*, aubergine salad.

He turns to me and asks: 'How do you have all this food? All we eat in Bucharest is potatoes and sometimes peas.'

My mother overhears him and for the first time she decides to address him directly: 'You can eat like this every day, Valentin, it's no problem for us,' my mama says with a voice so soft that I don't recognize it or remember that she was capable of producing it.

I want to laugh at her tone of confidence about the food, as if we were Party officials holidaying in the villas on the beach. She doesn't mention how she and Tudoriţa take turns standing in different queues from five in the morning, how they go round the Turkish neighbourhood in search of vegetables or fruit from local gardens, or how my father sometimes goes begging for a kilo of coffee or peaches, at the different restaurants that owe him their good hygiene ratings and that are sometimes unable to feed their own clients because of the shortages. But I guess nothing is too hard for my mother when it comes to her son. I feel I am becoming all crooked inside again, the way I was getting around Anushka and Gigi. I try to think of what Mariţa told me last night before I went to bed ready never to see my parents again, of her wise and harsh words.

To my surprise Valentin starts eating with an appetite that looks funny in contrast to his scrawny, delicate features and body. When he was last in our house he barely touched anything and my mother constantly wrung her hands in worry that her son wasn't eating enough, and wondered how he was surviving in that 'brutal capital'. He doesn't even breathe between bites, finishes all the courses before everybody else and asks for seconds. That's when my mother cracks. Seeing her son eat with a giant's appetite! She cracks just like the old walnuts we crack on the pavement with a stone. Because she could have fed him all these years instead of feeding the hundreds of silly tourists who were not him. She could have fed him since he was five. Her face is contorted from trying to hold back the tears and she looks a hundred years old. Suddenly her face is a tapestry of wrinkles. Thin, uninterrupted lines of tears are running inside the ridges. My mother's face is growing into a huge painting the way Anushka's did when I couldn't bear to see her next to Gigi. She is dressed in black for she is in mourning for the dead and misplaced children in our family, with a face like tree bark, long streams of water running down the ridges of the bark, and she is flying around the room in continuous circles. There is no sea, no water in this painting of my mother. Just gluey air. I don't feel sorry for my mother. I feel sorry for Aunt Raluca dying alone in a hospital in Bucharest. A beautiful house otherwise, I think, 'only Party people have better houses than yours,' Mariţa said. *But a cursed house and full of stupid secrets. What do you say to that, Mariţa? What good is it to have this beautiful house when your life is all crooked?* 'Life is only about learning how to endure the pain,' said Mariţa. Well, even Mariţa can be wrong sometimes. What about the pain that people stupidly and wickedly create for each other and serve on a poisoned plate just like this baked carp with tomatoes here?

Doru is smoking in between courses and telling loud stories from his construction sites in Europe, near accidents and deaths from cranes and heavy construction machinery. My father, though slightly overshadowed by Doru, is trying to match his stories with talk of the strains of dysentery along the seashore and the deplorable squalor of some of the restaurants at the coast. He is staring at his son in a daze. Aunt Tudoriţa keeps explaining and praising the different foods over and over again as if she was describing museum articles, and my mother is a cracked walnut in mourning flying around the room. Only my brother is truly serene. He is enjoying his food like no one else I have ever seen. This is our family. I see us all in a grotesque tableau.

'Uncle Doru tells me that by now you play the piano beautifully,' says my father.

'Oh, just so-so,' says Valentin modestly and blushes to his earlobes.

My brother is a bottomless box of surprises. He is like the magic box in a story Mariţa used to tell me. A box that a good and kind girl once got from a fish fairy because the girl didn't kill the fish but put it back in the water. In exchange she got a box with no bottom, from where colourful surprises came out non-stop every time she opened it: talking flowers, singing mice, walking violins. Why did she need all that? Then she got tired of it and threw it in the sea. And she and her family starved to death.

'Don't you remember our piano?' I ask quickly as I startle

myself out of my fantasies. *We are two artist children born into a demented family*, I think.

'That's right, I almost forgot,' Valentin says and he suddenly turns dreamy.

'It probably needs tuning but it still works,' I say proudly. 'It belonged to our grandmother, you know, the concert pianist.'

'I know, I remember that,' Valentin says in a shaky voice. He probably remembers the time he and I went into the basement when we were five and suddenly he approached the piano, touched the dusty keys and produced clear, melodious notes. I felt both happy and sad. I wished that the scribbling my mother always scolded me about produced beautiful sounds like those, instead of being so silent and the subject of quarrels in the house. I slammed the piano lid down on his fingers. To my amazement he withdrew them before the lid could smash them and only his middle finger got hurt a little. He had felt my thought, or heard my feeling. I felt so stupid after that, I rubbed his finger to make it better. I even spat on it and rubbed in the spit, believing that spit had magic properties. He didn't say a word, didn't complain about it, only stared at me with big suppliant eyes, just like he did when I pinched him in the street on our way to the boat ride.

I stand up and take Valentin out of the dining room and off to the basement. I am calling all the shots tonight. For one night, I direct everything. I am the mistress of ceremonies, Esma with her soldier's helmet. We go out to the back, where the entrance to our basement is, and the sliver of new moon is high above us, pure and golden. We go down the steps into the basement and I turn on the dim neon light. There are spider's webs everywhere in the room and old toys and furniture and tools and coats that must have been here for decades. And in the middle of the dusty chaos reigns my grandmother's grand piano. Valentin moves towards it like towards a shrine. He opens it and sits on the dusty stool. He strokes the keys, wipes the dust from them with the back of his shirtsleeve.

'I'll play this for you and our reunion, Nora!' he says, self-assured, with no trace of a squeak in his voice.

Just as Princess Esma must have painted her dream images on a canvas, so does my brother Valentin drip the notes from his fingertips until the air quivers and shines. All the thickness and stickiness of the past hours melts away and nothing is confused any longer. My brother's Moonlight Sonata rising from the dark basement filled with old junk since the time of my fierce land-loving grandfather moves through the house cleanly and sharply. All the people in my family are coming down one by one, noiselessly floating through the air down the creaky steps. They look almost elegant and noble. They align themselves around the piano and stare at the watery notes. For the duration of the song we live uplifted in the fragile, shimmering illusion that the last decade has not been tinged by absence and secrets and contorted life choices. Our pain is separate from us: an invisible string undulates around us, tying us to each other. This tableau is a little blurry like a picture under water, at the bottom of a wrecked ship. But we are surviving the wreck, and we are floating back up to the surface, for a gulp of fresh air. I will make this painting in the morning, at dawn when the sea is waking up, moaning and stretching lazily as if from a lover's embrace.

Our Communist Youth

First I hear his voice and rumbling laugh, and then I see his face. Gigi is surrounded by neighbourhood boys and girls from our town. Some of them are Turkish. The girls have a different air about them from the Romanian girls: sassy, sure of themselves and wearing tons of jewellery. They are all smoking and taking swigs from a bottle of something that they are passing from hand to hand. It could be *braga*, it could be vodka, it could be a mixture of both because they sound a little too loud, a little too rowdy. Gigi is smoking a pipe, not a cigarette like the others. His face is glowing and his eyes are shining in the halo of blue smoke. He laughs, he flirts, and he overshadows the others. They are all gathered around the steps that lead down towards the beach, right around the corner from our house. They click their tongues, and make the palm gesture that means good, '*iyi*'. What are they finding so good and wonderful? I look once, I look twice, I turn round, change my direction, then I regain my initial direction. *What is Gigi saying in Turkish?* is my first thought. *Do I know any of the girls who are with them?* is my second thought. I don't have a third thought because just then, on the cusp of my third thought, Gigi looks at me. All my thought processes dissipate and I stand with my mouth open. *Nora, go on, Nora, be brave, Nora, go into their midst and conquer Gigi*, says the voice in my confused mind. I didn't know I had to conquer Gigi. What's this all about, some courtly romance from the Middle Ages? I regain my composure and start walking again towards the centre, to the *alimentara* where my mother has sent me to get turnips for her soup. Gigi leaves the group and runs after me. He grabs my arm and turns me towards him. His eyes are shining in the July twilight like those of a wild cat.

'Weren't you going to stop and say hello?' Gigi asks with a mischievous smile.

'I'm in a hurry,' I say. 'I have to get something from the *alimentara*.'

'What do you have to get? Can't I come with you?' he asks.

'I have to get turnips,' I say and burst out laughing. It suddenly seems funny that I have to get turnips when all these young Romanians and Turks are having the time of their lives on the *faleza*. Gigi starts laughing too and he waves goodbye to the rest of the group. They are puzzled he is suddenly leaving them. Some yell in Turkish: '*Gule, gule*', goodbye, and wink at Gigi. He is still holding his pipe, which he extinguishes, shakes out and then sticks in his trouser pocket.

'Did you know Ceauşescu is coming to Mangalia?' he asks as we cross the street and approach the central square.

I had no idea Ceauşescu was coming to Mangalia. This summer, my sixteenth one, I have been consumed by painting and spending time with my brother. Gigi and I had grown apart a little since the previous summer, the Anushka summer as I call it sometimes. Valentin's arrival in our house has inspired me and spurred my enthusiasm for painting. I spend hours and days inside or in our front yard trying my hand at just about everything in a chaotic manner while Valentin practises his scales or his newest sonatina. I experiment with gouache, with watercolours, portraits, landscapes, dream images, abstract concoctions, portraits collapsed into landscapes. Gigi, on the other hand, has been spending more time with the local kids, though we still meet a few times a week to swim and dive and test our underwater breathing. But there is a melancholy underneath all our encounters, the nagging sense of something unfinished or of something not yet started.

'I had no idea,' I say absent-mindedly. As if I really cared that our leader is coming to our town. 'When is that going to be?'

'Next week, second or third of August. He is coming for the Navy celebrations and also for some kind of summit on the direction of contemporary art.'

I'm less than thrilled by the news. Last year we had French drama during the Navy celebrations, this year we have Communist apotheosis. I prefer Anushka and her Parisian ways to this year's news.

'We have to stand all day in the centre of town with our school,' Gigi announces, grinning.

'What if we don't go? We're still on holiday, aren't we?' I say in a whisper as we near the grocery store.

'We'll have our university exams soon, remember?' That's all Gigi says.

Of course, the Party and the secret police will take note of any high school students who aren't present at the 'welcoming demonstration' for our 'beloved leader'. They will put that information in a file, and then they will make it known to the school authorities, possibly to the universities where we hope to study. It's not every day that the leader comes to our little city of Mangalia. It must be important.

Every sector of our town suddenly bursts into a frenzy of preparations for the visit of Comrade Ceauşescu, from the elementary schools to the storefronts and the beach walk, the majestic *faleza.* At the last minute children and young people from eight to eighteen are stuffed with patriotic songs, taught how to make different formations and choreographed to spell 'Nicolae Ceauşescu', dressed in white, red and navy pioneer costumes for a welcoming parade in the centre of town. The storefronts, like that of the *alimentara* where I couldn't even find the turnips that my mother wanted for her soup a couple of days ago, are suddenly filled with displays of enormous cheese wheels, artisans' bread, fresh peaches and cantaloupes. While the traders in the bazaar and the Turks or Gypsies selling *braga* or corn on the cob like Mariţa are all asked to disappear and their tables are taken down, the mural with the couple raising their child to the sun is freshened up with bright yellows and blues. My father is asked to remain on call twenty-four hours a day but is forbidden to mention the cholera cases he has just found out about to any of the Party officials in town. The ship decorations for the Navy days are twice as bright as usual and the restaurants have displays of lobsters and huge sturgeons in their windows such as I have never seen in my entire life. Tudoriţa actually went to the *alimentara* and asked to buy one of the great circles of cheese but was told that they are not for consumption but for display. Also the bread in the window is made of plastic, not of dough. All the high school 'Communist Youth' in town are mobilized for the occasion and asked to appear in their best light blue and navy uniforms with the red Party tie. Gigi, Valentin and I are joking that they probably put more fish in the sea and instructed the fish to sing the National Anthem in case Comrade Ceauşescu felt like taking a dip or a walk on our beach.

On the arrival day, we are asked to gather in the centre, in front of the Communist mural, at six in the morning. When Valentin and I leave the house at ten minutes before six, a comrade is already in front of our door to make sure we head in the right direction. We meet Gigi and several of his Turkish friends from the other night halfway along the beach walk. One of them has filled his pockets with *baklava* and *rahat* for the day. Valentin and I have only our thermoses of cold water. The square is filling up with children, teenagers, schoolteachers, sailors, hotel workers – the backbone of our socialist paradise. Mixed in with the crowd, at a rate of about one in fifteen people, are men in suits who don't look like Mangalia natives, but are most likely comrades and secret police watching and listening. They are guarding our peace and prosperity. The sun is blasting out in full force today, not a single cloud in the sky, and the temperature is supposed to reach a high of forty Celsius later on. By ten o'clock we are already drenched in sweat and have finished our thermos water. The plastic cantaloupes in the grocery store window look appetizing. The leader is supposed to arrive any minute now, we are told by the officers in charge of the crowd. Every time there is a rumour he might be arriving, the loudspeakers pump out the National Anthem. Everybody is supposed to stand straight and sing along with the loudspeakers. The pioneers get into their prescribed formations again and again and some of the children look like lobsters ready to explode. Thank God Gigi and Valentin and I are beyond the pioneer stage and are now only Communist Youth. Some of the first-graders look desperate and start to cry. Mircea, one of Gigi's friends, is stuffing himself with *baklava* and is proud to have got through the crowd to bring back some water from the fountain at the other end of the square in a little folding plastic cup. We all take sips from it.

Finally, he arrives. A roar of motorcycles, cars and loud sirens is heard. The National Anthem is assaulting our ears, the pioneers, all soaked in sweat and red-faced, are writing 'Nicolae Ceaușescu' with their bodies as they wave red paper flags. First we see the endless delegation move across the improvised stage. Then the leader appears in a light grey suit and stands in front of the microphone. A podium has been set up for him and probably his speech is on the lectern. He first shakes hands with the city officials, then leans over the pioneers in the first row and touches some of their raised hands. One of them gives him a bouquet of roses. He strokes the child's head. I am standing between Valentin and Gigi somewhere in the middle and am trying to see the leader above the multitude of heads. He is smaller than he appears on TV or in any of the portraits. He starts talking in a bumpy, hoarse manner about the inspiration for socialist art. The working class and Communist Youth should be the only inspiration. He seems to be scolding everyone. He is a loving but tough father to all of us. Why did he have to come to Mangalia to tell us this? Now our art teacher will be even more fanatical about finding Communist topics for our projects. I look up at Valentin and his face is mimicking the face of the leader like a clown. Despite the heat, the sweat pouring from his face, Valentin is cheerful and merry. Gigi takes my hand and I squeeze it a little. His face is flushed from the sun and his freckles are more conspicuous. His eyes shine again like those of a wild cat, mysterious and impenetrable.

The leader keeps scolding the crowd about the sources of inspiration for contemporary art. Gigi looks at me and I see the smile in his eyes, mocking the leader's vacuous words and the grotesqueness of the situation. Something is tugging at my heart, a restlessness, a bitter sweetness. A seagull is shrieking above our heads and flying towards the sea. In its passage above the crowds it does a dropping right on the podium where the leader's speech is placed, missing his head by a couple of millimetres. The leader pulls back a little and for a second stares blankly at the crowd. The official standing on his right takes the bird dropping off the leader's speech and shakes his hand with a morbidly serious air. Then he wipes his fingers on his trousers. The officials in the crowd look fierce in order to make sure nobody in the crowd reacts inappropriately, such as by laughing. Valentin's face is contorted with laughter and I feel it rising inside me as well. Mircea whispers something in Turkish. The other Turkish kids are scrunching up their faces with laughter. I ask Gigi what he said. 'Now he is going to exterminate all our seagulls,' Gigi reports in a whisper. As he leans over I smell his salty flesh and breath. Gigi is squeezing my hand and when I look up at him I see he is all ballooned with laughter. I can't hold my laughter in any longer and as I shake with it Gigi pulls me to his chest. It feels like we are both going to burst into a huge peal of laughter that will blow up into a coloured explosion and sweep over everyone and everything in this square. We will take off in this balloon of laughter and fly above everyone like the white seagull that is now flapping its wings and moving towards the shore. The leader is finishing his speech at a fast-forward pace and his right hand is moving furiously up and down. He punctuates his very last word, 'the future', with a sharp move of his hand which remains in the air for a few seconds, and at that moment the loudspeakers burst into wild applause. We are all supposed to applaud and yell the leader's name.

Relieved that the ordeal is over, the crowds actually explode in what sounds like sincere applause and cheering. Only Gigi and I do not, because in the heat and hilarity of the moment, as if by accident, our two mouths, filled with bubbles of laughter, are searching for each other and kissing. Everybody around us is clapping and cheering for Comrade Ceaușescu, only Gigi and I are entirely absorbed in our first kiss. Gigi's lips taste salty. When the crowds have all dissipated, the two of us, wearing our heavy light blue and navy uniforms, drenched in sweat, hungry and thirsty, head for the beach and the cool silky waters, feeling lighter than ever.

My Art Training in Bucharest and the State Circus

The winds are blowing from the east, bringing cold rain and heavy clouds. Some mornings the sea is morose with a wicked steel grey encasing it all the way to where its normally clear line of separation from the sky is now blurry and indefinite. This school year, my father decided I needed to take special art tutoring in Bucharest if I was serious about being an artist and he hired an expensive art professor to give me private lessons on Sundays. My mother didn't oppose the initiative and I reluctantly went along with the idea. I was terrified of going to Bucharest by myself and having to learn about art so far away from the sea. But now Valentin and I both take the train to Bucharest early on Sunday mornings, then catch a bus to the city centre from the crowded station to where our ways part in the university square. I take a tram along the sinuous and dirty river that crosses the city, the Dîmbovița, to one of the older districts of Bucharest with buildings and villas from before the war, to attend my three-hour art class with Miss Anda Mantaș, an important artist and professor at the art school. Valentin takes a trolley bus and goes to the other side of town, to his old neighbourhood of Floreasca, for his piano lessons. We get back late in the evening and arrive, slightly dizzy from the long train rides and the rushing through Bucharest, in Mangalia station, which compared to the one in Bucharest looks like a miniature station built for toy trains.

Usually Gigi is waiting for us, his hands in his pockets, standing in the middle of the platform and turning his head right and left to see which carriage we will come out of. His face brightens with his mesmerizing, luminous smile when he sees us and although it has only been one long day, it always feels like I haven't seen Gigi for a long time. I am relieved to see him and know that he exists in this little town of ours by the sea, with its miniature station. Valentin has taken to Gigi as if he was also our brother and as the three of us leave the station, laughing and describing our long Sunday with arbitrary details, walking down the middle of the street towards the sea, you might even think we were a happy family.

Aunt Raluca died in November with my mother and Valentin beside her in the hospital, on a grey, rainy day in Bucharest. My father and I stayed home and during my mother's absence Aunt Tudoriţa lived with us and cooked every day. Some days my father even told me to invite Gigi for supper and it seemed as if I had slipped into a different family configuration, in which, instead of the fury and loud noises that always blew through our house, we were now wafted from room to room, from the inside to the outside and back inside, by a steady but peaceful breeze of melancholy and expectation. I had no inspiration for any paintings and my head was filled with an indiscriminate medley of pastels: light lime, washed-out orange, watery greys. Pastels and watercolours dripping lazily with the autumn rain.

It took me a while to get used to my art lessons with the famous and wickedly eccentric Anda Mantaş and to rein in my impulses to run away, take the first train back to Mangalia and never return. Her room was the most overwhelming conglomerate of disparate objects I had ever seen in my life, and she was an odd combination of old-fashioned elegance and incongruous modernity. She wore pink lacy tops over tight blue jeans, had dark make-up around her continuously moving small black eyes, red hair pinned in a bun and negligently loose around her face, an aquiline nose that made her look like a bird of prey, which, in combination with the small eyes, gave her face the air of a puzzled exotic doll. Her room was like her person: objects thrown in apparent disorder, fuchsia and dark green upholstered armchairs and sofas, Persian and Romanian traditional rugs, dark red velvet curtains with golden tassels, marble and bronze busts of unknown men and women, paintings of nudes, abstract drawings and conceptual sculptures, and a huge grandfather clock in walnut leaning forward and making you think it was going to fall on you at any moment.

In the first two minutes of the first lesson I found out that I knew nothing about art, that my fantastical fish and sea paintings were worthless, and that I had an inexhaustible universe of techniques and styles in front of me that I couldn't possibly master in time for the art school entrance exam in two years. She said that if it wasn't for the recommendation from Valentin's piano teacher, she wouldn't be wasting her time with me. I perched on the small wooden stool that she made me sit on as soon as I entered the room, stared at her without breathing and with every muscle of my face twitching out of control, and looked at the door from the corner of my eye, to catch the moment when she would turn away so I could make my escape. As if she had guessed my thought, she never turned away. She put a large easel with a sheet of paper on it in front of me, a piece of charcoal pencil in my hand, took my two hands in hers and stared for a second at their size, noticing they were different, gave a brief smile of satisfaction and to my surprise said: '*Bine, foarte bine*', good, very good. The only things about me so far that Miss Mantaş deemed worthy of fleeting praise were my unevenly sized hands.

She gripped each of my hands in each of hers and took turns in making them draw under her guidance on the white sheet of paper. She said I had the advantage of two kinds of hands and had to learn to use them both in order to get different effects. Hands have a mind, she said. I thought my mind had a mind, but she was fixated on hands. It was only thanks to that sudden closeness that I relaxed and decided to come back the following week despite the harshness of her manner and the deathly fear she produced in me. Her hands were little and soft yet extremely strong, and flew over the surface in front of us as if guided by magic strings. I felt strangely protected in that bizarre embrace in which my art teacher was making me draw in charcoal the chaotic landscape of her room. I was amazed at what came out of our joined hands: something that bore a striking resemblance to the actual reality in front of me and at the same time seemed like a mocking commentary on it all. The busts appeared to be grinning, the grandfather clock seemed to be levitating, the sofas and chairs were performing a ballet.

Then she dropped my hands and said that was enough. 'Just think about this until next time,' she said. Then she lectured me about proportions and perspective and depth and movements in the history of art and told me she was going to quiz me about every single thing she had said next time. When the lesson was over I wanted to go into a deep sleep. My mind felt short-circuited, as if connections in my brain had been rearranged. I went out into the grey and drizzling Bucharest afternoon and headed for my tram like a sleepwalker on a mission.

When Valentin saw me he noted I looked deathly pale. He asked me to walk a little bit so I would get some colour back in my face. He, on the other hand, looked happier and lighter than I had seen him in a long time. I understood that resuming the piano lessons had brought back his joy in life. He was running ahead of me and doing silly dance moves in the street to make me laugh. That afternoon after my first art lesson, Valentin guided me around the wide boulevards of the city that stretched for kilometres on end, its residential streets with turn-of-the-century grey stone villas and houses, the parks with hundred-year-old trees and see-saws squeaking and making the children going up and down on them squeal with excitement. Judging by the snobbish tourists that my mother had lodged and fed for a decade in our house and their spoiled, noisy children, I had thought I would hate Bucharest. But I found myself falling in love with its mixture of elegance and Balkan grittiness, such as the small streets with back alleys and antiques shops and people at street corners selling anything from Rexona soap and deodorant sprays to thick gold necklaces. We passed by the art school where I dreamed of being accepted if ever I mastered the mountain of knowledge that Miss Mantaş had presented me with, and I watched the students going in and out of the majestic building, talking, joking, strolling after their classes. I laughed out loud when I saw that most of the women wore an imitation of the clothes that Mariţa and the women in her camp usually wear: many layers of multicoloured swirling skirts, and scarves tied around their heads. Mariţa would die laughing when I told her that Bucharest women turned her kind of dressing into a fashion and she would probably say something like: 'Well, if them Bucharest people like our attire so well, they should try living here with us for a little while, see how they like that.'

I knew by the sparkle in Valentin's green eyes that he had something in store for me that Sunday evening. After strolling around the city, we took another tram and then another trolley bus and found ourselves in an enormous boulevard with a monument in memory of fallen aviators in the centre, and an endless park with birch and chestnut trees on each side. Then we stood in front of a huge round building made of glass and stone with a green roof shaped like waves of the sea. Joyfully, Valentin introduced me to the State Circus. My mouth was open for a few seconds and I stared at the building like it was the hanging gardens of Babylon. Then I looked at my watch and became worried that we were going to miss our six o'clock train back to Mangalia. I thought of Gigi who would be waiting for us at the station and wouldn't see us come out. His round freckled face with his special sad smile on it. Gigi's face never really looked sad unless you knew him. He had a smile for every mood, even for sadness. And then I didn't want to have that much fun without Gigi. Valentin said there was a show that night and we could spend the night at a friend's house, then catch an early train back to Mangalia the next day. He suggested I call Gigi from the phone booth at the corner and let him know. Why was everything pouring into my life all at once, like the flood in Noah's story: return of prodigal brother, death of aunt, art classes with crazy teacher, discovery of the capital, and the State Circus? Why couldn't some of this have been spread out a little more evenly throughout my life?

I couldn't resist it. As I stood in front of the building that looked like a white and green spaceship, looking at Valentin's sparkling eyes, the voracious curiosity about what I would find inside overtook me. I went into fast mode like the people in silent movies. Go to the phone booth and call Gigi, the coins in the slot, the tone, the ringing, the voice of Gigi's mother, sleepy, morose.

'Is Gigi home?'

'No, he isn't.'

'Please tell him that my brother Valentin and I are still in Bucharest and we missed our train, please tell Gigi not to wait for us.'

'What, you have a brother now?'

Oh my God, Gigi's mother doesn't even know I have a brother, no matter, yes, I have a brother, he fell from the moon just a few months ago.

'Just tell Gigi that, please, would you? We'll come with the morning train, yes, the morning train. Thank you, Mrs Malek, thank you so much.'

And then a quick call to my parents. They don't seem surprised, they just say: 'Fine, fine, we'll see you tomorrow.' What kind of sickness came over my parents so that they were suddenly all kindness and understanding?

I run with Valentin to get the tickets. What, no more tickets? It's not possible, two little tickets for us, please. Valentin is sticking twenty *leis* in the hand of the cashier as a bribe. Yes sure, go ahead, row 100, seats seven and eight. They are good seats, we'll see everything. The enormous cupola, round and filled with blinding coloured lights. Elephants, real live elephants, and white horses dressed like people standing on their hind legs. Ballerinas in shiny red, lime, purple sequinned costumes, standing on one leg on a galloping horse or hanging from the trapeze in the big cupola, lions jumping through burning hoops, little monkeys in tuxedos riding miniature bicycles, everybody hanging by every part of their bodies from the shiny cupola or from another part of someone else's body.

Then everything slows down with one twist of a shiny baton. And my brother Valentin leans over and whispers in my ear. 'It's the girl I love. There, see? My girlfriend.' Oh right, my brother is a real joker, how did I end up in such a confused family, such an upside-down, such a hula-hoop, hanging-with-your-head-down kind of family?

Valentin points to a coloured box. She used to live on the same hallway in the *bloc* where he lived with Raluca near the State Circus. They always met in the morning, as he was going to school and she was going to her circus training. She is two years older than him, a circus ballerina, and her name is Didona. She pops from a square coloured box, wearing a hot-pink sequinned outfit, she has coal-black hair, blacker even than Mariţa's relatives. Her family are all circus people. Can you be circus people in our country? Sure you can. The Party loves circus people, and even the President comes to the circus sometimes. A long string of black cars stops in front of the circus, Party and security guards make up half the audience and the President was even seen laughing once.

Valentin's girlfriend is being raised on strings, she is performing contortions in the air, she is dancing in the air. Violin music like a thousand wailing seagulls is filling our ears, music like a rapid sobbing, wailing, laughing and breaking of hearts all in one. It's Paganini. Ooh, Paganini! Then another tune, this time Romanian music, and then Gypsy music like in Mariţa's camp, harmonica mixed with accordion. It's funny how much people in Bucharest imitate the customs of Mariţa's people, even the circus people. Maybe some of the circus people are Mariţa's people. I have to tell Mariţa everything. And what will Gigi say about all this?

She is up there in her shiny pink ultra-sequinned suit swimming in the air like a swallow. Valentin has quite a girlfriend. I wonder if she is actually his girlfriend, or if he only thinks so because he has come to the circus many times and fell in love with her as he saw her twirl in those demented rotations in the shiny cupola of the State Circus in a pink sequinned suit. But after the show, as I stagger in the circus hallway and follow Valentin towards the exit, he wants us to wait. We wait until everybody is gone and the hallway is resonant with the post-show silence. I actually meet the astounding Didona. She is now wearing regular street clothes, a black turtleneck and jeans. She is staggeringly beautiful. She is a Delacroix painting. Today Miss Mantaş talked to me about Delacroix and showed me some reproductions in an album. *The Death of Sardanapalus.* Didona looks like the woman being killed in the painting only more slender. Maybe Mariţa is right when she says that everything is for a reason, everything comes together, colours, shapes, mountains of techniques I still have to learn if I want to get into art school. Didona bursts into my consciousness like an erupting volcano and this painting has the strongest, wildest colours: black background and glowing reds, Didona and Valentin are two angels with scarlet and purple feathers rising in the shiny circus cupola.

We spend the night in the apartment of an old schoolfriend

of Valentin's who happens to live near the station. It smells of cabbage everywhere in this building and the stairs are grungy. Everything is grungy and smelly. I feel guilty and worried, as if I had done something wrong. I want to be in Gigi's arms and near the sea. I sleep on the sofa in the first room, and my brother on a cot bed at my feet. We hear everybody snoring in the other room. What is this new life I've entered? It feels as though something dark and oily is waiting for us just around the corner, waiting to devour us. Street cars are running till late into the night and drunken people are yelling obscenities outside our window, the covers on the sofa are slimy and smell of rotting cabbage. I even miss my mother. Her clean, sharp voice when she yells at me.

Valentin and I sit in silence in our compartment on the train back to Mangalia. We watch the sun rise from the flat, flat Baragan plains, dark flat earth beaten by the winter wind. I am wondering if the previous day actually happened, or if I only dreamed it. I feel slimy from the cabbage-smelling sofa that I slept on. I realize my brother is a spoilt child, as if he were an only child. He always has his way; he is fragile but stubborn, and that's his strength. I ask him why he chose a circus girl for a girlfriend. He says you don't choose things like that. 'Did you choose Gigi?' he asks. His question puzzles me. Underneath his fragile looks, my brother is made of steel. I want to hug him nevertheless. Even though he keeps puzzling and confusing me. *Did I choose Gigi?*

I see him from the window as I lean out in the salty air, before the train has even slowed down. Of course I chose Gigi. I chose Gigi, and Marița also chose Gigi for me when she always took me to the Turkish area when I was little to play on the red beaten earth of his garden, because she said I needed to know what a boy was like. I chose Gigi every time when I went back to his garden and every time I swam with him under water, summer after hot summer. I don't believe in predestination but my brother Valentin does. He believes in predestination and in the State Circus. That's where he found his love.

Gigi is smiling his sad smile. His mother didn't give him the message till the morning, after he had already waited for us at the station. Then he went to my house and asked my parents if they knew we weren't coming back that night. They knew, of course they knew we were going to the circus after the art and piano classes, and spending the night at a friend of Valentin's. I go to school late and angry and get a poor grade in my geology class because I don't know today's lesson, which is about tectonic plates. I don't know my lesson because I went to the circus with my brother Valentin and met his girlfriend who is a circus acrobat and I had my first art lesson with Miss Mantaş who might as well work in the circus. Who cares about tectonic plates? Let them crash into each other and the earth explode. Then I get a poor grade in my Marxist economy class, because I don't know anything about the five-year Socialist plan and the means of production in the Socialist State. My grades are going to hell. This is a stupid country anyway. Valentin was right to force me into the circus like that. I learned more than in the Marxist economy class.

I yell at Valentin in our room tonight before going to sleep and tell him to never, ever trick me like that again, he should have told me beforehand of his plans. I'm not a toy, a plaything, a ballerina on a string.

'Just don't ever lie to me like that, yes?'

He laughs and says: 'Yes, all right, but didn't you have fun?'

I don't know what kind of person my brother is. Who does he take after with his cunning ways?

After I yell at Valentin I go back out into the salty wind and find Gigi at the end of our street, waiting for me. Gigi knows me better than anyone, he holds me and tells me he missed me, he never gets angry. Of course I chose Gigi, and I choose him over and over again, here in front of this wild green sea of ours.

About Life and Death

It started in Miss Mantaş's house, in my last year of high school, as she was quizzing me on Romantic realism and the Barbizon school. I knew my lesson by heart and words came out of my mouth smoothly and confidently, the landscapes of Corot, Courbet and Constable, the peasants of Millet, how these particular artists of nineteenth-century France and England abandoned formalism and decided to take inspiration directly from nature and society. Miss Mantaş was in one of her rare lighter moods, when even her voice had slightly kinder inflections. Maybe it was because of the particularly beautiful Bucharest autumn that year, red and orange leaves against a maddening blue sky, or maybe because I had come such a long way in the one year that she had been tutoring me. It didn't start with the nausea that some girls talked about, but with a sudden sleepiness and light-headed feeling. I knew right then and there, sitting on the little stool in front of the easel and facing the leaning grandfather clock, that I was confronted with what I had dreaded most: pregnancy.

We did everything we knew to avoid it, but there was a lot we didn't know. Nobody told you anything, and nothing that could help you was legal. We knew of one Turkish woman in town who helped girls like me. Gigi and I said we didn't want to have to resort to that. And here I was, ready to faint on Miss Mantaş's painting stool. I went on with my lesson, using every fibre of strength I had. I got to the works of Courbet and the Parisian salons of the period. I wrapped up my conclusion quickly and Miss Mantaş even smiled. Maybe I did have a chance of getting into the art school, she said. That was the highest praise she had ever given me. I didn't know whether to faint from joy at her compliment or from dread at my situation.

I became particularly dizzy and without saying a word I moved into the fuchsia armchair across from the window. I had never sat in that armchair and was struck by the scarlet tree that spread its dishevelled beauty in front of the window. I thought maybe I was hallucinating, and I had just had a fit of exhaustion. All the travelling, the studying till late at night, all the movements and techniques in art history, maybe it was too much. Maybe I was wrong about being pregnant. The tree swayed lightly in the wind and red leaves started their downward spirals and confused waltzing through the air. It was time to leave anyway, so I got up and thanked her as usual. She must have felt there was something wrong with me, because she actually asked if I wanted to stay for coffee. Her exotic doll-face with the red hair framing it looked slightly forlorn. I said I needed to catch my train back to Mangalia. As I ran down the squeaky old staircase in her building, the nausea started too. All my mother's gruesome stories about girls dying from illegal abortions are ringing in my head as I run along the Bucharest pavements through the crinkly blood-red and yellow leaves.

The first thing I ask Valentin when I meet him at our corner across from the university square is: 'Do you know anyone who does abortions?'

He is as serious as I have ever seen him, his face pale with what seems sudden worry for me. To my surprise he says simply: 'Yes, I do, I actually do.'

I find out that his girlfriend Didona has had an abortion by this doctor. He is safe, clean, but of course expensive.

'What do you want?' Valentin says when he sees me worrying about the expensive part. 'He can get life in prison or even death for this.' Valentin never ceases to surprise me. One moment he is a lunatic madly in love with a circus trapeze artist, the next he is all in control, knowledgeable about the most gruesome of practical things a woman can worry about in this ridiculous country of ours.

'Don't worry, we'll get the money somehow, and Gigi will help you, won't he?'

'Of course, what do you think?' I say proudly of my Gigi.

Not only is Gigi quivering with the desire to do everything he can to help me get through the ordeal, but he actually surprises me by starting to cry about it, all worried that I will die, because he knows the Turkish woman in town is not that safe, and he probably knows more than I do and doesn't want to tell me. This of course makes me feel tons better, to have all my anxieties about possible death or permanent damage to my womb confirmed by my boyfriend's nervous crisis. I comfort Gigi with the news that Valentin knows a safe doctor in Bucharest.

Sitting through my history class and listening to our grumpy teacher drone on about the glorious Romanian insurrection of 1945 as our forces joined the Soviet Army in liberating us and bringing the light of Socialism and Communism to our land, while my throat is gripped with dizzying nausea and my heart races with dread of tomorrow's 'intervention' by a mystery doctor in Bucharest, must be what a cruel God envisaged as a young woman's hell on earth. I have been counting the weeks, the days, the hours till the fateful event. After the initial shock Gigi has offered a constant flood of support and gentleness, treating me more like a sister than a lover, embracing me as if worried I might break, anxious that I might lose my balance. Sometimes I see Gigi and me from a distance, like an artist looking at her models, and it makes me laugh at how funny we are together: an unevenly shaped girl with crazy ideas and wild curls and a Turkish boy with red hair and freckles, me angry and feisty, him sly and shiny-eyed. There we are, just like in a family portrait: Gigi a tiny bit taller than me, wearing a starched white shirt, and me a yellow cotton blouse, both a little provincial, both a little burnt by the sun; Gigi with a smile, me with a frown.

Mariţa said prayers for me in her language and rolled her beads many times. She told me it was wise to go to Bucharest and not to the Turkish 'witch' doctor in town. I don't know why everybody is so set against our local midwife, obviously she must have helped many a girl in our town who is now running around and getting in trouble again. What if there are secret police at the door and I leave the place in handcuffs? What if police barge in just as I'm going through with the procedure? What if the doctor is a crook and he kills me? What if Valentin's girlfriend was lucky and I'm not? Wouldn't I have been better off with someone in our old town? What if, what if . . .

We set the date for the first Sunday afternoon in December, so it coincides with Valentin's piano lesson and my art class. It's going to take place in the doctor's own home, in an apartment in the district called Balta Alba, the White Swamp, quite an attractive name for a sea of prison-like grey blocks on the faraway margins of the city. My lesson with Miss Mantaş goes by in a fog and none of her biting ironies touches me today. In fact I am rather enjoying my foggy perception of her explanations of Pointillism, Impressionism and Van Gogh's dreary beginnings as a clerk and art salesman in a little mining town in Belgium. I start crying unexpectedly when she says that it was only when he decided to create beauty out of his despair and desolation that his paintings exploded with colour. Tears are flooding my cheeks when she points out he sold only one painting in his lifetime. I'm ashamed at my tears and my ridiculous lack of control, being someone who never cries in a public place or in front of other people. Miss

Mantaş is surprised as well but also moved by my being so moved. She pushes her red hair back when she is moved. Then I laugh stupidly at the title of his first painting, *The Potato Eaters*, and Miss Mantaş's face scrunches with distaste at my frivolity. I leave her apartment in a disorderly rush, eager to be in the presence of Valentin and Gigi. My 'two men' give me courage.

The cold December wind and drizzle is wicked this Sunday afternoon and it couldn't be better suited to my mood and the dreaded 'intervention' ahead. I try to appear brave and nonchalant in front of the two young men who are giving me all their manly support and kindness. In fact as the three of us walk down the dingy streets of the White Swamp district of *blocuri* I cheer up and begin to feel rather adventurous. Gigi is walking ahead with his hands in his pockets; Valentin is walking a little bit behind, gracefully and slightly out of balance as usual, me in the middle pulling at my coat collar and feeling like a confused anarchist. *Once all this is over, the three of us will even go and have a drink at the little tavern near the tram station and we'll laugh our heads off on the train all the way back to Mangalia. And I'll never get pregnant again until I really want to.*

I only remember when the lights went out. I was lying on his dining-room table. The lights went off and I lay there in the dark. There was groping. Something hurt more than before. I had told myself I would not remember anything. It was going well and step by step I was not remembering. But just when the lights went out my memory decided to flare up. The lights go off all the time in Bucharest because the State is economizing on electricity. The sound of metal instruments clicking against each other. He said I was done. I put on my clothes. He gave me a handful of pills, antibiotics, he said. I gave him the envelope with the money. All in the dark. He said it would come out later. Maybe tonight, maybe tomorrow. Not to be scared by the bleeding. It would start later. He was whispering. He smelled of vodka.

I found the door by touching the walls and the furniture.

Valentin and Gigi were waiting for me downstairs in the hallway. We walked in silence to the tram. The streets were all in darkness because of the State economizing on electricity. What do you do with the saved-up electricity? Are there barrels of saved-up electricity somewhere in Bucharest? The lights inside the tram hurt my eyes. Gigi sat next to me on the seat and Valentin was standing in front of us. A drunken man urinated in the back of the tram. I had never seen anything like that. I didn't know you could urinate on public transport. Everything is possible in Bucharest. I thought of Van Gogh's painting of *The Potato Eaters*. Gigi hugged my shoulders and stroked my hair. I was fine. I was going to be fine. I wanted to think of Van Gogh's painting but something kept taking my mind off it. Maybe it was the urine smell. Maybe it was the uncomfortable feeling in my groin. The tram ride seemed to go on for ever. Bucharest is a labyrinth. There were lots of drunken people in the station. Why is everybody drunk in Bucharest? Maybe because the electricity goes off all the time and people feel scared in the dark. Gigi and Valentin walked close to me to protect me. How lucky I am to have a brother. We got on the train to Mangalia and sat in a compartment in the last carriage, looking out of the window. The Baragan fields looked like a frozen black lake in the night. I remembered sleeping on the slimy sofa that smelled of cabbage after Valentin and I went to the circus. The feeling of something dark and oily coming to swallow us. Didona's face like that of the murdered woman in *The Death of Sardanapalus*.

Then it started hurting like a million knives. I didn't want to cry, so I kept thinking of Doru and his amputated arm. I am a lucky girl, my father always said. I was lying on the cold vinyl bench of the train with my head in Gigi's lap, sweating profusely, despite the unheated compartment. Valentin was sitting across from us on the other bench. He was looking at me with an anguished expression. They say twins are closer to each other than normal siblings. They feel each other's pain and happiness as if it was their own. I'm lucky to have a twin brother. I'm lucky all round. Sounds are muffled, I hear Gigi and Valentin telling me we'll get there soon, we'll be home in Mangalia any minute now. The sound of the train wheels on the tracks is covering their voices. Any minute, any minute, but I feel like dying right now. My groin is splitting into many pieces. And the face of Sardanapalus's concubine who is also Didona with coal-black waves of hair and rosy flesh is covering my entire field of vision and suffocating me like a creature with tentacles.

Somehow I find myself in Gigi's bed in his parents' house. His mother is hovering over me. Gigi and Valentin are hovering over me. Everybody is hovering over me like birds of prey. I want Mariţa next to me. I know Mariţa will make me feel better. Gigi's mother says they don't want Gypsies in their house. Somebody must have called my father because here he is hovering over me as well. Valentin, the traitor, he must have called my father. That shows you it's wrong what they say about twins, how they always stick by you. I'd rather die than let my parents know. But here is my father next to me with his doctor's bag. What does my father know about botched abortions anyway? He's just an epidemiology doctor who checks restaurants and hotels. He can't save me, only Mariţa can save me. And besides, I don't want to be saved. I'm shamed in front of Gigi's parents and my own parents for ever.

I'm lying here in a pool of blood in Gigi's bed like a grotesque circus spectacle. I'm the circus girl who didn't make it, she fell off the trapeze and there she is lying in a pool of blood while little chimpanzees in tuxedos and top hats are riding miniature bicycles round and round in the shiny arena. I knew something oily and black was going to swallow us all when I slept on that slimy cabbage-smelling sofa in Bucharest. It's all because of the circus. My father talks about septicaemia. I understand the word. In the painful bloody circus whirlwind this word is clear. Almost everybody dies of septicaemia. Mariţa told me about it, she called it blood poisoning, that's how Lili's daughter had died. That's how we all die. It happened in the dark, the metal instruments in the dark while the State was economizing on electricity. It's all because of the damn electricity. And because of the leader with his pig lips. In our country women have to make babies for the Communist future, to donate them to the sun, to the future, to the Party. To the State Circus.

We can't call any doctor or hospital because then the police will come too and we'll all be arrested. They will let me die and drown in my own blood. 'Don't call the doctor, don't call the doctor,' I keep saying. My own father is a doctor. He should be able to save me. He must have learned about this in medical school even if now he just verifies strains of bacteria in food and seaside epidemics. Camelia the Turkish midwife comes in. She is tiny and scrawny, with a white scarf tied around her head. I call for Mariţa. My father runs out. He says he'll be back, that I need a large dose of antibiotics. Gigi goes to get Mariţa. Only Gigi understands me. Gigi is part of me. Valentin is a stranger. He is skinny and pale like an angel of death. I want to live for Gigi. He is a magic fish. I'll paint Gigi as the magic red fish of the Black Sea, and we'll live happily under water.

I'm alone with Gigi's mother and the Turkish midwife and my brother Valentin. I ask Valentin to go out. He gets up obediently from the bed and leaves the room. The pain in my groin is unbearable. I don't care about how brave Uncle Doru was when the train cut off his arm. I'm not lucky, damn it. Screams and moans come out of my mouth. Camelia tells Gigi's mother to boil water for tea. She takes out herbs from her pocket. I should have let her perform the intervention. The Bucharest doctor smelled of vodka and Camelia smells of Turkish desserts.

First comes the smell of burnt leaves and dried plums and then Mariţa walks in. She holds my hands and calls me *porumbiţa*, little turtle dove. Camelia is making me drink a very bitter tea, and Gigi's mother is taking my temperature. I see that now we all get along, Gypsies and Turks and Romanians. My post-abortion agony is a pretext for world peace. I've never noticed that Gigi's mother also has freckles like Gigi and she is pretty in a surprising way. My father comes in with a large needle attached to a pump and sticks it in my arm. I have to hold it like that for a while, he says, so that the antibiotic gets directly into the bloodstream.

Gigi is kneeling next to my bed and smiling. I wonder what smile of Gigi's is this one. Maybe it's the 'I don't want you to die' smile. It's a bright smile with little stars in it. What kind of party are we having here anyway? It's my going-away party. The Turkish woman is telling the men to leave the room. Except for my father, he can stay. We don't need the men, they are always trouble. She and Mariţa clean off the blood. They take something cold from between my legs. My head is a burning oven. If I survive I won't make love with Gigi for a year. I'm a bundle of rotting flesh and blood, and this is a stupid country. If I survive I'll leave the country. What a pity if I don't survive though. I'll never paint all my paintings. And Gigi will be a wreck, he'll never smile again. And how about my mother? My mother will be for ever the cracked walnut she became when she saw Valentin eat her food with a ravenous appetite.

I have a funny thought that I have to survive for my mother. She's the meanest of all the people I know but I have to survive for her. So she doesn't become even meaner and kill everybody. I don't want her to be standing in the basement staring at grandmother's piano with a tear hanging from her nose for ever. I have to save the Earth from my mother's wrath. I see my mother's face at my own funeral and it's so fierce and so ghastly that the land around her will just freeze or dry up. And everybody else too. I have to survive for my mother. I have a memory of Anushka. Her face is sweet and bright like when she handed me her yellow scarf in the hotel room before going away. Anushka is a better person than Didona. Anushka is like Van Gogh's sunflowers. I ask Mariţa to tell me the end of Esma's story.

'How come you never told me the end of Esma's story?' I ask Mariţa.

My father puts more antibiotic in the intravenous pump. If I survive I'll never be seen lying in agony, bleeding, moaning and shaking like this. I'll never be sick again and when I die for real, I'll die all alone in a clean, tidy room with everything in order and well prepared for the guests to make their last goodbyes. Camelia gives me another cup of bitter tea.

Esma married the Grand Vizier Sokollu Mehmed Pasha and had a daughter by him, Mariţa tells me. She called her daughter Aysel, which means Flood of Moonlight. Aysel had the same gift of imagining on canvas as her mother Esma. But the viziers were envious of the power of the women and lied that Esma was unfaithful to Sokollu Mehmed Pasha. So Esma took Flood of Moonlight with her and ran away again on her black steed until she reached another city by the sea where she founded a colony of women who created beautiful images on canvas.

You are lying, Mariţa! There is no such thing as a colony of women making beautiful images on canvas, it's all a lie. Even you are lying, Mariţa. I am dying because of a pig-faced leader and the cursed electricity and I will never put another damn thing on canvas or on paper. This is not a fairy tale, this is our Socialist utopia, Mariţa, and you live in the damned camp next to the cement-box buildings with your desperate people sitting around the fire all the time, and it's all a big circus even when you don't go to the State Circus. No wonder the President was seen laughing once. He is proud of his circus, he is the big ringmaster.

Mariţa, hold my hand, please hold my hand! Your stories are beautiful even if they are lies. My father keeps taking my temperature, and he is putting cold compresses on my forehead. Where is my mama? Look at us all here having a big party, except for my mama. I want my mama, mean as she is. I want her here with me. I don't care that she knows, and that she will kill me, let the whole world know. The sea will be very, very cold and dark when I go under.

They say I slept for two full days. They say I was lucky, that very few survive septicaemia. I'm a goddamn lucky woman. They say if this one didn't kill me, nothing else will. My mother is walking around the room in silence. She is a silent phantom, gliding about in a green gown. I am so happy to see my mama, I don't care that she is bitter and angry all the time, she's the only one I've got. She looks at me sternly. I've never seen her in a green gown with her hair down. Her brown curly hair is just like mine. My mother walks with a softer tread since she has both her children near her. I've never painted my mama.

We never spoke of anything that happened during those days ever again. Not even when the investigations started. We always acted as if it didn't concern us, as if it was someone else, the neighbours. Not us.

The first day I could go out, Gigi and I went to the sea. Everything was icy and blue. There was snow on the beach, and the seagulls were shrieking and diving into the sea for fish. The water was blue the way it is only in the winter: dark, serious blue and the sky hurt your eyes with its cruel light. We walked on the beach in the salty gusts to clean ourselves, to forget. I might just make a new painting of my mother in her green gown, walking on the snow-covered beach. She is coming towards me through the snow, her green gown perfectly contoured against the white beach and the dark blue sea, and she embraces me.

The Investigation and the End of Fairy Tales

They always come around dinnertime: two men in black raincoats. They wear raincoats even when it's not raining. They ring the bell first, then immediately knock on the door too, just to make sure. Usually it is my mother who answers the door. She wipes her hands on her apron and puts on her fiercest look. In her opinion it is better not to show them you are intimidated, or they will get you. It is during the investigation that I know my mother really loves me. Although she is still furious with me for having got into so much trouble, she is standing up to the secret police like a tigress, like a Roman matron, like an Amazon. My father usually gets up a little after my mother and stands behind her, protectively. Valentin and I remain sitting at the table, pretending we are eating our food as if nothing has happened and it is just a benevolent neighbour calling on us. This is the scenario we had decided on, once we heard from Gigi that someone had interrogated his father about a girl having an abortion in his house.

'But it wasn't in your house,' I yelled when Gigi told me.

'Technically one could say it was, that's where you bled, where you actually aborted the foetus, where your father and Camelia treated you, where you convalesced. They know everything.' I saw that Gigi could indeed make ship's captain. He was cool, precise and in control.

My parents and the two secret policemen go into the sitting room where my mother keeps her sewing machine. She usually perches on the edge of the chair in front of the sewing machine, casually, as if she was just making something: a new curtain for the living room, a new tablecloth for our lacquered dining-room table. Valentin and I try to be very quiet and go on pretending to eat, hoping to catch some phrases from the interrogation next door. We hear words such as 'large doses of antibiotics missing, unaccounted for, an intravenous pump nowhere to be found', from which we deduce that my father, in his desperation to save me, actually went at night into his clinic and stole the antibiotics and IV equipment that saved my life. Then they ask my mother the same question over and over again, if she knew where I was on the evening of 5 December and who performed 'the illegal procedure'. That's when my mother plays her part best. She tells them in clear and resounding words that yes, of course she does, her daughter was right here next to her, trying on a new dress she had made for her. Then she reprimands them harshly for insinuating anything dirty about her daughter. And what procedure are they talking about? She doesn't even seem to understand what the procedure is, a tonsil operation, a pedicure, is that illegal? When I hear my mother saying 'my daughter' in that voluminous and stern voice, I want to crawl on the floor with shame for what I am putting my family through and in love and gratitude towards my mother. Valentin is always serious and pale, and winks at me from across the table, as if to say: 'Don't worry, we'll be all right.'

They are trying to prove that both my father and Gigi's father were accomplices in an illegal medical intervention forbidden by the State and Party, and to find out who the principal culprit in Bucharest was. The main villain! As if this was about nuclear weapons or other State secrets and everyone involved knew something of this unfathomable mystery. Two families and several Party employees all drawn up in a battle about a desperate eighteen-year-old girl not wanting to have a baby. We have got used to the visits and we are almost worried on the evenings when they don't turn up. We call them the raincoat men and we even laugh about it sometimes. It was only when the *securitate* began paying us regular visits that we saw my mother actually laugh at dinnertime.

'They are playing with us to lower our defences, to drive us crazy,' says my father.

'We just have to go about our life as usual,' says Valentin.

'I'm not going to give them the satisfaction. Over my dead body,' yells my mother, after which she immediately calms down as if upset at her own outburst and not really sure herself what kind of satisfaction she is referring to.

I am always quiet. I don't say a word. I would just like to melt inside our lacquered hardwood floors and disappear from everybody's vision like in a cartoon. Now I'm here, now I'm not. It's a funny thing they never ask to talk to Valentin and me. Maybe because what they really want is to punish a whole lot of adults and ruin several lives, knowing that our lives will also be ruined in the process. I'm glad I don't know the name of the doctor in Bucharest who performed the operation. Valentin was clever not to tell me anything other than the number of the building and the apartment. Or maybe he didn't know it either. I don't ask, I don't talk about it. On the other hand, maybe if I had known it and just told these raincoat men his name, they would leave us alone and not try to destroy all our lives.

Gigi is more involved than ever in his studies for the naval school and acts as if nothing special is going on. When I visit him, he is always hunched over a ship diagram or a physics problem. His mother looks at me like an enemy whenever I show up, but Gigi raises his head from his books, his red curls all over his forehead, and smiles one of his most welcoming smiles. When he says that someone came again to interrogate his father, he talks as if he was mentioning something he has just read in the newspaper. Suddenly I see my Gigi turned into a grown man overnight, as if the trials of the last months have tested all his strength. From the boy who was crying at the prospect of my abortion, I see him as the man who would lay down his life for me. A real ship's captain. I love him more than ever and everybody's proofs of love in these nightmarish days feel like a huge burden.

It's all because of my carelessness, I shouldn't have got pregnant in the first place, I should have done this, I shouldn't have done that, I'm ruining everybody's lives. I am my own worst nightmare, a black silent scream just like my first fish painting.

The lessons with Miss Mantaş are my only refuge. I welcome everything that is harsh and biting these days. Screams, cold rain, late-night trains, insomnia, my self-inflicted punishment. I take all of Miss Mantaş's criticisms and reprimands with great joy and call for more. I ask her stupid questions or pretend I know less than I actually do, just so that she can raise her voice at me and tell me I'll never take the entrance exam. I even study Socialist Realist art on my own because I know they will stick a question or two about that into the exam. Then on the way back to Mangalia I read my art history book for the full four hours without looking out of the window once, under the dim neon light, until my eyes hurt.

I don't see any more paintings in my head either. That's my worst punishment. There is a silent, oily blackness in my head like the blackness that grabbed everything around me the night of the abortion in the doctor's apartment when the State was economizing on electricity. Maybe the Party has finally achieved its mission as far as I'm concerned: it has installed darkness and immobility in my own mind. What bad timing, just now, when everybody loves me so much, for me to be walking around with a big black hole in my brain.

They stop coming and we all become irritable and edgy, as if we were missing the routine of the raincoat men visiting us around dinnertime. My mother resumes her morose ways, staring at the weeping willow and eating by herself, my father writes notes in his doctor's notebook at the dinner table and Valentin gets up in the middle of dinner and goes into the basement to play the piano. *They must be up to something, right now silence is worse,* we all think but we never say it out loud.

Spring is more painful than ever this year. The yellow forsythias strike you with their nonchalant brightness; the shimmering cobalt blue of the restless sea throwing off her wintry greys is a sharp dagger through your soul, the strident screams of the seagulls sound like the infinite reverberation of our own worries and sorrows. Sometimes Gigi and I walk along the shore at dusk, and breathe in deeply the painful blues, the bittersweet spring gusts. He wraps me in the sailor's cloak that he borrows from his father and for a short moment we become each other's rescue boat in a round, tight embrace in the dwindling light.

But then they start visiting my father at his clinic and Gigi's father on his ship. They ask my father if he has heard of a certain Dr Niculescu. If my father had any connections with this doctor, if he provided antibiotics for him and his 'illegal operations'. As if this Dr Niculescu needed a provincial epidemiologist three hundred kilometres away to provide him with antibiotics.

'And what's the big deal with antibiotics anyway?' I hear my father argue in front of my mother, as if he was arguing with the raincoat men. 'I didn't know they are illegal too. Maybe it's illegal to provide treatment for bronchitis; maybe aspirin and cough syrup are illegal, too.' My mother just stares at my father when he goes into speeches like these, and says nothing. Sometimes she turns round and does something at the sewing machine, and the little boom-booms of the machine punctuate my father's perorations like sonorous commas.

So it was Dr Niculescu who operated on me in the dark, smelling of vodka. Once I find out the doctor's name, everything that happened that night suddenly becomes very sharp in my memory: the silent walk through the White Swamp district in the dark, between Valentin and Gigi; the long ride in the glaring lights of the tram and the smell of urine from the drunken man. I wish I had never known the name of this doctor. I was starting mercifully to forget and now it's all hideously alive in my head again.

It's also now, with this new piece of knowledge, that my brain seems to unclog from the oily blackness that has filled it over the past few months. I see us three in the Surrealist style of the twenties and thirties. Valentin and Gigi and I are in a tram, sitting in a row and caught in glaring light, our eyes huge and staring into it. We are all dressed in cobalt-blue suits and I am wearing a huge scarlet hat with feathers and a yellow parrot on it. Miss Mantaş is standing at a distance, wearing leopardskin and carrying a whip. The tram is also the circus and Didona is making pirouettes in a pink sequinned outfit. There is something that looks like a ball of raw flesh in the corner of the tram. The glaring light is coming from the huge face of the leader which is in fact the same as the sun blinding us from outside the tram windows. My mother produces a sharp scream when she walks into the sitting room and sees my painting. She says she wants to know why she was punished with such a demented child.

I want to tell my mother that it's not me who is demented, but the world we live in. I'm just scared and angry and unevenly built. I move towards my mother and have a terrible desire to embrace her, but she pushes me away and leaves the room. I long for the evenings when the *securitate* men were visiting us and my mother stood up for me like a tigress. That must be a sad day in someone's life, when you long for the visits of the secret police just so you feel loved by your mother.

One evening at dinnertime when my mother is slowly masticating some noodles while staring blankly at the weeping willow in our back yard, we hear Valentin play the waltz from *The Merry Widow* in the basement. Such glorious joyfulness sounds like an insult. I leave everything and rush to the back of the house and down into our grungy basement and there is Valentin caught in a sentimental swirl of notes, crying profusely as he plays. Why am I surrounded by crying men? I think, and feel annoyed and embarrassed by the incongruous spectacle. Everything in our lives, though, has been an incongruous spectacle, a Surrealist painting in the making, a circus on wheels. I run to the piano and stand in front of Valentin, placing my hands on the keys to make him stop. He looks at me through his tears, continues to play softly, and tells me over his own piano-playing that it was his girlfriend Didona who turned us in to the police about the abortion. I want to say I knew it, I knew that Sardanapalus circus girl was trouble from the night I saw her, trapeze acrobatics and all. But the pain on Valentin's face forbids me from saying even one word.

I find out she took a friend of hers to the doctor in Balta Alba, they were caught and her parents were threatened with losing their jobs in the State Circus unless they provided a lead to the doctor. They had no idea of anything, because Didona had found out about this doctor on her own, and she had to tell the police to save her parents. Everything is going round and round in the shiny arena, white horses in red velvet robes standing on their hind legs, ballerinas hanging by their teeth from the dizzying cupola of the State Circus where even the President comes once in a while, and at the very end of this human and animal chain is a miserable alcoholic doctor performing illegal abortions on desperate teenage girls while the State is playing hide-and-seek with the electricity system.

The doctor was caught and is in prison for life, but now they are following all the leads and want to find out about everyone who has had even a remote involvement with anyone connected to this Dr Niculescu. They are after Camelia now and will probably arrest her, since she is the one with a history of 'illegal interventions' in our town. Camelia who helped save my life with her special teas and cared for me, who would probably have done a better job and not got me into the trouble I'm in. Isn't there any important work to be done in this country, textile factories and shipyards to be run, school and university students to be taught, trains and bulldozers to be driven, acres of land to be planted, food to be cooked? Why are so many people spending so much time on a dead foetus?

Valentin accompanies his story with the *Merry Widow* waltz. He tells me of this raw chain of people and events. He has lost his girlfriend, his love and his trust in the world. I try to get him to tell me more about Camelia, I want to save Camelia, I want to stand up for Camelia, and this music is so wrong for the occasion and my brother is so out of synch. He tells me they are in town again, the raincoat men, and have gone to Gigi's house. I leave Valentin in the basement playing his *Merry Widow* waltz and run to Gigi. It seems I've been running almost non-stop for some time. Everything has been a cruel, jolting merry-go-round. My brother has been a wicked box of surprises but I can't imagine my life without him in it any longer. He is my twin brother who is tied to my flesh since our crooked embrace inside my mother's womb. I'd better get used to the ways in which he keeps twisting our lives.

I find Gigi staring at a cargo ship diagram but from the glossy veil over his brown eyes I know he is not thinking about the drawing. He says they've been asking questions about Camelia and her work. I tell Gigi we have to try to get to Camelia and warn her, maybe she can run away somewhere, maybe Mariţa can hide her in her camp. Gigi agrees and as soon as he looks at me with his clear shiny eyes I start feeling even and normal again. We take all the short cuts that Gigi knows to Camelia's house. We go through the Turkish cemetery with its stone turbans and the little child tomb, the walls and the tower lit for the evening prayer, we run across the yards of red beaten earth and the vineyards and get to a small stone house with a thatched roof at the edge of the district. We barge right in and find Camelia in her kitchen stirring a bowl of soup. Pungent smells of herbs and condiments envelop us. We tell her the secret police are after her and she has to run somewhere. We offer to take her to the Gypsy camp. She says we are crazy, she is not scared of anyone, she isn't doing anything illegal, she is just helping Turkish women with their babies, that's all. And she has a nurse's job in the hospital. She's a respectable woman, she says without even turning round from her soup-stirring. We insist and tell her someone told the *securitate* that she had helped me with my abortion. She puts on her white scarf and decides to follow us. We run through the empty fields at the end of town. The corn and sunflowers have barely been planted and we step on the little shoots sticking out from the hard earth. We see the campfire from a distance and smell the burnt leaves. Mariţa is in her tent with her daughter, drinking tea from a thermos. She asks me: 'What's wrong, *porumbiţa*?' Mariţa always knows if something is wrong. She sees Camelia and she knows.

'You can't stay here,' she tells her, 'you'll get us in trouble too. We have enough troubles of our own.'

Camelia is ready to go, because Turkish women are proud and it's a big insult to be refused hospitality. I beg Mariţa to take in Camelia. We are all in trouble, I say, what will become of us? I curse the laws in this country, and Mariţa tells me this is no time for cursing. She gets up from her mattress and asks Camelia to follow her. She tells us to wait there, that she'll be right back. But I have a bad feeling in my throat and in my heart, and suddenly I don't want to be separated from Mariţa. I say I'll come too and

Mariţa doesn't insist this time. Gigi comes as well and we follow Mariţa outside the camp, on to a dark road in between two rows of dilapidated wooden fences with dilapidated houses behind them. She says no one will find her over here; a cousin of hers lives in this calamity of a neighbourhood. The road is filled with potholes and the houses and fences look like they are about to crumble to dust any second.

We take a turn on to a wider road and Mariţa is ahead of us. A set of headlights suddenly appears out of nowhere and comes towards us. I see Mariţa starting to cross the street. She is slow and I scream at her to get out of the way. The car is screeching on to the dirt road and the next second I see Mariţa thrown in the air and fall on her back in the middle of the road. A hollow silence sets in and everything moves very slowly: people coming out into the street from their dilapidated houses, the man at the wheel reeking of bad alcohol getting out of his car and looking down at Mariţa, then turning round and running away on the dirt road. I am screaming to call an ambulance but no sounds seem to come from my throat. Camelia leans over Mariţa and touches her jugular. 'She is still alive,' she says.

She is alive, Mariţa is alive. I hear the thought in my head but something is not connecting. How come she is alive if she is lying here motionless, with a thick streak of blood on her forehead? There is a gooey whiteness in the unlit night dripping all over us. Gigi is trying to pull me away from the middle of the road, I push him aside. He sits next to me, on the dirt in the road. My scream finally comes out of my throat, and more people emerge from their houses, staring at the body in the road. I lean over Mariţa and stroke her face and whisper in her ear to please not die. Mariţa, you are not supposed to die, you are a witch, a magic Gypsy. 'You'll be all right, Mariţa,' I whisper hoarsely.

Gigi says he's going to run and get an ambulance. Is she still alive, Camelia? Keep her alive, put your scarf over her forehead and keep the blood from flowing. Mariţa smiles at me, she makes a sign to come closer, she whispers to bring her daughter over. She is whispering, she is smiling, and she is going to live. Who said Mariţa is going to die? Women like her don't die so easily. Call her daughter, someone go to the camp and call her daughter Gabi and tell her to come quickly. Some kind of whitish gelatin seems to be filling the black night and filling my mouth and nose and ears as if I were drowning. How come the night is not black like the night should be? Everything is wrong and upside down.

I hold Mariţa's hand and for some reason huge hiccups are coming out of my throat. Mariţa is making a sign to me again, I lean over her and she whispers in my ear, she whispers a secret. She says it's only for me, I'm her special *porumbiţa* and not to forget what she says. Yes, it's only for me, Mariţa! The ambulance will come any minute now, you know how fast Gigi can run, and you'll be fine and then we'll laugh and talk about all this and about the secret. Camelia says it stopped. What stopped, Camelia? Don't talk nonsense, this is no time for nonsense. Did the blood stop flowing? Then it's good, it's all good. No, her breathing stopped, her jugular is not pulsing. Camelia too can be wrong; in fact she is wrong so often, she messed up young women and Lili's daughter died because of her. You are a bad woman, Camelia, it's all because of you, she was trying to help you and look what's happened now. Mariţa, you never told me all your stories, you have one big story to tell me, you'll be alive, you'll be fine. I know Gigi will come with the ambulance any second. Oh, here it is: the ambulance with the siren *nee-no, nee-no* and all. Camelia is crying and wringing her hands. She's not dead, damn it, she's just in a coma, I tell the young doctor who comes over. I lean over Mariţa and I am not going to let anyone take her from here, she has to rest and she needs my body warmth, she's just cold, that's all, it's a cold bloody night.

They drag me from Mariţa's body, and the ambulance lights are cruel and white. Some Gypsies I recognize are running from the camp and Gabi, her daughter, is ahead of them. People's faces are scrunching in hideous ways as if crying a most desperate cry. Mariţa's family is here. She has a big family and they are all crying. But I don't see why they are not letting me warm up her body. They take Mariţa in the ambulance. The whitish stuff is drowning me again. I'm going to drown and I'm not even in the water.

As I am standing here at the funeral with the Gypsies playing their heartbreak accordion music I'm wondering how I will stand all the greyness in my life without her. How will I bear my mother's madness, my brother's weirdness, my father's outbursts at my mother, this whole bloody investigation, Miss Mantaş's harshness, without ever hearing Mariţa call me *porumbiţa* and tell me to stop wailing myself to death and go on and paint my crazy paintings and be kind to my mama?

After the funeral the police raid the Gypsy camp. They tell them they can't live there any longer. They have to live in the *blocuri*, in the cement boxes for good, they cause too much trouble, they disrupt the city order, they should be grateful to the government that gives them free places to live. It's a good and generous government. The Gypsies can't live in the cement boxes, didn't you know that, you stupid police in a stupid country? They tell the police all right, they'll move back into the *blocuri*. But I know them better. At night, when I go back to the camp, everything is dark. The cement boxes are gaping and empty with hollow windows like many pairs of huge gouged eyes. There is just beaten black earth where the camp was. The Gypsies are all gone. There is no fire and no smell of burnt leaves. I wonder if it has ever been and if Mariţa ever existed. But from the big aching hole in my heart and from the smell of dried plums still lingering on my clothes I know she did. I have no paintings in my head and my longer arm is hanging beside me uselessly. I am walking towards the cobalt sea as the forsythias burn my eyes with their insolent brightness and Mariţa's secret is ringing in my ears.

Blue May, Cold June

I write a letter in my head to Anushka Pomorowska. I can't send it because it would be censored and Anushka would never get it anyway. But I indulge in this childish activity of writing an imaginary letter. At least if she's not going to get it, it's because I never sent it, not because the police took it away. Living in this country stunts your maturity, and you want to stay in your childhood for ever, even when your childhood is also a mess. I write to Anushka:

My dear Anushka Pomorowska,

I think of you often and of our summer together here at the beach. I still wear the scarf you gave me quite often and I treasure it because I always remember the moment in your room when we talked so honestly and we cried and because it's the most beautiful thing I've ever owned. It has the same colours as Van Gogh's sunflowers. After you left that afternoon almost three years ago, I went back home and painted your portrait. I made you as a bright sea deity, the saviour of desperate suicidal people. You are bright as the sun in the middle of the storm in my painting. I hope you are no longer suffering so much from the death of your boyfriend, and that maybe you have a new boyfriend you can love.

You know, sometimes I wish you could have packed me inside your suitcase with colourful soft French clothes and taken me with you to Paris. Our country is getting stupider than ever. I've had a very great sadness in my life recently. My oldest friend in town, the old Gypsy woman Mariţa, died after she was hit by a drunk driver one night, when we were trying to hide Camelia the Turkish midwife from being caught and taken away by the secret police. Camelia helped me after I had an illegal abortion. Things like this only happen because we have such absurd laws that are trying to destroy the people instead of helping and protecting them. When you have to slalom between bad laws, more bad things happen, because more people are desperate, drunk, careless, angry or just plain stupid. Here we are all cursed in multiple ways. Since Mariţa died it's like everything lost colour. Even the sea that I love so much seems greyer. And everything that used to bother me before now bothers me ten times more. I sometimes want to strangle my mother.

Since the abortion Gigi and I haven't made love at all. Every time we tried, I remembered the intervention in the doctor's room, or the night when I almost died from blood poisoning, or the months of the investigation that ended with Mariţa's death and Camelia's disappearance. And then I can't go on with it. I want to so much, because when Gigi and I made love everything in the world and in my body seemed in its right place and I stopped thinking about the awful things in my country. But Gigi says to give it time, and that I'll feel like it again one day. Camelia the Turkish woman disappeared. We don't know whether she is hiding somewhere with her Turkish people, or if she managed to leave the country, or if the secret police got her and took her somewhere. I hope she is hiding and fooling the secret police. She did help save my life after all. I don't have any painting ideas in my head either. It feels like a fountain of life and joy in me has dried up. At the source of this fountain there is only dry sand. And to think I'm only eighteen and a half. How will I be at thirty, I wonder? Maybe I'll be like my mother: a dried-up black walnut in mourning. I hope I can make love to Gigi again. I hope I can paint again. I hope to see you again in my life some time, Anushka. I hope for so many things but who knows what will happen with all my hopes. So far it doesn't look too good.

Take care of yourself, Anushka, and give my greetings to Paris. Nora Teodoru.

I seal and send my imaginary letter to Anushka via an imaginary mail box, *par avion imaginaire.* I actually ended my letter by saying to give my greetings to Paris. That would have made Anushka laugh if she ever got such a letter from me.

Imaginary activities are helping me. I try to put little imaginary activities in the black hole left in my life and heart after Mariţa's death. I know it's what Mariţa would have wanted me to do: to keep filling that hole with colourful things like the myriad of things that she sold at street corners and in the market, until it was packed full and I wouldn't feel it as a big empty hole any longer. That's how you learn to endure the pain of life, Mariţa would say, by filling it with many little colourful things.

Easter is this week and we all move into a frenzy of egg-colouring. Even Gigi is colouring eggs, just so, for the sake of tradition and because he likes coloured hard-boiled eggs. My parents and Valentin and I go to the midnight Easter service at the big Orthodox church in town and Gigi comes with us without telling his family. I tell him he has to do the same for me, sneak me into the mosque for the celebration at the end of Ramadan. I'm dying to see the mosque ready for the holiday. We walk three times around the church holding our lit candles and singing, and the smell of hyacinths, daffodils and lilac erupts with a vengeance in the spring night air. I feel this is an important spring; after all the dark events of the last years, maybe there is hope for us, maybe we too are blooming in the night like the purple lilac. Walking home with my candle lit amid the large crowds, it seems to me I see Mariţa far away. The round swirling rainbow skirts swishing this way and that, the hurried walk but with a slight, almost imperceptible limp, the red scarf around the head tied at the back. I forget Mariţa is dead and I run after the woman, my heart pumping with joy like hyacinth bulbs erupting into flowers. I leave my family and Gigi and run after the woman, I follow her through the market place, the square of the old bazaar, and I catch up with her and grab her shoulder. It was all a bad dream, Mariţa never died, what was I thinking, I knew women like that don't die. She turns round and I see it is Gabi, Mariţa's daughter. She looks older and heavier. She smiles when she sees me but I am ready to collapse.

I hold in my tears and tell her: 'For a second, I thought it was Mariţa.' In fact I can't hold my tears, they are soaking my face.

'Miss Nora, I was wondering if I was going to see you.'

'What are you doing here, Gabi? I thought you had left the area.'

'We did, we went down closer to the Danube, there are more of our people over there, but now we are thinking of coming back near Tekirghiol, the salt lakes. I just came back here for Easter, to pray for my mama's soul. She always liked the Easter night. My man is waiting for me over there at the end of town, in our old cart.'

Now I feel a great confusion about the dead and the living. I want to tell Gabi to send Mariţa my love, but Mariţa is dead and Gabi here standing in front of me looks almost like Mariţa, but she is not and she doesn't know any of her mother's stories.

'You wouldn't happen to have some money to spare? We aren't

doing very well, Miss Nora, you know,' says Gabi with a shy smile. I take out a ten-*lei* note and hand it to her.

'May God bless you, Miss Nora. My mama loved you dearly, she always said you was a special girl, with visions and a special calling.'

Gabi goes away and I stand in the middle of the market place watching her leave, holding my Easter bouquet of fragrant hyacinths, daffodils and purple lilac, and it is all wintry in my heart. I miss Mariţa so much that this seems like the cruellest Easter of all. I see Gigi in the distance running to meet me. How come Gigi always finds me when I'm lost? I hang on to my Easter bouquet and let Gigi hold me until that red wound reopened by this unexpected encounter slowly closes.

On 1 May, International Workers' Day, Gigi turns nineteen. I used to sometimes make fun of this coincidence and tell Gigi he should lie about his birthday and say it was 2 May. But this year I want to give Gigi a big birthday party, Workers' Day or not. Two days ago I woke up with a sudden wild hunger to live and be happy again. I knew it was Mariţa pushing me ahead and telling me to move on, to let go of the black hole in my heart, to be young again. She showed herself to me that morning, dancing a Gypsy dance in the middle of her old camp, with a red scarf round her head as always, only this time her scarf had golden coins sewn all round it. Mariţa was young and more nimble than I knew her and danced like a magic flame with castanets in her hand and bare feet on the earth near the fire. She was a classic Gypsy figure like in some of our Romanian traditional paintings, a colourful idealization. She winked at me from that portrait and told me to forget about life being all about learning how to endure the pain, that life is also about living and enjoying it. When the radio in our house started howling the 1 May workers' song early in the morning the day before, in anticipation of the day to come, that's when I thought I wanted to give Gigi a big party, dance, be joyous, wear a colourful dress instead of the funereal clothes I've been wearing lately.

I tell my mother about my plans and I don't wait for her to tell me how it's a bad idea and she's tired of my caprices and she's exhausted from her miserable work at the school.

I just say bluntly: 'Mama, I'm going to have a party for Gigi's birthday tomorrow night.'

She says: 'That's what you think, Nora!'

And I say: 'Mama, that's exactly what I think, and I'm going to do it. You don't have to do a thing, I'll take care of everything, and we'll stay in my room or outside in the garden.'

'You will get pneumonia partying outside at this time of year.'

'That's all right, Mama, if I get pneumonia, at least I'll know I've lived a little,' I answer more impudently than ever.

Valentin is listening to us in the doorway, holding his music scores under his arm, and he says: 'That's a good idea, let's have a party for Gigi. We have never had a party in this house and soon we'll go to university in Bucharest.'

My angry scrunched-up face relaxes and I turn a sweet smile towards Valentin, thanking my fate this time for the existence of a brother. Valentin is my never-ending box of surprises.

My mother sweetens her tone as well and says: 'We'll see about that!'

After our mama leaves to get ready for work, I tell Valentin he should make up with that Sardanapalus concubine of his and invite her to the party as well. Has she ever in her life seen the sea? He is staring at me because he has no idea who Sardanapalus is and I realize I am speaking from my own fantasies.

'I mean Didona, your circus girl.'

Valentin becomes stern; he takes on his no-nonsense serious pianist face and says: 'First of all, she's not "my circus girl", secondly I will never make up with her. She's an informer.'

'Ooh, relax a little, Valentin!' I say wisely, as if some of Mariţa's old wisdom had seeped into me as well. 'She had no choice; she was forced to do it. What would you have done if they had threatened you that both your parents were going to lose their jobs? Hmm? What?'

Valentin's face becomes fierce and he says, tensing like a big feline before it pounces on its prey: 'I would rather have died, I would have killed myself rather than turn anybody in, I would have taken poison, sliced my wrists . . .'

Great, I think, *Valentin is a psycho too, besides being the world's weirdest brother, he is also a psycho. That's how he pushed me there in our mother's womb for the full nine months of our close cohabitation, to where I became a less than normal person; he pushed into me like the fierce crazy cat that he is, wanting everything, wanting all the space for himself, all the air for his lungs alone, all the food coming down that umbilical cord for himself alone. He wanted to swallow me whole and annihilate me so he could grow alone all fat and strong in our mama's belly.*

I say only: 'Valentin, stop being so theatrical about everything! Just invite her and see what happens.'

It's the first time I stand up to my brother and put him in his place. I expect he will pounce on me and we'll start a big fight. But Valentin doesn't really know how to fight. He only gets ready to pounce and then withdraws.

'Do you really think so, Nora?'

'Do I think what?'

'Do you think I should invite Didona to the party? Do you think we should make up? And why did you call her my Sardanapalus concubine?'

'I'll tell you another time, Valentin, but yes, I do think you should make up. Just go into the sitting room and call her. We'll have a nice party,' I say. I am a round oyster of wisdom and common sense. I am stronger than my brother, he only acts stronger.

Gigi is so happy about the party that I think it's worth all the trouble with my mother just to see his full golden smile bubble all over his face. We invite our few friends from the high school, but mostly kids from his Turkish neighbourhood. We invite Yafsin, the Arab man who helped me get my blue jeans from the port of Constanţa, and his girlfriend Jasmina. Valentin is radiant after making up with Miss Trapeze and my father brings us different restaurant foods from his many faithful clients. My mother even relaxes a little when she sees Valentin so happy and makes her famous plum dumplings and salty cheese pastries for the party. We set the time of the party for eight o'clock.

Today the sea is like burning sapphire. It moves hypnotically in sharp, edgy plates of deep blue. With just the right amount of light green to make it not really blue, but an illusion of blue. The chicory flowers at the edges of the beach are brighter and glow like a precious necklace around the whitish-yellow sands. The May sun is warmer and in the afternoon Gigi, Valentin and I take a break from the preparations and sit out in the front garden, soaking up the balmy air and chatting about the people we have invited. In a little while Valentin is going to the station to wait for Didona, who was 'bubbling with joy' on the phone, so Valentin reports. This is going to be a good day. I feel Mariţa's joyfulness and Esma's wildness and Anushka's brightness move through me and make me light and ephemeral.

The evening is fragrant and filled with the whimsical promise of summer. I am wearing my Van Gogh Anushka silk scarf over my new light green velvet dress and I feel like an alert crocus that just came out from under a thick layer of snow. That's the exact image I have of myself this afternoon as I'm laughing and being silly and frivolous with my 'two men' in the front yard of our house, and as the sharp blue point of the sea glittering through the blooming vegetation winks at me from a distance: an impertinent yellow crocus emerging from the snow.

We choose a combination of LPs and tapes for the party. My French and Italian tapes of pop music, Gigi's collection of Romanian and Turkish folk, Valentin's tapes with Dire Straits and Fleetwood Mac that he copied from a friend in Bucharest. Besides being a prodigy pianist he also keeps up with the newest and weirdest American music. Valentin is a baroque personality, a combination of old-fashioned and stridently modern, of steel harshness and break-down-cry-till-you-drop sentimentality. He is the complete one of the two of us. I am the incomplete, uneven one who keeps making and remaking herself in new colours and surprising shapes, like the images you see through a kaleidoscope. I am my own sculptor, my own ringmistress. Gigi is like neither of us. He has become the man of every girl's dream and that's also what gives me shivers of anxiety once in a while when I see him talking to or smiling at a girl who is not me. He has harvested the roughness of that red beaten earth of the Turkish neighbourhood and the luminous smoothness of our sea. Gigi, Valentin and Nora are a trio worthy of a masterful painting, of a stunning circus act, of a Hollywood movie, if ever any important Western movie person with a taste for the Balkans or a suicide wish should one day stray into this part of the world and discover us.

The party starts in a swirl of loud talk, boisterous laughter, unleashed dancing and lots of plum dumplings. My mother rises to the occasion and keeps bringing in trays of her best snacks and my heart fills with renewed love for her the way it did at the time of the investigation. *Ah, the good old times of the investigation by the secret police which brought our family together.* She is wearing the dark green dress she wore when I saw the painting of her walking on the frozen beach.

We make up for all the parties we haven't had in this house. Valentin and Didona are dancing languorously even to the fast tunes. Didona surprises me by not being dressed up at all. She is wearing the same black turtleneck as when I first met her at the circus and a pair of jeans. But she walks, moves and talks as if she were wearing a ruby-studded dress. Her black hair falls in waves like a hallucination. I feel a sudden burst of admiration for her and no tinge of jealousy, as I sometimes do next to a perfectly built and beautifully crafted female form. The way I did next to Anushka, for example. It's as if Didona actually stepped down from my own imagination, from a painting that I could have painted or that I will paint some time in the future. The concubine of Delacroix's Sardanapalus has melted into the dark meanders of my own thoughts and there she is dancing in front of me fluidly like the very incarnation of a dream. I don't even feel angry at her for having been partly responsible for the misery of the investigation. I don't see what else she could have done when she was made to choose between her entire family's survival and turning in an abortionist doctor who was an alcoholic crook anyway. But tonight I don't want to think of anything as nauseating as that experience. I want to catch one last flicker of my youth before it dies out and we all go our separate ways.

Gigi is playful and rowdy tonight. He is lifting me up in a crazy dance to the music of the Algerian singer Enrico Macias that Yafsin brought over for the party. He has grown stronger and more manly, his muscles tighter, his chest wider: I'm crazy about him. Didona's hair seems to be flying around the room like a flock of black ravens, inciting all of us to rowdiness and hot embraces. Yafsin is embracing his petite, brown-haired Jasmina as they are dancing in a trance, Gigi is holding me until I can't breathe, Valentin is all over Didona, kissing and stroking her. In my dizziness from the wine and the dancing, everything seems to be swirling around like a huge carousel. A new idea comes to me in a flash. I stop in the middle of my dancing and I scream: 'Hey everybody!' Everything stops, and they all look at me as if frozen, exactly in the midst of a dance move, a lifted arm, a bent knee, a lock of hair twirling in the air. 'Let's go to the basement so Valentin can play the piano and we can play the music even louder.'

As if on command, we all leave the room chaotically, and

run through the yard towards the back of the house and the basement entrance. The spring night air hits our lungs with its saltiness, its raw purple smells. This is a Romanian movie in the making, a movie about Romania's confused youth, the Ceauşescu generation, trying to live in a strident pretence of freedom. Pretended freedom feels almost like freedom. My parents come out of the sitting room, alarmed by the noise, and stare at us in consternation, as if they were faced with a crowd of loonies freshly escaped from the local asylum. They are speechless and motionless, hands in the air and eyes wide open, a Goya portrait in the early stages.

We turn on the basement's neon lights. Whoever had the bright idea to put neon lights in the basement? It all looks charmingly decrepit. We throw ourselves on to the old sofas, raising clouds of dust in the already dusty air, coughing and laughing at once. Valentin sits at the piano and starts playing a polka, a goddamn Polish polka, while jumping and shaking on the piano stool like a Charlie Chaplin impersonation.

I feel nationalistic tonight, and I say: 'Don't you have some Romanian music you can regale us with, Brother?' We are already hopping to the rhythm of the polka when Valentin changes his tune midstream and starts a hora, a goddamn Romanian hora. We hop to that too. We arrange ourselves in a hora circle and twirl round and round doing the little hora steps, not really knowing how to do them because we are such bad Romanians, such bad sons and daughters of our country, and we hang out with foreign students and Arabs like Yafsin and we know better how to dance to American music than to the music of our own ancestors. Ancestors like my crazy grandfather who loved his land more than his own children. Maybe he shouldn't have said: 'That'll be the day,' and he should have given away his wretched land and then he wouldn't have been lifted brutally from the dinner table and killed in a grungy basement by a bunch of Bolsheviks. Then my mother would have been a sweet and normal mother playing joyous and melancholy piano pieces at the grand piano which would be occupying our dining room instead of the stupid lacquered dining table that is in it now.

My thoughts are a wild rollercoaster and come and go angrily in strident colours as I'm twirling like mad in the Romanian hora. The Turkish kids are making their own circle and do a Turkish version of a hora, with jumps and slaps of the calves, and we are the most international house in the neighbourhood and we'll probably have to pay for it one day.

'Didona, do some acrobatics for us!' I yell as if possessed.

She was waiting for nothing less than that command. Didona turns into a firebird, a panther, a wreath of palpable music: she somersaults around the room and high-jumps over our heads, she does backflips on top of the piano. We all stop, except for Valentin, who keeps playing the hora faster and faster while Didona is jumping around the room in an ecstasy of reckless moves. We have our own Nadia Comaneci right here in our basement.

How is this number going to end? I wonder. Suddenly I have a bad feeling that Didona is going to hurt Valentin somehow, some time, somewhere. That Valentin is going to reel from the pain. I look at his pale face and his wide, ecstatic smile, that 'I'm living it all up as if I will die tomorrow' kind of smile. Didona suddenly lands in front of us on the basement floor and bows as if she really is at the circus. Valentin slams down his last note, and we are all quiet. Didona's face is inexplicably, excruciatingly sad, but then it widens into a broad smile as if sadness didn't even exist in the world. It's an act. Didona is all an act, now she's sad, now she's happy, a real circus girl. Who is she really? One of the Turkish boys claps and says, 'Bravo.' Everybody starts clapping, the neon light seems even dimmer, clouds of dust are floating in the air, the last piano note reverberates under Valentin's pedal, like a drawn-out moan. We make a fine spectacle of desolate Romanian youth.

The spring night is filled with restless rustles from the sea and blooming trees shaking their buds in the salty gusts. We finish our party outside, breaking the cool darkness with our laughs and loud talking. I decide to go to Gigi's house tonight. The Turkish boys are rowdily walking ahead of us, mixing Turkish and Romanian words, a medley of honeyed consonants and wavy vowels, *baklava* and plum dumplings united. The long street leading from our house deep into the city and towards the Turkish neighbourhood is quivering with our bubbling laughs, mixed languages and the bittersweet colours of the last shimmer of our youth.

When we get to Gigi's house, we see it is all lit up and loud voices in Turkish are bursting out through the open windows. There is laughter and oriental music that sounds like a mix of Gypsy melodies and Romanian folk but is different from either of them. Smells of Turkish desserts are oozing out into the street. Everybody's having a party tonight. The apricot tree in front of the house is shaking its pink blossoms so that they fall on us like sweet snow. Gigi makes a sign to me that he will go in first and for me to come into his room through the back window. He makes his Turkish sign of beckoning, with the palms up. He stares at me and his eyes are shiny in the spring night. With Gigi life is both sweet and adventurous, a mellow carnival, a playful ballet. I do as he says and in a couple of moves I'm in his low-lying bed. He takes a while and I hear him talking Turkish with the guests, bumpy, juicy sounds in his voice that is both soft and manly, a velvety medley of new sounds that wake up my longings and caress my body like playful fingers. Gigi comes in and whispers to me that Turkish relatives are visiting from Istanbul. Luca's brother Lemi with his wife Seda have arrived tonight and are visiting all their relatives in Mangalia and Constanţa. I have never heard of these Turkish relatives before, but I don't really care. Gigi speaking Turkish had an enthralling effect on me just now, like Mariţa's stories, like my fantasies of Esma the princess, like Dido's soulful eyes in the small reproduction of the mosaic in our history book. Gigi locks the door.

Tonight we make love secretly, quietly, to the sound of Turkish words and music, in the smell of baking *baklava* and apricot blossoms, feeling and tasting every sweet part of each other's bodies like hungry thieves in the fragrant spring night. Curling next to Gigi like a greedy cat, on his low hard bed, feeling his honeyed tight-muscled body and his quick breathing, I want to go through all the trials of life with him, watch him pilot his ship across our violet-green waters, while I make hundreds of magical paintings of us and of all the people and places I know, like Princess Esma used to: a Turkish-Romanian fairy tale, dictatorship be damned.

Late into the night, we whisper, we make plans for our future, we caress and kiss like real lovers. My body feels full and sufficient to itself. When Gigi touches and strokes my arms and my breasts, my nape and the small of my back, I even out instantaneously and turn into a continuous wave of watery pleasure. We decide it's best for me to go home before everybody wakes up. Gigi pulls on the smart brown trousers that he wore for the party, the white shirt buttoned all wrong, I get into my green velvet dress giggling in the dark and we both jump out through the window on to the hard earth. We walk into the night back to my house, holding each other by the waist. Stray cats are mewing on the pavements, a few dogs start barking as we pass neighbours' houses, and we hear the shrieks of the first seagulls waking up on the beach. I tell Gigi I want us to get married as soon as we pass our entrance exams this summer. Gigi doesn't say anything, just walks with his head down, staring at his tennis shoes and the dark pavement.

I say: 'What's the matter, lover boy, now that you've had your pleasure with me you don't want to marry me any more?' I laugh at my own joke and my laughter rings stridently in the quiet streets.

'That's right, I just want to use and misuse you over and over again, Nora,' says Gigi, smiling his mischievous smile, and I want to greedily bite the sound of my own name off his fleshy lips.

But then he gets serious, stops me in the middle of the street, lifts up my chin gently to make me look at him, and says: 'Did you ever think that my parents would expect you to convert, if we are to get married?'

I burst into laughter again and say: 'Convert to what? What the hell are you talking about?'

'Become a Muslim, become a Turkish woman of sorts,' he says seriously. The expression 'of sorts' in his mouth, and after the other things he just said, sounds particularly humorous.

'What is a Turkish woman of sorts, Gigi? Is that like a pretend Turkish woman, or maybe like a cross between two species, or a jug of *braga* with a little bit of Romanian *ţuičа* in it?' I could go on and on making fun of what Gigi has just said and he knows it and silences me with a long warm kiss. After the kiss I start again though, still thinking he is joking.

'So I'd better start going to the mosque with all the Turkish women, I guess, hm?'

'Nora, I can't help what my parents are, you know that, just like you can't stop what your parents are. What do you think, that your parents aren't going to want me to become a Christian if you tell them we want to get married?'

I had never in my life pondered this problem until Gigi brought it up. With all the mad things happening throughout my adolescence, like almost dying in a storm while saving a distraught French woman from the sea, having my prodigal brother return to the family nest, having an almost fatal abortion, our whole family going through months of a nasty and absurd investigation and Mariţa's violent death, religious conversions were the last thing on my mind. I look him in the eyes and smile my own crooked 'you are not fooling me' smile back at him.

'It's not like our families are really devout religious people,

Gigi. How often do your parents go to the mosque except once in a while on Muslim holidays? And how often do my own parents go to church except at Christmas, Easter and for someone's funeral or wedding? I think we should convert to Marxism, Gigi,' I say, giggling and proud of my humour. 'I think we should get married in the name of Papa Marx and Papa Lenin and have Papa Ceauşescu seal the deal. Then we should dance to the National Anthem for our wedding party.'

I'm proud of my vivid imagination too. Gigi is serious and doesn't smile. A soft breeze is stirring from the sea with the approaching dawn and a streak of bluish light is moving in above the sea, as we approach my house.

'You don't have to be super-religious and a devout Muslim or Christian to hold on to old prejudices, Nora, you know that. But when it comes to marriage people are really tested. I dare you, just go ahead and ask your parents about it and see what they say. How do you think my mother got to marry my father, hm?' Gigi asks earnestly.

'How? I'm dying to find out, Gigi, how did she?'

'She converted, that's how. My mother is not Turkish, she wasn't a Muslim, she is Romanian from Tulcea,' he says, almost whispering, as if revealing a great secret. 'But now she's more Turkish than the Turks.'

Oh, just wonderful: Gigi's mother is from the same town as my mother's relatives, we are practically kin already. Maybe her parents knew my crazy landowner of a grandfather. And me who thought all along that Sabina, Gigi's mother, with her quiet, slightly secretive ways, feline steps and talent for drawing world maps from memory, was just your regular Turkish woman. Maybe Romanians are really Turks, maybe we aren't Romanians at all, and who cares anyway what the hell kind of nation we are, if I can't marry the only man I would ever want to marry because of some pretence of religious devotion in a Marxist country.

I push Gigi away from me and start running down the middle of the street, as dawn is thrusting its wild pinks through the horizon. There are no fairy tales, they are all lies, even Mariţa's stories are all lies, and Mariţa knew it too, she just went on and on about Esma and her magic drawings to take my mind off the squabbles in my house and the crazy secrets and child-swapping in my family. Maybe Mariţa also told me stories to take her own mind off the misery of her people, who are begging at street corners with their newborn babies hanging on to their necks, being forced into the Socialist concrete boxes like cells for prisoners. The Gypsy woman in her red scarf with golden coins dancing with castanets is also a fairy tale that has never existed except in the mind of some Romanian artist who knew nothing of how the Gypsies really lived. And maybe Nora and Gigi are also a lie, an improbable love story, and the only truth is that black scream of my first fish painting. I am crying now and my sobs sound just as strident in the empty street as my laughter sounded a few minutes ago.

Gigi runs after me and grabs me with force, pulls me to his chest and does not let go. I wriggle and thrash in my fury but Gigi is stronger and doesn't ease up. I am forced to calm down. I am a meek feline holding in my rage for now. He whispers into my hair, into my brown coiling curls: 'How silly can you be, Nora, to let this upset you? What does it all matter? Christian, Muslim, Marxist, you know you are the only woman for me in the whole world, ever. Why do we need to marry with our families' blessings anyway? We can simply go to the Justice of the Peace after we pass our exams this summer and tell them afterwards. I just wanted you to know the truth about everything, in case you were thinking of some glorious wedding with a big family party and all.'

Gigi speaks wisely, like an old man and an adventurous teenager all in one. He manages to calm me down with his slow, determined kisses. But I feel a trace of lingering sadness in Gigi's voice and caresses. I understand that Gigi is truthful and will always love me, but that he would have liked to marry me with his parents' blessing, not like an act of vengeance, not spitefully, not in secret, but smoothly, roundly, with everyone on all sides clapping and dancing in a big circle like that silly hora we did last night.

I decide to let go of this for the moment, maybe we are too young to get married anyway. And really, in the larger scheme of my life right now, marriage should be the least of my worries. What matters is that I have Gigi's love through and through, his rainbow of smiles and his tight embraces. And I'm certainly not converting to any other religion. I'm not even too crazy about my own. Inside one of my paintings Gigi and I get married floating on the sea at dawn, with a flock of seagulls swirling around, a fishing boat sailing by and throwing its large nets into the rustling waves, and the two of us with pearly shells and green algae in our hair like two unheard-of sea creatures, our own special fairy tale.

Valentin is awake when I get into my room through the window. He has been sleeping on a sofa bed in my room since he came back into our family, though he uses our sitting room during the day to study in or just to sit and think. He also derives special pleasure from watching our mother work on the sewing machine in the sitting room. I find him studying music scores and music history, cross-legged on the sofa and crouched over his books. Nothing sways Valentin from his ambitions, not even Didona with her mythic raven hair and formidable acrobatics, not even the spring fragrances and pastel blossoms, nothing. Whereas me, everything sways me this way and that like the willow in front of our window. I should be studying my own art history book instead of thinking about marriage. Miss Mantaş is going to break a vocal cord and burst a vein yelling at me next Sunday. I tell Valentin what Gigi has just told me, that I would have to convert to his religion if I wanted a proper family wedding.

Valentin starts laughing wholeheartedly the way he does only rarely when he finds something really funny. His nose scrunches up and his whole body is shaking, producing a rumbling kind of laughter, like an avalanche of hiccups.

'What's wrong with you two, are you deranged? Why the hell would you even want to get married now? Don't we have enough worries as it is?'

I'm not as amused as he seems to be. 'It's not that, Valentin, it's the principle of it, you know.'

'Oh, who cares about the principle of it, Nora? What matters really is the thing in itself.'

'Like what? What the hell "thing in itself" are you talking about?' I ask, irritated.

'Like the fact that you don't need to worry about having to convert for a big wedding because you shouldn't be thinking about marriage in the first place. And who in their right mind worries about religious conversion in our country when the only accepted religion is Marxism anyway?'

I know Valentin is right, but I want to know. Gigi has just dared me to ask my parents about marriage. I want to talk to them this very morning. I want to know what my family is really all about. Valentin is humming scores to himself, Chopin, Liszt, Mendelssohn, the classics. I decide to wait patiently until my parents wake up and I can ask them. I sit in front of the window and try to find the opening through the trees and bushes towards the sea. It is larger now before all the vegetation erupts, and I stare at the iridescent sapphire surface swaying lazily and sparkling in the rising sun through an embroidery of rose and white blossoms, light green young leaves and budding grapevines. I fall asleep with my head on my crossed arms, on the windowsill, with the morning breeze cooling my face. My sleep is deep like a dark mushy tunnel, with no dreams, just a black feathery cloak over my tired consciousness. A light tap on my shoulder pulls me out of it and when I look up I see none other than my own mother, wearing a beige woollen dress that I have never seen before. Maybe a huge miracle has happened in our lives while I was asleep and now we will all start a gentler, more normal existence. The same thought that I went to sleep with is fully awake, persistent, stubborn, a wide-eyed creature with feathers. A thought like a fantastical bird. This is the perfect moment to present it to my mother.

'Mama, I want to marry Gigi,' I say softly, groggily.

'Marry a Turk?' she says without blinking, without flinching, without a moment's pause, standing in her beige woollen dress in front of me like a stone statue.

'Yes, marry a Turk, that's right. Mama, what have you been thinking all these years, who else should I marry? What makes us so superior to the Turks anyway?'

I notice that Valentin is still in the room, lying on the sofa bed, an arm over his eyes as if sleeping. I don't know if he's sleeping or awake though. My mother turns her head and looks over to him and her face softens like a statue come to life. She has never had that expression for me. But I'm not jealous, I'm glad my mother looks softer and less threatening, even if it's not out of affection for me but for my brother. Valentin is a beneficent presence, he brings the best out of my mother, and some of it trickles into my life too.

Mama turns her face back to me and now I see she has a melancholy, pained expression, like the one she had when I caught her with the tear hanging on her nose by the piano in the basement. All sorts of miracles are happening in my family lately.

'Nora . . . fine, marry a Turk if that's what you want, his family are nice people, really it's not that. But not now! Wait a while, see what happens with the art school, you have time to marry . . .' she says.

I'm about to fall off the chair, because I can't believe my mother is actually having a conversation with me and not threatening or scolding me or telling me she will kill me with her own hands, or that I am demented and hopeless and what did she do to deserve it. It must be the spell of Valentin, his presence, his feline steps around the house, his piano music filling the house from the basement every day, the completeness she must feel again in her body from having both children near her. Maybe before she gave away Valentin to her sister, my mother was the sweetest, most reasonable person on the street. Maybe we had a few good years, Valentin and I taking turns suckling at our mama's breast, wrapped in the warmth radiating from her body, all cuddled together in one bed, with my father snoring on the other side. Maybe there is a memory of happiness in all of us that's been awoken and is struggling to push its head through all the messiness and fears of our lives. I want to say: 'You are right, Mama, I'm going to listen to you, I'm going to devour those art history books and pass the exam in the top group, and not worry about marriage at all right now.' And I want to embrace my mama the way I did in my painting on the beach in the snow, when she was wearing the dark green dress in the icy afternoon. But I can't bring myself to do it. I am not used to saying words like these to my mother, to agreeing with her and being a good, obedient daughter. I know my mama is right, and I want to tell her, but my mouth stays shut. She takes my silence as my usual defiance and determination always to do the opposite of everything she says.

'Fine, do what you want, it's your life, play with it as you wish,' she says, regaining her familiar harshness.

That's when my mouth cracks open and I yell just as she is about to leave the room in her off-white woollen dress, with the brown curls that are also my brown curls falling down her back.

'*Da, Mama, da, bine, sigur*', yes, Mama, yes, of course, sure, I yell. She turns her head so that I can see her profile, her majestic Roman profile framed by the brown curls, unmoved, impenetrable. Maybe she believes me; maybe she's heard me and believes what I just said. Valentin takes his hand away from his eyes and I see he has been awake all along. Valentin is a cunning ferret, a ringmaster in disguise.

One evening when I come into Gigi's house for desserts, Seda and Lemi show me some photographs of Istanbul and I don't know why I feel I've seen them before, though I haven't. The Blue Mosque with its enormous round cupolas and towers, reigning in the vicinity of a sea that is even bluer than any of the bluest days of our sea, seems to emerge from somewhere in a dream. It must be Mariţa's stories about Esma and her travels and paintings of magical mosques rising from the sea. She must have told me stories about these places when I was little and sitting cross-legged on the pavement in the market place, listening to her in a wide-eyed trance. I tell Gigi when we go out into the street, on the way back to my house, that maybe, if we pass our exams and all is well, we should try to take a tourist trip to Istanbul next year, and visit his relatives and see those fairy-tale blue and golden sights. We might be lucky and get passports and tourist visas after all. Gigi smiles his adventurous happy smile and says nothing would make him happier. I already see myself walking with Gigi on the Bosphorus Bridge with a golden painting blooming in my head, and buying ruby rings in the Turkish bazaar.

I never mention anything to Gigi about marriage any more and he doesn't either, as if we had made a tacit pact. He studies for his exams, I study for mine. Valentin practises his piano day and night except when he's in school. We enter a frantic rhythm like the relentless wheel of my mother's sewing machine, on and on through the end of spring until the summer hits us with a wave of torrid heat and suffocating, sand-filled winds. We are almost at the end of high school and are counting the days till it's over. Our university exams are in a month and we are already making plans for what we will do this summer if the three of us are all successful. It seems like the threshold of a real possibility of independence and happiness. Except I don't know how I will manage living in Bucharest, far away from the sea and far away from Gigi, who will go to the Naval Institute in Constanța.

Gigi's Turkish relatives are staying through the summer. Often in the evening his house is a crowded, chaotic mixture of the two languages, and several kinds of spicy and non-spicy meals, honeyed and sugary desserts, depending on Sabina's mood to cook Romanian or Turkish meals, or both. Aunt Seda and Uncle Lemi apparently brought many cans and packages of dried foods, condiments and preserves from Istanbul, so Gigi's household actually knows a blessed period of abundance. They also brought twenty-four-carat filigree gold jewellery set with rubies and sapphires that they are trying to sell to Romanians in town. People can buy gold because there isn't much food they can get with their money, so they wear twenty-four-carat filigree gold rings set with rubies and eat dried bean stew every night.

Luca has to go out more often to work at night on the ship and has to make unexpected trips. Gigi says for some reason his father's work is getting tougher by the day, his superiors in Constanța more demanding. He also tells me they are building a new ship in the Mangalia shipyard, a cargo ship that will beat every existing record in the Romanian naval industry. I'm wondering why Romania needs to beat its own records in shipbuilding while we are surviving on beans and bread just a few hundred metres from the port. Maybe we should all get on that ship when it's ready and sail away to Istanbul.

On the evening of our high school banquet, we feel crazy and hungry for adventure. Valentin has gone to Bucharest to see his old high school friends there and of course to be with his circus beauty Didona. After the party, Gigi suggests that we take a swim at night. It is 15 June, the air is vibrating with linden and petunia smells and the sea is a glossy mirror crossed by what we call '*puntea lunii*', the moon bridge: the shiny reflection of the full moon stretching across the waters. I am wearing a new dress that my mother actually sewed for me on her sewing machine, the first time she ever made a dress for me. I treasure it more than a ruby-studded, twenty-four-carat gold ring. It is light green, which is my best colour, of thin gauzy burnt cotton that feels almost like silk, and has a dark green lace trim around my neck. My mother even lends me her soft brown leather belt and I feel like I am walking on fluffy clouds, not just because of how pretty my dress is but because everything I'm wearing carries my mother's mark and I can tell everyone: 'My mother made this for me.' This is the one time in my school life that I can brag about something my mother made for me other than the plum dumplings that I sometimes take with me for lunch.

We are heated from the dancing, light from all the laughing, a little tipsy from the wine and the couple of 'depraved' cigarettes we indulged in. I have my bathing suit in my bag and Gigi is wearing his trunks. We walk hand in hand on the beach, take off our shoes and walk on the cool sand towards the water. But then Gigi has the idea to walk on the pier with the lighthouse for a little while and then swim off the rocks at the end of it. I go along with everything Gigi suggests tonight. We walk towards the flickering lighthouse and decide to swim off the rocks closest to the port. Gigi says the water will be a little warmer there. This year the water has been icy cold despite the extremely hot weather. I am so light and feathery and blissful tonight that I don't feel like resisting anything that Gigi proposes, even though I would prefer to swim out into the sea, far from the ships and the shipyard, cold water and all.

We leave the pier and climb down on the rocks leading to the sea. The waves are splashing carelessly against the side of the sharp rocks. We drop our clothes on the rock closest to the water and slide into the cool darkness of the sea. We swim in wide, slow movements, almost touching, stroking each other's sides, and try to keep within the moonlit path. Suddenly I feel a jellyfish touch my thigh and its gooey softness in the dark jolts me and makes me cringe. Now I don't think this is such a good idea and I start swimming quickly in the direction of the port, trying to get to the strip of sand instead of having to climb back out of the water from the rocky side. I tell Gigi I was stung by a jellyfish and I want to get out. He laughs, telling me they are harmless, I'm silly to be scared. I don't care. I want to get out anyway. I am cold and anxious suddenly. I swim in the direction of the big ship they are building, the one that's competing with the entire Romanian fleet. Gigi is swimming behind me and I hear his soft edgy moves cutting the water and his regular swimmer's breathing. We almost reach the enormous naval construction site, where we shouldn't even be going because nobody is ever allowed to swim there. We hear voices and see several naval officers and guards standing on the sandy strip. A patrol boat is right next to us and we realize there are officers on it too. Gigi catches up with me and makes a sign to be as quiet as possible. We stop swimming and Gigi holds me right next to the patrol boat while we tread water and try to hear what all these officers are talking about and mostly try to figure out a way to get out of the water without being seen or heard. The water is cold and the side of my thigh where the jellyfish touched me feels itchy and stingy. For the first time ever I feel repelled by the water and the opaque surface of the sea scares me. Someone is speaking in Russian, orders, short questions and answers in Russian, then a Romanian officer says a sentence involving an anti-ship missile launcher and the code SS-N-2C/STYX. Romanian sounds as foreign and scary as the Russian tonight from down here in the freezing water. The Russians are saying '*Potomushto*', why, and '*Niet harasho*', not good. The Romanians are explaining something about torpedo tubes and more surface space.

The lower half of my body is starting to lose feeling. I think I am crying from the cold and the fear but I'm not sure because my body feels so numb. I am angry at myself for going along with Gigi's stupid idea to swim in this direction. We are both going to either freeze to death in the water tonight, or get shot by one of these officers in what seems like some kind of Soviet-Romanian naval coalition. I whisper to Gigi to swim back out towards the lighthouse from where we started. He agrees. But I am very slow in the water because of my half-frozen legs. I don't know how far I will be able to swim before I sink altogether. Gigi says he will help me and take some of my body weight. He whispers some more. I don't understand what Gigi is saying as he is whispering in the dark, in the freezing water, next to KGB and Romanian naval spies and military. Gigi is speaking a foreign language too, another language just like Russian. I try to move my feet and legs under water as quickly as I can so I don't lose feeling completely, while doing breaststroke with my arms. The first rock seems unattainable, the distance to it impossible to cross. Gigi has got underneath my body and is swimming with me almost entirely on his back.

What the hell are anti-ship missile launchers? I wonder, as I try to make it easier on Gigi and swim mostly with my left arm, my longer arm. My physical abnormality serves me well on certain occasions, like painting, and this particular situation of swimming halfway with one leg and one arm, while hoping I won't become a block of ice in June or be turned to dust by a missile launcher or a torpedo.

I hear Gigi panting in the dark, as he is swimming for both of us. I keep moving my left leg and arm, heavily, desperately. I keep asking questions and thinking, to keep my mind alive, to keep my mind from growing numb too. What is an anti-ship missile launcher? What are all those letters and numbers, the Ss and Xs? How many metres to the first rock? Why are they building such a ship? What kind of Romano-Soviet plot is this? Is my green dress still there? Why am I not feeling the itch and sting from the jellyfish any longer?

Gigi says we are almost there. We still hear voices behind us, but they seem further away. It means we are getting closer to the pier. I still hear some Russian words. And a Russian peal of laughter. I'm sure it's a Russian laugh, a Slavic laugh: low, deep, gurgling, not like a Romanian laugh: rumbling, open, higher. Latin people have better laughs. But Romanians are just as bad as the Russians, they are all Communists, building anti-ship ships when we are starving and eating beans and freezing in the cold water. This is not a good painting. It's an anti-painting painting, it's all black with no light, not even a streak.

'Here we are, Nora, just a little bit more and we'll have made it.'

I trust Gigi, even when he pushes me to do stupid things because he wants to show me he is still manly under his sweetness and gentleness. I don't need manly to push me to do stupid things and get killed by the KGB. We reach the first rock and Gigi grabs on to it. He tells me to hold on to him. But I say I can do it by myself. I want to be manly too. He pulls me closer, I grab on to the sharp rock covered in algae. I can't get on to it because of the slimy algae, and because my legs aren't strong and alive enough. He climbs on to the rock and then helps me up, dragging the weight of my body, while whispering to me to keep quiet. Don't I know I have to keep quiet? Did I look like I was starting to sing a serenade to the Romanian and Russian officers?

I realize we have come out far away from where we left our clothes. I need to get my dress. I whisper to Gigi that I need to get my dress. He says forget the dress, I say I can't forget the dress, my mother made it for me. I will never have another dress made for me by my mother, or any other object made for me directly by my mother's hands. I am going to get my dress. I have to climb from slimy sharp rock to slimy sharp rock until I get to the one where I left my dress. Gigi says not to do it, I tell him to leave me alone. I crawl from rock to rock, and my legs are starting to get a little bit warmer. What a night, hot summer outside and cold winter in the water, and the two of us ready to freeze. Which is stupider, I wonder, to die from an illegal abortion or from freezing to death in the Black Sea in June because you swam in an illegal area and ran into some big State secret? And why is the area illegal anyway? Why is everything we do illegal? They must be building something really bad on that ship, the atomic bomb, for example. Compared to this, dying from the illegal abortion seems quite noble now that I think of it. I have only two rocks left and I see the light spot made by my green dress on the rock. I suddenly slip on the third rock before the one with the dress, and cut my leg on it. I let out a scream without meaning to. I hear the soldiers' voices get higher, and in a second a circle of bright light envelops me. Gigi yells at me to run, I don't listen and climb on to the last two rocks until I reach the one with my dress. I see the patrol boat starting to move in my direction. I put on the dress in a second, my leg is bleeding and I can hardly walk. Gigi is down to where I am in a few moves, like a nimble cat, like a cheetah on a mission. I hear the Russian word '*ostanoviti*' and remember from my Russian class that it means to stop, and then I hear a Romanian saying to stop. Are these people crazy, why would I stop? Gigi is helping me to get up, the patrol boat is near us and I see Gigi stare at it as if he just saw the Four Horsemen of the Apocalypse. I turn round and see Luca. He is equally stunned to see us and to realize he is chasing his own son.

The officer standing next to him looks at him and yells: 'Get them, what are you doing?'

Luca says: 'Leave them, they are all right.'

'No, they aren't all right, they are spies,' yells the officer. He pulls out his gun. I didn't know that naval officers carried guns.

Luca keeps repeating: 'Leave them, I tell you, just leave them!'

We are up on the rocks, trying to get on to the pier so we can start running. The naval officer aims at us. We are in an action movie. Even Romanians can make action movies, not only the British with their Roger Moore. We have a Soviet-Romanian KGB action movie right here.

Luca pushes the officer's arm down while yelling at the same time: 'He is my son, he is all right, damn it!'

We hear the gun go off into the water, a shot and a splash. A shot in the water probably killing lots of fish and jellyfish. Serves them right, it all started with my jellyfish sting tonight.

We are running on the pier, I am leaving a trail of blood behind me. I am running miraculously, despite the numbness of my feet, despite the cut in my leg. We fly through the town all the way to my house. We walk in through the front door and try to reach my room quietly, hoping my mother isn't around. We pass by the sitting room which is all in darkness except for a tiny light like that of a cigarette. Who can be visiting? I wonder. Only Uncle Doru smokes in our family. My mother is sitting in the dark, in her sewing-machine chair, and smoking. I had no idea my mother smoked. Although my leg is bleeding profusely and I am soaking wet and we both look like a couple of escaped criminals, the sight of my mother smoking in the dark has me transfixed.

I say: 'Mama, I didn't know you smoked.'

She takes a slow drag then puffs the air out and says: 'I don't. I'm just smoking now.'

I don't know what to say. My mother looks like a ghost in the dark room, her face illuminated slightly just when she drags on her cigarette.

I look around the room and see that my father is also there, in the green upholstered chair, and Aunt Tudoriţa is sitting in the big beige armchair and staring in the dark. It's a good thing our house is filled with beautifully upholstered chairs, some of them left over from the time of the landowner grandfather, the martyr in the family. Everybody is staring in the dark with their eyes wide open like a family of scared owls. I don't see Tudoriţa's little boy anywhere. My heart clinches: not another child tragedy in our family!

'Who died?' I ask brutally.

'Uncle Doru stayed in Germany on his last trip,' says my mother calmly, blowing out cigarette smoke. Oh, Uncle Doru stayed in Germany, that's not dying. Well, that's not so bad, compared to anything else that might have happened.

'He asked for asylum last week,' my father adds, passing his thin fingers through his hair. I can see in the dark that my father is tired, his busy season has been going on for a while and there are more diseases and hygiene problems on the seashore every year. Dysentery is beginning to threaten Romanian seaside holidays and I heard my father again say he suspected a couple of cases of cholera near the resort of Eforie. Communism is the new Middle Ages, soon we'll start dying of the plague and then the great ringmaster with the pig lips will celebrate because he'll be ruling over a dwindling, hungry, disease-ridden population. You can impose any crazy rules on such a weak population.

I toss this bit of information about our latest family crisis into my half-frozen brain and try to understand the consequences, while applying pressure to my bleeding leg. Tudoriţa could ask for first-degree-family reintegration in a couple of years so she could join her husband. Our family would get smaller, but at least it wouldn't be because someone died. Uncle Doru and Aunt Tudoriţa would send us food packages with freeze-dried coffee and Toblerone chocolate from Germany like I saw some families get in the post from Turkish relatives, if the customs officials haven't got to them first. So it's not so terrible after all, I think. Why is everybody moping here in the dark while I am bleeding?

I know my father always feels better when he is doing something useful, something medical. So I yell: 'Tata, I cut my leg on a rock, I'm bleeding, look at it.'

My father jumps up from his chair and tells me to come into the living room. I am relieved when he turns on the lights, I'm sick of all the darkness and misfortunes tonight. Gigi is following me from room to room and now when I see him under the chandelier lights I am amazed at his face: it is so pale that even his freckles seem to have lost their colour, and his curls are redder than usual and stick up wildly. Gigi is a stunning apparition tonight, some kind of devilish angel. Only now do I understand the full magnitude of what has taken place, of what we have witnessed and of what almost happened tonight. It's all inscribed on Gigi's face, in his glowing pallor.

My father looks at my wound, then stares at me and I think he is going to ask how in the world I received that gash. But he doesn't. He just opens his mouth and then he closes it, looks at my wound again and all he says is: 'You need stitches.' He gets his first-aid box from the cupboard and asks Gigi to help him. My father cleans my wound carefully with alcohol and then starts sewing the cut in my leg slowly and methodically, not even asking me if it hurts. He knows I'm tough and that I've been through worse. Gigi is getting paler as he watches my father sewing my leg, right below my knee, trying to pretend he is tough too. He hands whatever my father asks him: gauze, stitch, gauze, thread. I am turning into human embroidery. The clean, sharp pain of my leg being stitched up calms me down and creates order in my thoughts like an efficient vacuum cleaner. When my father tells me it's all done and affectionately taps my hands, their chubby fingers clasped obediently in my lap, I look at Gigi and I see in his shiny brown eyes that he is also wondering, just like me: how will we stitch the huge gash we just made in all our lives tonight? And it all started as an innocent little adventure on our last day of school. You can't have innocent adventures in our country. Everybody's guilty.

Last Family Portrait

Our exams are next week and everything is frighteningly quiet. Gigi and I have been waiting for naval officers, droves of secret police and the Romanian army to swarm around us and for all of us to find out our dreadful destiny. We don't talk about it and act as if nothing had happened. We walk around all day with a big lump of fear in our chests. We hear each other's thoughts. As we slip into the silky waters at dusk after a day of relentless studying, I hear Gigi think as he is *not* looking in the direction of the port and of the torpedo-launching monster.

The man walking on the faleza *with his hands in his pockets is after us and is carrying a gun,* Gigi is thinking. *People don't get shot in the street in our country; that only happens in the free world. We are safe from guns here,* I think back at him. Holding Gigi's hand as we glide into the waves, I dare him to pick up my irony by telepathy. I think he does, because Gigi is all smiles as he makes his sharp dive.

We swim the two kilometres to the line of ships in the distance and back swiftly, quietly, fiercely engaged in a mental dialogue. We swim ourselves into oblivion and by the time we are back on shore we don't care about the man walking up and down the *faleza* any longer. We almost don't care.

When I get home Tudoriţa is in our house, and her son Florin is running around, jumping on the furniture, and talking in unstoppable rivulets of squeaky words. Since Doru's defection, she spends most of her time after work in our house, trying to make herself useful. She kneads dough for my mother's pastries, dusts our lacquered furniture and polishes our lacquered floors. Everything is spotlessly, sparklingly clean in our house since Doru asked for political asylum in Germany. My mother stopped having Bucharest tourists in our house in the summer when Valentin came back to live with us, and she uses all her unemployed energy to cook and clean furiously for us. Despite the shortages she manages to find ingredients for her favourite dishes: roasted pepper and aubergine salad, baked carp and mashed potatoes, red cabbage salad and fried *guvizi* and her epic plum dumplings. The earth opens its arms for my mother alone, despite the national starvation. Valentin is still eating in the same greedy and formidable way that he did on the first night he returned to our house, and for the duration of his rushed meals my mother does nothing but stare at him with shiny eyes, with a blank face and quivering lips.

Three days before Valentin and I have to leave for Bucharest to begin our week-long exam ordeal and Gigi has to leave for Constanţa for his, Tudoriţa is sacked from her nursing job at the hospital. Luca is demoted from his position as ship's captain to ordinary sailor on the cargo ship he has commanded for fifteen years. And Sabina is fired from her post teaching geography at the school and given a secretarial position. Everybody's falling, like the little lead soldiers Gigi and I used to shoot in his back yard when we were kids, with a gun made from a stick or with a water pistol: *pac, pac, pac.* You're dead, you're dead and you too are dead. What is next? Who's next? We are waiting for my parents to lose their jobs now. And what will we do when all the adults in our families are demoted or lose their work? We'll have to sell our lacquered furniture and maybe we'll even have to steal in order to eat. Or fish and dive for sea treasures and sell seashells and pumice stone at street corners.

Valentin plays the piano like a madman from morning till night, all in a disorderly medley: Chopin's études and Beatles songs, Romanian folk and Beethoven's piano concertos, Enescu's Romanian Rhapsody and circus music. He always comes back to circus music: the entrance of the clowns, the horses' and dogs' parades, the trapeze numbers, when all the acrobats invade the stage with their hula hoops and sparkling multicoloured outfits. My ears cannot sustain Valentin's musical hysteria any longer, and in revenge I bring my easel into the dining room and paint the darkest, most bizarre and violent paintings that make my mother gasp and shake her head and cross herself in revulsion: decapitated fish lining the seashore, chimpanzees in tuxedos selling pumice stone, our family having dinner in the dark with big round owl eyes, aboard a torpedo-launching ship, Mariţa dead in the middle of the street with a big crack in her skull, a white liquid filling the air and dull faces staring blankly in front of dilapidated fences. We are engaged in an artistic war that is driving our parents crazy. Somehow, though, my silent grotesque paintings upset my mother a lot more than the deafening and strident musical carnival that my brother produces at all hours of the day. She tells me to move my easel to my room, but I stubbornly leave it in the dining room for everyone to see and be scared.

The night before our departures to Bucharest and Constanţa, my father comes home from work looking happier than usual, with no news of cholera or other deadly diseases. He tells us to get dressed because he is taking us to the restaurant of the Ziemens Hotel, the manager owes him for season after season of good hygiene ratings and he says we are all invited tonight. We'll eat pizza, my father says, now the Romanians are making pizza too, it's a new thing, has any of us ever eaten pizza? Nobody in our family has ever had pizza. Valentin and I are particularly happy for the distraction, since we are both quivering with anxiety at the thought of our exams. My mother doesn't really want to go, we never go to restaurants, first because there is hardly anything any more that they can serve, secondly because for years our own house was a restaurant, feeding hundreds of Bucharest tourists, and my mother can't conceive of going somewhere else to eat anything other than her own food, and in her own house. Even though she hardly ever enjoys her dinner anyway because of her bad memories.

'You all go, and I'll stay,' says my mother and waves her hand as if pushing us all out of the house. My father won't hear of it and takes my mother by the shoulders affectionately like I haven't seen him do in years.

'Come on, woman, take a break from your cooking for one evening, and let's see how it goes. If the man has invited our family we have to accept. We can enjoy a restaurant meal in our country too; you don't have to defect to Germany to do that. We too can enjoy ourselves in this blessed country, what the hell!'

Tudorița laughs wholeheartedly at my father's speech, for the first time since the news of Doru's escape, and she says she wants to go so she's going to her house to change. My mother leaves the room untying her apron, which suggests she will come after all.

We all leave the house dressed up as if ready to go to someone's baptismal party or wedding, and walk down the stone steps towards the Ziemens Hotel. Going down the steps, I almost stumble and fall on my face. Valentin grabs my arm and prevents me from falling, then starts laughing.

'What's the matter, Sister, are you trying to break your neck before your exams?'

'Don't worry, I'll go even with a broken neck,' I say proudly.

My mother, who is walking on my father's arm ahead of me, turns her head a bit and says: 'You would, Nora, wouldn't you?

That's just like you, the recklessness and then the bravado. You'll paint well with a broken neck.'

It seems to me I almost see a flicker of a smile. *My mother is actually trying to joke with me, it's a good sign, I'm going to do well in my exams,* I think and don't want to open my mouth any more so as not to upset this moment of mild hilarity in our family tonight.

The manager of the restaurant is all smiles and leads us to a corner table especially set for us with starched napkins inside tall glasses. The restaurant is almost empty, except for a few foreigners in colourful shirts and a couple at the other end of the restaurant: a man in a black suit and across from him a woman in a shiny, tight cyclamen dress. Romanian folk music is playing in the background. Now I agree with my mother that we would have been better off eating at home. Nobody eats at restaurants like this except foreigners and secret police. But my father is so proud that he is able to take us out for once to one of the hundreds of restaurants and cafés he inspects in the summer that I do my best to look cheerful and grateful.

He suggests we take the mushroom pizza, it's the best, or the ham pizza, that is good too. He tells the waiter to bring us a mushroom pizza and a ham pizza. The waiter says they are out of both the mushroom and the ham pizza. What kind *do* they have then, asks my father, passing his fingers through his hair. Only the plain cheese one. My father looks around the table at us, shakes his head and tells the waiter to bring us two cheese pizzas then, and some tomato and cucumber salad. They don't have that either. What do they have then? *Salata orientala,* potato and onion salad, says the waiter.

'Fine, bring us some of those,' says my father with a sigh.

'We are going to eat some fried dough with cheese and potato salad on the side?' asks my mother disdainfully.

'I love *salata orientala,*' I say quickly.

'Well, most people on our street would be happy with such a meal. And for free!' says my father.

Florin is wriggling in his chair and says he wants cake. Valentin winks at me from across the table. I feel like bursting into gales of laughter but I try to abstain so as not to upset my mother, who is sitting with her arms crossed, staring into the distance as she has been doing at dinnertime for her whole life. Half an hour later, when Florin is so bored and restless that he is hiding under the table and tickling our feet, the waiter and the manager appear, each carrying a large round pizza with melted cheese on top and potato salads for everybody. The waiter slices the pizzas carefully and places a slice on each of our plates. My father says pizza was invented by poor Italians. Initially it was the poor man's food in Italy, like *mamaliga*, corn mush meal, is for our people. 'Pizza is for Italians what *mamaliga* is for us,' he concludes.

I discover I love this Italian poor man's meal and find it quite a bit more interesting than our own poor man's meal. Somehow it seems less poor. At first, my mother doesn't even want to try it, but my father actually cuts a small piece for her and feeds it to her. I watch my mother, transfixed, to see if she likes the famous Italian meal. She chews and swallows and then says: 'I can make better than this.' She ends up eating four full slices, while still pretending she is not crazy about it and she can make a better pizza. We greedily finish the pizza, but when we get to the potato salad, Valentin says his potatoes are raw.

'What a restaurant,' whispers my mother, 'serving us raw potatoes!'

Indeed, we all try Valentin's salad and realize his potatoes are rather raw. My father looks embarrassed and sad, but my mother actually starts laughing.

'Don't worry, the pizza was good at least,' she says. 'I'll make you a good potato salad when we get home.'

I have never seen my mother laugh at dinner, ever in my life. My father starts laughing too and Florin is eating the raw potatoes on Valentin's plate. This is a good family portrait. At long last a cheerful portrait of our family, on the evening before

Valentin and I set off to discover our fate and seal our future in Bucharest. Maybe we'll have a good spell, a happy string of days for a little while. My mother has undergone a metamorphosis while eating Romanian pizza in an empty restaurant. She is a fish fairy, granting wishes for everyone, her bony tanned face rounded up into an impish laugh, her brown curls framing it. She is handing out magic wishes for everyone at the table: chocolate cake for Florin, a ticket to Germany for Tudoriţa, lucky exam tickets for Valentin and me, and a one-month summer holiday for my frazzled father. She has apricot blossom in her hair and we are greedily eating fresh golden peaches. It's a summery, fresh and juicy family portrait in fleshy pastels. My first pastel painting ever! It's the upside of Van Gogh's *Potato Eaters*. We are no potato eaters, no raw potato eaters, we are peach and apricot eaters and my mother is granting us wishes.

I walk with Gigi along the *faleza* tonight, to give each other courage for what's ahead.

'You show them, Miss Michelangelo,' says Gigi and kisses my face warmly.

'And you show them, Mr Captain Munhauser,' I answer back and bury my face in his wide chest.

I know Gigi is heartbroken because of his father's catastrophic demotion, but as always he is trying to appear light and cheerful and tough. A few days ago, he told me his parents are a pathetic sight: they sit and stare at the dinner table without taking one bite, without saying a word. His father comes home after his day as a sailor on the cargo ship and changes from his sailor's uniform back into his captain's uniform, and sits at the dinner table in it, not eating, not talking. He even saw his father fall asleep in his captain's uniform.

'Gigi, let's marry right here, right now,' I tell Gigi suddenly, as we reach the white Greek columns. 'Right here by these Greek ruins.'

Gigi knows and understands me. He gets it right away. He

takes my hand and pulls me in front of the columns, right in the middle of the space between them. He picks two dried wreaths of algae from the beach and places one on my head and the other on his. There is a crescent moon tonight: a perfect bold slice of golden moon. The sea is rustling and humming its spellbinding chant. Suddenly I feel incredibly beautiful, Dido of Carthage, Esma the Turkish princess, Flood of Moonlight, my own magical feminine creation. We take shells from the beach and make our own vows that no seas and no earth will ever separate us, that no political plot will ever break us apart, that our flesh will stay chaste for each other. We give each other the shells, like rings, no ruby-studded Turkish gold but pearly white shells with tiny holes so we can pass a thread through them and wear them. I am not scared of the future any longer.

The next day it smells like melted tar in Bucharest and my heels sink into the pavement on my way to the art school. Valentin and I parted in front of the School of Architecture this morning and he left whistling a Chopin étude. Before parting, though, he embraced me warmly and for a long time like he had never done before.

He whispered: 'Thank you for everything, Nora. You are a hell of a sister. Knock them dead, you have what it takes!' And then he left in the direction of the conservatoire, whistling, his hands in his pockets.

There are crowds of frantic students filling the pavements around every single university building in the city, parents with worried faces saying goodbye and wishing their kids good luck and inspiration, and good fortune, and powers of concentration, as if they were sending them off to a brutal war overseas. Romania's university exams are a kind of war and everybody is desperate to get in, to obtain a university diploma, even though jobs in any field other than engineering or medicine are more scarce every year, or scattered outside the cities in the deep countryside, or obtainable only through relatives and nepotism and contacts. But the harder it is for degree holders to get jobs, the fiercer the competition becomes every year to enter the university. Everything in our country is a masterfully crafted circus with masks, somersaults, formidable acrobatics and then huge crowds falling on their faces right in the middle of the arena, with the ringmaster swinging his curly whip in the air. *Olé!*

As I am standing in the crowd in front of the school of art, melting in the merciless heat of Bucharest in July, I see Miss Mantaş pass through the crowd trying to enter the building. She is wearing a lime linen dress and an enormous pink straw hat. Strands of red hair are coming out from under the hat like irrepressibly nimble flames. I hear people around me whisper her name and point to her in awe. My heart jolts with affection and pride for Miss Mantaş and I feel superior to those around me, having done my two years of *meditaţii*, private lessons, in that neo-baroque apartment of hers. I know she can't give any sign that she knows me, since it looks like she is going to be on the exam committee and invigilating exams. Maybe my luck really is turning now. Perhaps my mother's attempt at joking with me and her granting us wishes were good omens indeed.

For the theoretical part of the exam I get one of my favourite and best-known subjects, Romanticism versus the Barbizon school. My pen is flying almost on its own for page after page after page until it is time to hand in the exams. Delacroix, Millet, Constable, Corot, all the painters and styles that Miss Mantaş stridently stuffed into my greedy brain on Sunday afternoons are erupting on to the page like phantoms bursting into life.

After the exam I meet Valentin in front of the Intercontinental Hotel and he is glowing, radiating contentment. His topic was not one of his favourites but he worked at it beautifully until he actually ended up liking it: the Russian modernists, Rachmaninov, Prokofiev, Stravinsky. I hadn't heard Valentin play much of these composers on our basement piano but I should have got used by now to my brother's never-ending box of surprises. We decide to cool off after our exam and have a beer at the outdoor café next to the School of Architecture. I feel mature and adventurous here with Valentin in this swarming, liquefying city, a real artist. We compare music to painting and try to find all the similarities and differences between the two forms of art, until we veer on to a playful slope of absurd comparisons.

I say: 'Painting is a silent music that you can only hear with your heart.'

Valentin says: 'Music is loud painting that you can only see with your soul.'

The street around us is swarming with students coming out of their various exams, some crying, others screaming with joy that they got their favourite topics; the beer is getting us tipsy and drowsy.

'Notes are colours with an attitude,' Valentin says.

'Colours are notes under a bell jar,' I say.

As we hunch over our beers with laughter, I see Valentin smile and wave to someone approaching on the pavement behind me. I turn round and see the friend at whose house and on whose slimy cabbage-smelling sofa I had spent the night long ago after Valentin showed me the State Circus. He stops at our table and chats with us about the exams; he has just finished his in maths.

Then he whispers to Valentin: 'I'm so sorry about Didona.'

Valentin opens his mouth in surprise and so do I. Maybe Didona had an accident and died falling off the trapeze.

'You didn't know?' the friend asks.

Then he leans over to Valentin's ear and whispers something. Valentin's face becomes pale, almost translucent, that of a ghost. I remember the feeling I had at Gigi's nineteenth birthday party that Didona was going to hurt him willingly or unwillingly and he would be reeling from it. He is reeling right in front of me. Then Valentin leans over to me and whispers that Didona and her parents all stayed on in Italy and asked for asylum there when on tour with the State Circus last week.

I have developed a good habit of always thinking first that someone has died whenever I hear bad news. This way, whatever the news turns out to be other than death, I feel relieved.

'Well, at least she didn't die,' I tell Valentin.

He stares at me in disbelief. 'Oh, you are something, Nora, you really know how to console someone in distress. It's *as if* she died,' he says and I hear his voice quivering as if he is about to cry.

'No, it isn't. It really isn't. Aunt Raluca is dead, Mariţa is dead. Didona is not dead, she has just left the country,' I say.

'She has a point, Val,' says the friend, still standing on the pavement. He says he is sorry again and goes away.

'How about if you just found out that Gigi had suddenly disappeared to Turkey?' Valentin asks wickedly. He too has a point, and I realize that I would be ready to lie down right here next to this brasserie on the melting asphalt and howl in pain if a passer-by had just whispered in my ear: 'Gigi left on a boat to Turkey and asked for asylum.'

I want to console Valentin but when I try to open my mouth I don't really know what to say. My lips are moving with no sounds, with colourless quiet movements. Valentin had his heart set on a capricious firebird. He is not a blood relative of hers so he can't undergo the ordeal of first-degree-family reintegration the way Tudoriţa is going to. Once gone, Didona and her family can't ever come back, or they will all be thrown in prison for life. Or even executed. They left with all the circus equipment and while on an official State-sponsored trip. Thinking about it again, how is this different from death? Our relatives and friends are leaving one after another, and our population is thinning rapidly. Some kind of plague: the running-away-from-your-country plague. What's the point of taking exams? What's the point of doing anything?

'It's terrible, I knew she would make you suffer,' I say, touching his hand across the table and realizing that I've gone from bad to worse.

But Valentin's eyes sparkle with anger and he says: 'How could she do this? I knew she was a traitor ever since the story with the abortion doctor. Well, if that's who she was, then good riddance!'

Valentin is in control even when he is out of control. I am wondering again if he really loved Didona, or whether it was a fancy he had because she was so exotic and unlike any normal girl one would meet at the local high school. I tell Valentin how the minute I saw her in the hallway of the circus I thought of Delacroix's painting *The Death of Sardanapalus.* Her profile and the amazing black hair falling in waves down her back seemed to me then the exact live copy of the woman in the foreground of that painting, as she is being held captive, naked, seized from the back by a bearded man with a sharp knife pointed at her throat, and I always saw her as both victim and executioner, as Sardanapalus and his concubine, only more athletic. My imagination always continued the painting and saw her break free from the man's hold, pick up his knife and slice his throat instead. The unknown Delacroix! I tell Valentin it seemed to me her body was just as majestic as that of Sardanapalus' concubine, though really he is the one to judge. I smile a silly smile at my poor joke. Valentin takes it lightly and smiles too, as if touched by a fleeting memory of holding Didona's naked body in his arms.

'See, you foresaw her future, you knew she would die somehow. At least for me, because she is dead for me,' he says, resigned. Then he smiles: 'Sardanapalus! You are something, Nora, you know that? And did you know you had the gift of seeing the future?'

'Like hell I do,' I answer right back. 'If I had that gift I wouldn't have got into so much trouble before I was even twenty.'

We move slowly through the crowded city and try to find the

apartment building near the Patria film theatre, where our father found us rooms for the period of the exams, through a doctor friend of his. Despite the beds of roses and chrysanthemums and the heavy chestnut and linden trees lining the boulevards, the city is dusty and the air is sticky, smelling of petrol and burnt tar. We take the longer route to our address, going through parks and side streets. I wonder what Gigi is doing in Constanţa, how his first day of exams has been; I think of our pastoral 'wedding' of two nights ago and his playful Adonis face with the wreath of dried algae in his hair. My parents and Mariţa were right to say I was a lucky girl.

Miss Mantaş is invigilating for my exam the next day, for the drawing and painting tests. The first one is the assigned drawing, where you have to copy as faithfully as possible a drawing or painting they give you, and the other is a painting on a theme in a medium of your choice. For the assigned one, we get a painting by the famous Romanian artist Sabin Bălaşa: the Ceauşescu couple with a crowd of children in the background. He is waving with his right hand high in the air, looking ahead into the distance, probably at an 'adoring' crowd. Elena Ceauşescu is a step ahead of him in an immaculate white dress, her arms lifted a little away from her body as if she is ready to fly. The children on one side are also wearing immaculate white costumes and are all flying somewhere, just like the people in the mosaic in the centre of Mangalia. The children on the other side are like statues staring in a trance. Everybody flies and is immaculate in our country. And those who don't are turned to stone. Communism gives you wings, endows you with purity, and enables you to fly.

I get to work, and set out my pencils and tempera paints next to me on the desk. I draw without stopping for a full hour, Ceauşescu's slender rectangular figure, the raised hand, the curly pig lips, Elena's immobile face, the immaculate dress, the flying children and the stone children. I hear Miss Mantaş's steady steps back and forth in the classroom, and the hardwood floors squeaking under her feet. I follow every contour and every shape with precision and try my hardest not to think, not to remember the middle school art classes when I drew page after page of geometrical flowers and shells to avoid drawing precisely something like this, not to remember the grotesque fish painting with the big black howling mouth meant to cover the curly pig lips that kept haunting me.

I rest a little before my next assignment. The theme for the free painting is 'Family'. I smile to myself, and think of my bizarre family full of heavy secrets and troubled lives and rage and upside-down decisions and I wonder how I can draw my family in a way that will be original but not too bizarre. This is what Miss Mantaş has advised: she said to show my ease and my talent in making portraits, creating a space, using a certain technique, being consistent, adding an edge of originality and also making sure it is within traditional conventions. 'Not one of your extraterrestrial frightening pieces, Miss Nora,' she had told me in her room. When she was pleased with my work she would call me Miss Nora and I knew she liked the fierceness of my paintings although she often made fun of them. Miss Mantaş is in the same lime linen dress as yesterday, and I feel a gush of gratitude for this wicked fireball of a woman who taught me so much during the two years of private classes. I look at my uneven hands and try to feel lucky about them too, and to feel lucky all round.

I draw my family of two nights ago, in the fancy empty restaurant when we had our first pizza with a side dish of raw potato salad. The family portrait I saw in my head that night. I relive Miss Mantaş's artistic embrace during our first class, the way she held my hands tightly in hers and how our four hands were flying across the paper, reproducing the baroque landscape around us but with a touch of irony, with a wink and a snap.

My mother's bony, elegant face with the brown curls framing it dominates the painting. My father is in profile, distinguished, his thin black hair combed carefully and his hand holding his chin, looking at my mother. Valentin is looking straight at me and winking. He has his playful mischievous look, black strands of hair falling carelessly on his forehead. Next to him is Tudoriţa with her round face and short bobbed hair, her dark eyes slightly scared and worried, but her mouth actually opens in a wide laugh as she is holding Florin in her lap and he is stretching across the table to get a slice of the Italian poor man's meal, his eyes sparkling. 'Never forget the depth, don't forget the atmosphere,' Miss Mantaş used always to tell me. 'Always create a world, depth, depth, and depth again.' I draw the waiter in the background, almost flying across the room with several plates on his outstretched arms, and I fill the restaurant with people: the man in the black suit with the woman in the shiny cyclamen dress. Everybody is happy having their first pizza tonight. My hands are flying and I draw using both of them, just like Miss Mantaş taught me. I'm using each hand differently: the left one for the lighter, more sinuous touches, the right one for the hard and precise lines. The other teacher invigilating the exam stares at me in wonderment once in a while because nobody draws with both hands, and everybody in our country is right-handed. But then nobody has two hands of different sizes like I do. I place myself between my brother and my mother, my right arm almost touching my mother's left arm, and I am leaning towards her a little as I bite into a slice of pizza. My hair is falling on my shoulders and my tanned face is glowing, just like my mother's, we could almost be sisters with our huge mass of curly brown hair like brown sheep. My face is as I imagined myself on the beach 'marrying' Gigi between the two Greek columns: Flood of Moonlight. My mother's hands are stretched out as if she is offering food. That's where I make the wink, the snap, the special edge: a subtle splash of colour, of peach and orangey pastels, a vagueness and a pink haze floating across the table, as if my mother is gifting magic fruit and special wishes to all of us. I title the painting *Family Portrait: The Peach Eaters.*

Mariţa's Secret

Valentin and I arrive back in Mangalia in the evening, exhausted, sweaty and thirsty for the sea. When we get home, we throw our luggage into our room, quickly tell our parents we think we did very well in our exams, now we'll just have to wait for the results, and we are off: Valentin to the beach where he says he wants to clear his thoughts and think about the last few days, and I rush to see Gigi as I'm dying to find out about his exams in Constanţa.

I freeze when I see the dark house and find the door locked. I walk around it, searching for a trace of life. I step on the ripe apricots fallen from the tree in front of the house, stumble over the tree stump on the side, see the shovel stuck in the earth at the back where they have their tiny vegetable garden as if someone has been digging recently. Just when I'm about to leave the place limp from worry, I see a tiny light moving like that of a torch in the back window. Then it goes out the second I move up to the window. I go up close and tap on it, calling Gigi's name softly a few times. No movement, no answer, no sign of life. Maybe I have lived in a parallel universe all this time and nothing that I thought I had experienced actually happened. Maybe I am in the fairy tale where the hero goes in search of life everlasting and comes back to his native village hundreds of years later, which to him has seemed like only one year, to find nothing but dust, rubble and graves. And my ambitions weren't anything as lofty as life everlasting when I left for Bucharest, just to pass my art exams. I get ready to leave, thinking that Gigi's family has been made to disappear because the two of us ran into multi-State secrets. But just when I'm about to go I hear the front door being unlocked. I run to it and see Gigi's mother come out looking like she's just woken up, squinting as she lets me in.

From now on we start our rollercoaster, our run for cover, our no-nonsense Romanian action movie. Luca is sitting on the side of his bed in his sailor's outfit, smoking and staring in the dark. Gigi is sitting on his bed in the last room, holding a small torch.

When he sees me he says: 'We are all finished.'

'What do you mean all finished, what happened?' I ask breathlessly.

'They didn't even let me take my exams, Nora. Two guys were waiting in front of the Naval Institute and they told me not to bother going in. We don't even know if my father can hold on to his bloody sailor's job.'

This is a new Gigi that I didn't know until now: hopeless, angry and defeated. But a few seconds later, the one I know looks up at me in the dark and asks me how my exams went. He calls me 'my love'.

I say: 'I think I did well, I knew my topics, Miss Mantaş was there. What's happening?'

He places his finger on my lips. He takes my hand and guides me to the door and then outside. He tells me to climb the apricot tree, we can talk there. Maybe Gigi snapped, maybe something went really wrong in his brain and he lost his reason. We haven't climbed the apricot tree since we were kids. But climb the apricot tree I do. We sit on the first branch, our legs hanging. Gigi whispers that they are being followed almost all the time now, there are people passing the house at all hours of the day.

'We ran into something bad that night, Nora. And I'm to blame for it. I'm the idiot who asked you to go that way.'

'How come they were so careless talking about all that stuff out in the open like they were having a grand old party if it was so important and such a secret?' I whisper, picking an apricot and eating it quickly out of nervousness.

'First, Nora, remember we were swimming in illegal waters; if they are illegal and nobody is supposed to go there, then they can talk as they please. And secondly, why should they care anyway? They know they can squish anyone with a snap of their fingers, just like that.'

He snaps his fingers, the only sound higher than his breathless murmurs.

'We are lucky not to all be locked up in some political prison in Northern Transylvania by now,' he says.

Again the luck thing. How lucky are we? I don't think we are so lucky, after all. Things are pretty bad, and I don't know why we always have to compare ourselves with prisoners and maimed accident victims or casualties of war in order to make ourselves feel lucky when horrible absurd things keep falling on our heads.

'That's the kind of country we live in, Nora,' says Gigi directly in my ear, as if having heard my thoughts. Instead of whispering words of love and passion in my ear on a summer night perched in the old apricot tree in front of his house, Gigi is whispering resigned aphorisms about our stupid country. And why are we sitting and talking in the apricot tree at ten o'clock at night anyway?

'The house is bugged,' says Gigi. We don't need to talk. Gigi and I can just exchange thoughts. We could spend our lives perched in the apricot tree having silent dialogues. I see Gigi's face in the dark and the disorderly red curls covering his forehead. We haven't even kissed tonight, yet I feel the way I did the night in Gigi's room after we made love and his Turkish relatives were in the next room eating *baklava* and listening to Turkish music. Even in the midst of this terrifying misery, I feel weirdly happy and safe next to Gigi. I could be locked up with him in the worst of political prisons, hiding in the belly of a ship, running for cover across dark fields and I would feel happy and almost safe. But Gigi is miserable, his career as a naval officer is over before he even had a chance to start. How are we going to carry that burden? No wonder people die before they turn fifty in our country. Our oldest people are infantile and the young ones are ancient and laden with a heavier past than they can carry before they even turn twenty.

Everything is dark for the rest of the summer. Even the brightest days are dark. We are counting the days till all the university exam results are posted in Bucharest. Our house is quieter than usual. Sometimes the only sounds you hear are my mother's sewing machine and Florin's flood of shrill words. Only machines and children speak, the adults are quiet, the houses are bugged, the sea is dangerous and filled with jellyfish. My mother is sewing everything she can put her hands on: old tablecloths turned into covers for the upholstery, old curtains turned into tablecloths, unused fabrics she bought years ago and just now found in some old drawer turned into strange old-fashioned dresses for me. I've never owned so many dresses in my life as I do now when we are on the brink of a final and irreversible catastrophe: paisley red and green cotton with a bow, yellow-orangey acrylics with ruffles, white lacy gauzy cotton like a wedding dress, royal blue tight and short like a bridesmaid. She sews trousers for Valentin, she takes in my father's old shirts that don't need taking in, my mother is on a sewing rampage that keeps us all from having to talk and she makes us look like we are on parade in a never-ending carnival. After she is done with a new piece, she throws it imperiously under our eyes and all she says is: 'Here, put this on!' We don't dare disobey her. We are hoping for a cholera epidemic, a flu pandemic, a natural catastrophe, an earthquake like the one in

’77 so that we can escape the constant surveillance, so that those who are after us get distracted by a national emergency.

Will this last the rest of our lives? I wonder. Will someone get killed, the way Mariţa did at the end of the abortion investigation? What will our final punishment look like? My father’s work is indispensable to the city and the whole region, so he is still employed. He had been right about the cholera cases he had suspected. Now he has to devise plans to quarantine tourists on the coast while Party officials try to stop him from doing that so as not to encourage rumours about cholera and give a bad name to our resorts. My mother wouldn’t care if she were fired from her school job. She’s saved enough money from her decade of housing and cooking for Bucharest tourists to keep us for a while. Besides, there isn’t much to buy with your money anyway, except for agricultural tools or Turkish rings on the black market.

We travel to Bucharest on a Monday to see the results. Gigi comes with us, wanting to take a break from the gloom in his house and exchange it for gloom on wheels during the train ride there and back. We are followed on the train too. We are used to the relentless surveillance by now and even make light of it. Gigi kisses me passionately in the compartment as he’s never done in public before. We spite our followers with our show of lust. Valentin is staring out of the window and tapping his long fingers on the little table in front of him. We go first to see my results. Bucharest is hot and crowded just as we left it after our exams. There is an interminable line in front of the lists. Gigi pushes through the crowd and I’m following in his wake and holding his hand tightly. I am sweating and my head is spinning. We arrive in front of the lists, and at first I want to scream with joy, from a distance I see my name pretty high up where the successful candidates are listed. But when I get close I see that I am below the line.

The first name below the line: Nora Teodoru. I am the twenty-sixth on the list. Only twenty-five accepted. Gigi is squeezing my hand. He is not smiling. Everything I had thought was a good omen turned out to be a bad omen. Even good omens foresee bad things. After all, my family portrait was right in its predictions of peachy beneficent things: I did do well in all my exams, only that is irrelevant in the country where I was born. Why wasn't I born in France, like Anushka? Or even in Turkey like Seda and Lemi? Why was I born at all?

Valentin's face moves into a grimace when I tell him I failed.

'If you did, then I did too. They are everywhere,' he says softly as we move away on the hot pavement. 'They get into everything.'

We don't talk until we get to the conservatoire. The crowds are smaller here, the street quieter. Valentin approaches the wall where the results are listed at the same steady pace, his hands in his pockets. He goes to it, stands in front of it for less than two seconds, turns round with a happy face and moves towards us. *At least one of us got in*, I think, maybe my failure was honest failure, not secret-police-intervention failure.

'*Niet harasho*,' says Valentin in Russian of all things. 'Not good.' Valentin is laughing at his own demise. He is also the first one below the dreaded line. He says the last one above it is the son of a *ştab*, a big Party official. He went to school with him in Bucharest, he was a nullity in music, says Valentin. Now we can truly say we are twins: both below the notorious line, both equally guilty and equally punished.

Valentin thinks his failure is due to his relations with Didona and her family. Gigi thinks mine is because of swimming in illegal waters and hearing what I shouldn't have. And this comes on top of a history of illegal abortion and a family member having recently defected to the West. We are all guilty as the guiltiest of criminals, there is no place for us in any of Romania's universities and schools, and we are the pariahs of all pariahs. In our misery we try to think of our options for the future: we could live for another year in our parents' houses and take our exams again. Maybe next year we'll make it. Maybe one year of punishment will be enough. But maybe not, maybe our fate is sealed for ever, all university doors closed to us for the next half-century. Why would they let us in next year? We could all move to Bucharest and get factory jobs until something better happens, like the collapse of the government. Work in the paper or textile factories at the margins of Bucharest. We would have access to free paper or free fabrics. We could all become fishermen in Mangalia. We could move to Constanța and work in the port there as *hamali*, dock porters, carrying stuff from the ships to the shore and from the shore back to the ships. We have some alternatives after all.

We sit on a park bench and laugh at our list of choices. We haven't mentioned becoming involved in the black market, being *bişnițari* in Constanța or Bucharest. Oh yes, there is always the black market. We could sell Turkish filigree jewellery that Gigi would have to get us from Turkish relatives in Mangalia. Or we could sell fried *guvizi* by the seashore to people more miserable than us who can't even fish. We could join the Gypsy camp by the salty lakes of Tekirghiol. This is how Gypsies become Gypsies. Now I know.

There is a lull in the Bucharest afternoon as we sit on this park bench watching two children go up and down on the squeaky see-saw. As if everything suddenly slowed down and became quiet. Marița's secret is crackling in my head. The one she whispered in my ear right before she died. I take out a crumpled piece of paper from my purse and the black pen I wrote with for the theoretical part of my art history exam and I write slowly in small capital letters: LET'S ESCAPE TO TURKEY. That's what Marița said, she said: 'Run away to Turkey,' and then she said something else that was not clear: a name, a place, a word that started with the letter L but the rest was blurry. I brush that vague memory aside and think only of the very clear order: 'Run away to Turkey.' Marița knew we would be on the run and that more trouble was coming our way. I nudge Valentin and Gigi with my elbows both at the same time and I show it to them.

They look at it and then start laughing as if I had shown them an obscenity. They are doing it on purpose, precisely to mislead anyone who might be watching us from behind a tree or a bush, making them think that we are drawing obscenities. Gigi takes my pen and writes: HOW? I laugh out loud, oh what a bad word, shame on you, Gigi, and then Valentin takes the pen from Gigi's hand and writes: SWIMMING! The three of us are shaking with laughter, bending down with laughter, choking with laughter. What to do with the piece of paper now, not to leave any trace of it? Gigi understands and first tears it into little pieces, then starts eating some of them.

'Mmm, good,' he says. 'Want some?'

'Sure,' I say, 'I'd love some. Here, Valentin, you have some too.'

We are eating Mariţa's secret and now our own secret, chewing at it and swallowing the softened pieces of paper with dry gulps. We run to the water fountain in the park to wash it down. We each take a long time leaning over the anaemic jet of water. A short man in a white shirt with rolled-up sleeves passes by without looking at us. He is hard at work, for he has rolled up his sleeves. We know it's one of them, by the steady step that's a little too steady, by the look straight ahead that's a little too straight ahead. We start squirting water at each other as a distraction. In our country we are like both old children and infantile adults. We live in a game with masks more dizzying than the circus. We are the acrobats to our own public.

My mother cries when she hears our news. I don't remember when I last saw my mother cry. Maybe at her sister's funeral. But not like this, not with gulps of enraged crying that make you think that next she is going to burn down the whole city. She is crying with rage. When she stops she tells us it's our fault, we are all idiots, we destroyed our lives, and we lived recklessly in a place where you can't afford even a little bit of inattention. Now we are paying for it, it's done. When my father comes home from work and hears the news, he drops his doctor's briefcase on the floor. He is quiet like when he picked us up from the hospital after we had almost drowned.

He pulls himself together after a second, then he says: 'Well, it's not the end of the world, we are all still alive.'

'That's some consolation!' yells my mother. 'What good is a life badly lived?'

'Oh shush, woman, there is some value in being alive even if you haven't passed your university entrance exams.' Thank God our parents are arguing so their attention is diverted away from us.

During the next several days, Gigi, Valentin and I meet at different places in the open air, and think of ways to plan our escape. Sometimes we go to the beach and swim out together. It is still the safest place to be, unless they've found a way to insert listening devices in the jellyfish. We have to find out exactly how many kilometres it is to Turkish waters. What's the border patrol schedule? Are there any Turkish ships that sail close by? Does the Romanian cruise ship ever go close to Turkish waters? And once in the Turkish area, what then? Where will we go then, who will pick us up in the very middle of the wide, wide seas where the depth is two thousand metres? We study the history, the layout, the ecology of the Black Sea from Sabina's geography books. There are no deadly species in the Black Sea, the salinity of the water is lower than most seas, temperatures are steady across a certain distance.

One day the three of us are sitting on Gigi's bed crouched over an old geography book of his mother's and I let out a sudden scream: the Limanu cave. There is a page that describes a certain cave near Mangalia, on the way to the village of 2 Mai, where artists and students go and live in the houses of the peasants and visit the nude beaches. Limanu was the name that Mariţa whispered in my ear that night. Now the syllables in that hoarse whisper of Mariţa's last breath arrange themselves in that exact order:

Limanu. It says in the geography book that the cave is a labyrinth unique in the world, that in it are traces of dwellings as old as the Thracians and the Dacians, there are prehistoric rock engravings and at times thieves and smugglers used to hide in it. The cave is supposed to be four kilometres long and reaches all the way to Turkey. So the legend says. But what if it's not a legend and there actually is a long cave that opens into the Bosphorus at the other end? Mariţa never said which way to leave for Turkey: by water or by land. She just said: 'Run away to Turkey.' And then: 'Limanu.'

We divide our duties: I am supposed to find the location and entrance to this cave. Valentin is supposed to hang out in the port and find out the schedule of the cruise ship and any other news he can gather about possible Turkish ships passing nearby. Gigi has to find the meteorological information for the rest of the summer: the warmest days and nights for the rest of July and the whole month of August, which of the warmest nights will be moonless, what storms if any are predicted for the rest of the summer, what is the timing of the rotations of the lighthouse rays. We all have to find out how many kilometres it is to Turkish waters from our shore. We devise ways of misleading our followers. The three of us go to the market and spend time buying silly trinkets, sesame sweets and Turkish *braga.* Then suddenly one of us pretends they forgot something at home, or that we have been hit by an attack of diarrhoea. Then we split up and go about our research. We meet up at my house and listen to loud music: Fleetwood Mac or Romanian folk. Then we go back to the beach for a swim and share our information. We are after all carefree, with no worries about exams or starting a course of study in the autumn. We are Romania's parasitic youth wasting our lives in pointless adventures.

Not so pointless though. We are hard at work, determined to find ourselves in Istanbul and send news of political asylum through a secret source to our parents by the end of the summer. That's how fanatical about escaping we have become.

Limanu, End of the World

'Yes, there will be a Turkish ship passing by on the night of 11 August, near the border, near the village of 2 Mai, approximately twenty kilometres from the shore and four and a half kilometres from Romanian waters,' says Valentin when we meet on the beach for our usual afternoon exchanges of information. 'There are two hundred and sixty kilometres from the Mangalia shores to Istanbul; the length of the Bosphorus is thirty-one kilometres, the Black Sea part alone is ten kilometres – that's a lot of swimming. It's probably impossible. We have to connect with a ship, a boat, a vessel of some kind. I found this out from a Turkish man called Bekta, who pilots the tourist cruise ship. He seems to know everything about the passing ships and distances and schedules, a clever Turk and kinder than most sailors I've met in the port.'

And I whisper in my turn: 'I found it, boys!' We are standing next to some tufts of thistle and chicory bushes. I wrap my arms around their shoulders happily. 'I know how to get there, prepare yourselves!' Their faces stretch out in a smile, a mixture of incredulousness and contained joy. Failing our exams has given us wings. We are the Romanian Roger Moore team and more. The sea has the colour of lapis today, dark blue-green with a brownish streak, and she seems to be winking at me.

'How did you do it, Sister Witch?' says Valentin, laughing and performing a cartwheel on the beach, which I had no idea he could do. Gigi picks me up and throws me in the air, then picks me up in his arms like a ball. The circus has rubbed off on my two guys, they are real acrobats. Oh Didona, in what corner of the world are you slicing the air in your hot-pink sequinned suit?

'Today I found out that the biggest storm of the summer is predicted for the beginning of August,' announces Gigi proudly and goes on with a long stream of news and explanations. 'We'll have to plan our escape around the middle of the month; it's a good time, the middle of August, just when the tourists are thinning out. There will be no moon on the tenth, eleventh and twelfth of the month. Between the waning crescent and the new moon there will be three moonless nights. We will have to leave on one of those days, the darkest of them, probably the eleventh. Val is right, we have to be taken onto a ship. Mr Bekta is going to take us on his cruise ship on the day when the Turkish ship will sail close to the line. Hey, Val, isn't that on the eleventh of August?' asks Gigi almost conspiratorially. 'It coincides with one of the three moonless nights, it's perfect.

'Now that we are planning to leave for Turkey, my father's stories from when I was a child are lighting up in my memory: the six minarets of the Blue Mosque, the round cupolas above the sea so blue that your eyes hurt, Hagia Sophia with its ancient brick walls, the maze of streets in the great bazaar sparkling with mountains of jewels. I will tell my father about our plan and ask him to help us. I don't see how we can do it without help. He will talk to his friend Mr Bekta to try to get us close to Turkish waters, he will hide us on his ship during one of his cruises, and he will plan it so it coincides with one of those three nights,' concludes Gigi and winks at me exuberantly. I don't think Gigi has ever talked so long in his life. He is my magic red fish, as I always thought, but now he is outdoing himself. Who said there was no life after failed university exams? Oh, my mother, right, she always sees the end of everything, a good thing we aren't listening to her these days. Well, Mama, it seems like life is just beginning.

The Limanu cave was discovered in 1975 by a team of experts from the Speleological Institute in Bucharest. 'It's on the way to 2 Mai village across from Lake Mangalia and under a hill,' I report, lying on my back on the beach between Gigi and Valentin. 'It seems unreal, apparently there were Dacians that took shelter and lived in it almost two thousand years ago. It really is a labyrinth and you can even find creepy traces of cults, animal bones lying around and other cheerful stuff like that,' I say with matter-of-fact ease, though I was trembling and sweating with every centimetre of my body when I found that information in a book on the history of our city at the municipal library. And when Gigi's mother disclosed to me all the historical wonders that are apparently hidden in the cave, I shivered and sweated some more. When I shared our plans with her she started drawing maps and researching for us with a fury, as if it was she who was planning to escape. She drew a map of Limanu village and how to get there from memory, like she does all her maps, hunched over the table, squinting and drawing in continuous swirls without lifting the pen off the paper. I have got quite close to Sabina lately, now that we are planning our big escape. There is steel and sparkle underneath the sweet docile manner. She puts all her fury into her maps, particularly now that she's been sacked from teaching geography. You can sack everybody in the country, you idiot Communists, but you can't stop people from thinking, imagining, drawing maps, helping others to escape!

'That's very beautiful, Nora, but how is it going to get us to Turkey?' asks Valentin. Just when you think he is going to do something unexpected like a cartwheel in the sand, Valentin surprises you with something so logical and practical that it takes your breath away.

'It doesn't matter if it does or it doesn't,' I say self-importantly. 'Maybe we can hide in the cave for a while in preparation for our big escape by sea. It's better to leave from that part of the coast anyway, we might trick and confuse the imbeciles following us, you know. Mariţa knew what she was talking about when she whispered to me in her last moments.'

Gigi is staring at the sky and lying on his back too. He seems calm and secure as if he was living in Turkey already. How come we are all suddenly so calm and so carefree, what has happened to us, what has happened to our surroundings? Aren't we still being watched, aren't we still being followed? Maybe they've got tired of it after having almost ruined our lives. And why are we so desperately set on this escape? I don't share any of my hesitations with Gigi and Valentin, though. I just continue to stare at the sky.

After all, why does it matter so much where you live? Maybe this freedom thing is just an obsession we inherited from our parents, who were traumatized by the war and that whole post-war Stalinist period. Maybe freedom is all in our minds. Who says we aren't free? Look at us running all over town, on the beach, on the pier, swimming, performing acrobatics on the sand, and listening to Dire Straits! Look at how much I learned from Miss Mantaş: the history of Western art, out of old books, slides and the imagination. What is freedom really? Can someone take away your freedom, or do they just condition people to think they are not free, and then everybody acts unfree, scared, paranoid, looking over their left shoulder, looking over their right shoulder, looking in their shoes or under their pillow for a listening device? What if everybody just started acting freely, as if there *was* freedom, as if the secret police and the pig-faced leader and the Communist Party and the Socialist Republic of Romania did not exist? What if we acted as if we lived in France, for instance? How was Anushka freer than I am? She came all the way from Paris to commit suicide on these shores. You are even allowed to kill yourself in our country and we provide that facility for free, even for desperate foreigners. I want to know what freedom really is, damn it!

'Let's just go and live there for a few days, boys,' I say lightly. 'Let's find this cave and see how we can live in it. And then swim away.'

We tell our parents we need to take a short holiday, to explore the countryside, to go backpacking, we've never been backpacking. Gigi's parents, who now both know about our escape plans, are helping in any way they can, sending messages to their relatives in Istanbul, deciphering maps for us, giving us important addresses. Beaten up by the system and with no better hopes of a tolerable future, they want at all costs for their son to accomplish what they haven't been able to. They want to sublimate their own misery in Gigi's future in a bright corner of the Western world. However, there is no way Valentin and I could let our parents know, miserable or bright future. My mother would lay her own body on Mr Bekta's ship as a manifesto and we would all end up in a prison for political detainees, for enemies of the people, the way my land-loving grandfather Octavian was first tortured and then killed with an axe. My mother believes if you are clever and cunning enough you can still make something meaningful of your life in this country. It's just too bad her children don't seem to be able to accomplish that dream.

'Oh I see, you need to celebrate all your failures this summer, don't you?' says my mother with a clean shiny face that she raises above a pot of lettuce soup she is making. My mother has even been mean to Valentin since she found out the results of our exams. We are all failures in her eyes.

'That's right, Mama, how did you guess? We have to celebrate these events somehow and now is the time.' I too have been shamelessly impertinent with my mother lately. Our house is again the battlefield it used to be, strings seem to be stretched out ready to pop everywhere: our nerves.

It's 6 August, and the 11th is just around the corner. We decide to prepare for the big departure. The village of 2 Mai is closer to Turkey than Mangalia. Mr Bekta's ship will go a little bit out of its way; the tourists on it won't know the difference. On the 11th, around midday, we will swim out towards his ship. We'll pretend we've gone out too far and one of us is drowning, Mr Bekta will help us and take us on board. For the benefit of the tourists on the ship, we'll pretend to be foreign students. Foreigners love the peasant housing and the nude beaches in 2 Mai village. Mr Bekta will take us to his own cabin to offer us food and a place to rest. We'll wait there till the night. Until 22.45 to be precise. Luca and Mr Bekta have calculated everything. At 21.45, when most people are going to their cabins for the night, he will take his ship towards the Turkish waters and let us slip into the sea four kilometres from the line. Between 22.30 and 22.45 the Turkish ship will pass by, almost entering Romanian waters. We can't be there too early or too late. We have to calculate it so we don't wait in the water for more than a few minutes, or the frontier patrol boat will spot us. And shoot us. Luca was very clear about that. Don't we know it, Gigi and I, from our freezing late-night adventure close to the anti-ship missile ship.

'You were lucky it was just jellyfish that got shot that night. Next time it won't be fish, it will be you,' Luca had said one night from the edge of his bed, crouched over a map of the sea, smoking his pipe and wearing his captain's cap.

'Is that boy, Valentin, capable of going through with this plan?' he asked afterwards. 'He seems kind of frail.'

He talked about Valentin as if he wasn't also present, lined up on the bed like the rest of us. We told Luca we had trained him, he was tougher than he seemed. Valentin didn't mind being talked about as if he didn't exist. We whispered mostly and talked in signs, while loud Turkish music was playing on the turntable. To confuse whoever might be listening. Then one of us would burst out laughing, say an obscene joke, or swear at someone.

We managed to obtain three wetsuits from Yafsin, who works in the Constanța port and can get just about anything on the black market, from French perfume to birth control pills to wetsuits. We spent all the money we had ever saved on them. But the wetsuits were the most important thing; we would have no use for Romanian money anyway. Valentin and I also stole money from our mother's savings that she had hidden inside the piano, under the lid. The money she had saved from the summers of cooking for the Bucharest tourists. Apparently Valentin had known that the money was there since his first night at home, because he could sense that a foreign object was inside the piano from the way the chords sounded. But only now did he let me know about it. We took only enough to pay for three waterproof fluorescent watches that Yafsin got for us as well. We needed those so we could be precise about the timing on the escape night. Yafsin never asked why we needed such-and-such an object, he just scratched his head and said: 'Give me some time and I'll see what I can do.' The next day he would appear with the stuff. He would call Gigi or me and say something like: 'Want to go for a swim around five this afternoon?' Then we knew to meet him at the beach near the columns, at five o'clock.

It is the evening of the 6th and we have told our parents we are leaving for our holiday tomorrow. Valentin and I are preparing our backpacks in the kitchen. Mama is grudgingly helping by choosing her best preserves for us: pickled green tomatoes, honeyed whole walnuts, *zacuscă* – the red pepper, aubergine and tomato paste – and lots of plum dumplings that she places in a square tin box for us. When she asks us exactly where we are planning to go, we tell her we want to explore the Delta, we've never been there and we think we should know our country a little better. We'll stay with peasants or in our tent, we say. She tells us to be careful in the tent, that there are all sorts of *lighioane*, monstrous creatures, in the Delta. Even scorpions, she says.

I look up at my mother and I see her face is furrowed with deep lines of worry. I realize this is it. I may never see my mother again. My father walks in and stands looking at us from the threshold, one arm propped on the door. I may never see my father either. Valentin's green eyes are mirroring mine at the other end of the room. There is something sparkling in his eyes. Something I don't know. I see my father look at Valentin and smile proudly. I haven't paid much attention to my father's relationship with Valentin, obsessed as I always am with how my mother and I are getting along and how she is dividing her affection or lack of it. Valentin looks like my father, only he is thinner and has green eyes. He responds to my father's smile with an open, luminous look. Something between father and son, a certain need for strength, a reassurance of manliness. I feel the green of Valentin's eyes as a force in itself, a light that is suddenly moving around the room and injecting us with a new understanding of things. The sharp and sparkling realization of this moment, of its fleeting nature, of the past hanging on it and the uncertain future opening from it like the black mouth of my first fish painting.

My mother slams the tin box with plum dumplings on the table and says: 'Here, you two, you should survive on this in the Delta for a few days.'

So many things are left unsaid between my mother and me, so many things I wish I had done with her and said to her; we haven't taken a long walk on the beach together in ages. Did we ever even walk on the beach together, Mama, just you and me? I drink it all in like a snapshot and blink at the image of everything and everybody in our kitchen.

I can't accept the thought of 'never'. I fast forward it all into a happy ending: Gigi, Valentin and I disappear in a few days and get to Turkey by swimming across the frontier line on the night of the 11th in Yafsin's wetsuits, Gigi's parents let our parents know about the whole escapade, they get news from Lemi and Seda in Istanbul that we are safe, we eventually write to them, our parents are actually relieved, they say: 'They are better off there, at least they have a future. What were they going to do here? Good for them, smart kids'; they apply for the reintegration of the family with first-degree kin, article number three hundred and something, wait a year and there we are, Valentin and I, waiting for them in the station or port or airport in Istanbul, it doesn't matter which.

Close the lid of that tin box over the plum dumplings, Mama, close the lid. You are the most beautiful mother in the world and I only realize it now when I am parting from you and you are preparing your green pickled tomatoes and honeyed walnuts for us without even knowing why. Will you ever be able to forgive me, Mama?

I will not say goodbye as if I wasn't coming back, I will not look back, I will not take another look at every corner of our house and at the weeping willow in front of the kitchen window, I will not cast even a furtive look at my parents sleeping next to each other under the rays of the waning moon which will fade out entirely in another three days.

We meet Gigi at the corner of our street at dawn. I walk with my head down. We take the bus to 2 Mai village and get off it just before the last stop. The sun is moving upwards and we are walking towards Limanu, carrying our backpacks and looking at the map Sabina made for us from memory. I breathe in the salty morning air. I'm waking up, I'm excited, and so alive.

We walk on dirt roads and between thick undergrowth of reeds and thorny bushes. Gigi is a few steps ahead, and Valentin a few steps behind. We walk on a bridge across a lake of silvery blue water, towards the gentle hill ahead of us. We take the road to our right. There are stray donkeys and ducks going down the middle of the road, a dusty dirt road. An old woman with a black scarf holding a round-faced tanned baby is staring at us from behind a green iron fence. Even though the sun is getting higher and hotter, the time does not seem to be passing. The air is golden and unmoving. We keep going up the hill looking for the rocks that Sabina had indicated for us on the map. Our steps are slow and sink into the soft earth. A seagull passes by with a shriek, a sign that the sea is near.

This is the end, the very end of the world and the beginning of history. We first see a patch of trees in the distance, then the rocks. We run towards the white rocks neatly packed together. We see it: a black open mouth in the bowels of the hill. Not too big, but big enough for a person to get through. We sit down and rest at the entrance. Take off our backpacks. Valentin wants to eat. Gigi gently reprimands him and tells him it's not eating time yet, but he can drink some water. We have rationed every meal until the middle of the day on the 11th, and have provided for an extra one. Just in case. I am bursting with love for the two men accompanying me. I want to feed Valentin from my own hands but I also want to listen to Gigi and protect our meals for later. Here we are in front of this cave: rock, man, woman, brother. The basics.

The mouth of the cave is black and wide open. The quiet air is hanging in the afternoon heat. Another seagull passes by, shrieking and darting east towards the sea. We look at Sabina's map of the hill again to make sure this is indeed it: the prehistoric cave of the Dacians. The beginnings of our history curled up in a dark cave. We delay entering the cave and explore the area, the hill, the lake, the village. In the late afternoon we eat our ration of bread, *zacusca* and honeyed walnuts. We walk through the village with our backpacks on, pretending to be Bucharest tourists. Three donkeys stare at us in the middle of the dusty road, each at a distance from the other in a triangle. We meet the woman with the black scarf and the round-faced baby again. We ask her about the cave. 'It's a cursed place, dark things have gone on in there,' she says. The baby looks at us with dark round eyes without blinking. Valentin makes a face at him and the baby produces a twinkling laugh in the quiet afternoon. 'There's bats and altars with animal bones in there, pagan satanic dealings,' she says slowly. We tell her we are students in archaeology; we want to see the cave. Does she know someone who can show it to us?

'It's a labyrinth,' she says, 'many people have lost their way in there.' She is avoiding our question. Valentin makes another grimace, and the baby is shaking with laughter like crystal bells. The donkeys are quiet, staring at us too with wide blank eyes, set in their triangular formation. We offer the baby a plum dumpling from the supplies my mother prepared for us and carefully placed in the square tin box. The woman decides to take us to a man in the village who knows the cave 'like the back of his hand, he saved them children who got lost in there once and scared their mamas to death'.

We follow her down the middle of the dusty road to another house in the village. She stops in front of a small house built of yellowish stone, with a yellowish fence and vines hanging all round it and climbing on to the roof. A man with a long white beard like Father Time comes out of the house and the woman tells him we are students, we need to see the cave. He looks us up and down, wipes the sweat off his forehead and yells to someone inside that he'll be gone for a while. There is no answer, the man slams the front door and is coming over to us.

'Have you got cave lights?' he asks.

At first we are taken aback, we don't know what to say. Then Gigi says: 'Torches, you mean? Yes, we've got a couple, thank you.'

Gigi is taking on the speech of the man, I realize, he understands him and is trying to talk like him. The old man looks at me and asks Gigi: 'Is the girl coming too? She'll be scared out of her wits. There was another girl student a while ago and she fainted inside the cave, we had to fetch people from the village to bring her out.' He is talking to Gigi as if I was either absent or deaf and dumb. But I decide to keep quiet, let Gigi deal with him. This is not a time for female pride.

'She is a strong one, she is stronger than both me and our brother here,' says Gigi, slapping the man on the shoulder. I realize Gigi is trying to be gentle on the mores of the local people and is indicating we are all siblings. The old man smiles and trusts Gigi.

I do want to faint but I bite my lips to stop myself losing consciousness. The air in the cave is neither hot nor cold, it's stale and unmoving. Piles of animal bones are set in grottoes built into the cave wall. A flock of bats darts from a corner. We see a peculiar arrangement of stones inside one of the grottoes. The man says they are Dacian altars. He tells us the story of the tribe of Dacians who took refuge from the Romans inside the cave. The Romans blocked up all the exits from it. A whole village of Dacians died in there. With their cattle. They made altars, they sacrificed their cattle, and they all died of suffocation inside the cave. I hold on to both Gigi and Valentin's hands, like a little girl with her bigger, older brothers.

I am confused about time and history. I hate the Romans and I don't like being descended from them. Dido with your soulful eyes, maybe I have a different lineage, maybe I am an offshoot of your Carthaginians and I skipped the Romans. I touch the altar of the Dacians. The rock is smooth and cold. I see the women and children and the tall blond Dacian men kneeling by this altar, smearing it with the blood of their cattle, praying to their god Zalmoxes. The Dacians were not afraid of death, they laughed at it. But they didn't like dying in a dark cave, seeing each other suffocate in darkness. They were solar beings, walked the beaches proudly, grew grapevines and wheat, and worshipped the sea. They thought that in death they were going to meet Zalmoxes. He had taught them about the immortality of the soul. Maybe they lay down quietly as if to sleep, breathing their last breath.

What about the last person to die? How about that last person left breathing who has to see everybody else lying in the dark, a pile of lifeless flesh and bones?

I see this last person as a tall blonde blue-eyed woman stepping among the dead bodies in a trance, in a daze, her eyes glassy in the darkness of the cave, stepping over bodies, young, old, children, her own children, her parents, her brothers and sisters, a mass of dead flesh. The last Dacian alive. She is going further, deeper into the labyrinth of the cave, she doesn't want to die squashed among so many bodies, she wants her freedom in death. She wants to die standing against the furthest wall of the cave, in hatred of the Romans. She wants them to find her just when they think they have trapped everybody and all the Dacians are dead. They will come to the furthest wall in their Roman armours and helmets and will have to face her standing: dead, glassy-eyed, hatred still sparking from her lifeless stare. The Romans think she is a Dacian deity, a witch, a supernatural creature. They run away. They are not so brave after all, those Romans, they are just bloodthirsty.

I try to remember why I wanted so much to come here and live in this cave with Gigi and Valentin, why I wanted to take this detour from our main plan of escaping our country by swimming to Turkey. I wanted to find out what freedom really is, to push everything to the limit, see what the three of us are really all about. The graffiti written on every square centimetre of the cave walls' yellow stone is staring at us mindlessly among encrusted animal bones and upside-down crosses. Liliana, Grasu, Viorica . . . everybody wants to leave a trace, scratch their name, leave a stain in the shape of a finger, in a voracious and crass need to be remembered. The old man is asking us if we've seen enough, if we want to go further. We say yes, as far as it goes. Curves, circles, labyrinths, guano, bats. Could this possibly go as far as Turkey? I don't want to know or try.

'Aah the bats, they's something!' says Father Time. 'There is this woman Marioara, in our village, she started digging a well for her family, a well in her back yard, and instead of water, what do you think comes out of the earth? Bats, hundreds of bats comes out of the earth instead of clean drinking water. She's dug into the top of this cave here. They's covered up the hole and nobody's digging for water anywhere near there.' The bats are protected. 'They too is coming from the same God as water is, we've just disturbed their place, that's all.'

I'm still confused about freedom. Were the Dacians free, the ones who hid here from the bloodthirsty Romans? Are we free, walking through the labyrinth of this cave and trying to escape investigations, failed university exams, families, our country, ourselves? Valentin is pale and I think he is going to faint before I do. Gigi is holding my hand and sweating despite the cool air. I feel nauseous like I did when I was pregnant. Only I feel the opposite of pregnant in this cave: empty, sterile, stale. The taste of dust and raw history is bitter on my tongue. I spit in a corner of the cave. I pass my hand over one of the walls. My nails feel the need to scratch something, to leave a mark, now I understand the vandalizing need of graffiti artists, to scratch your name, your initials, imprint your face on the yellowish stone of this millions-of-years-old cave. I take both Gigi and Valentin by the hand and drag them outside. The old man is shuffling his steps behind us. At the exit from the cave we shake hands and give him our last *leis*.

I've never welcomed the sun as greedily as I do now. I run to the top of the hill where we can see the village and the lake, I touch the grass, and breathe in the salty twilight air. I tell the boys: 'Let's set up our tent over here on top of the hill, right above the cave.' Our tent is small and cosy, almost like a teepee on top of the grassy hill above the cave swarming with bats and quivering with the souls of murdered Dacians.

I sleep between my two male protectors like the first woman in some primordial nest, motionless, my head on Gigi's shoulder, feeling Valentin's quick breathing and the warmth of his body right next to me. Like in a strange kind of womb. An incestuous womb in the centre of the earth. We are covered in bats and they make a velvety blanket over our bodies. The bats are protecting us. Gigi and Valentin are protecting me. I am a hard kernel of life in the centre of the earth. I am quiet and warm and will live for ever if I can only stay motionless like this for the longest time. This is my freedom, in this kernel of life, not on an aeroplane to Paris, not on a ship to Turkey; it's in this round walnut that is me, that is the centre of me, this warmth enveloping me between my lover and my brother. Rock, man, woman, brother, freedom. It's the right equation.

The sun is up when we wake and we are all sweating in our small tent. Time passes without appearing to pass, in a gelatinous roll. The air is golden and thick. At noon, after we've had our ration of aubergine salad, bread, plum dumplings and water, Valentin tells Gigi and me that he cannot come with us to Turkey. He cannot swim four kilometres in the dark, but mostly he cannot leave our mother.

'I cannot leave Mama, not again,' he says seriously, hunched with sadness like an old man. I don't fully understand the meaning of his words. We are sitting on top of the hill in the blazing sun. The air is visible, tangible, time is passing slowly, and all is golden. Valentin's face looks like the clown in the circus, he is laughing with tears, crying with giggles. Valentin is my otherworldly twin brother, an angel of death. Is he even alive, does Valentin exist or has he been an illusion, a creation of my mind all along? Gigi's mouth is moving slowly as if he is talking too, but I can't make out what he is saying. His red hair is on fire, is a flame in the blazing sun, soon Gigi will burst into flames on top of this hill above the cave filled with bats. The blonde Dacian woman, the last survivor of the tribe, is gliding around us glassy-eyed. She is telling us to stick together, not to part, we are a sacred threesome, we are a kernel of life, and together we form the mound of earth from which everything started. But I have to stick to my plan, we have to do what we had set our hearts on, we have to find our freedom. We have to get to Turkey, Valentin or no Valentin.

At noon on 11 August, Gigi and I put on our wetsuits, our fluorescent watches, tie maps and addresses to our bathing suits underneath our wetsuits, and I tie the tin box with our birth certificates to my back. I had an idea that we needed some proof that we exist, that we were born. I am a marine camel, ready for our trip. In the midday sun my brother and I embrace on the sand at the edge of the waves gently splashing against the shore. I hold his scrawny body, his spidery arms. I feel his heart beat against mine. We once filled a whole womb. We break apart and whisper our last goodbyes.

Gigi and I walk into the sea without looking back. We swim smoothly, effortlessly, the sea is at its gentlest and most soothing, a mother like I've never had. Mr Bekta's ship appears in the distance, swaying in a dream across the gleaming waters. Gigi and I speak French, we laugh, we play our parts well, we get on board the ship, the hours pass slowly. Everything is shiny and oily.

The moonless night envelops us. When the time comes Mr Bekta guides us to the lower deck, and sends us off into the dark waters. Gigi and I swim. Everything is going according to plan. We are one. Every move is synchronized. Now I know what freedom is, next to Gigi in these dark waters swimming like red fishes to the adventure of our lives. We are getting close to the line. We see the patrol boat move to our right towards Bulgaria. Our fluorescent watches are showing 22.30. The Turkish ship should be here any minute. There it is. We see it in the distance. We are swimming at the same pace, every breath in synch, every stroke perfectly aligned to the other, like a dance, like a love dance for survival. We are getting closer. We are two slick silvery eels cutting through the moonless, pathless waters. By our calculations we have about half a kilometre left. The patrol boat is still turned towards the other shore. We keep gliding, we are magic fishes swimming freely. The patrol boat has finished its round in that direction and is turning towards us. It seems a little earlier than expected. The Turkish ship seems a little slower than planned. We have less than two hundred metres. We'll make it. We see the patrol boat increase speed and move in our direction. So is the Turkish ship moving in our direction. The ship that will pick us up right on the line separating Romanian Black Sea from Turkish Black Sea and take us out into the Bosphorus. An invisible line of life and death. We are almost at the line between our present and our freedom. The waters are moving in the wake from the two ships coming our way. We look in both directions. We are almost touching each other. We swim faster. We swim for our lives. Freedom is only a few beats away.

Excuse Me, Is This Istanbul?

A red light kept flashing in my head. That was all I could remember: a red light cutting the surface of the black waters at night. Two ships on each side of me. The bright light was growing like a stain on the black sea. Then I found myself sitting on a low bouncy chair surrounded by round-faced, dark-eyed people speaking a different language. There must have been a shipwreck, a plane crash, a police chase, an almost drowning incident, all of that but I was not sure which one in particular. I kept trying to grab on to the image in my head but whenever I tried to hold it for more than a second, it eluded me like a slippery fish.

I stared at the rugs in the room. The floors were covered in red, blue and purple velvety rugs. I was stunned by their beauty and felt like I had seen rugs like those before, though not the same ones. I couldn't remember where. Hold on to the rug pattern, a voice in my head kept telling me.

I heard myself say: 'My mouth tastes like metal. I want to get rid of the taste of metal in my mouth.' The language I spoke felt foreign to me and I seemed to speak automatically. The words rolled off my tongue without my control and I was surprised by how light they were. 'Am I speaking French?' I asked and everybody in the room smiled lightly.

There were whispers, looks, eyes, smiles, a shuffling of steps all round. At some point I felt like I should be running away but my knees buckled when I tried to stand up. And immediately someone brought me a cup of apple tea that I had not asked for. It was hot and tasted sour, but I enjoyed its warmth seeping through my body.

The rug pattern gave me a sense of balance and I decided to stare at it, hoping it would trigger other images that had a meaning, hoping the budding memory it had tried to conjure up earlier would come into full bloom. But the rug pattern failed me again and again.

A woman wearing a flowery dress came and started talking to me. I lifted my eyes from the rug pattern and they projected the lines and circles of the rug on to her face. She looked stunning, like a live painting, with a face filled with coloured lines, squares and circles.

'You are safe and you can rest now. Do you want to rest, Nora?' She had a sweet low voice that seemed familiar.

'I'm not tired. Was I not safe before?' Again the words rolled off my tongue and I delighted in the sensation. I kept thinking more words would come out of my mouth and bounce in the air like before, but it didn't happen.

'You were in danger, you swam for a very long time and you were almost caught by the police. But you are fine now.' Hearing the woman in the flowery dress speak in her low voice was also delightful and familiar. Her name was Seda and the man standing by the fireplace was her husband Lemi. She kept calling me Nora, and telling me I needed to rest. Then she told me that I should take a bath. I didn't want to take a bath, I didn't feel dirty. I wanted to stay on the bouncy chair and see if more words would come out of my mouth.

The lamp on the little table produced a red light and the image came back to me: a watery image of being swung in the air and hoisted on to the ship. That's why I was thinking that maybe I had escaped a plane crash, because at some point I was flown through the air, above the water, but I had no memory of ever having taken a plane. A girl I once knew took a plane to Paris, she was French and gave me a beautiful scarf. Funny I should think of that.

'How did I get to this house? I was swimming and then suddenly I was flying through the air and being hoisted on to a ship. Someone yelled: "Stop!" and threw a bright light on to the water. A red light like one of the lamps in this room. Not really on me but right next to me. The light seemed to be cutting an exact line between me and someone else who had been swimming next to me. How did I end up here in this house, Seda?' Words and sentences were a true miracle. Since I could speak so well, the rest would come back too, sooner or later. If only that clumsy, embarrassing moment of sitting there in the middle of a room full of unfamiliar people would pass more quickly.

For what seemed like a long time I was not sure of my exact position in the world. My relationship to space and time was skewed and broken up in chunks. I didn't remember how I got up from the bouncy chair and how I ended up taking a bath, for example. When I was climbing into the bath I asked Seda: 'Excuse me, is this Istanbul?'

She said that indeed I was in Lemi and Seda's house in Istanbul.

'Seda, did you once show me a postcard of a mosque?'

'Yes, Nora, I showed you postcards of the Blue Mosque and Hagia Sophia when we visited Mangalia, your home town.'

'Can I see the places on the postcard?'

'Of course you can, just take a bath and rest a little and then we'll all go and see the city.'

The bathroom walls were covered in mirrors and red tiles and the water in the tub was transparent and clean. I had never been in a bathroom such as that one. The red tiles were shiny and the water in the tub glistened and reflected them. I must have started to fall asleep because at some point there were three women in the bathroom trying to get me out of the beautiful glistening tub. Seda was telling me that I had fallen asleep and almost drowned in the tub. *Why didn't they let me drown?* I thought. *They should have let me drown.*

I didn't know how much time passed between then and the next day. I was in some kind of tomorrow because at some point I woke up and the sun was blinding me. The light was coming into my room through rosy silk curtains with a flower pattern on them. The light was rosy and there was a fragrance of sweet spices floating around. Seda came into my room with a tray of bread rolls, pistachio and nut pastries, dates and figs.

'Seda, today I want to go out and walk around the city of Istanbul. I want to see the mosque with the six towers that you showed me on the postcard. Am I really in Istanbul, Seda?' For a brief moment I had the disturbing thought that everything could also be a trap set up by the army or the police who were flashing their red light that night of the crash, the accident, the wreck. But I took another look around me, at Seda's radiant face, and decided I was not going to be paranoid on top of being amnesic. I was just going to trust the people and things around me to be what they appeared to be.

'Seda, can you show me around Istanbul today? I feel fine, I am strong today.'

'Yes, today is a good day, Nora. I have some work to do in the morning and then we will go into town. We will go with Lemi. Eat, eat, you need your strength. Here are figs and pistachios, they'll make you strong.'

Seda showed me her wardrobe so that I could choose something to wear for my big outing. Of all the coloured silks and rayons, I chose a loose black dress made of several layers of cloth. Seda was surprised and said women wore that only when they went into the mosque sometimes or out in the countryside, particularly in the east. That seemed perfect. The thought of wrapping myself in all that black cloth seemed quite comforting. It seemed like the only appropriate thing to wear. I also chose the black scarf that went with it. It felt warm and cosy inside the black dress like a larva in its cocoon. The black layered dress fitted well with my forgetfulness.

I blinked at the dazzling sunlight. I covered my ears to protect myself from the clashing noises. I called for the quiet in my head. Too many colours for the eyes to contain and too many noises for my ears! I saw a street sign and tried to remember it in case I got lost: Eminonu. I was on Eminonu Street, which reminded me of a name from my country. A grind of people, noises, colours, foods, jewels, silks, orangey glazed desserts, pastries, trinkets, rugs, plates. I wanted to run back into the house. I was in Istanbul for real. Lemi and Seda were smiling and each took me by the arm again. Seda was wearing a tight red skirt and a white satin blouse, Lemi was wearing black trousers and an embroidered white silk shirt. I was more Turkish than they were. I liked being Turkish and being wrapped in black sheets, my body felt at rest, nobody stared at me; the Turks knew, they made good clothing for uneven women.

'I'd like the big coiling orangey glazed dessert over there,' I told Lemi and Seda. They taught me how to say thank you in Turkish: *teşekkür ederim!* I repeated it perfectly and Lemi and Seda smiled. I was a blank slate, they could write any language on me. I wanted to learn more. They told me useful Turkish expressions: *afedersiniz*, excuse me; *lütfen*, please; *evet*, yes; *hayr*, no. With each combination of syllables something made a little sound in the brain like that of a tiny bell. Several syllables arranged themselves neatly in my head, then on my tongue and formed the name Gigi Malek. His parents' names were Sabina and Luca Malek. Turkish words filled my brain quickly with a rumbling sound. Words like *evet* and *hayr, iyi* and *gule gule* from a summer day when I saw a boy named Gigi Malek amid a group of Turkish boys and girls on the beach walk in my native city. His eyes sparkled in the sun like those of the white cat right there on Eminonu Street. Amber eyes in the afternoon sun. A warm memory flooded me like honey. Cat's eyes, hot July afternoon, Turkish words, Turkish boys and girls, dangling jewellery. I needed to buy turnips. The amber-eyed cat on Eminonu Street was staring at me. I saw the slow lazy walk through my native city, laughing with Gigi Malek about turnips. Now that I had that memory, what was next, when would it all come back so I could make sense of what was going on in my brain? I thought the cats would help. Istanbul was full of cats.

'Where is Gigi Malek?' I asked Seda in the middle of the street. They looked at each other, terrified, as if hiding something from me.

I felt a big lump of blackness pressing on my brain, covering up something very important, something that had to do with a boy called Gigi Malek. Lemi and Seda walked with me through crowds and rugs and silks and glazed sweets, on narrow cobblestone streets, on wide streets pumping like a crazed heart, up and down and in circles. 'Look!' said Lemi. There was the image from Seda's postcard, only magnified thousands of times. The Blue Mosque with greyish blue and milky white cupolas and minarets. I saw a streak of the Bosphorus beyond the Blue Mosque. Blue until it hurt. It was the first time that something actually hurt since the crash, the accident, the red light. I was alive after all. But where was Gigi Malek? I kept wondering. I felt as though I should have wondered, yearned, longed for him, but couldn't remember the reasons why, as the black lump pressed on my brain and I had a fierce desire to scratch it and tear it apart. Only I felt too lazy to do anything other than stare at the Blue Mosque. The blue hurt was all I could take in one day.

'Look at the water and the ships, Nora, and there, that part where the water shines is called the Golden Horn because of how the light falls at dusk.'

It was dusk, and the water, the ships, the mosques all glowed in a honeyed glaze. Next to me was a line of men polishing shoes. People stopped in front of them, sat on a high chair and had their shoes polished for a few coins. I tried very hard to imprint everything on my brain: over there was the Golden Horn, the honey-glazed light over the Bosphorus, ships, mosques; over there were shoe-polishing men. Had I ever seen anybody polishing people's shoes in the streets of my country? The pungent smell of the polish they were using on the shoes touched a nerve; there was something familiar about it. I looked at the water one more time and saw that at one point, close to a three-decked ship leaving the port, the sun was making a golden puddle, like a magic mirror. I felt the desire to paint.

'You used to make such beautiful paintings back in Mangalia,' said Seda, echoing my own desire. 'Do you want to start painting, Nora dear? We'll buy you an easel, watercolours, oil paints, charcoal pencils, brushes of all sizes. It will be good for you to start painting again. And go to the beach, don't you want to see the beaches, Nora?'

Some days later Lemi and Seda took me on a bus to Kilyos beach on the Black Sea. The beach was tapestried with colourful towels and umbrellas. I recognized the water because it ran through my veins with my blood. I ran to it in an agile slalom through the hundreds of beach towels and umbrellas and glided into it like the first woman on earth entering the primordial ocean. I stood in the silk dress I had borrowed from Seda that day. I stood motionless on the shore, right where the sand was mushy and the waves were breaking with delicate foaming ripples. The waves kept gently hitting my ankles and the setting sun bled its scarlet rays into the water. I had once stood like that on a shore in the golden sun, the waves gently breaking against my ankles. The red light started flashing in my head again and with it the face of a red-haired boy. He was being plucked out of the water, up in the air, his eyes staring wildly. He was shoved into a ship opposite where I was, and smaller than the ship I was being taken on. He was thrown into it like a toy by angry men in army uniforms. The name of Gigi Malek clung to the face of that red-haired boy and the two became one. He was being swung in the air in a net like the ones used for catching fish. Now I knew why I was supposed to yearn for Gigi Malek. He was the same boy who had once stood on the beach walk with shiny eyes like amber and walked me to the store to buy turnips in the Black Sea twilight. He was the boy next to whom I was swimming that golden day, that red night.

'Look at her, how she enters the water in her silk clothes!' Seda and her family exclaimed as I walked into the waves without bothering to take off the red and blue paisley silk dress I was wearing. The water was entering me and I swam far away towards the cruel blade of the horizon that separated me from everything that I had been before the red night. I went far towards the horizon, thinking that maybe now I could take the road back. I was going to repair everything. They sent out boats and swimmers to save me. The Turks were kind and hospitable. I didn't need saving. They brought me back to shore as if I were a drowning victim. I laughed.

'I'm fine, I didn't want to drown. I just wanted to get to the other side, to see my mama for a quick moment. I wanted to see Gigi Malek.' Saying his name out loud made me want to run to the sea again and swim the full length of the Bosphorus, but Lemi and Seda and two other men who had brought me back held me like a prisoner. We walked back slowly through the coloured umbrellas. I smiled at the sea. I smiled at my entire life story.

Lemi and Seda bought me paints and an easel. I remained oblivious to the passing of time and I measured the hours and the days by the number of paintings I made. I painted people on a big ship waving goodbye in multicoloured clothes. A suggestion of the Blue Mosque and the blue Bosphorus was visible far in the distance, a haze over bluish spheres and towers. Whole canvases in one colour. The blue phase. The yellow phase. The red phase. The grey phase. There was a painting of a massacred family all in yellow. Maybe my own massacred family. Sickening, light yellow, rotting bones in the sunlight, my people yellowing the world and the waters of the sea. The painting of the red-haired boy as he was being flown in the air was the red phase painting. His red hair had set the night ablaze: the naval police, the two ships, the light cutting a line in the black water. Everything was in three shades of red: burning red, dark blood red, plaintive purplish red. Gigi Malek was a red fish caught in a huge net. Only his eyes were shining.

I mixed the media and the paints in no order other than my wild desire to absorb everything in my thirsty canvases and to remember. I made myself remember through my paintings. I used all sizes of brush as well as my own hands and fingers; I made collages on paper, canvas, and cutouts from old pictures I found in Seda's rubbish. My fingers and palms were always streaked with colours and became raspy and sore.

There was a painting of me in blacks and greys. I protected myself. I hid in the Turkish night, underneath black sheets. I went back to wearing the black clothes. The only spot of colour was the gold Turkish slippers with the red pompoms that Seda gave me to wear around the house. I painted myself as a black nude. The black nude looked extraterrestrial; it was turning into something other than human, it was opaque and transparent, at once gooey and metal-solid, watery and blank. A lonely meteor moving aimlessly through space with gold Turkish slippers that shone like whimsical stars.

'There is the painter woman in the *hijab* who makes crazy art!'

I heard whispers and rumours and gossip in the streets of Istanbul. Some people bought my paintings, just for the weirdness of it. Some tourists were intrigued, they found them avant-garde. A French tourist bought the nude painting for one hundred Turkish liras. I saved the money for a rainy day. Throughout the painting madness I kept looking, I kept trying to catch that part of myself that eluded me like a slippery silver fish. Now I was holding it and now it had glided from my hands and was nowhere to be found. It was floating somewhere in the waters of the Bosphorus. Everything was raw and right at the surface, as if I had been skinned alive, but beneath the skin there was a black screen that was keeping me from myself. Whenever I painted in Lemi and Seda's living room in the smell of Lemi's pipe smoke, another warm memory with pipe smells enveloped me. I was in a room covered with red and purple rugs like the ones in Lemi and Seda's living room, sitting on a low bed with three men. One of the men sitting on the bed was smoking a pipe just like Lemi always was. Another one seemed to be Gigi Malek. And there was another boy sitting at the very end of the bed, staring absent-mindedly at the wall. He had black hair and was very thin. The four of us were planning something, it looked like fun. I had a faint desire to be with them, to repeat that moment. Then the face of the thin black-haired boy came back to me. I was sitting on a rock on a hill in the sun. There was a golden glaze surrounding the two of us on that hill. The boy was telling me that he couldn't come with us. But where was it that we were all going? I always became too tired and lazy to search further in that memory.

One day I'd had enough of the black *hijab*. 'I want to wear your colourful dresses, Seda,' I demanded shamelessly. Silks, cottons, Turkish polyesters and rayons, you name it. I was ready for colour and texture.

'My clothes fit you well, Nora. We are both of medium height, tight and plump.' Seda had a raspy full laugh. 'You've got a little plumpish since you came to Istanbul, Nora. It's good, Istanbul agrees with you and you look healthy!' When she said that, Seda made me think of my mother in the kitchen. Of how she always wiped her hands on her apron and then passed her fingers through her hair, just like Seda did then.

'Seda, I want to see my mama.'

'You can't. Your mama and your family are all fine. We already sent them word about you, Nora.'

'And the red-haired boy – Gigi Malek – is he fine?' Seda turned her head away. He was not fine then; why didn't they tell me? Seda looked me in the eyes and like never before stared at me fiercely, almost angrily.

'He is fine, he is alive, don't ask again!' Maybe Seda was puzzled by the irony of it all, how *I* had made it across the border and their flesh and blood hadn't. Seda was right. I was not going to ask any more, I was going to live with the lack of knowledge. I had to relearn everything. I had to live with bits of knowledge, new burdens and holes in my memory. At least I remembered that I didn't remember everything, there was hope for me. I told myself: *I'll go back to painting my blue pain, my red memories and yellow bones, my black nude.*

Struggling for Memory in Istanbul

I don't remember turning twenty, but I know it happened while I was living in Istanbul with Lemi and Seda. It turned out I had spent more than two years living amid the dizzying mirages of that throbbing city, painting in coloured phases and cooking Turkish sweets. Lemi said I suffered from a form of amnesia due to the trauma I had experienced; my psyche protected itself by refusing to remember the traumatic night and with that came a wave that washed over the rest of my memory. Most likely there will be things I will never remember or will only remember if I have another shock. Lucky me, I may have to go through another psychological big bang in order to remember what I have forgotten as a result of the first bang. The ironies of life never cease.

Lemi was a paediatrician in one of the children's hospitals in Istanbul and he often received visits from his patients at home too. Parents with pale-looking or fat and swollen or red-faced feverish children walked into Lemi and Seda's house at the oddest hours and they always welcomed them as warmly as if they were their own family. Lemi had an office in the house and did not mind being called on for emergencies at any hour of the day. There were also aunts and sisters and other children growing and living in their house and I never got to know who was whose relative or child or sister and what their names were. I just remember a large group of people staring at me and smiling with wide smiles during the first few days after they brought me to their house. Sometimes I found a child hiding under my bed in a hide-and-seek game, or sitting on my bed and sucking his thumb. You were never by yourself in Lemi and Seda's house. After a while I got used to living among a constant swarm of people of all ages and wandering around their many rooms all filled with heavy red rugs, velvet cushions, dark sculpted wooden furniture and wide shiny mirrors. The hard colours and the uninterrupted throb of human life and voices was precisely what I needed during that period of complete disconnection from myself.

Their house was situated on a sloping street in the old historic district called by the delicious name Eminonu, close to the Egyptian Spice Bazaar. I spent hours every day in the spice market, inhaling the fragrances of the multicoloured condiments, pastes, desserts, hoping that if I exposed my dormant memory to pungent smells and tastes, it would slowly awaken and come to life. I had my special spice and dessert man, who always welcomed me with a smile and let me taste from his multitudes of Turkish delight. I inhaled the smells of the Iranian saffron, the cumin, the coriander, and then went back to tasting *baklava* and pistachio-filled crunchy cakes. My memory was waking up in little spurts and it was the same scenes that would flash in the fogginess of my brain: Gigi and I stealing *lokum* in the bazaar and then running away and laughing, Gigi and I eating the *baklava* that his mother Sabina had made fresh on a Friday night, in the front room looking out at the apricot tree that guarded the house. The images floated and were not connected to what had happened before or afterwards. I knew almost everything I knew about myself and my family from the meticulous story-telling that Lemi and Seda did every evening.

They kept telling me my own story over and over again: where I was born, who were my parents, who was Gigi, who was Valentin, my mother Rodica, my father Sandu, describing the beach near our house, the mosque and the Turkish cemetery, the tourists that my mother had lodged and fed for many years. I knew all that after a while, but I couldn't really see it. I knew it in my head, because someone had recounted it to me.

Seda had the idea that contact with raw substances, spices and pastes would help me remember and bring me closer to myself. She taught me how to cook Turkish foods, and how to recognize and use all the spices, the condiments, meats, pastes. I learned how to make the *kebabs*, the *koftes*, the *pilafs*, the aubergine salads, the potato pastries, the vine-leaf *dolmas*, the desserts: the *halvahs*, the *baklavas*, the *kadaifs*. The whole family ate my meals. After dinner I sometimes went out in the street and gave the leftovers to the poor. My resources were endless. I was feeding all of Istanbul with my scary paintings and juicy *dolmas*.

One day in the spice bazaar, I met a woman who was a street artist. She was from Mongolia, which sounded almost like my native city of Mangalia. She walked around with a small easel, wearing a black frock in whose pocket she had a collection of coloured chalks. She asked me if I wanted to have my portrait drawn and I laughed, then I asked her if she wanted her portrait done by me. We both laughed heartily. Her name was Chernega and she was living in Istanbul for a while, trying to make money with her portraits, to send to her family in Mongolia. She lived in a one-room apartment on the Asian side, in a neighbourhood called Taksim that was filled with electronic and hardware stores. Whenever the two of us walked through those streets, carrying our portable easels and paints, the shop owners, all men, stared at us with a mixture of disapproval and curiosity. The neighbourhood seemed harsh and unwelcoming to me and the massive mounds of wiring, nails and pliers grated on my nerves, like a sharp object scratching the surface of an old wound. It reminded me of something unpleasant from my home town, a threat, a group of angry men in uniforms surrounded by lots of metal and electrical equipment. I couldn't get to that memory, just the unpleasant feeling it generated. But Chernega stopped at a different store each time, to buy a small object: a handful of nails, a transformer, a pair of scissors. She said she was actually building her clientele, the neighbourhood appreciated her for supporting their businesses, and one day some of those self-important men might want to have their portraits done by us. A portrait of a stern, moustached man standing proudly in front of barrels of nails and orange electrical wiring.

We teamed up and started joining the Bosphorus cruises, which we knew were filled with both Turkish and foreign tourists. Invariably, a young woman or a teenage girl would stop us and ask how much we charged for the portraits. We did our portraits in tandem, Chernega in chalk, me in charcoal, the way I had learned from Miss Mantaş. Our double act, and the speed at which we could do the portraits in competition with each other, was what mostly attracted tourists. We said we made two portraits for the price of one. We always charged one hundred Turkish liras for the double portrait, and never bargained. This way we achieved a certain reputation and respect. We went on a cruise almost every day, and with Chernega I didn't feel the obligation to rummage through my memory. I didn't have to try to stimulate my mind through all sorts of sensory experiments. I just lived in the moment, like a woman with no past or with a hazy, unclear past. Memory is also a burden, and there was a certain wild freedom in living without one. Because big chunks of my memory had been eviscerated, everything in the present had an unusual intensity: the salty cool wind coming from the Bosphorus stung my nostrils every time, the tastes of roasted aubergine or *ekmek* honey-soaked cake filled my mouth and soul with delicious sensations. The colours were sharp, the sounds penetrating and the smells inebriating. While part of my brain felt dead, my senses were doubly, painfully alive. I connected to the natural world of Istanbul in a visceral way: the water, the stray cats, the pigeons in front of the mosques. Chernega took me to street corners and palace gardens with lots of cats and told me the Turks loved cats, but hated dogs. I sometimes went alone to the garden of the Topkapi Palace and painted the congregations of cats sitting in mysterious formations, quiet and confident as sphinxes on the cobblestones. The self-contained animals and the many pairs of glittering eyes deigning to look at me with unperturbed calm also tapped at the surface of my memory. I tried to outstare the cats until my eyes were full of tears and the cats always won. I felt if only I could look long enough without blinking, something would emerge: an important memory with a cat in it.

One day when we were on one of the Bosphorus cruises and Chernega and I were doing the portrait of a tall thin Turkish man from the eastern part of the country, I heard two of the crew tell the story of a group of several Romanians who had tried to escape on a Turkish ship by hiding below deck, inside one of the small cargo rooms, and how they were found dead from lack of air and water, and from breathing in toxic fumes from the engine. Somebody mentioned the length of the Bosphorus: thirty-one kilometres, and then the narrowest part of six hundred and sixty metres – a breeze to swim across. I knew those numbers, they were familiar sounds which served no purpose now. I raised my head from the portrait I was drawing and stared at the two men recounting the story. I took particular note of the swaying of the ship on the waves. From their faces it seemed that the men derived a certain pleasure from the story. I thought I detected a malicious smile on the face of one of them. The image of a man dressed in an army uniform giving orders on a ship in the dark, his face in the centre of a circle of glaring light, struck my consciousness. I carried around useless information in my head such as the length of the Bosphorus, or the distance from Mangalia to Istanbul of two hundred and sixty kilometres; Gigi and I had gathered information like that and then we failed miserably. Not as miserably though as the Romanians whom the crew were talking about on the Turkish ship, for they had all died, suffocated and thirsty. Kilometres weren't important, it was luck that mattered. A sharp pain went through my chest. I bent over and knocked over the easel, and then my easel knocked over Chernega's easel, all our materials went flying in all directions, and the client who was having his portrait drawn stared at us with his mouth open. I wasn't ready for that memory, not like that, not alone and in the absence of the rest of my memories that could explain that moment. I picked up every bit of chalk and charcoal off the deck with the rapidity of a circus juggler, made everything look as tidy as before and resumed my portrait. I never wanted to talk to Chernega about it.

Lemi and Seda were wise enough not to pressure me into taking any decisions about my future until I was ready to. They let my days drift by at their own pace, sometimes frantic, at other times in something of a sleepy lull, as my mind and searches were dictating.

Seda came into my room one evening, tiptoeing and smiling as she always did, and told me she had word from someone who had been to Mangalia, a Turkish relative of Mr Bekta's, that Gigi was in prison. He was in jail as a 'class enemy' somewhere in Transylvania. He was alive but in prison. Yes, that's what she had said, 'alive but in prison'. Not 'alive *yet* in prison', not 'alive *and* in prison'. 'Alive *but* in prison'. I knew what that meant. Romanian prisons were dreaded locations, particularly if you were in there for political reasons. He was barely alive. His imprisonment had turned his life into a form of non-life. I knew Gigi had almost bottomless resources of endurance. I had watched him grow and develop into a man the way he had watched me grow into a woman. He was tough and wiry and would not let himself die and leave me in the world without him. He could endure thirst and hunger and physical pain. But I knew what they did to people in prison. My grandfather had been killed with an axe in the Sighetu prison and that only after long periods of torture. They got tired of torturing him because he wouldn't die and that's when they resorted to the very efficient axe method.

The thought of Gigi being tortured, kept on a starvation diet, in a cold prison cell made me want to tear down the whole city of Istanbul with one swing of my arm. Blue Mosque and Hagia Sophia and all. What good were the beautiful buildings when people were being tortured and turned into mud? But the swarm of people moving with inexhaustible energy through the meandering streets of that city seemed to contradict my philosophy. People did move on, life did go on, cities progressed and worked even while people were tortured in prisons and children were lost and lovers were brutally separated and families broken apart. And even the most miserable in this city still journeyed on and on through the coloured rugs, the shimmering silks, the sparkling sapphires and diamonds, and the mouth-watering honeyed desserts: the insane murmuring and conversing with their own imaginary associates, the desperately poor stretching out trembling hands for the smallest coin, the widows, the cheated lovers, the street children curled in a corner begging for a coin, the street women selling themselves for a few Turkish liras, they all went on and on in the shadow of indomitable towers and cupolas, in the blue light of the Bosphorus and of those entangled seas that washed the shores of the city.

I decided I was going to go on for as long as I felt that Gigi would go on in his prison cell. Or outside it, if he ever made it beyond its thick walls. I decided I was going to move on through life for as long as I felt Gigi was still breathing, whether in prison or at liberty. I asked Seda about my parents and Gigi's parents and she said they were all fine, 'given everything'. I knew what that meant too. They were all alive, and the secret police had not killed any of them. Not yet. But they were all drowned in varying degrees of misery and suffering. What good ever came of anything? Where was I going? For how much longer was I going to stay in the swirl of Turkish pleasures wrapped up in amnesia?

The answer came one evening when I was drowning in the sweetness of one of Lemi and Seda's post-dinner tea and dessert moments. An autumn evening with the setting sun slanting its rays through the silky mauve curtains in the sitting room, and resting on one of the red and gold velvet cushions. Seda's white cat Bambina sat purring by the window. She was a special kind of odd-eyed cat that the Turks considered to be semi-magical because that type of cat had been loved and protected by President Atatürk, the founder of modern-day Turkey. He had predicted that an odd-eyed cat would bite the ankle of his successor. Bambina stared at me in an unusual way. She had one amber eye and one green eye. The sun shone in her eyes and I couldn't stop staring back at her. I had seen eyes like that, only in a person. The sun shone on her white fur and it made sparkles of different colours in her amber and green eyes. I had an unusual feeling of warmth both physical and mental, as if an inner sun was shining from within me.

Seda started showing me family albums and a Turkish melody was wailing its last notes on the record. She went on and on telling me the names of her relatives, the places where the photos were taken, until we reached one page that she went over quickly as if not wanting me to see it. I put my hand on her hand and turned the page back. There, looking at me from a black-and-white photograph, were none other than Gigi and Nora. We were looking straight at the camera with a wild hope and a gauzy light spread on our faces. Then I looked at Bambina again and the combination of the picture and the way the sunlight shone at a slanted angle in the cat's odd-coloured eyes untied a knot in my head. It was the picture that Lemi had taken of us during their two-month-long visit to Luca and Sabina's house. It was taken in front of Gigi's house next to the old apricot tree in bloom.

You could see the little white blossoms like shiny globes in the tree and Gigi and I were standing proudly next to it, leaning slightly into each other as if we were tied together, made of the same hard, sunburnt salty flesh. The images that until then were only specks of light in an overpowering blob of darkness now triggered other images and they all rushed into my consciousness like an invasion of hungry birds. Bambina moved and the sun stopped shining in her eyes. I felt a seeping through my heart, an overwhelming sadness.

The string of months and years running through my childhood and adolescence, until the last days with Gigi and Valentin in the golden heat of 2 Mai village on top of the bat-filled cave, glared and erupted in my head: our family dinners with my always angry and depressed mother, the rare and memorable visits of my brother, my father's summer raids along the epidemic-infested coast and his cholera investigations, the abortion in the dark by Dr Niculescu who smelled of vodka, my relentless and angry passion for painting, the bazaar with the Gypsies selling trinkets and corn on the cob, Mariţa and her Turkish stories, Mariţa and her unnecessary death, the enchanted summers by the sea, Gigi and I diving and diving again and holding our breath under water, the two of us swimming in cold illegal jellyfish-filled waters next to the half-built anti-missile ship. It all cascaded together, rumbling mercilessly in my head. The amber in Bambina's left eye was the exact colour of Gigi's eyes and the green eye was like mine. Bambina was an uneven creature like me that contained both Gigi and me in her visual field, she had Gigi's and my eyes put together. It was something of an improbable coincidence. The asymmetry, the coincidences, the intersections of light and darkness in that moment woke me up and I was ablaze in memories and associations. I understood Gigi better, his feline movements, the way his eyes shone in the August afternoon when I met him on the *faleza* surrounded by Turkish kids from the neighbourhood. The music stopped, the sun set, the room was almost in darkness. Lemi turned on the lights, the coloured chandelier. Seda held my hand in silence.

I asked Seda three questions one after the other, breathlessly:

'How old am I, Seda?'

'You are twenty-one and a half, Nora.'

'What year is this?'

'It is 1986.'

'How long have I lived with you?'

'A little more than two years.'

'I want to go to Paris, Seda.'

At that particular moment I was sure I wanted to go to Paris. Anushka bloomed in my consciousness like the pure salvation to my confusion, amnesia and pain. Anushka in Paris.

'I have enough money for the plane ticket,' I said. 'You know I saved from my painting and cooking,' I added proudly.

'We know, we know, Noricica dear, you are the most courageous and enterprising girl we know.' They often called me by this diminutive they had made up, something to make me feel warmer, loved, protected. 'But we are worried about you going by yourself to Paris. How do you know that French girl you met six years ago at the beach is going to be of any help? What will you do there by yourself, our Noricica?'

Seda had a point, but I didn't care. My brain became unclogged when I saw the picture of Gigi and me in front of the old apricot tree. I saw myself standing on a sharp line between the past that was contained in that photograph and a future that was nothing but a greyish, whitish blur. I now saw the past with great clarity and the future in a fog. The balance had changed. Only the present was solid and nice-smelling. Somewhere through the blur I saw Anushka's face with her squinting blue eyes and round doll-face, amid Paris-postcard emblematic sights: the Gothic towers of Notre Dame, the round neoclassical cupola of the Sacré Coeur and the upside-down metal Y of the Eiffel Tower. I also had an image of Anushka standing in front of the Eiffel Tower behind a curtain of falling snow. I believe that image derived from the memory of a gift I had once received from Uncle Doru after one of his European trips: a glass globe with a tiny Eiffel Tower inside a liquid that became filled with snowflakes when you shook it. Between the painfully clear contours of the past and the irritatingly unclear vision of the future, one thing was plain: for all practical reasons I couldn't go back to Gigi. I had to keep going forward. I had to start something. I had to carry out a plan. All through my adolescence Gigi kept telling me to go to art school to become the artist I wanted to be. I was twenty-one, had no real work, and no formal schooling beyond the pathetic Mangalia high school. What would he want me to do? Go back, to be taken directly from the airport by the secret police and put in another cell for enemies of the country? Stay in Istanbul enveloped in amnesia, *kadaifs* and *hijabs* for ever? Or move on to doing what I was meant to do in life? What was I meant to do in life? I was meant to paint and love Gigi. I could pursue the first goal if I moved to Paris. First, in order to be closer to Gigi I had to get further away from him. I had to go on living for as long as I felt he was alive.

Seda and Lemi decided that they would get in touch with Uncle Doru in Germany, ask him to take me to Paris and help me get settled there. He was good at this sort of human problem, just like he had taken care of Raluca when she was dying, and escorted Valentin from Bucharest to our house in Mangalia. He had the special kind of strength needed to make huge life transitions such as moving from one city to another, from one family situation to a new one, from life to death, and appear light and immaterial through it all. Like a game. With his fedora tilted to one side, his curled black moustache, his roaring laugh and his elegant empty right sleeve carefully tucked inside his coat pocket, he made you feel like you were just playing roulette and nothing merited too much anguish or attention. Except the black ball, keep your eyes on the ball. I was glad at the thought of seeing Doru, a family member. He inspired vital energy, and he would be good for my mental well-being.

Lemi contacted Uncle Doru by phone. His address and phone number, together with Anushka's address and phone number, were among the papers tied to my bathing suit underneath my wetsuit when I swam across the border into Turkey. As were the three birth certificates I had carried in my mother's plum dumpling box on my back like a camel of the sea. I had ended up with Gigi's and Valentin's birth certificates on top of mine and now I had to keep carrying them with me wherever I went. I didn't mind carrying the light burden of the proof of their identities; I placed mine in between theirs and thought of the nights in the tent on top of the Limanu hill, of how deliciously safe and full I felt during those moonless nights with everything I needed to be happy within reach: love, kin, earth and water.

As in my childhood, I first smelled the fresh lemony fragrance of his special cologne and then I heard his huge laugh fill the hallway. I got up from the sofa with a jolt in my heart and ran to him, forgetting for a second where I was, thinking I was at number 9, our old stone house in Mangalia, and Uncle Doru had just returned from one of his adventurous architecture tours through Europe. When he saw me his mouth opened in his most explosive laugh and he lifted me up with one sweep of his left arm the way he always did back home. When I could look at him better I saw he was much thinner and had an almost sickly air about him, though his manner was still that of the *bon vivant.* He proudly showed me his new prosthetic arm and hand and then punched me with it to show how hard it was. He laughed at his own coarse jokes as he always did. When I saw him amid the Turkish décor that was not the décor of our old house, the absence of my entire family stabbed me suddenly with a sharp pain. I pictured Tudoriţa fidgeting and walking around in her confused-mother-hen manner, my mother coming in from the kitchen and wiping her hands on her apron with a frown and the suggestion of a welcoming smile, my father passing one hand through his dark shiny hair, Florin running through the maze of everybody's legs, and during the last years, Valentin coming in with a slightly sleepy look, green eyes sparkling with a playful smile, dishevelled dark hair all over his forehead. With Doru's entrance into Lemi and Seda's house, the last bit of my amnesia was finally cured and I had nowhere to hide any more. It was time for me to move on indeed. I felt the proper amount of pain and longing. I was now the regular traumatized refugee trying to make it in a new world with a small bag of belongings, a cartful of useless memories and a throbbing ball of chaos and confusion in her mind.

I was nervous as I held the phone in the hallway of Lemi and Seda's house while I waited for Anushka to answer. It rang several times and nobody answered. Just when I was about to hang up I heard the childish high-pitched voice pointed in a question mark: '*Allô, oui?*' I gasped holding the receiver in my hand and heard again: '*Allô, qui est là?*' Then I rushed to say something for fear she would hang up and I wouldn't have the courage to call again. '*Anushka, c'est moi, Nora. Nora de Mangalia.*' For a second I was weighed down by the brutal provincialism of that expression, 'Nora from Mangalia': a Balkan girl with a peasant grandfather, an imperfect body and a naïve desire to become a painter. An encounter at the beach, a little summer drama and a silk scarf to remember it by. But Anushka's voice in the receiver was melodious, as if this was exactly what she had waited six years for: a phone call from Nora from Mangalia. She said: '*Nora, c'est toi? Tu es à Paris?*' Her voice had an echo as if it came from inside a barrel and it did not sound real. There was a gooey slowness to her speech as if there was something wrong with her. But I became excited at the sound of her voice even if it had a strange echo and I told her I was in Istanbul and wanted to come to Paris. I had escaped from Romania and was thinking of trying . . . of just trying . . . to live in Paris. Could she help me? She said in an almost unctuous tone that yes, yes, three times yes, come right away, could I come now? For a brief moment I thought that maybe Anushka was completely out of her mind. But then I brushed away the idea and thought that she was just shocked and excited by the news, quite remarkable news, that after six years I was calling her from Istanbul with a request that she put me up in Paris. I told her I was making preparations to come, taking care of my papers and tickets, and I would probably arrive in Paris in a week. I would let her know exactly when, and if she could meet me at the airport that would be so kind of her. '*Vraiment très gentil de ta part.*' Then she brusquely said goodbye, as if suddenly tired or annoyed, and hung up.

After I put down the phone, I sensed that something was wrong. What if Anushka wasn't really going to help me, what would happen to me in Paris? I felt a strange shiver go through my body as I played back the conversation with Anushka and stood in the hallway surrounded by Lemi, Seda, Doru, an aunt living in the house, and a dark-skinned shiny-eyed child. Everybody was staring expectantly at me, waiting for news from the French capital. 'What did she say, what did she say?' they were all asking. They didn't want me to leave and were afraid that something awful would befall me in Paris. I felt as if the Anushka I had just spoken to was a fake. But I shook off the feeling. I smiled, for besides learning how to cook colourful Turkish desserts, in Istanbul I had also learned how to smile. I never used to smile before. I would either instantaneously burst out laughing or I would be serious and frown. But in Turkey I learned all the nuances of smiling. 'She can hardly wait to see me,' I said and smiled, suggesting that everything was just fine. 'She will meet me at the airport,' I added and produced an even wider smile, trying to convey that I was relieved, I was worry-free, don't anybody worry about me now.

The three hours on the plane from Atatürk Airport in Istanbul to our first stopover in Frankfurt were destined to be my last pleasurable and carefree hours for a long time. It was my first time on a plane and I delighted in every minute of it like a great adventure. The impeccably dressed and made-up stewardesses showered you with more smiles than even the inhabitants of Istanbul did. They offered you drinks and snacks and food that far exceeded my need or appetite but kept me entertained. And mostly I delighted in the sight of the infinitude of thick white bubbly clouds in the midst of which our plane's Boeing engines roared. Once in a while the image of Anushka Pomorowska in a slinky red dress or a flowing blue gown standing in front of a flying Eiffel Tower would make its appearance from one of the cottony clouds and reassure me with a giggle that everything was going to be all right and I had no reason to worry. When the plane landed, hitting the ground with a short thud, I did have a moment's worry about the way in which Anushka had answered and talked when I called her a second time and gave her my arrival details. She sounded distracted, did not repeat the information as someone normally would to make sure they had got it right, and quickly said: '*Oui, oui, bien sur.*' She hung up abruptly like the first time. But I brushed the worry away again, followed Uncle Doru out of the plane and into Frankfurt airport and told myself I was on the verge of a new beginning and could hardly wait to see Anushka after all those years.

When we found ourselves halfway to the gate from where our plane to Paris would leave, Doru hugged me fiercely, wished me luck and said goodbye. At first I thought he was going to buy cigarettes or take a tour of the airport. But he was actually staying in Frankfurt, he said. There was no need for him to accompany me to Paris; if I had made it across the Bosphorus and survived for two years in Istanbul, he had no doubt I would be fine in Paris, which was a much easier city than Istanbul and where I had my good friend Anushka willing to help me out. I remembered the time on top of the Limanu hill in the glazed morning light when Valentin told me he was not coming with us after all. What kind of cruel and strange fate was governing my life? I thought, trembling with fear and the shock of the news. I was holding on desperately to Doru's prosthetic arm with my smaller hand, the right hand. In what kind of terrifying dream was I caught? Surely I was going to wake up and find myself in a safe, solid place surrounded by those I loved. Such as what? Where were those I loved? Far away beyond an impassable line. Nothing could turn back time, this was my own living nightmare and I had to confront it. Droves of busy travellers rushed by me and brushed against me with their luggage. Standing in front of Doru in Frankfurt airport and holding on to his hard artificial limb, I felt my face become like the cracked walnut that my mother's face had been when Valentin arrived back in our house. Huge bubbles of tears were blocking my sight and my cheeks felt contorted and twitching.

'Uncle Doru, please come with me to Paris, just for a little bit. You have to help me,' I said, hiccuping from the crying.

He looked at me with a sad expression like I had never seen on him before and said: 'I wish I could, Nora dear, really. But I am sick, you know, and I have to hurry. I'm really ill, not much time left. I have to get back to my treatment and make sure I finalize all the paperwork so I can bring Aunt Tudoriţa over here for a while. So we can see each other a little bit more. Before, before . . . you know . . . Be good, be strong. You'll make it, I'm sure. Watch out for those Parisian men though, they are trouble, and a pretty girl like you . . .' He produced one of his roaring laughs, only softer than usual.

Before disappearing in the airport crowd, he turned one more time and told me to try to get into the Ecole Nationale des Beaux

Arts, the best art school in Paris. 'Don't waste your talent!' he said. 'Grab on to it like your life depended on it. Your life *does* depend on it!' He moved on through the crowd, his prosthetic arm neatly tucked into his silver-grey elegant coat, fedora tipped to one side, cigarette in the corner of his mouth.

At that point I had no idea what talent he was talking about and what any art school had to do with me. My talents be damned! People seemed to derive a cruel pleasure from giving me big existential advice just before dying or parting with me. Leaving me empty-handed when I needed them the most. Mariţa with her big secret on her last breath, Valentin telling me he couldn't go through with our escape hours before we left, Doru dropping me in the middle of this crowded airport on my way to Paris and letting me know he was dying. *I should have stayed in Istanbul; Lemi and Seda were right, their worries were all fully justified and I haven't even set foot in Paris yet. I could take the plane back to Istanbul and forget about Paris.*

I stood in the same spot where Doru had left me and thought about my situation. I counted my money and saw with some satisfaction I had almost five hundred Turkish liras. Doru had paid for my plane ticket to Paris so I could keep everything I had made from selling my paintings and desserts in the streets of Istanbul. I smiled for a second, proud of the memory. In my amnesic state I had done some worthwhile things and actually led quite a productive life. Maybe I should force myself back into amnesia. But forgetfulness was not something you could impose on yourself. I counted the money again: four hundred and ninety-three liras. It cost less than that to buy a plane ticket. I looked left and right, trying to find a sign for a ticket counter. There were only signs for exits and other gates and baggage claim. Airports were a sanitized labyrinth.

A voice announced that my plane to Paris was embarking at Gate 96. I saw people rush towards the gate and was caught in the wave. I thought 96 was a good number, our house in

Mangalia was number 9, and I had known Anushka for six years, it contained my past and my future in one. Walking fast in front of me was an African woman in a multicoloured dress and turban, wiggling her hips and buttocks in a most delightful way. The colours of her dress made me think of Mariţa and I followed her to the embarkation gate. *What would Gigi advise me to do?* I wondered as I watched the African woman walk like she was dancing on clouds and wrapped in bright yellows and reds. He would say: 'Pursue your art'; he would say, like Uncle Doru, that I must grab on to my talent as if my life depended on it, because my life did depend on it. I realized I would probably never see Doru again. I held on to the last image of him walking through the crowd as nonchalant as ever, laughing at Death itself with a cigarette in the corner of his mouth. I kept walking behind the African woman to Gate 96, still not sure whether I shouldn't just turn round and find my way back to Istanbul. And then drown in Turkish desserts and become a fat amateur painter and cook. I felt as though I was moving towards my plane solely because I couldn't stop following the African woman in the yellow and red dress, while at the same time Istanbul was beckoning me with its wrenching blues and dazzling shine. This was how I got on the plane and found my seat, which luckily was right next to the woman. My seat was by the window and hers was next to me. I saw her face only when we were each getting into our seats. She had a wide-open face with enormous eyes that were calm and confident and she didn't smile either, just like I had never used to smile. She laughed though when the man behind us tried to help her place her bag in the overhead compartment. And when she laughed it was like a gust of spring suddenly touched and enveloped you.

I wanted to know why I was going to Paris. For the first fifteen minutes of the flight, I sat upright with my bag tight against my chest as if ready to leave the plane any second. Even after taking off, I still felt as though I could just walk out and take a leap into the thick rolls of cloud and trot back to Istanbul. I pursed my lips, closed my eyes, and tried very hard to concentrate on a list of reasons for going to Paris: 1. It was the city of art and I had always wanted to be an artist; 2. The artists who had meant most to me and my own artistic formation, with the exception of the fairytale Esma the Painter Woman, were French or had worked in France: Corot, Van Gogh, Gauguin, Delacroix, Dalì. 3. I knew French better than any other foreign language; 4. The Romanian sculptor Constantin Brancusi's greatest dream had been to live and work in Paris and he had walked there from his village in Wallachia with a small bag on his back and a walking stick that he had carved from the branch of a birch tree; 5. I knew a young woman called Anushka Pomorowska in Paris who had once made a promise that she would help me were I ever to come to Paris.

I had five strong reasons to go to Paris, besides the recent real or imaginary urgings of Gigi and Doru. It seemed as though the whole world was collaborating with my journey to Paris and my trying to settle there. I relaxed and looked over at the white immensity of sugary clouds. The best-known edifices of Paris were floating again over the feathery bubbles and Anushka reigned in the midst of it all in a silky red dress. A little miniature girl who looked like me and who had kept appearing to me during my amnesia period in Istanbul was also sitting on a cloud, cross-legged, her face scrunched up as if crying profusely and sorting out dresses that my mother had sewn: the red ones to the right, the yellow ones to the left and the blue ones in the middle. This was a mixture of the national colours of my birth country. It was a nationalistic painting.

I felt a gentle touch on my arm and someone pushing me lightly back in my seat. It was the African woman sitting next to me, who told me I had fallen asleep and I would be more comfortable that way. '*Tu es fatiguée*,' she said. This wasn't an astonishing observation but in the way she said it, in the low, serious pitch of her voice like the sweetest of lullabies, it sounded as if it contained some fundamental information about life and death. Indeed I was tired to a degree that would have required an uninterrupted year-long or century-long period of sleep. My whole being was shattered to its foundations, to the point where I wasn't sure who I was and where I was going and what the purpose of my life was.

'*Je m'appelle Agadira,*' said the woman, and she let me know that she was from Burkina Faso, a country I had never heard of in any of my geography lessons in Romania, nor had I seen it on any of Sabina's maps, and which sounded like an enchanted kingdom: a territory of princes and astounding flora and fauna. A territory in light browns, mellow blues and feathery pinks. This is how I imagined Burkina Faso. After I told Agadira my name and she laughed, saying it was a beautiful name, I wanted to know why she was going to Paris. Was she visiting someone? No, she lived in Paris, she was a refugee and her husband had brought her over three years ago. He had left first. She had visited her family in Burkina Faso and now was returning to Paris. Lucky her, I thought, she could go back and forth to visit her family in the savannahs of Burkina Faso, then come back to Paris where a husband waited for her. I could never go back, I had no idea what was happening to my family.

'Why are *you* going to Paris?' she asked, wrapping herself more closely in the aircraft blanket.

My mouth was clamped shut, unable to open. I conjured up the reasons on my list and the mythic and venerable Constantin Brancusi appeared in front of my eyes with his Father Time beard and walking stick, like the man who had guided us through the Limanu labyrinth on that sun-glazed August afternoon. Yes, he was the father of conceptual sculpture, a genius now known and revered all over the world whose works rested serenely in museums from Paris to New York. But so what? How did that concern me? What I had once thought in my country before escaping did not hold true any longer. I did not want any of this freedom. I didn't know what it meant, and what to do with it, since I felt so broken and without purpose.

I stared blankly at Agadira and all I could think of was that it would be so unimaginably comforting to lie next to her in a bed or a tent in Burkina Faso or on another planet, to cuddle next to her plump body the way I had once cuddled next to Mariţa in her tent the night I had found out Valentin was coming to live with us for good, the way I had slept next to my mother the night I was agonizing over Gigi and Anushka. And if I did that, somehow, miraculously, I would be put back together. I just needed a deep sleep next to a woman like Agadira here, who smelled like the sun and earth of Burkina Faso. I didn't know what the sun and earth of Burkina Faso smelled like but I imagined they smelled like Agadira: slightly sweet and mellow, a little pungent, like the spices Camelia was cooking when Gigi and I walked into her house the night of Mariţa's death.

She stroked my face and said again: '*Oh, tu es fatiguée, ma petite, tu dois te reposer.*' Just like Seda had kept saying I needed to rest in the early days of my stay in her Istanbul house. Becoming an immigrant is an exhausting business, because you are always on the run. Then Agadira asked me if I knew anyone in Paris, who was waiting for me at the airport? I said Anushka was waiting for me. Who was Anushka, a friend? I said, yes, a friend, I had saved her life once. Agadira said that meant we were family, we were kin, '*parents*', she said. I thought *parents* meant your mother and father. Certainly Anushka wasn't anything like that to me. But Agadira said once you saved someone's life you became '*parents, famille*'. Parents also meant family in French and Anushka was now family to me. Certainly she had to help me when I went to Paris. Agadira gave me her phone number and address and told me to call her if I needed anything. This is what people did to me: they gave me their phone numbers, they told me important secrets and existential advice and then they left or died. They left me alone to deal with the wide world. When we parted after leaving the plane, Agadira told me I was in charge. 'In charge of what?' I asked. 'Of your life,' she said. And she wiggled her luscious body draped in bright yellows through the crowd.

The closer I got to the waiting area, the more certain I was that Anushka would not be there. The passage through customs and immigration was agonizing. Three different men came and looked at my Turkish papers. They talked among themselves, smoked, laughed. What entertainment to have a confused refugee as the target of jokes! I didn't want to go to Paris and start my life in that great city of art after all. The officer who was smoking asked me if I was '*gitane*', a Gypsy. I guess with my wild brown hair grown wilder and darker since my escape, my weathered complexion from all the time I had spent in the sun and wind of the Bosphorus peninsula and on the streets of Istanbul, I could pass for a Gypsy. Maybe I had acquired a certain ease of manner too from having been unhinged, unleashed, hit by forgetfulness and then by remembrance like two merciless waves striking me on the head consecutively and pulling the earth from under my feet. A hoarse whispered '*oui*' came out of my mouth. In the whole misery and humiliation of that moment, closed up within a glass cubicle with three French customs and immigration officers smoking their stinking Gitanes in my face, I experienced my first moment of hard crystal joy in a long time. Taking on the identity of the most wretched of the earth. If I was to be wretched I might as well be so all the way. Then I could be truly defiant at the whole arrangement of this world as I knew it. Ride my own caravan of misery through the streets of that art-filled Paris and flaunt all the colours that seethed in my brain in a relentless swirl of ragged skirts and shredded heart.

Holding my suitcase in my smaller hand and my bag over my larger shoulder, stinking of the Gitanes cigarettes of the three callous customs officers, and emboldened with anger and a new pride in my poverty as part of my recently acquired Gypsy identity, I walked through the swing doors of international arrivals in Charles de Gaulle Airport looking for Anushka but prepared not to find her. My instincts had been right, for she was not there. Valentin too was right: I knew how to read people and therefore could sometimes predict the future. There was no witchcraft, just sound intuition. Anushka's ups and downs on the phone and her vague, rushed answers about picking me up at the airport told me there was something wrong with her, with the person I knew as Anushka. That she might not be the person I thought she was.

After changing my Turkish liras into many notes of French francs I went out into the October air. I had Anushka's address and phone number and a handful of French money, not bad for a Romanian Turkish Gypsy girl taking on Paris. I found out from the bus driver that Rue Lecourbe was near Trocadéro. We crossed the city in the falling dusk. After the delirium of colours and the throbbing life of Istanbul, Paris seemed grey and drab. It reminded me of Bucharest, the large boulevards and all the grey, grey stone buildings lining them. Yes, it was beautiful, classic, romantically decadent, but where was the sea? The absence of a large body of water that glimpsed from a street corner and that burst in your eyes and consciousness, the way the sea did in my native town, shocked me. The sluggish Seine with all its stone embankments and baroque bridges didn't really count as water for me. I howled inwardly on the bus that made its way towards Trocadéro because of the absence of the sea. I understood now that Paris was a city where you could think of suicide and actually pursue it. Between the romantic glamour of Notre Dame and the bustle of the glittering Champs-Elysées, there was a sad, liminal area: waterless streets and districts weeping with loneliness and desolation, drunken men propped against a pole, street women on the lookout for emerging clients, a woman with a lost, hopeless air, walking with her face to the ground, a stray dog, someone with his hands in his pockets, not caring about anything. You saw how it might all seem so hollow and colourless, how in one second you would want out and it would seem a relief.

The bus left me a little way from Rue Lecourbe and I thought I would just walk. It turned out to be a longer walk than I had expected but the autumn evening air revived me after my wretched day in airports and planes. Modern, clean, promising. I pressed on the intercom button for number 10. No answer. I pushed again and again. No answer. The concierge was getting ready to leave and asked me who I was looking for. I said Anushka Pomorowska. He said no one by that name lived there. I said her name again, slowly, like talking to a deaf person. He said again that nobody by the name Anushka Pomorowska lived in that building. He left lighting a cigarette. The earth was shifting under my feet at an astonishing speed. I had to hold on to the building's wall not to faint from dizziness. What now? Where was I supposed to drag my tired person at this hour of the evening in this city of lights?

As I was leaning against the building staring at an old woman walking her dog on Rue Lecourbe, and reviewing my options, it seemed I heard a whine, something like a thin wail, produced by an animal in pain and yet human. Almost obscene. I looked to my right, to where the building ended and a small alley started, and I saw a woman propped against the wall of the building, coiling, writhing, embracing the wall and moaning in a most troubling way. I stared at her too, in the absence of anything else to do, and had a feeling I knew the woman. In fact she looked like Anushka. She turned round with her back to the building and her face looking upward at the greyish October sky. It *was* Anushka. Only she appeared smaller than I had remembered her and she seemed drunk and in some kind of pain. I didn't care if she was drunk, I was just happy to see a familiar human on my first evening in Paris after a day when everything seemed to have gone so wrong. I rushed over to Anushka and stood in front of her, trying to hug her. But when I looked closer she terrified me. Her face was gaunt and yellowish, her teeth were chattering and her pupils had a strange way of gliding loosely and showing the whites of her eyes. This was more than drunk. I had been right: it was her, but she was not herself. She smiled when she saw me and then I could recognize the old Anushka I had known at the beach six years ago. There was something so infinitely sad and terrifying about her face and her entire demeanour that I forgot how lost I was and worried about what I could do to help her. Maybe she was dying of a deadly disease. Maybe she had developed serious mental problems.

The first thing she said was: 'Do you have some? I am missing.' I didn't know what she could possibly be missing, and what it was that I might have. Maybe she still missed her motorcyclist friend who had died, maybe that had been such a powerful love that she really was destroyed by his death. But then she grabbed me by the collar of my coat and said again if I had any, to give her some. '*Je suis en manque*,' she kept saying.

How wrong I had been to believe that because I had saved Anushka's life once she would now 'save' me in some way as I was starting a new life in Paris. Life didn't work that way, it wasn't like the fish fairy tale where the little girl saves someone and that someone does something for her in return. I had to try to save Anushka again and could expect no help from her. She was a heroin addict, and was ferociously looking for her fix every hour of the day. I had indeed been to the building where she had her apartment, but the name on the intercom was still that of the previous owner, or boyfriend, or a rich uncle, it was impossible to get a straight answer about anything from Anushka. A man called Guy Laurent had owned it before and the new concierge had no idea of the names of all the people living there. The flat had been a nice modern space at one time, with all the utilities, and a pretty view of red and grey Parisian roofs and back yards. Now it was filthy, and strewn from its little entrance hall all the way to the potentially charming kitchen with anything from syringes and needles to human refuse of the most disgusting kind. This was some kind of hell I had to go through and it wasn't clear why. Maybe entering the space of that prehistoric Limanu cave on those August days had roused some really bad cosmic energies, the revenge of the murdered Dacians on a descendant of the criminal Romans. Maybe the entire mechanism of my destiny on this planet had been broken at some point and had gone haywire: the brutal separation from my twin brother as a very young child, the ferocious anger and pain that my mother had poured into me over the years, the abortion I had had in the apartment in Balta Alba, the mistake I had made in asking Mariţa to help Camelia that led to her death, the leap into the Black Sea on 11 August. Something was out of kilter, the right equation had been lost and I was spiralling down into a dark tunnel towards the lowest of human misery.

I didn't want to touch anything in Anushka's apartment, as everything made me sick even to look at it. I didn't know how and where I was going to sleep, where I was going to stay. At some point in my first night in her apartment, somebody rang the doorbell and a tall man dressed in a trench coat brought over her dose for an immediate fix. I was drifting in and out of a painful, terrified sleep. I had found a small sofa in a corner of Anushka's front room that seemed to have less filth on it, pushed everything off it on to the floor with the tip of my shoe, found some medicinal alcohol in the devastated bathroom, poured it all over the sofa in an attempt to disinfect it and wrapped myself in several of Seda's dresses and shawls that I had brought in my little red leather suitcase. Since I had landed in Lemi and Seda's house in a wetsuit and with a tin box as my only possession, almost everything I owned had come from Seda. The rolled-up paintings I had made were mine, and a set of colours and a paintbrush I had bought with my own money in Istanbul. I had a few coloured silk dresses, a couple of sweaters and the *hijab.* I wrapped myself that first night in Anushka's apartment in the Muslim dress, as a protection against the reeking filth and degradation all around me.

Like never before in my life, I called on the names of the figures known as divinities: Jesus, Allah, the Virgin Mary, St Peter. I conjured up forces I didn't really believe in, on the off chance they might actually exist and felt neglected and vengeful at my lack of respect for them. I figured the united forces of Jesus and Allah might be more helpful than either of them alone, and I needed the help of all the divinities in the world to get me out of the mess I was in. Why had I saved Anushka from the sea? I kept asking myself between a fitful sleep and an agonizing wakefulness. After she got her fix and had her rush late into the night, she became joyful and played obnoxious loud music on the tape recorder. She tried to get me up from the sofa where I had made my nest to dance with her. I hit her so she would leave me alone. I pushed my nose into Seda's fabrics which smelled of Turkish desserts and incense and slept until a grey dawn seeped its sad light through the windows of Anushka's apartment.

Paris Street Corners

I look for the sea at every street corner. I walk fast through the busy Parisian crowds, my head to the ground and with only one goal in mind: to get to the end of the street, to get to the corner, because maybe once I turn that corner I will look up and the sea will stretch out in front of me and I will finally be able to relax. I will drink it all in and my tense body and achy eyes will be soothed by the sight. But it's always a deceit, it's never there. Boulevard Saint-Germain, yes, beautiful stores and cafés, famous cafés once frequented by famous existentialist authors who apparently drowned in cigarette butts, elegant women in high heels, architectural masterpieces of Haussmann, lots of traffic, keep walking, keep walking, you will eventually hit the corner, just a little bit more, there, you see where the street curves, then you will probably get to the sea. But it's just more architectural masterpieces and stores and cafés and no sea in sight. The same if I go on the smaller streets, La Huchette, or the in-between streets, Richelieu, or the very street where I live, Lecourbe, it's always the same game of looking for the sea and never finding it. It's how I push myself to move through this city so heavy laden with grey stone and marble buildings and with so many cars and buses. I have to tell myself that if I keep going I will eventually find the sea.

I know there is the famous Seine, in whose waves all the architectural masterpieces from Gothic churches to baroque palaces to modern apartment buildings sway and shimmer in languorous reflections and along which so many lovers walk hand in hand or in which some dejected lovers have ended their days, but the Seine is not the Black Sea. Sometimes, as an extension to my game of 'find the sea around the corner', I stand on a bridge and stare into the distance down the long, flowing river, imagining that at the furthest point, where it all becomes blurry with trees and small buildings, the sea might actually surprise you: the sluggish river might in fact erupt like the Danube into a tumultuous delta and open up into an immense expanse of water that surrounds you on three sides. And there you will be, looking at Notre Dame from the middle of the violet Black Sea. This game works well on foggy days, when the far end looks vague and watery and the boats gliding on the Seine may just fool you that they are sailing towards the salty waves.

I delay as much as possible getting back to Anushka's apartment on Rue Lecourbe, sometimes until late into the night. As sea-deprived as the streets of Paris may be, I prefer them to Anushka's apartment. On some nights I ask Mme Tournelle, at the *boulangerie* where I work on Rue du Cherche-Midi, to let me clean up and close the store. At first she thought it was because I wanted to steal bread and cakes and I heard her tell her husband on the phone that '*La petite roumaine est un peu bizarre . . . elle veut rester après . . . oui, je sais . . . les roumains, il faut faire attention . . .*' When I heard her say that you had to watch out with Romanians, I filled my pockets with croissants and my mouth with half a white bread roll and pretended to cross the store quietly with large thief steps, as if wanting to get away. Then I turned round, took out all the croissants and said: '*Oh, excusez-moi, madame, est-ce que je peux voler tout ça?*' I wanted the satisfaction of that silly prank even at the risk of getting the sack. The twenty-something refugee that I was, acting like a bratty teenager! Mme Tournelle turned as scarlet as the ripe raspberries on our tarts and stared at me for a few seconds, not knowing what to do. Then she actually apologized, she said: '*Je suis desolée, vraiment, ma petite Nora, excuse-moi, je parle des bêtises.*' After that she told me to call her Mimi and we became good friends. A classic immigrant-in-France story, I guess, first they insult you by telling you that you don't belong and you are a thief, and then they befriend you because they feel sorry for having insulted you. And at the end they always call you 'little'. I loved Mimi from the *boulangerie,* though, she reminded me of Gigi's mother Sabina: she was thin and freckled and apparently subdued, particularly when her moustached loud-voiced husband appeared. But she had a wild streak and I suspected she had a lover, from some phone calls she received near closing time and which she always answered in her most velvety, alluring voice, as if cream and chocolate mousse were flowing on her tongue. Once I found her dancing by herself in the back of the store to a Johnny Hallyday song. She didn't stop when she saw me, but grabbed me and had me dance with her in the little space filled with golden baguettes, fruit tarts and almond croissants.

'*Oh, ça fait du bien,*' she said afterwards. Then the phone rang and her voice became chocolate mousse again and she left an hour earlier than usual, telling me she had a doctor's appointment. I winked at her and thought to myself, *Quite some doctor, I hope the treatment is good.* Then I felt limp the way I always do whenever I do or say something funny or engage in something pleasurable. Because immediately the thought of Gigi and what he would have done or said, or how he would have smiled, erupts in my head. Gigi is my constantly erupting inner volcano. My inner voice, my alter ego, my shadow. Sometimes I have a bizarre feeling that he is actually watching me from somewhere and I become particularly self-conscious. Especially late in the evening when I am all alone in Mimi's store and the street is quieting down and I see the silhouettes of people passing by one after the other. Suddenly I think that one of those shadows is going to be him, that somehow he escaped from prison, or they let him go, and by some miracle he ran away by hiding in the belly of a Turkish ship and made it to Paris right here on Rue du Cherche-Midi, because of all the streets in Paris he would know I would work or live on a street with a nostalgic name that was code for something that had to do with the sea, with our home town, with our love: Rue du Cherche-Midi, Search for the South Street.

The very day after my arrival in Paris, I engaged in a fight for life with Anushka and with myself. With Anushka to get her to break away from the hideous monster that was heroin and with myself not to jump into the Seine or slice my wrists with the kitchen knife the way my Aunt Raluca had tried to do. Agadira was my saviour during those first months. When she came over the next day after a desperate phone call from me, begging her to help me out, she first said: '*Oh mon Dieu de la France, que c'est sale, ça pue!*' Agadira was always calling on the God of France. She thought God had helped France more than other countries and the French had made good use of their resources and the help of the Almighty. Considering how badly some countries were doing, in her opinion France was pretty good. Here almost everybody could read and write, while Burkina Faso had the highest illiteracy rate in the world. She laughed her coming-of-spring laugh, saying that at least her country came first in something: the number of illiterate people. But in the few photographs she showed me of her family and home town, everybody looked joyous and everything was bursting with colour. I was yet to become as appreciative of my new city and the French Republic and its God as Agadira was. I sometimes thought that the Communist propaganda that was injected into our brains in the Mangalia high school and in high schools across the country with the same perseverance that Anushka was injecting the noxious heroin into her veins, about the capitalist world and the Western countries being centres of decadence, drug addiction, pornography and ruthless consumerism, was not too far from the truth. I had never believed one word of it then and was craving a taste of that decadence, as I listened greedily to the music of Pink Floyd and Abba, Johnny Hallyday and Edith Piaf, Queen and Dire Straits and fantasized about a free world filled with rhythm and opportunity through which I would walk nonchalantly, my hands in my pockets, or my easel under my arm, painting, dancing, loving Gigi.

After she made her salutation to the God of France, Agadira ran to the nearest store to buy detergents, then got down on her hands and knees and started scrubbing the floors. She had flooded them with soapy water first, so the lemony smells of the detergents were slowly replacing the stink of vomit and rotting refuse in the apartment. I got down on the floor with her and we scrubbed and cleaned everything furiously, while Anushka was slowly waking up from her drugged slumber and starting to feel the withdrawal effects. She stared at us, puzzled, and uttered French swear words. Her speech was slurred and her pupils miniscule which made her eyes look even smaller, like those of a bird. Agadira got up and stood in her way. She grabbed Anushka by the straps of her negligee and told her she had to promise right there that she was going to give the drugs up. I still couldn't figure out what kind of inexorable pain, madness or dissatisfaction could have pushed Anushka on to the hellish road of drug addiction. But Agadira understood it all, she had seen everything, she had seen worse, she said, and I couldn't imagine what exactly could be worse than where Anushka was except death. And in comparison, maybe death was better. I told Agadira I didn't believe there was worse. And she stood up proudly and stubbornly in front of me and said: 'Trust me, there is worse.' Agadira knew about life's worst miseries and darkest places.

This is why I run and walk quickly through the streets of

Paris, always hurrying to get to the corner, trying to keep myself occupied every moment of the day, to fill the holes and the abyss with colour and substance and little trinkets and fruit tarts and almond croissants in Mimi's *boulangerie*, when I am not helping Anushka through her withdrawals. She says every time: 'This will be the last, I promise I will stop, may God hit and strike me, this one now is the very last and I will pull through.' And even when she does manage to keep her promise for a few days, she always goes back to the drug in less than a week. Agadira told me there was no rule for how to save someone's life, or what you could expect from people, that Anushka was like family, that life had brought us together in a most unusual way, and that I had to help her out. Just because I had pulled her out of the water during a storm, which is what every human being should want to do when they see a fellow human drowning, there was no rule which said that I could expect anything back from Anushka. Right now, I just had to keep on saving Anushka, and that was all. Agadira is like a goddess of wisdom pronouncing immortal aphorisms, shining in her bright African dresses and singing praise to the God of France. I sometimes thank the God of France too for Agadira.

On my way back from the *boulangerie* on Rue du Cherche-Midi, I walk slowly, delaying as much as I can my entry into the lobby of Lecourbe 27 and into apartment 10, wondering whether Anushka is going to be on a new high, dancing on the tables, immersed in her rush, or writhing on the floor and begging for a fix. Tonight I play the 'find the sea in the middle of Paris' game with more intensity than ever. The spring air is waking up something in me, I am not sure if there is anything left in me to be woken up, but my nostrils are alert to the smells and my ears are catching the sounds: young people greeting each other with explosions of laughter, an Edith Piaf song trailing its way out of a brasserie, traders advertising their hot crepes or glow-in-the-dark bracelets, artists calling out to tourists for quick portraits or caricatures, scents of fresh bread and hyacinths, the sour tar smell from a newly paved road and jasmine perfume from an elegant woman rushing towards her lover. Tonight I sort of understand Paris and the big deal people make about it. I kind of get why Brancusi wanted to come here and why he set out walking towards it for a month with his birchwood stick. Tonight I am grudgingly starting to like Paris. Out of my pain and confusion, and fear and weariness, solidarity with the other sad, desperate people of the city is starting to emerge and a feeling that you should hang on to life in this Parisian spring night.

I am standing on Pont de la Tournelle, one of the less glamorous bridges of Paris, asymmetrical like myself, and built over an asymmetrical part of the river bank, with the austere statue of St Genevieve thrusting towards the Parisian sky. It also has the same name as my boss Mimi. The similarity gives me an enhanced sense of familiarity with the city, as I can connect the name of someone I work for, who is becoming something of a friend, with the name of a place. Connections make you grow roots in a place, just like I always connected piano music in Bucharest with the State Circus because that's where Valentin and I went on the evening of my first art lesson and of his resuming piano lessons. I am squinting the way I always do when I play this game. I am staring into the distance, trying to guide my mind towards a sea painting, working on my usual fantasy of having the Black Sea emerge out of the Seine, far away where the weeping willows on both banks almost seem to merge with each other and with the sky and the pointy Gothic towers. The *bateaux-mouches* are starting to glitter on the Seine, the lights are flickering in the distance along the river, and there she is: the Black Sea, *my* Black Sea, dark violet and brooding, rustling in the Parisian night, unfolding its capricious waves on the right bank and on the left. In the centre of it Nora and Gigi's fishing boat is gliding towards sunrise, and the two of them are embracing in the moonlight, wreaths of algae in their hair, Flood of Moonlight floating nearby: a Parisian Balkan water wedding with day and night combined.

Art, Drugs, Dresses and Emigrés

I have not been to the Louvre, or to the Musée de l'Orangerie, I have not been to the Jeu de Paume Museum, or to the Rodin Museum, I have not visited the Ecole Nationale des Beaux Arts for possible classes, and I have not pursued my talent as Doru had advised me or Gigi would have urged me to do. Surviving in Paris and struggling with Anushka's addiction are occupying all my time and energy. I might as well be living in Siberia for all the culture and excitement I enjoy in this great European city.

I am now convinced that death is better than drugs. If anybody asked me right now to choose whether to be like Anushka or to die, I would say without a second's hesitation: 'Take me out, shoot me, poison me, hang me right now, only don't let me be like Anushka.' She does not cling to her life but to her drug addiction, she does not care about her body and her needs but about serving this serum that goes through her battered veins for the few hours of a demented rush. Her face is ashen, her body a tapestry of red and blue needle marks, and her speech an incoherent flow, a blurred wailing complaint, an outburst of obscenities, or a rushed high-pitched series of broken sentences. Sometimes when I remember how radiant and luscious Anushka was at the beach six years ago when Gigi and I saved her from the storm, and I look at her now, between her false ecstasies and her pitiable withdrawals, I want to sit down and cry for her decay. But mostly I want to cry for my own bad luck in starting my Paris life in the miasma of a heroin addict. I also wonder where is Anushka getting all the money to pay for her drugs, who owns or pays for her apartment, who is this M. Guy Laurent whose name is on the mailbox and the intercom?

Once a week I sleep at Agadira's place so I can get a good night's rest. When her husband Hajid works the night shift at the hospital, I get my wish: I sleep next to Agadira in her low hard bed covered with coloured blankets from her native province of Boulgou and I delight in the feeling of safety and comfort that her full, fragrant body exudes. Agadira treats me as if I was her child, she feeds me an African dish made of lamb, peanuts and okra, and she gently pulls the covers over me at night. She lives in an old apartment building near Pigalle Street and the Moulin Rouge, the neighbourhood native Parisians like Mme Tournelle refer to as the district of prostitutes and immigrants, delinquents and drug dealers. Mme Tournelle always lumps immigrants and delinquents in the same sentence when she talks to me about social problems in Paris, and then giggles with a little shrug of her shoulders. The building where Agadira lives is not the cleanest in the world, but the two rooms of her apartment are spotless and shiny. It is filled with colourful hangings, cushions, pottery and masks from Burkina Faso and it smells of incense and spicy sauces made with saffron and cardamom.

I give Agadira a full report of my week and tell her that once I have saved enough money I will move out of Anushka's apartment and she can rot there, choking on her own heroin puke. Agadira never says anything to that, she shakes her head, serves me the food, but then later on says something wise like: 'We have to care for those who are fallen and cannot rise by themselves,' or cryptic riddles such as: 'When you are at your weakest you are strongest.' Agadira combines her Sufi Muslim beliefs with shreds of Catholicism and native Burkina Faso superstitions, and this religious medley gives her the strength to walk proudly and wiggle her plump body through all the hardships of life and the seedy streets of her neighbourhood, while also caring for those even more in need than her. Those like me.

I sometimes revolt at Agadira's implied messages that I should keep on helping Anushka until I die of exhaustion or burst with disgust and I tell her that I wish I had let Anushka drown that summer afternoon at the beach in Mangalia, and that she would be better off dead. Agadira doesn't say anything but I know what she is thinking.

One day she raises her shiny black eyes to me and says: 'Let's make a plan about Anushka. Let's work together and get her off the drug. But this time really stick to it. We'll take turns being with her during the withdrawals. Are you ready? And if we can't do it by the end of the month, you can move in here with Hajid and me and find a place for yourself when you can afford it and let her die as you wish.' She waits, eats another spoonful of the lamb stew, and then she asks: '*C'est d'accord?*' It sounds a fair arrangement to me, and I particularly like the finite quality of this deal, the fact that there is an end in sight, one way or another.

Agadira tells me to arm myself with all the patience and compassion I have left, and I am thinking that I have none left, but I just nod and say: '*Oui, oui.*' She tells me to find as many things to do as possible during the days I am off duty and also to sleep well on my off nights, as it will be a day-and-night operation. She talks as if we were setting out to build the Eiffel Tower all over again, but she insists that this is hard work and I should look on it as work. Saving someone from destruction is work just like any other, only more important, she tells me. Because I know this plan will be carried out in a month and then I'll be free, I say *oui* to everything Agadira imposes.

I buy myself an old sewing machine from an antique shop, and lots of coloured fabrics from the Marché aux Puces at St-Ouen, where Agadira takes me for a pre-ordeal fun afternoon. I buy drawing paper, canvas, watercolours, tempera and oil paints for some painting I want to do on the 'off days', as Agadira puts it. And I buy a clown costume I find in a pile of old clothes, in a moment of nostalgia for the circus days in my country. Maybe I can even have my own little circus on the 'off days'. Let the show begin; let the lions leap through the hula hoops.

The month of April is a wild carousel of excruciating struggles with Anushka's illness on the 'work' days and demented rushing from one activity to another on the 'rest days' so I can fill every moment with something that occupies my mind and hands. I sleep only every other night, and then for an hour or two in the afternoon during the days off. Paris is bursting with tulips and roses and everywhere you look the city is acquiring a little more colour. I do what my mother did during our investigations to keep myself from crumbling into a million pieces: sew dresses and curtains, tablecloths and bed sheets. But mostly I sew dresses, loose skirts and blouses that are easy to tailor. Some are coloured like Agadira's clothing, others checkered black and white, others pink-based pastels. Anushka's apartment is becoming almost cheerful and I get to look more and more like a circus performer every day. In Mimi's shop, I start introducing all the Turkish desserts that I learned to prepare in Istanbul and her clientele is growing. When an old customer compliments her on the little pistachio and almond paste cakes, she laughs and says it's '*la petite roumaine*'. She says that I am talented and the risk of hiring me paid off, although I looked like a *gitane*, a Gypsy girl, when I first walked in. Whenever I hear her say something insulting like that from the back room when my hands are sunk deep in a gooey blob of dough, I come out all covered in flour and say that I *am* a Gypsy, a Romanian Gypsy, and everybody had better watch their wallets, don't they know all Romanians and all Gypsies are thieves? And I am doubly that, being a

Romanian Gypsy refugee. Mimi Tournelle invariably blushes to her earlobes and I never understand why she plays this game of pretending she doesn't know I can hear every nasty word from the back room. Her customers laugh and think I am '*si drôle*'. Lack of sleep and the fight with Anushka make me unstoppable. I sweep over everyone and everything like a tempestuous wave. Paris might be sorely deficient where the sea is concerned, but I am becoming my own Black Sea.

I go to the Louvre for the first time and join the groups of art students copying the various masterpieces as part of their training. I sit a little bit at a distance yet close by as if I was part of the group, but not really, and I do everything they do on my drawing pad: copy the figures of women in Rubens paintings, the Madonnas in the Italian Renaissance section, the busts in the Greek and Roman classical section. I take a break from my own style of unleashed fantastical forms and colours, and follow the art students at the Ecole Nationale des Beaux Arts, pretending I am pursuing a course of study. Pretending I am with them. The revered Venus de Milo at the top of the marble staircase gives me shivers of anger with her perfectly shaped, perfectly even breasts and thighs and that tilted head fabricated from a man's vision of female perfection. I delight in her missing arms! That's my favourite part of the Venus de Milo.

I get nauseous and dizzy at the sight of the hundreds of larger-than-life naked female bodies bursting from every room in the Louvre like cascades of useless flesh. I am raw and have my hands sunk deep in a woman's personal tragedy and I want to slap the Mona Lisa with her smug smile. What did those painters know of a woman's despair, passions or self-loathing? And where are the women painters, I keep asking as I move frantically from one salon of canvases as big as boats to another salon of canvases by Romantic or Renaissance painters gone wild on female flesh? The Delacroix paintings infuriate me now that I see them life-size. I am outraged that the concubine of Sardanapalus looks as if she is enjoying herself and stretching out in ecstasy while a ferocious bearded man plunges a knife into her jugular. The much larger-than-life dimensions of the oil painting, three hundred by four hundred centimetres, its chaos of raw carnality and violence in bright reds, blacks and flesh colour, throw me into spasms of rage. How wrong I have been to make fun of Didona and call her Sardanapalus's concubine. It is Delacroix who is making fun of Sardanapalus's concubine and her humiliation by representing her as if she was in ecstasy while being raped and killed. I wonder what arenas and cupolas of the world Didona may be twirling in right now?

Why did everybody send me to Paris, didn't they know that women don't get into the Louvre unless they are naked models or eager visitors? I think of Anushka's emaciated figure, once similar to the shape of this Venus de Milo with arms and all, of the map of needle marks on every joint of her body, of her trembling arms holding on to me and begging for 'just a little bit of a dose, just this one time and that's all, I promise, Nora, I swear to you'. And Anushka's eyes . . . the eyes are the worst, as they beg, cry, bulge in fury, watery in infinite sadness. I see Anushka sweating, Anushka shivering and her teeth chattering like she was either under the African sun or naked on the Alaskan ice. It is now, as I run through room after room of rosy, fleshy, curvaceous, dull-eyed female bodies on gigantic canvases and think of Anushka in the Lecourbe apartment, that I am gripped by an unbearable pity for her. What and who could have pushed her into such a reckless path of self-destruction? What is Anushka's story? Why does she not have anyone but a post-amnesic Romanian Turkish Gypsy refugee and an overworked Burkina Faso immigrant to help her?

It occurs to me as I am staring at another batch of rosy Rubens females, that Anushka is so frighteningly alone in her apartment on Rue Lecourbe, and despite everything I have been through I have never been as lonely as she is. It is now, as I am copying portraits and nudes and imitating the students at the Parisian art schools, pretending I am pursuing my painting career, and seeing that I can sketch those nudes and portraits better and quicker than any of them, that I start to love Anushka and pity her misery.

I run through the hallways of the Louvre searching for the Millets, the Courbets, the Barbizon school, the Van Goghs. I am searching for the desperate painters, the artists of the wretched and the unfortunate, of golden flowers bursting out of misery and suicidal wishes. But they are nowhere to be found. I must be in the wrong museum.

In the prints and drawings section of the Louvre, I run into Goya's sketch that portrays a scrawny human figure carrying a frightening burden on his head. It's the first work that speaks to me. It's about Nora and Anushka and Agadira, about them carrying burdens much heavier than they have strength for and yet they are still breathing, crying and holding each other in that grey dusk that descends every evening over the apartment in Rue Lecourbe. With an ominous, back-breaking bulk of suffering that looks like a giant's fist on their heads, just like Goya's man. This little sketch by Francisco Goya is the first that makes me happy and I search for other Goyas in this labyrinth of a museum. This painter knew about female anguish. I sob in front of the portrait of the Marquise de la Solana because she looks so much like my mother: dark, fierce, severe, staring at you without shame and dressed in black. My mother could have dressed like that and looked like that if she had been the pianist she had wanted to be, and if her father hadn't been killed with an axe for a sentence he had uttered, and if she hadn't torn from her breast her green-eyed boy and given him away. Except maybe for the pink bow in the marquise's hair. I don't think my mother would ever have worn a pink bow in her hair. But she would have looked just as proud and majestic, a fierce matron of the Black Sea. Playing Chopin's études and Italian tarantellas on our grand piano on a wintry day, notes flying from under her fingers in waves like those of the tumultuous sea. It is only now that I start forgiving my mother for unleashing her cruel words throughout my childhood and adolescence, as I imagine she is starting really to love me now that I am so far away. Now, when we are irreparably separated, my mother is painfully blooming in front of my eyes in the poetic incarnation of Goya's Marquise de la Solana in a black dress and a pink bow.

I am at the end of the twentieth day of our common struggle with Anushka, and today's crisis is in its calming phase. She has been through the shivers, the sweating, the vomiting, the arching of the back and the excruciating hurting and throbbing. Sometimes we are engaged in a life-and-death wrestling match, with our bodies entwined, Anushka trying to destroy everything around her and tear her own body apart, and me holding and tying her down, lying on her, even punching her in order to exhaust her. Once we actually started this ferocious game, I was shocked to discover that the monstrous craving for a fix gives Anushka equally monstrous physical strength.

We were set back a few days because once when I was in the bathroom taking a shower, Anushka was able to get another dose from someone who must have arrived at the speed of lightning when she phoned. I also learned that drug addicts have an intense social life, huge networks of other addicts and dealers. When I got out of the shower Anushka was calm, rosy and humming the '*Alouette, gentille alouette*' song. I knew her rush would soon fade and the sadness and drowsiness would set in and then the vomiting would start. I wanted to beat her up and tear out her blonde hair. She promised again it was going to be the very, very last fix, '*Je te le jure, Nora.*' When Agadira came for her shift we made a pact that Anushka couldn't be left unsupervised for even a single moment. We weren't going to shower on our work days and we would go to the bathroom with the door open. We couldn't take naps while we were taking care of Anushka either. The lack of sleep made me want to kill people and eat raw flesh. Often in the very second before plunging into sleep like into black water from where I never wanted to come out, a thought would sting me: how much better than this my life in Romania was! Even under the dictatorship, even with my neurotic mother, even having failed my university exams, even with the illegal abortion, even with the investigations, it all seemed like a lost fairy tale compared to this Goya nightmare. What universal sins have I been expiating and why did I ever want to leave my country, and then once I had left, why did I have to leave Istanbul where everything seemed so sweet and easy? I would have had a better life in Istanbul. I cursed this city of lights, which had been just darkness for me.

It is six in the evening and I have two more hours before Agadira gets here from her work as a cleaner in the hospital where her husband Hajid is a nurse. I am counting the seconds until I see her luminous round face and shiny eyes and hear her exclaim about the good God of France helping us all. Anushka has just dozed off after her withdrawal peak. I go to the kitchen to make myself a sandwich and throw some cold water on my face. I let the water run, the sound is soothing. I try to imagine the waves of the Black Sea rustling against the shore. On a spring night in April with forsythias in bloom and chicory flowers on the golden sand. I slice the baguette I brought home from Mimi Tournelle's *boulangerie* with the big kitchen knife and put whatever I find in the refrigerator in between the halves: cheese, tomatoes, onions, ham, fruit, vegetables, trying to get all my nutrition at once. My sandwich is salad and soup and dessert in one. I am wearing three of my home-made dresses one on top of the other: the longest black and white first, the pink and mauve one with geometrical shapes second, and the last one made of orange and cyclamen flowery cotton right on top of the other two. The many layers of cloth and colours make me feel protected and my own circus-like appearance helps me push along my cartful of miseries.

I am also wearing a red bow in my hair, like Goya's Marquise de la Solana is wearing her pink bow, right in the front, on the left side. Although it is spring and I am inside the apartment, I am wearing the boots that Agadira gave me at the beginning of winter: heavy, brown thick leather boots up to my knees.

I am standing in the kitchen enjoying my sandwich and staring at the Parisian roofs glistening in the sunset when I hear voices in the other room: Anushka's voice, plaintive, almost crying, and a man's voice, edgy, hoarse. I hear Anushka begging: '*Guy, je t'en prie, seulement cette fois.*' Guy says: '*La pute est là?*', is the bitch here? I don't wait for Anushka's answer but pick up the kitchen knife in my right hand, my smaller, stronger hand, and the long ice pick from beside the sink in my left, my longer hand. I am not sure how but before either of them can say another word, I am holding this Guy character, a small, balding man, by the collar of his maroon leather jacket with the kitchen knife pointed at his jugular and the ice pick at his scrotum. I poke him with the ice pick while still holding the knife at his jugular. All my unslept nights, all the vomit I cleaned off Anushka, all my crushed dreams of becoming an artist, the horror of having lost everyone I had once loved, the black fantasy of Gigi lying in a prison cell and being tortured, the memory of the red light cutting the waters in half on 11 August 1984, the lingering echoes of last words uttered by people I loved, the murdered Dacians in a cave, all of that is giving me titanic strength to take down this little Guy monster who has been the provider for Anushka's self-destruction and misery. I want to kill him and throw his liver to the crows. I stick the kitchen knife in his shoulder and the sight of his blood makes me even wilder. I see Anushka's blue eyes sparkle with fire and fury like I had never seen them before and she picks up the heavy Buddha statue from the little bedside table and hits him over the head with it. Though dizzy from the blow, Guy is trying to fight back with his hands. Only he can't do much with the tip of my knife right on the vein where his blood is pulsing. Anushka is kicking him and with every kick she yells a reason: 'For killing Roland'. 'For stealing my money'. 'For getting me addicted'. 'For destroying my life'. 'For lying to Aunt Natalie'. As I hear all this while both my hands are holding lethally sharp objects next to parts of Guy Laurent's body, I am thinking that one day Anushka will have to explain all this and tell me her convoluted story.

Suddenly Agadira appears in the doorway, takes a look at the scene and exclaims: '*Oh mon Dieu de la France.*' She understands right away. But to my surprise, Agadira laughs and says: '*Bon travail, les filles!*' Then she brings her round face very close to that of Guy Laurent and tells him in her lowest, fiercest voice: 'You will never set foot within ten square kilometres of this apartment or anywhere near Anushka. Or my partner here and our big boss will cut you to pieces first and kill you afterwards. Did you get that through your bald head?' Guy Laurent says that yes, he gets it, and Agadira asks him to repeat word by word what she has just said. Only change the pronouns. 'I, Guy Laurent, swear never to set foot within ten kilometres of this apartment or anywhere near Anushka Pomorowska, or the women here and their big boss will cut me to pieces and kill me afterwards.' Agadira tells him to repeat 'ten square kilometres', then turns to us and says it's important to make that clear, that it is *square* kilometres. We throw him down the stairs and shut the door. Then we slowly fall to the ground, trembling. Anushka is still holding the wooden statue of Buddha and embracing it. Agadira is wiping the sweat off her forehead and invoking the gods of France and of Burkina Faso combined. I start cleaning up the blood. We clean everything up. Anushka looks at me through teary eyes and says: 'What kind of fashion is that, Nora? Do you know you are wearing three dresses on top of each other?' Agadira bursts into her melodious laughter. We laugh and cry through the evening. Anushka says she will do everything we tell her from now on, she will get off the '*putain de poudre*'. 'For ever,' she says. This time she means it and I know she is telling the truth. Then Anushka asks

Agadira, who is the big boss? Agadira laughs and says no one, God maybe. We laugh again. All I need right now is an eternity of sleep.

By May, Anushka is freed of her heroin addiction and Agadira has won her bet. Now I have to cook a hundred Turkish desserts. I was the one who set the conditions, and if I had won, that is if Anushka hadn't been clean by the end of the month, then Agadira would have had to take me into her apartment. And I would have let Anushka die. I am twenty-two years old and I feel like Mother Time. I am wiry and punchy, and I walk the streets of Paris like they belong to me now. I don't press Anushka with questions about her past. I know she will tell me everything when she feels ready. The one thing she does do is change the locks to our apartment and when I ask her if we are safe from Guy Laurent and if he is the owner of the apartment, she tells me not to worry, she'll explain later, he's out of the picture for ever.

Once she became determined to be free of the drug, she went through the last throes of withdrawal stoically. In the evening, after the shivers and the sweats, she sometimes just wanted to hold my hand for a full hour. I sat next to her on the bed watching the spring sunset envelop the roofs and listening to the noises of the Parisian street. Anushka's hand was small and sweaty, trembling in my hand. I now experienced waves of love for this mysterious suffering creature who must have spent most of her adult life trying to end it. Agadira had been right, Anushka and I were family. I had acquired a sister. Caring for her gave me a reason for my own confused life in Paris. I cooked enormous lamb stews and pilafs for Anushka and made sure she ate three times a day. One evening, when I came home exhausted from my ten-hour day in Mme Tournelle's bakery, she was waiting for me with dinner ready for the two of us: *salade niçoise* and *boeuf bourguignon.* 'It's time to learn some French cuisine, Nora dear,' she said with a mischievous smile.

Now I have plenty of time to grieve for my lost love and family again. To agonize in the darkest fantasies about what the secret police may be doing to Gigi in prison. To ache for the absence of my dear Valentin and his cascades of dazzling music. To yearn for the sea again. To lick my wounds in the Parisian spring. The one new element now is that I know I am surviving. I know I am carrying that giant's fist on my head, the burden of my hardships like Goya's man. I make a plan with Anushka about both our futures and we have Agadira witness our deal. I am supposed to start some kind of education or art training and Anushka is supposed to start teaching in her field: literature or philosophy or both. By the end of the year I will move into my own apartment. Before the end of the year, Anushka, Agadira and I will take a trip to the sea: the Mediterranean.

Like Mariţa used to fill her days and smother her misery with many coloured trinkets and fantastical stories, so I start again filling my days with a myriad of jobs, errands, activities, projects, coloured dresses, fluffy pastries, fantastical paintings. A lot of free time is not advisable for an overly traumatized refugee. First I make a plan for my art studies. I decide to go to the Ecole Nationale des Beaux Arts and see if I can register for classes, or for an exam to get into it in the first place. I call from Anushka's apartment to enquire about the entrance exam and a woman with a guttural voice and an irritated tone recites to me breathlessly everything I need to have and do to gain admission: proof of high school diploma, baccalauréat, certificate of registration in high school, and a portfolio of work. The exam consists of a practical, drawing test and a history of art and culture test. I also have to be no younger than eighteen and no older than twenty-four. She says *au revoir* and hangs up.

I have none of the documents she has listed. All I have to prove my existence on the planet are my Romanian birth certificate and my immigration papers. As for a portfolio, I have my package of manic paintings from the Istanbul amnesia period and the ones from the Anushka on drugs period. Anushka tells me the birth certificate is a gem because I can at least prove my age, I am younger than twenty-four. She says we'll put the portfolio in order, and I have to ask for special permission to take the exam without proof of high school graduation. Anushka calls the school again, pretending to be me, and asks for an appointment with the school director, a certain Professeur Duquesne. On the day of the interview, I borrow one of Anushka's dresses, a brown and light pink velvet dress, severe yet feminine, because amid all my clownish recent creations, the Muslim *hijab* and the few Turkish silks and cottons, I couldn't find anything that would make me look both interesting and stable, original and hardworking. Anushka has all of that and more in her wardrobe. At the last minute, before I go out of the door, she puts a peach-coloured crinkly scarf around my neck. Anushka and her scarves will enter history. She says I must have a little bit of '*folie*', craziness, added to my appearance. Just the right amount of colour and *folie*, for I am going to the art school, not Sciences Po. Today she is also set on finding a job teaching in the lycée system and she is wringing her hands and biting her lips from nervousness. She is wearing long sleeves and a buttoned-up shirt to cover all the needle marks that are slowly fading away. Her face has resumed a little of its former radiance but she looks much older than when I first knew her at the beach. There is a gauzy shadow of sadness spread over her face. Her blue eyes are more fiery and determined, though, and she has lost her childish air. We kiss and wish each other good luck for the day, like an old couple, like twin sisters.

Professeur Duquesne's office is also his atelier and is filled with abstract semi-cubist paintings in all shades of brown and female nudes in many colours. He is bald and has a white goatee and when he sees me standing in the doorway, he makes a cryptic sign to me with his right hand without any words and goes on with his painting. I remain standing in the doorway. I stand motionless, with my roll of drawings and paintings under my left arm.

He lazily lifts his eyes towards me and says: 'You are the new model? Strip . . . over there.'

The rage I felt in the Louvre in front of the gigantic Rubens paintings is choking me and Anushka's crinkly scarf is burning my neck. I put my right hand around my neck and say: 'Are you the old model? Don't bother!'

This time he puts down his brush and looks at me for a few seconds. He starts laughing with a roaring laugh that reminds me a little of Uncle Doru. Only Doru was actually handsome and charming.

'*Qui êtes vous?*' he asks as if I was a talking orangutan.

'*Je suis Nora Teodoru et je veux m'inscrire à l'examen d'admission de cette école.*' I had practised that sentence in front of Anushka many times, only using the conditional, '*je voudrais*', 'I would like.' But I didn't want to extend my politeness to this Professeur Duquesne so I replaced it with a simple 'I want'. I want to take the entrance exam.

'*Ah bon?*' he says.

I don't answer. What intelligent thing does one say to an empty idiomatic expression like 'really'? I am staring at him with a smirk, the Mona Lisa smirk. I repeat my first sentence, about wanting to register for the entrance exam.

Jacques Duquesne wasn't the ogre he appeared to be, he was just used to women stripping and posing for him at the merest twitch of his little finger. He took his time looking at my paintings and drawings. I was sweating like Anushka during her heroin withdrawals as I stood in her brown and pink velvet dress and almost did feel like stripping. After looking at each piece of my work for a couple of minutes from up close and from a distance he said: '*Tu as de la veine.*' You have guts. He particularly liked my 'Black Nude' and the 'Red Night' paintings from my Istanbul period. His second favourite was one from the Anushka period, an acrylic and tempera combination in yellows, with Agadira by Anushka's bed wiping her face with a cloth and both of them placed on a huge lotus leaf in an ocean of clouds. He asked me who I was studying with. This time it was my turn to laugh. So I laughed first and then I said: 'No one.' Then he asked who I had studied with. Then I stopped laughing and said: '*Mlle Mantaş, Université de Bucharest.*' At which he raised his eyes with great interest and said: '*Pas vrai! Elle enseigne toujours!*' She is still teaching! Not that he was younger than she was, but he must have felt immortal, ageless.

Now I just stood with my mouth open. It turns out Professeur Duquesne was a great admirer of Brancusi and also of what he called the Romanian school of artists. I must have missed that school when I was struggling with my entrance exams and trying to avoid or rather survive the Socialist Realist school, the only one I knew of. He had been to Romania in the seventies to see Brancusi's work in its natural habitat, his early work. Then he stopped off in Bucharest, which he sensitively called '*une moche de ville*', an ugly city, and actually met with faculty from the art school including Miss Mantaş, who had left a powerful impression on him. For a fleeting second the image of Miss Mantaş lecturing me amid the baroque delirium of art and old pieces of furniture in her apartment, with strands of red hair falling all over her face, grips my heart. Then I think of her in her lime linen suit on the day of the practical examination. All the hope flickering on that day in lime colours and then all shut out by darkness. I put away the thought and try to listen to M. Duquesne. He says he had appreciated the work of Ceauşescu's famous official portrait painter, Sabin Balasa, the one whose painting of flying Communists I had to copy for my entrance exam. I let that pass and don't say what I really think about this great master. I find enough courage to tell him I need his help to waive all the requirements of high school diplomas and baccalauréat and the rest, that I don't have any such documents, and that my entry into the free world was effected in my bathing suit through the Bosphorus, in the middle of the night. However, I produce my birth certificate and show it to him, proving that I am the right age. He is baffled by how I managed to bring my birth certificate. I know he will never believe it travelled in a tin box tied to my back underneath my wetsuit as I was swimming from the Romanian to the Turkish Black Sea, so I just say it's a long story, and someone from Turkey helped me out. He looks at me attentively again and says: '*Tu es une drôle de fille*,' a funny girl. Just like the customer in Mimi's bakery had said. Yes, I am a real clown, a bona fide circus girl entertaining the Parisian crowds with my tricks: I somersault from country to country, from one trauma to the next, one side smiling a Turkish smile, one side screaming an international scream, and always landing on my own two feet. I am a Muslim cat, a Gypsy witch, a cunning ferret as my father used to say. Who am I? Guess the riddle, M. Duquesne!

Jacques Duquesne agrees not only to help me out but to prepare me for the exams over the next several weeks. He grabs my chin in one hand and touches my shoulder with the other. I tell him that's very nice, when can we start? I shake off his pawing and tell him my body is off limits. And no modelling! He says no one ever talked to him like that. I tell him maybe it was time someone did. He produces his roaring laugh again. We set the next meeting time, then I fly down the marble staircase, through the classical square courtyard and in between the two huge heads of artists guarding it like stern lions. After the encounter with the great master of the Ecole Nationale, I decide to visit the Atelier Brancusi, the workshop of my famous Parisian compatriot.

I decide to use my Métro francs for the entrance ticket and to walk back to Lecourbe. I go in sceptical and cynical, proudly hardened by my recent trials and unleashed boldness. And three hours later I leave the place in tears, trembling with the mixture of joy and sadness that you are moved to by a certain kind of art which speaks to you, which thrusts its spiralling blend of form and emotion right through your soul. I study for a long time each one of the small and large tools, the wood-carving knives, the stone-carving knives, the chisels, the long thread with a marble ball at the end proving gravity in its downward straight flight, and all the round and square and oval shapes in all the shades of wood, in creamy stone, in glistening, sunny bronze. I imagine Brancusi at the turn of the twentieth century, a young man from a faraway village in a little-known country with a wild passion and a mythic beard, walking through foreign towns and villages to reach Paris, star city of Western art.

I am best starting to understand Paris through Brancusi's journey, through what I imagine was the shining light at the end of his itinerary, the longing for his native landscape combined with his hunger to embrace the entire world and the universe of human thought in smooth, round, glowing shapes. The oval stone eggs make me think of my perfect sleep between Gigi and Valentin the night before our irreversible separation, the full kernel of life that I thought I was then. The two wooden halves kissing are Nora and Gigi in their incomparable union on the golden sand, in the violet waters, in a complete confusion and reversal of body parts and selves. I recognize myself in ecstasy and pain in Mlle Pogany's pensive roundness folded into herself, the sensuous thoughtfulness of her huge head and the suggestion of a body wrapped in itself and not revealed, bird, fish, woman in one.

Anushka comes back to life in the May gusts and blooming gardens of Paris. She starts wearing her sultry dresses and diaphanous silk scarves, and teaches French literature in a small *collège* in the *sixième arrondissement*, not too far from where I go for my pre-exam training at the Ecole Nationale des Beaux Arts. She introduces me to a group of émigré artists, among whom are a few Romanians: writers, painters, playwrights, musicians, each trying desperately to absorb the Parisian artistic vibes and survive without being completely crushed by the needs of the body. The Romanians, unlike any other group of refugees, party and drink a lot, badmouth the French, each other, and almost all other émigrés, and engage in depressive existential musings and arguments. But somehow the sound of my language, the recognition of jokes, gestures and of a certain cultural universe give me comfort, particularly on Saturday nights, when I am half blind with exhaustion from the work in the bakery, the studying with Professeur Duquesne and the non-stop business of keeping in check all my longings and worries about the world and the people I left behind several years ago.

A struggling Romanian playwright, Virgil Teodorescu, whom Ceauşescu had apparently tried to have killed during the seventies because of his dissident writings, is always at the centre of the discussions and arguments. He drinks glass after glass of vodka mixed with wine, and then washes that down with French cassis, and uses large gestures as if he was lecturing to an entire stadium full of people.

'The French are finished,' says Virgil one Saturday evening as several of us are gathered in the Rue de Montparnasse, in the small smoke-filled apartment of Aleksey, an aspiring Polish poet, journalist and essayist. 'Look at them; they are just living off their past glory. Besides, most of their modern artists are foreign anyway.'

Aleksey, a blond, frail-looking man who smokes incessantly, contradicts him in a high-pitched voice: 'You couldn't be more wrong, Virgil. You are speaking like the fox who couldn't reach the grapes because you are having a hard time making it here as a playwright. Why are you here in Paris? Why is any of us here? The French have created modernity, they reinvented humanism for Europeans, and they are always initiators of new trends. They are more alive than ever, if you want to know.'

Except for Sartre, whom we learned about in high school in my French class because he was a left-wing writer and a Trotskyist,

I don't recognize any of the names that Aleksey is so passionate about and lists to prove his point: Albert Camus, Jean Giraudoux, François Truffaut. I feel ignorant and peasant-like amid this intensely intellectual talk. Not only am I poor and traumatized in Paris but I also have an entire history of Western civilization to catch up with.

'First, I am making it as a playwright, and my new play is being produced in the Marais. Secondly, the bloody fable is shit because foxes don't eat grapes,' yells Virgil, taking another swig of vodka and laughing at his own remark. 'Third, the most innovative modernity was created by foreigners. The people you mention are old news. The newest theatre – you have a Romanian and an Irishman: Ionesco and Beckett. Painting – Chagall, Kandinsky, Miró, Picasso – Spaniards, Poles, Russians. Conceptual sculpture – Romanian again – Brancusi, right? It's the foreigners, the émigrés with their broken selves, their duplicitous identities, their refusal of tradition and raging nihilism, who–'

'You are both wrong,' interrupts a woman's voice with what seems to be an American accent. 'It doesn't matter how many of the artists in Paris are foreign or French. Paris is Paris, it's a cultural magnet, it always has been and it always will be. It attracts brilliance. Of course it's full of foreigners, because it's a Mecca of ideas. And it's not just because, as Aleksey said, the French are trendsetters, but because Paris is classical and modern at once, rational, irrational, surreal, romantic . . . it's a space for ideas to clash and germinate . . . It's not even the most beautiful city in Europe, other cities are more beautiful than Paris – Amsterdam, Florence, Rome, but they are not Paris.'

'Oh Sally, give me a break with the French and the Parisians,' says a Romanian-sounding woman from the other end of the room. 'If it hadn't been for the British and the Americans, the French would be speaking German right now. I'm so sick of hearing about how great the cultural life of Paris is and how great the French are. They are so incredibly snobbish and full of themselves even when they are not creating great art. There are other great cultural Meccas, you know, Sally. You should go to London to get a taste of rocking modernity. And yes, Amsterdam, it would blow you away. Other cities are actually more welcoming to foreigners than this one. Here, once a foreigner, always a foreigner, the French never fully accept you as one of theirs until the second or third generation. And do you think they like you? They hate Americans, but they steal all the popular culture from them. I wish I had emigrated to America, frankly.'

'Shush with the Americans, Roxana,' says Virgil. 'They have no sense of history, they are ignorant and fat. Except for you, Sally, who must be the one beautiful, slender, intelligent American there is.'

'Thanks, Virgil, that's really kind of you,' says Sally. 'How many Americans have you met in your life to make such stupid generalizations?'

'Two others before you, and it's been enough,' says Virgil, laughing.

'How about if I said all Romanians are thieves and racists? How would you like that, Virgil?'

'They are,' says Virgil. 'Except for the few brainy ones who emigrated to Paris. Actually, now that I think of it, it isn't the French who are trendsetters as you put it, Aleksey, it's Romanian exiles who are trendsetters: Surrealism – you've got Tristan Tzara, a Romanian Jew; conceptual sculpture – Brancusi; theatre of the absurd – Ionesco; modern opera – Enesco; modern history of religions – Eliade; modern philosophy – Cioran. There you have it: when we aren't thieves or whores, we Romanians are trendsetters and creators of movements. Not bad for a miserable unknown country in the fucking Balkans, wouldn't you say?'

Everybody laughs at Virgil and his absurd arguments. Apparently they are used to him always being on some kind of offensive and producing the most extreme statements to get people all riled up. Sally is a sassy blonde New Yorker with short hair who stands up to all the men in the room like she was one of them. She invites us all to her apartment for a special slide show the next day. She says she has a surprise for us.

Sally lives in the revered Montmartre, where I haven't yet been in the full half-year of my Parisian life. I take Anushka with me to Sally's party and I find myself liking this part of Paris more than any of the other districts I've crossed so far, either in a tired daze or a manic rush or a hazy depression. The hilly narrow streets filled with cheap poster and print stands, incongruously framed by the formidable white structure of the Sacré Coeur looming in the distance, and all the sentimental music echoing from crammed piano bars reminds me strangely of the State Circus the night Valentin took me there for the first time. Maybe because it's the first real burst of colour I've experienced in Paris, maybe the roundness of the Sacré Coeur triggers the image of the plump circus dome inside which Didona was flying in her hot-pink sequinned dress, maybe the stridently dressed women in tight clothes seem like a cross between circus dancers and prostitutes. Or maybe it's just my desperate need for colour and stridency after so many months of grey and drab.

Sally's apartment is on the top floor of an old five-storey building on a sloping street. Virgil is already on his fifth vodka or cassis of the evening, Aleksey is finishing up his pack of cigarettes, Roxana is both smoking and drinking while dancing by herself to the music of Charles Aznavour. Only Sally is sober, fresh and lively in a sexy black mini-dress and focused on setting up what looks like a slide carousel and projector. Anushka talks and flirts with everyone a little, just the way she did at the Black Sea so many years ago when Gigi and I rescued her: a part of her bubbly and radiant, and a part of her absent and somewhere else. As I look at her through the swirls of smoke I am wondering, as I often do, what are Anushka's secrets, what mysterious past is wrapped around her soul?

At some point during the party Sally turns off the music,

shushes everybody and tells us to take a seat, because she is going to show us something. What follows is a slide show of paintings that startle me as if I had found a lost part of myself expressed in ways that I haven't yet been able to explore. Portraits in earthy greens and reds, cobalt blues and shameless yellows: a woman who looks like Didona only with enormous eyebrows, self-portraits of a woman shaping her screams of pain and anger in clear, blade-sharp lines: woman tree, woman deer, woman with two bodies, heart cut in half with sharp scissors. Her name is Frida Kahlo and she was a Mexican painter in the forties and fifties, Sally tells us excitedly. She was the lover of another Mexican painter, Diego Rivera, who obviously made her life a living hell, because his image is carved in her brain while her eyes are about to burn down the whole world. I ask Sally please to show again the slide with the two Fridas with their hearts pulled out.

I see myself: Nora split in half and doubled up with pieces of heart throbbing open, scarlet blood, liquid fire. There is Nora on the night of 11 August 1984 on one side of the red line in the black waters, with the red-haired boy on the other side, on the bad side. I see the story of Queen Marie of Romania with her rambling heart, with her heart stolen by Communists from its resting place, with the empty space where it once lay, it all fits in this artistic orgy of women's hearts and veins. Only the colours on the canvas remain: the Mexican greens, the Balchik blues, the Black Sea emerald plates. The heart wanders from place to place. The heart is pulled out of its nest. Stick with the colours.

I find out from Sally that Frida was a passionate Communist, a Trotskyist even. She had an affair with Trotsky before he was assassinated. I don't care, I love her anyway, she must have had her reasons. History is the biggest circus of all: loud-voiced ringmasters running nations like acrobats on the trapeze, like bears on bicycles, everybody falling flat on their faces in the end and then wondering what happened. How come we let the concentration camps happen, why didn't anybody stop the gulags, how could the atomic bomb occur? Oh I forget, we were busy jumping through hoops, we didn't see, we had to work the trapeze, do the acrobatics, be good Christians, be good Marxists, be good parents, don't look left, don't look right, just look straight ahead like the horse with the red bow and the white cape, just listen to the ringmaster's whip and do the steps. I want to be like Frida Kahlo, paint like her, Communist or not, I don't care about the politics any more. I just want to scream my red nightmares in sharp lines like Frida Kahlo.

We decide to go out into Place du Tertre for more drinks and to see the artists make portraits of tourists eager for cheap thrills. The colourful square is bubbling with streams of curious visitors coming and going, desperate artists trying to earn a few francs with their instant portraits, the smells of *steak frites* and *crèpes*, the ebullient chords of a piano inside a bar where they serve fresh oysters on the half-shell. Everything is on the cusp between the sadness and the joy of being alive, between a bohemian feel and a cheap, strident call for pleasure and immediate gratification. In one corner of the square, a crowd of people has gathered to watch a street performance. Wailing violin music that awakens a dark point in my memory is making its way persistently through the general din of the evening.

I walk over in that direction with my group of newly acquired émigré friends. A man in a worn-out tuxedo is playing the violin with extraordinary contortions of his face and of his entire body, a woman in a shiny black sequinned gown is accompanying him on a miniature harpsichord, producing high-pitched notes that create an assonant echo to the violin. Between the two: a round pedestal like that of a music box is turning slowly and on it a young woman with cascades of black hair in a white lace dress like a vintage bridal gown is performing the most extraordinary acrobatics while pinned to one spot in the centre of the pedestal. More and more people are gathering, some throwing money in the hat placed on the pavement, others just stopping for a few seconds and going away with an amused smile. Others, like me, stand transfixed.

A feeling of apricot trees in bloom passes through me, apricot blossoms falling like snow on Gigi and Nora on a spring night with a cobalt sea and Turkish desserts. The ballerina in the lace wedding dress is draped over herself, a giant fantastical black and white bird, her head glued to her right ankle, her left leg perfectly straight in the air. A flutter of seagulls and ravens passes through me, the topaz sea rustling in the twilight, a wedding with algae wreaths in a frame of Greek columns under moonlight. The violin is breaking strings, wailing a familiar melody of love and despair, the pretend harpsichord is winking at the violin's heartbreak, everything's a joke, everybody is a clown. The bird bride is folding and unfolding, curling, breaking in half, feathers, roses, doves, a wizard's tricks – and there appears Didona in a bridal gown. A feeling of dark cave shadows and bats envelops me. My eyes throw darts; Didona blinks quickly, looks right at me and smiles. Didona, past lover of my twin brother Valentin, heartbreaker, circus ballerina, is smiling at me in Place du Tertre.

Nora, Come Home!

Soon after my birthday in January 1988 I received a thick envelope from my mother that seemed to have been opened, read and glued shut. Given its contents I was surprised it ever made it across the Romanian border. Maybe things were changing, or maybe my mother just didn't care. It was a rainy day in Paris and I opened it with wet, cold trembling fingers rushing like mad up the stairs to the Lecourbe apartment. A long letter from my mother was something miraculous or frightening; it had to announce either someone's death or a radical event of some kind. I couldn't tear the envelope fast enough. It was addressed to me and me alone with an endearing line: 'Nora, my dear girl.' I gasped, my mother had never called me that before.

> The evenings are the worst. When the house gets darker and is full of shadows, that is when I want to scream the same refrain in every room: 'Nora, come home, my Nora, please return!' Now with Valentin also gone our house feels like a large tomb. The wind is whistling through it and it sounds hollow at every step as if we are also dead. Sandu comes home more tired every evening and reads medical reports through dinner and then falls asleep in his armchair. We

hardly talk to each other any more except to exchange information about what needs to be done, who called, what to stand in line for at the empty grocery store. What else is there to say? I often think, Nora, that if I had made your life more peaceful, if you had felt more loved, you might not have run away. You would have married that Turkish boy and might even have passed the university exam if you took it again. Just like Valentin did. He tried again and again, and just about tore that piano in half from playing it so much. In the end he succeeded. He went in the summer session and then again in the autumn session, for two years in a row until they let him in. Nora my girl, you would have succeeded in the end too. You were just as talented.

When Valentin returned alone from the trip which was supposed to be your exploration of the Danube Delta (you all really fooled me with that one) and told me about you and Gigi, I didn't believe him at first. I thought he was joking as he often has the habit of doing. But when his face scrunched up and large tears started flowing from his green eyes, I knew he was telling the truth. I held on to Valentin and howled in his face, asking why he let you go ahead with the escape. For more than a week, until I heard from Luca and Sabina that you had made it to Turkey and Gigi had been taken to prison, I wanted to destroy everything. I smashed all the bloody china in our dining-room cupboards. I cut down the willow tree in our back yard with an axe, all by myself. Then I became numb and even lost feeling in my hands. I was literally becoming numb, paralysed. Sandu put me on a special treatment for a month, gave me injections, took care of me. I didn't feel a thing. I was like a half-dead piece of flesh with only my eyes staring wildly at the nothingness ahead of me.

Then I took a journey back to the beginning, trying to understand: Raluca and I growing up in the big house by the Danube in Tulcea, with a fierce father who hated the Russians and the Communists so much that he sympathized with the Germans, and a passionate mother who hated the Germans so much that she cheated on our father with a Communist Party activist during the war. The forests of reeds, the swamps, the vineyards of our childhood and the endless hot summer days that we spent by the harbour, bathing in the Danube, or perched in an apricot tree in our large orchard while our father tended to his grapes or to his rye and wheat fields. Then came the war, the Germans first, the Russians afterwards, and everything became confused and chaotic. We all had to move and leave everything more than once. I remember long trips in horse-drawn carts, with Raluca constantly whining and complaining about the heat. I remember our mother arguing with our father that she wasn't going to leave the house without the piano, and our father yelling at her and then slapping our mother. Then my memory fades, the images become more and more confused, overlapping each other: our mother standing by the piano with tears smearing the kohl make-up around her eyes and saying they could kill her but she wasn't going to leave without her piano. Our mother yelling that she hated our father, and that she loved another man: a Communist. Our father striking her again. Raluca clinging to our mother's skirt, and I clinging to one of the piano legs. I didn't want to let go of the piano either, I wanted to play the piano like my mother did. But for some strange reason only Raluca received piano lessons because she was the older one.

I remember a long trip in a dirty train with Romanian and Turkish peasants, cages with chickens and geese and urine smells everywhere. Then came our short-lived period of relative happiness in a small village house. For most of the day we were alone with our mother, who played the piano from morning till night, while our father took a horse from the village to go back and check on the old house and the land. There was always his land. Sometimes, in the afternoon, a young man in army uniform stopped by and our mother would offer him rose petal preserve. One time I heard them laugh in my mother's bedroom and the young man saying: 'I will take you away one day, Irina. I swear, when the fight is over, when we win, you will be all mine.' My mother moaned. A while later she came out of the room with her beautiful chestnut hair coming undone and her face all flushed.

Then my memory fades again. We were back in the old house and having dinner. Our mother was at one end of the table and our father at the other end. Three men in the new army uniforms that looked like those of the Soviets came in and asked our father if he was Octavian Moraru. He looked at them defiantly and said: 'Yes, what do you want?' One of them, the younger one with the moustache, asked him to follow them. Our mother looked at him straight in the eyes as they were taking him away and said nothing. We looked at her. She got up from the table and ran after them. Raluca and I heard her say to the men: 'Please let him go, we are good Communists!' The younger man with the moustache answered: 'Not good enough!' Our mother came back in and with a sweep of her right hand pushed everything off the table: the white and blue china, the soup bowls, the roast, the crystal glasses, the plum cake. I looked out of the window again as they were pushing Tata into a black van. I recognized the young man in uniform with the moustache. He was the same young man who always visited our mother in the afternoon, when we lived in the little house in the village near the Danube.

Later in her life, when we were already living in this house, our mother became very strange: she wouldn't take off her black recital gown: she slept in it, ate in it, and cleaned the house in it. She stopped caring for herself and was talking in sentences that didn't make sense. One day a team of doctors came and took her away. They took her to the local sanatorium in Mangalia. Raluca and I visited her on Saturday afternoons and she always looked right through us at something in the distance.

I tried to teach myself piano from her music scores, but my playing sounded hollow and dissonant. Then I started to replace the feel of the piano keys under my fingers with any work that filled the void: sewing, tailoring, cooking, planting, lacquering the furniture. Raluca, who had taken five years of piano lessons, never touched our piano. She collected flowers and weeds and pressed them in an album. One day when I came back from school, Aunt Elizabeta told us that our mother had died in the hospital. She had had a stroke. She died calling for her girls, Elizabeta said. I didn't feel anything except a strange relief and I did not cry at my mother's funeral, although Raluca sobbed and sobbed and threw herself on top of our mother's dead body. She was buried in her black recital gown with the long string of pearls around her neck. I never mourned for my mother and it grew in my chest like a tumour. I transferred all my mourning and grieving to my father. Because he had been killed by Communists, we turned him into a saint, a martyr dying for his land. What did my mother die for? She died alone in a sanatorium, without even her children near her, with a heavy conscience, a wasted talent, a confused past.

Something in me became numb, atrophied, after my mother's death. When you and Valentin were born, though, you filled the void in my heart and in my life. But there was still a numb part left inside me, I just didn't know it. The period when your little bodies were both next to mine, breathing in unison, was my one happy spell. Nora, you were always drawing and scribbling and painting on every surface you could find: furniture, walls, doors. You sometimes withdrew completely inside your own world, staring at your own visions. You could draw anything from memory. One time, when you were about six and your brother was in Bucharest with Aunt Raluca, I took you to the market with me and while I was choosing tomatoes at one of the stands, I saw you stare in fascination at a Gypsy woman who was selling plastic bracelets and beach balls and pumice stone. When we came home, you drew the portrait of the Gypsy on the white tablecloth on the kitchen table. You even drew the red slippers she wore and the coloured scarf tied around her head. It was a stunning painting, precise yet fantastical, with just the right colours and lines. I scolded you then, saying that you had destroyed the tablecloth. I should have encouraged your art more, and I should have scolded you less. My whole life is a huge pile of 'I should haves'. I think that lump of numbness in my heart was also the reason why I was so passive and docile in allowing Raluca to take Valentin to Bucharest permanently, until she became his mother more than I ever was. I just let things happen to me. Then I punished you for Valentin's absence and the pain I felt from missing him, from not ever playing the piano, from not crying when my mother died, from the horror of my father's murder. You were always there, with your squeaky voice and your scribbling and your wild mane of hair like mine, a more independent and wilful version of me at that age.

Before we know it, summer will be here. I dread the month of August, because that's when you ran away. Valentin always goes to Limanu on 7 August; he has been going there every summer since you left, as some kind of sinister commemoration of your separation. He misses you terribly, Nora, but he has always stood by your decision. He returns in the summer and spends his days swimming and walking along the beach, and playing the piano. One good thing we have done in this house is to bring the piano up from the basement. It takes almost all the space in the dining room, but it's much better to see the piano fill the room than our old lacquered table. Sandu has even asked me to take up playing again and I have timidly accepted his encouragement. I have learned my first sonatina from beginning to end.

I heard that Gigi was released from that dreaded prison and returned just a few days ago. Tudoriţa told me she saw him in town looking like a frightening shadow of his old self: with a long red beard that apparently makes him look like a Viking, only skin and bones, a walking skeleton. He did almost four years of prison and forced labour in that jail in Bucharest. Tudoriţa said she heard he is working in the shipyard with his father.

I kept all your old paintings, Nora, and I periodically take them out and stare at them, trying to understand you better: the one in the tramcar scares me the most, the ghastly light coming from the window, the woman in the leopardskin. I think it must have arisen from the time you almost died of septicaemia. But there is one painting that is bright and joyous and that reminds me of the time we all went to the restaurant to eat pizza. Do you remember that happy time, Nora? I am thinking that from the way you have portrayed me, maybe you were starting to forgive me. Maybe you have forgiven me. And there is another crumpled painting. I think this must be your first real one. I found it in one of your drawers, next to the yellow silk scarf you used to wear. And there are grains of sand stuck to this painting, as if it was forgotten on the beach. Nora, my mystery girl, come home! Your loving Mama.

I sat holding the letter and crying over it until it got dark in the room and Anushka returned home, bringing in a gust of fresh, wet Parisian air. She thought something awful had happened when she saw me staring out of the window in a catatonic state, and she took the letter from my hands. When she saw the name on the envelope she thought that maybe my mother was writing to me with news of the death of my father, Gigi or Valentin. I told her it wasn't about death, it was about forgiveness.

Stealing the French Landscape

After defecting from Romania with aerial nets, hoops and cubes, Didona and her parents had spent some time working for travelling circus troupes and at carnivals throughout Italy, Germany and Switzerland. Eventually they made their way into France as part of a three-wagon circus that contained sea lions, tigers, one elephant and many white doves in addition to an abundance of clowns, illusionists, a family that made a seven-person human pyramid, and tightrope walkers. Didona's trapeze acts of hanging and twirling in the air from every possible body part in brightly coloured sequinned outfits were unique and the real selling point for their family. By the time I found her rotating on her head in Place du Tertre, her family had exhausted their resources, were tired and homesick. They had decided to leave the circus business and try to make it on their own, as individual performers in the various entertainment venues of Paris. Soon enough they found that the best they could get was small gigs in seedy concert halls and cabarets; that the dark complexions that betrayed the dreaded ethnicity of Gypsies, and their poor immigrant status, gave the owners of these places complete freedom to mistreat, insult and eventually sack them. Didona was the only one who earned real money, particularly once she started dancing in a nightclub in Montmartre called Chez Toto, where she ended up shedding more and more clothes every night until she was asked to strip completely. That was when she left and the family began their street-performing career.

Agadira, who, with the exception of two ten-day trips to Burkina Faso, had been working as a cleaner at the hospital for three years almost without a break, decided to try teaching *école maternelle*, starting in the autumn. She quit her job and went on unemployment benefit for the summer. Anushka was relatively content with her teacher's job at the middle school in the sixth *arrondissement* although she said the children were '*barbants*', a pain, and was dreaming of taking her first real holiday with the money she had earned.

As for me, I had added to my work in Mimi's *boulangerie* a set designer's job in the little theatre in the Marais district where Virgil Teodorescu sometimes had his plays produced. Although I got paid a third of what I made by baking croissants, almond and pistachio pastries or fruit tarts, I loved the idea of earning even a few francs from my drawing and painting. Among the actors in the theatre, I felt more at ease than I did in any of my classes at the art school, where for the most part I felt lonely and an impostor. Oddly enough, M. Duquesne, although he was a pathological Don Juan, was the only one who made me feel like I was worth something and had a chance of becoming a 'real artist'. The lists of important alumni posted in the hallways only increased my feelings of being a fraud. It was sort of improbable that I was studying art at the same school where Delacroix, Renoir and Monet had studied, but in those days there had been only one woman painter, the American Mary Cassatt, and a Swedish woman sculptor who started as a model. All that made my presence in that art school seem like an illusion. I periodically checked my registration status with the secretaries in order to make sure I was in fact a student of the Ecole Nationale des Beaux Arts. Each time I asked them they looked at me with greater irony and irritation. Some days in the art school I experienced an uncanny sensation that I didn't exist within the parameters of those buildings and in the eyes of my professors. I felt immaterial, irrelevant, with a heart dislocated from my body and lost somewhere among changes of regime and appropriations of territory, like Queen Marie of Romania. I wondered if posing as a model might make me feel more real and relevant. But Anushka howled in indignation at the idea.

Whenever I complained about feeling so marginal in the school, Anushka replied: 'Well, they let you in, didn't they? They must have thought something of you since you were admitted to the most competitive art school in France.'

To which I always answered: 'Yes, they let me in so they could feel good about themselves for letting in a "poor refugee" and now they are making me feel like one.'

To which Anushka replied: 'Nobody can make you feel anything you are not!'

And then I always said: 'But I *am* a poor refugee, that's the problem.'

At this point Anushka would tell me to stop feeling sorry for myself and go out and paint something. The theatre people who put on obscure avant-garde plays by Romanian or Czech playwrights, or delicate eighteenth-century dramas with lacy costumes, never doubted that I was already a 'real artist' and always welcomed my ideas for sets with superlatives: '*C'est chouette, Nora, tu es géniale*', Nora, you are amazing! That was where Didona also found work as an actress, dancer, singer and acrobat, and where she found a lover, the dark-haired and charming Marcel, who always played roles of delinquent men miraculously transformed by a woman's love. Didona admitted to me that Valentin had been for her a dream of her youth, a fantasy, an illusion, a Pierrot dancing under the moonlight. At first I felt betrayed and angry on my poor brother's behalf, but then I understood Didona and was actually relieved. Valentin and Didona would have eaten each other alive, were they ever to be together.

For a few weeks after I ran into Didona in Montmartre, Anushka and I joined her in different parts of Paris for performance pieces that she invented and we were as happy as little girls with the money we made from our street art. Didona was always the centre of the act, with a few of her best acrobatics, while Anushka and I created a background. I sometimes drew Didona as fast as I could during her performance, with large dramatic gestures, wearing three or four of my best home-sewn dresses on top of each other and a painter's beret, while Anushka wore my old clown costume that I had bought at St-Ouen during her heroin period and pretended to play heartbreak music on a violin whose sound we had recorded beforehand and that we hid under Didona's rotating pedestal. We opened our act in Montmartre, in front of the Louvre, in the Jardins du Luxembourg, in the Latin Quarter. The best moments were when a child would ask its parents to stop and watch and then pulled its parents' hand or the hem of their coat to make them throw money in our top hat. If the parent was in a hurry or was simply stingy, the child would beg: '*Je t'en prie, maman, une petite pièce*...' The parent would blush and throw a coin or two in the hat. I liked the Parisian children more than most of the adults in the city and wondered what made the adults so on edge, so stuck up. What did they want, what did they need? Would all those nice children be like them one day? They had Paris, they had freedom, they had French citizenship and stable jobs, they had the 'God of France', many had lovers or spouses and adorable children, what more did they want? What did one need to be happy and calm?

I discovered with horror, guilt and shame that for the first time since the fated night of 11 August 1984, despite the four-year-long separation from my family and from Gigi, despite the painful knowledge that Gigi, the man who was irreplaceable, my only imaginable male companion, had been spending dark day after dark day in a dreaded prison and was now an out-of-prison ghost wandering around Mangalia, despite all that, I was happy. It seemed immoral and out of balance. How could I be happy when my family and my love were far away and miserable? Yet happy I was. During the Parisian spring and summer of 1988 it seemed like I had taken a huge bite into some forbidden fruit. I was continuously bubbly and light, moving from my art classes to kneading dough and making Turkish-French desserts in Mimi Tournelle's bakery to drawing Surrealist backdrops for a group of Bohemian actors in the Marais, to the time I spent laughing or performing in the street, or cooking in my minuscule kitchen with my priceless collection of sisters: Agadira, Anushka and Didona.

As planned, in the summer of 1988 we decided to travel by train across France and eventually to the Mediterranean. And we added a fourth to our group of female musketeers: Didona the circus performer. We planned first to move south-west towards the Atlantic and then south-east to the Mediterranean. More than the Atlantic, though, which seemed in my imagination too overwhelming to be a welcoming sight, I wanted to see the prehistoric caves that I had read about in one of my art history books. Anushka and Agadira wanted to see the Atlantic, they said the ocean was grandiose and the west coast filled with enchanting fishing villages and magnificent beaches. My heart was set on the prehistoric caves, where the first *Homo sapiens* left marks of their artistic cravings and dreams by painting wild horses and bison on the walls. And then I was set on the Mediterranean, a sea, a body of water that was neither too big nor too small and that might make me feel as if I was on the shore of my beloved and painfully missed Black Sea. Didona didn't care where we went, she was just thrilled to be travelling and seeing anything without having to either hang by her teeth in some circus tent or dance with no clothes on in order to pay her way.

We put everything in black backpacks that we had bought in the flea market at St-Ouen and carried our money in little pouches tied round our bellies. We were ready for the joy trip of our lives, and felt like the four musketeers setting out to save the king and a hidden treasure. The four of us must have made quite a striking spectacle because we noticed that people and particularly men would stare or whisper about us. Some tried to approach us. We did our best to look angry, serious, no-nonsense to scare away any possible troublemakers. Anushka, after overcoming three years of drug addiction, had acquired a certain brash toughness of manner. Occasionally, whenever such unwanted admiration came our way, she would take out her large Swiss army knife, open it, cut an apple with it and then lick the knife with lascivious gestures. Agadira would shake her entire body in a full laughter that she couldn't control whenever she saw Anushka attack her pocket knife in that way. And Didona, who always wore jeans and a tight shirt when she wasn't performing, if we happened to find ourselves in a little station in Normandy, would do a quick back flip as easily as some people stretch out an arm or scratch their neck. Then people would move away and make unsuccessful efforts not to stare at us.

We were determined to see each one of our dream places and finally arrive victorious on one of the Mediterranean beaches. En route to the city of Brest, as we were crossing the mellow green countryside of Brittany and dozing off with our heads nodding to the rhythm of the train, Anushka started talking as if to herself. Her head was stuck to the window pane and her words came out smoothly and effortlessly. Agadira rubbed her eyes in surprise, Didona stretched and opened her eyes wide and I stared at Anushka and took her hand, having known this would happen sooner or later.

'*Ma mère s'est suicidée dans la baignoire. J'avais cinq ans,*' she started. My mother killed herself in the bathtub. I was five. Her story rolled on for hours, punctuated by the monotonous yet precise rhythm of the train wheels, and when she was done we were numb, tearful, confused. I was still holding her hand. Anushka was not her real name and it had been given to her by the Polish French woman who crossed the border into Hungary with her wrapped in a blanket in 1965. Anushka's real name was Eniko, and she was a Hungarian Jew from the Sighetu region in Northern Transylvania. Her parents had miraculously escaped being loaded on to a train going to Auschwitz-Birkenau camp in 1944. They had sneaked out of the ghetto where most Jews in Sighetu had been placed. When Romania had lost part of Transylvania to Hungary and Austria under the Second Vienna Award in 1940, most Romanians had fled, and two Jewish ghettos were created in Sighetu. Although nobody knew for sure where all the Jews were being taken during those infernal early months of 1944, the young couple, Ilinka and Miklos, felt that something ominous was going on and one night they hid in the back of a truck that was leaving the ghetto with several bodies of people who had recently died. They were both eighteen. They had both left their parents in the ghetto. They jumped off the truck in the middle of a field and hid in a nearby barn. They lived there for months on leftovers that a young boy kept bringing them from his parents' house, one of the rich peasant homes in the area. In November, the boy gave them news that Romania had changed sides. But for the Jews it was too late – the Hortyst Government had already speedily, frantically and efficiently sent most of the Jews in the area on death trains to the camps during the spring of that year, Ilinka and Miklos's parents included. They too had been loaded onto one of the sealed trains to the camps. Everyone was crammed into sealed trains.

The young couple walked back to Sighetu and found Ilinka's parents' old house wrecked, the furniture, the picture frames, the mirrors all smashed. Their parents would not be returning, nor would any of the other Jews in town. By now Sighetu and the area of Northern Transylvania had been given back to Romania, as a result of King Michael's coup of 23 August 1944.

When the Soviets arrived with their vociferous troops, tanks and Communism, Ilinka and Miklos were two of only one hundred Jews left in town. More than twenty thousand Jews from that area had been deported and mostly exterminated under the Hortyst Government. Ilinka and Miklos decided to repair their house, pretend they were not Jewish and live as Hungarian-Romanian gentiles. Soon the Communists turned the old prison in town into a prison for both 'class enemies' and 'enemies of the people'. Students and intellectuals were thrown into it first and then anybody else deemed to be an 'enemy of the people'. Some Romanians, who came back to Sighetu after the war, or those who had never left, recognized Ilinka and Miklos from before 1940 and said that it was the Jews who had brought the Communist plague down on their heads. They would whisper things like that to Miklos while getting their ration of meat for the month, or while standing in line at the post office for a package. And then some of those very Romanians who blamed the one hundred Jews in town for having brought Communism joined the Communist Party, or the secret police that was being formed as the Party's most trusted and feared organ. The Romanians said they had no choice, and that they were forced into it because of the Jews who had brought Communism down on everybody's heads, the Jews with their Marx and Engels. Miklos and Ilinka never said anything and pretended that none of the words uttered under people's breath pertained to them. People were being taken away and put in political prisons, or killed for the smallest reasons or for no reason at all. Ilinka and Miklos both worked in the local timber factory and were making ends meet.

We were now nearing Finistère, the point on the French map which looks like a huge nipple, the area of Brest that sticks out into the Atlantic. The train soothingly continued its monotonous roll. The brilliant summer light was melting slowly into crepuscular shadows and Anushka's voice was growing stronger. Much of what I had always thought to be some kind of frivolous childishness was Anushka's mask in the face of life and history, her way of coping with the gloom of her past. Agadira kept giving Anushka jasmine tea from her thermos, to make sure she stayed hydrated as she related her devastating family story, while Didona was all curled up with her legs around her neck, which was what she always did when she was nervous and excited. I was holding and stroking Anushka's hand.

Anushka was born in 1960, which made her five years older than me. When she was born, her parents Miklos and Ilinka were living in the same third-of-a-house apartment that they had lived in since 1945, and instead of fading away, the shadows of their parents who had disappeared during that hideous year of 1944 were becoming more overpowering. News of Jews from their town, such as Elie Wiesel, who had been freed from the camps and ended up in America or in France, was getting to them and Miklos sometimes bitterly said that they would have been better off if they had taken one of those trains. Then they might have had a chance of getting to America instead of living a dreary life in an anti-Semitic town under a Communist dictatorship. But of course Ilinka always sobered him by reminding him that most likely they would have been gassed and that Wiesel had just been among the lucky ones. His family hadn't been so lucky.

At some point when Anushka was three, Ilinka and Miklos decided to take a holiday by the Black Sea, using the money they had been saving since after the war. If they couldn't go to France or to Israel, at least they could go to the Black Sea, to the city of Mangalia, which they had heard that Romanians were starting to visit because of the beautiful beaches that were opening up. That must have been her parents' only happy time, because of her entire five years of life in Romania, Anushka remembered only the summer at the Black Sea and the one photograph that they had taken on the beach one sunny afternoon. That photograph had stood on the cupboard in their main room until the afternoon when her mother killed herself in the bath. In that picture, her mother Ilinka, who had wavy dark blonde hair coming down to her waist, was sitting on a beach towel on the sand and laughing. She looked happy and relaxed, her eyes squinting and her body perfectly shaped in her swimming costume. Her father Miklos was lying on his side behind Ilinka and smoking, with one arm wrapped around her waist. He was smiling an irresistible smile. Anushka was playing in the sand right next to the towel on which her parents were sunbathing and was looking straight at the camera.

Nothing worked for them after that, everything disintegrated, just like in a Greek tragedy, said Anushka, just like those families who because of some absurd curse go spiralling down towards total destruction. Anushka found her mother in the bath in bloody water, her head thrown back with her waves of blonde hair touching the floor and wearing her bathing suit. She had not wanted to be found naked, obscenely dead in the bathtub; this is how thoughtful her mother had been, said Anushka with a sad smile, she wore her swimming costume to kill herself. Her father lost his mind in an instant and Anushka went out into the street in front of the house. A neighbour saw her whimpering and sucking her thumb in the middle of the road, and asked her what had happened. She couldn't speak. She wouldn't speak. The neighbour went into the house and discovered everything. Anushka didn't speak for two years after that. There was nothing to say. Since Miklos never recovered and was taken to the local sanatorium, the neighbour, a Romanian Polish woman whose family had left Sighetu in 1940, before the Hungarians started deporting the Jews, took her in, fed her and looked after her for a few weeks as she tried to find a home for her. Larisa was old and sick and couldn't take care of a traumatized five-year-old child. She remembered a niece of hers, Natalie, who lived in Paris and with whom she exchanged an occasional letter that would reach her weeks late, after having been opened, read and glued shut by the secret police. But Larisa had no political secrets to tell, just trivial information about health, weather and family relations. She contacted Natalie by phone and told her she had something for her, that she should come on a visit.

A month later, Natalie Pomorowska arrived in Sighetu from Paris and was presented with five-and-a-half-year-old blonde Anushka, who wouldn't speak. The two women tried to devise a plan to take Anushka out of the country. They decided they had to risk smuggling her out on the train going to Budapest through the Transylvanian city of Oradea. The hardest point was the Romanian border, where the customs officers searched every crease of your luggage. Natalie Pomorowska decided she was going to transport Anushka in a quilt. Anushka was tiny and scrawny, and Natalie had heard of another young child who had been saved from the Nazis by being wrapped in a blanket, and thrown as if carelessly on the overhead rack of a train. Natalie Pomorowska was a devout French Catholic and put her trust in the Catholic God, the Pope, and her good looks, which could charm any male authority figure.

So Anushka was to set off for Paris with her new protector, the beautiful aspiring actress Natalie Pomorowska. Natalie bought a first-class ticket for the sleeping car that was going to Vienna through Budapest. Although Anushka still didn't speak, Larisa the neighbour explained everything to her, and prepared her for the trip she was going to take with Aunt Natalie. She told her to act as a lifeless pancake, wrapped in one of her home-made *plapumi* quilts. Anushka nodded to everything.

The awaited night arrived. Natalie was lying in bed in the sleeping car in her pink frilly negligee. When she heard the customs officers approach she arranged the *plapuma*, inside which Anushka was draped like a lifeless pancake, over her body. She pulled the *plapuma* a little bit higher than her waist, so that the low-cut negligee could do its work. She feigned extreme sleepiness and grogginess when they came in. She smiled, whimpered, moaned, yawned and invited the two Romanian and Hungarian customs police to check everything, every bit of her luggage. She pretended to be shy and pulled the quilt up to her chin, but she kept letting it slip back down so that the two men were suitably excited by her perfect rosy décolleté. She had a French passport and French citizenship after all, they respected her more than if she had been an ordinary Romanian citizen going to Budapest and then to Vienna. The two customs police left the compartment laughing and in a good mood, even slid the compartment door back attentively and wished Natalie a good night, winking lasciviously. Natalie held and stroked the *plapuma* that contained the frightened Anushka once they were gone. They descended on Paris three days later and Anushka was formally adopted by Natalie Pomorowska. That was how she became French and how she got her Polish name.

Later in her life, in the spring of 1980, Anushka received a phone call from someone who did not want to disclose his identity but who said he had something of value to give her. They met on a bench in the Luxembourg Gardens. He was an old man with a strong Hungarian accent and he had taken care of her father in the asylum where he had spent the rest of his life. He had managed to leave Romania on a trip to France and was not going back. Mr Sandor handed her a thick envelope and told her that her father had begged him to keep it and if ever he was able to get to France to give the envelope to his daughter Eniko who had become Anushka Pomorowska. The envelope contained the story of Ilinka, Miklos and Anushka's first five years of life, handwritten in Hungarian by her father in the asylum where he had died that year.

Nineteen eighty was a wild year, equally good and bad, a terrible year in fact, Anushka said, looking straight at us in the growing dusk that was leaking in through the train windows. It was also the year when the one man she had ever loved, Roland Giraud, died in a motorcycle accident on the Champs-Elysées as he was being chased by Guy Laurent in a car, for a payment he owed him. A payment for drugs. Roland had taught Anushka everything she knew about love, sex, motorcycles and photography. He had brought thrill and passion into her life with Aunt Natalie, who was always in an emotional crisis or rehearsing a new part for the theatre but who had treated her like the most tender of mothers. Anushka rode on Roland's bike across Paris, her blonde hair flying wildly in a swirl of emotion and wind. When I asked Anushka who Guy Laurent was, her face and eyes took on the furious shine they had acquired the evening when I put a kitchen knife to his jugular and she hit him on the head with a wooden Buddha. He was her ex-stepfather. He had married Natalie Pomorowska when Anushka was twelve. It was not clear why Natalie had fallen in love with him. Anushka thought it must have been because, conman that he was, he had a certain ease and confidence about him which Natalie, the vulnerable, naïve aspiring actress, in her late thirties and eager to marry, was lacking. He had married Natalie mostly for her inheritance. He swindled her out of her money, tricked her into signing over to him the apartment on Rue Lecourbe that she had been keeping for when Anushka came of age. When Anushka reached twenty and fell in love with Roland, Guy took advantage of her desire to be free and have a place of her own. Natalie had divorced him by now but his name was still on the apartment contract. He said she could live in the apartment with Roland if she paid him rent. Anushka used her monthly allowance to pay rent for an apartment that was already hers but really not hers any longer. Then Guy tempted Roland with a little bit of heroin. One thing led to another, as it always does when it comes to drugs. Roland and Anushka got involved with a bad crowd of heroin users and bikers. At first Anushka resisted the drug and only used a little bit occasionally, and not in intravenous form. Roland was already shooting up and suffering from the withdrawals when he was killed, plus he had no money and was willing to do just about anything to get his fix.

That was when Anushka, then a philosophy student at the Sorbonne, decided that there wasn't much point in living. At least not for her. That was when she also decided to go back to that beach on the Black Sea, to the place where she and her parents had enjoyed a month of happiness. Maybe she would find meaning there. She became obsessed with her family's story as revealed in Hungarian in her father's handwriting and, added to her own memories of the month spent in Mangalia and the recent death of her boyfriend, her trip to the Black Sea seemed an absolute necessity. She did not come to Mangalia that summer with the idea of killing herself. She wanted to see the place where she had once been happy with her parents and to get away from Paris, from the gang of bikers and heroin addicts and from Natalie's despair at her crumbling love life. She wanted to find some meaning.

From the balcony of her hotel room in Mangalia, Anushka watched Gigi and me that afternoon in August, the day before the Navy celebrations in 1980, as we swam happily, as we chased each other on the shore, as we larked about in the waves. The image of the two of us made her think of the family picture: her mother Ilinka laughing happily with her heavy waves of blonde hair down her back, on that same beach, more than fifteen years earlier; her father holding Ilinka by the waist and smoking with an alluring smile; of herself playing in the sand next to her parents and looking straight at the camera. She thought of her life in Paris and of Roland with his skull crushed against the curb on the Champs-Elysées. She thought again of her mother with her wrists sliced in a bath filled with blood and wearing her swimming costume. The storm started and Anushka stopped thinking. Nothing made sense. Life was a big joke, history an even crueller joke, happiness an eternal illusion, and philosophers, no less than her ex-stepfather Guy Laurent, were all conmen. She put on her bathing suit and headed joyfully for the violent waves, thinking it would all be over soon. She welcomed the force of the waves hitting her and pulling her under with sensuous pleasure and the anticipation of complete oblivion.

'*Et puis tu es venue dans ma vie . . .*' Anushka concluded and smiled her most ravishing smile ever. She smiled as if only now had she fully come back to life after that near-drowning incident of eight years ago. Then she opened her little navy blue leather purse and pulled out a photograph. Agadira, Didona and I all leaned over the black-and-white photograph like hungry birds: there was a woman with thick waves of shiny blonde hair down to her waist. She was sitting on a beach towel, her legs under her, and laughing with her head back in a way that reminded me of Anushka. The man lying behind her and smoking was thin and looked almost emaciated, but he had an irresistible smile and wavy silver hair. The little girl squatting next to a bucket and spade in front of the couple was smiling dreamily but with a tinge of something that looked like anxiety. In the background was an expanse of sand, a corner of sea and the bushes and rocks at the edge of the Mangalia beach where Gigi and I had spent hundreds of hours of our youth.

Agadira, Didona, Anushka and I spent that night in Brest, the westernmost part of France, the nipple of France washed by the Atlantic, in an old house converted into an inn with four bedrooms for guests. We shared one large attic room and laughed and talked like young girls into the night. Anushka was like a new person, or maybe just fully herself: joyous, funny and free in her manner. When the first rays of sun shone through our triangular attic windows and we looked outside we were left breathless at the sight of the rocky shore in the distance, the sloping streets and the medieval castle on the water. Agadira and Anushka had been right to pull us in this direction and we ran to the beach without breakfast, such was our wild desire to touch the waters of the Atlantic. For the first time since I knew her, Agadira wore jeans and not one of her African coloured dresses and a more youthful and playful woman seemed to emerge with the Western attire. Didona barely wore anything at all over her pink bathing suit, and Anushka and I each threw one of my tailored concoctions over our bikinis. It was the first time I was on a real beach since I had been in Istanbul and swam in the Black Sea at Kilyos. I ran to the water like a thirsty animal, wanting to drink it all and be submerged in it body and consciousness. This water was rough and stirred up and the algae were thicker, curlier, the shells bigger, the sand harsher, the tide tricky and quite a novelty for me. This water matched the new me well and what I had become after four jagged years of searching and struggling and scratching the walls for survival.

We found out to our amazement that Didona did not know how to swim. For all her aerial swimming and breathtaking acrobatics, she had actually never learned how to float in a body of water. She had grown up in a Gypsy family on the outskirts of Bucharest and spent her entire childhood and adolescence as a circus girl; her family had made the transition into a more stable lifestyle when they were hired by the State Circus, but that hardly gave her the opportunity to learn how to swim. We vowed that by the end of that day Didona would swim. She might be the unknown circus version of Nadia Comaneci and an émigrée in France, but swimming was survival, I told her. We spent the whole morning teaching Didona how to float and it was Agadira's eternal wisdom that convinced her to let go. Because Didona just did not want to let go. We would hold her gently on top of the water and tell her to keep her body straight, her lungs full of air, then we let go and she didn't. At the last second she would grab on to one of us and we would all end at the bottom of the ocean on top of each other. We would come out choking with laughter and salty water, mixing limbs and torsos in a liquid confusion of bodies. Didona could fly but couldn't float. When she was six or seven, her father's idea of teaching her how to swim had been to throw her in a lake on the margins of Bucharest where they were camping with a caravan, and she almost drowned because her father couldn't swim either. She was lucky that a good citizen who was fishing nearby jumped in and pulled her out by her hair.

Agadira said to her: 'Didona my dear, do in the water exactly what you do in the air, God will take care of the rest.'

To which Didona answered: 'I'd like to see you let go in free fall from fifty metres high. Would you, if I told you to let go, trust that God would take care of the rest?'

Then Agadira added some pragmatic information to her spiritual wisdom and told her to use the skills and the muscles she used when she did her flips in the air, and do in the water what she did in the air, that is, keep them tight and then relax. Imagine she was held up by invisible strings just like in her circus acts. Water and air were both God's elements, Agadira said, at which Anushka and I laughed and asked mockingly if they were universal elements of God or of the God of France. She ignored our irony as she often did when she wanted to have the last word. Whether it was the God of the universe or the God of France, the fact was that Didona miraculously started floating.

As the four of us were splashing and laughing wildly in the French Atlantic to celebrate Didona's mastery of her own body in the water, images of Gigi and me swimming, splashing, embracing, kissing, competing with each other in that magical topaz sea of our childhood burst in on my memory. They passed before my eyes in their full luminosity like a carousel of coloured slides under the silvery blue sky of Brittany. The fullness I felt with my three sisters in the dizzying tide of the Atlantic was overpowering and the presence of Anushka's round blonde body next to mine in the water comforted me. I had never dared ask her if there had been any physical closeness between Gigi and her that summer at the beach when I was almost devoured alive by the fever of my jealousy. But I didn't care any longer. It had also been the jealousy that awoke in me my love for Gigi.

As our trip continued through little towns with Gothic churches and cafés in the centre or big towns with baroque architecture and large avenues like Bordeaux, through hilly regions with stone houses hidden deep in the shade of pine trees or by rocky seashores and beaches, in the rhythm of our own steps or of the monotonous train wheels taking us across the French countryside, I found myself starting to reconnect to my Romanian past and to the landscapes of the nineteen years I had spent in my country that was no longer my country. Because I had no country, I took possession of all countries. France was just a continuation of Romania with a stupid political division between them. The Atlantic was going to be my Black Sea, the Dordogne valley with its broad river cutting through green forests was going to be my Dobrogea Mountains with the broad Danube undulating between sandy shores and reeds, and the Mediterranean, whenever we got to it, was going to be my Black Sea too. It wasn't my fault, after all, that I hadn't been born in France but under a silly dictatorship to which a bunch of fat old presidents at the end of the Second World War consigned the Romanian people. No wonder the native French were afraid of refugees, for not only did we take away French people's jobs, as the saying went, but we greedily took away their mountains and oceans and lavender fields, their Gothic churches and classical theatres, and transformed them into as many countries as we had come from. I saw it in Agadira's concentrated eyes too as she was staring at the landscape rushing by the train windows: how the little French stone houses in the Dordogne were also the round huts along the Black Volta river in Burkina Faso, how the markets with fruit and vegetables were also the small shops by the side of the road to the capital, Ouagadougou, that sold a modest mixture of products from grain to soap to cooking oil. We swallowed everything in our hungry stomachs and psyches, us refugees, and jumbled up frontiers and borders, mixed languages, wore strident clothing and spilled our violent and messy stories all over neoclassical cities and shiny green countryside.

As we were waiting for our train in a small station in the Perigord area, and were talking about the stereotypes the French had about refugees being 'thieves' and delinquents, Agadira said to our surprise: 'And the French can be thieves too.' Given that Agadira usually had only words of praise for the French, their republic and their God, that seemed rather radical.

'That's right, everybody can be a thief, but refugees are the best thieves because they are the hungriest,' I said proudly.

When our train entered the station we got on it laughing and the people that we had shared the waiting room with looked at us admiringly. We were off to a little town called Les Eyzies. We had heard it had some of the best prehistoric caves. I was hungry to see how far back the craving to scratch the walls and leave your mark went. We got off the train in a tiny station surrounded by rock formations and woods and walked to the centre of town in single file on the side of the road, with our black backpacks from the flea market on our backs and our hearts ready to explode in excitement and curiosity. The cars going by honked at us, and a group of young men in a Peugeot estate actually whistled at us and made obscene gestures. No wonder women in the past used to travel dressed in men's clothes.

For sure this was going to be my Limanu village, cave, end-of-the-world rediscovery. Jagged rocks with dark pines on top and asymmetrical hills with taupe stone houses and dark red tile roofs surrounded us on all sides. Anushka carried a tent in her backpack and we all had sleeping bags, so we decided we were going to camp by the river, to save money but also to experience a primitive life.

Everything became an echo reverberating across time and space from the days of my Limanu trip, when I was walking, sleeping, eating next to my lover and my brother in the heat of August 1984. Now I was walking on narrow roads between rock and water, sleeping under sharp stars in the fresh air of the Dordogne valley and sharing frugal meals by the river with my refugee sisters. The murdered Dacians with their altars encrusted with animal claws, and the prehistoric humans who had dwelt right under these same rocks of Les Eyzies, leaving delicate drawn or sculpted contours on the inside of their homes of animals kissing and licking, were all part of the same continuum of fierce determination to survive and even more fierce hunger for immortality. Leaving a trace, scratching the walls! It wasn't all about survival, it was also about love. And I was somewhere on this axis of time and space, a speck of humanity frantic in my desire to leave my mark and be that egg of life and love. I stood for a long time in the Grotte de Fond-de-Gaume staring at the deer on the walls or at their prehistoric kin kissing, tongues, antlers, only a thin line of fading red remaining from the colouring of twenty thousand years ago. That art had meaning. I understood why people painted and why I always wanted to paint, why Esma and Frida wanted to paint: to tell the colours of our loves, of our nightmares and dreams, of everything that words could not describe and that was encrusted in flesh but did not evaporate the way flesh did.

The last place we visited was a prehistoric shelter turned museum dating from the Perigordian period of twenty thousand years ago, when our Cro-Magnon ancestors lived. I was tired from all the walking that we had done that day and my head was burning from the hot August sun and from the hot memories of another August. I almost didn't go inside. It was 11 August; four years had passed since the fated escape that started under the blazing noon sun in the shimmering waters washing the 2 Mai beaches. Agadira, who took notes of everything and methodically like a schoolteacher informed herself about every landmark we had planned or were going to see or had already visited, said we shouldn't leave before we saw the last one. She had it in her travel guide as an important site.

'You never know what you may find right at the end of your journey,' she proclaimed. So I turned and told Anushka and Didona that I was going in after all.

The layers of encampments stretched out like terraces slicing through prehistoric eras in reddish porous stone. It was like falling through time. When we were back in the one-room museum section, looking at the objects displayed under glass, my eyes became glued to a thumb-sized carving of a female figure in a cone-shaped rock. There was almost hesitancy in the carving, as if the frozen miniature female wasn't sure of her existence in stone across thousands of years. But there she was, winking at me from the porous stone and reflecting me. At first I didn't understand why I felt reflected in that unassuming attempt at a statue. I kept staring at it and felt waves of emotion towards what seemed like a woman egg, a woman embryo emerging out of stone with her head slightly tilted to one side, her legs glued tightly together like the tail of a mermaid, and one breast larger than the other. One bulging breast and one timid breast attempting to emerge. She was called Venus, just like the Venus de Milo. But this was no Venus de Milo. This was me, Nora from Mangalia, with my uneven breasts and arms in a foetal dream, an adult form in embryo size floating through the universe and rotating through the millennia, woman fish, striving to create herself and to scream her assonant song across time. At one time an uneven-breasted female body was thought to be beautiful and worthy of eternity. I stood shaking in front of the magic Cro-Magnon Venus and for the first time ever I thought of myself as fully, gloriously normal, stunningly beautiful *because of* my unevenness and not despite it, sister of that tentative yet so confident Aphrodite of twenty thousand years ago.

'Look, girls, I found my prehistoric double,' I said to Agadira, Didona and Anushka.

'It just goes to show that you always have to listen to Miss Prophetess Agadira here,' said Didona with her grinning circus face and her low cabaret voice.

When we travelled to the Dune de Pilat we climbed up to the top of the soft, golden sandy formation and then rolled down into the ocean curled up in foetal balls of thirsty flesh. The light was glazed and honeyed the way it had once been on top of the Limanu cave throbbing with swarming bats in its belly. Only white seagulls shrieked across the gleaming horizon of the Atlantic. Maybe I had travelled through the centre of the earth and of myself and had emerged on the other side, at another point of existence, another experience of freedom. Next we were off to the Mediterranean. She was waiting for us viciously and neurotically blue, impossibly blue in the majestic city of Nice. I kept looking for the tinge of green to mellow it and make it into my mysterious Black Sea, refugee thief that I was. My three fellow musketeers and I mocked the pebble beach in Nice out of existence until we peed in our bikinis staring at the French women tiptoeing on the hard grey pebbles in a variety of awkward ballet moves until they reached the water. We decided to try the sandy beaches on the coast: Antibes, Cannes. We were on the Côte d'Azur, at the exact same latitude on the map as my native city of Mangalia, with our old house at number 9, with Greek columns and a Turkish mosque, and with a mad love left unfinished and scattered over every stone and across every wave like a fiery dragon shedding its many skins and its many bleeding lives.

Music like Water

Another Parisian spring with tulips, lilac and roses sweeps fluttering through the city, after the long cold winter this year. A winter with more snow than usual, said the Parisians, and now a spring with more abundant tulips than usual. I am hurrying to my afternoon gouache and acrylic techniques class, concentrating on a new painting I am trying to create in mixed media: a painting of Anushka, Agadira and Didona as a parody of the Three Graces represented throughout history, on a ship in the Mediterranean, with the three of them at the helm, like protective sea deities in circus outfits. They are protecting me and Gigi, who are sleeping on the higher deck of the ship, in a hammock, under the Mediterranean sky. It will be a grandiose, tragi-comic painting of unfulfilled wishes, nostalgia and fantasy. My three 'muses' actually posed for my painting in my small studio apartment on Boulevard Rochechouart.

As I pass the Fontaine Saint Michel a large poster board on the pavement catches my eye. It grips me in a tight claw: *Orchestre Philharmonique de Bucharest. Valentin Teodoru – piano; Beethoven, Chopin, Berlioz. Théâtre des Champs-Elysées.* I stand in front of it and reread the information several times: Valentin Teodoru – piano – playing works by Beethoven, Chopin and Berlioz. The

Romantics. In Paris, at the Théâtre des Champs-Elysées. Maybe there is another Valentin Teodoru who is not my twin brother and who also plays the piano. Or maybe this Valentin Teodoru on the poster is another twin brother I didn't know about, a twin of my twin brother, a deeper, darker secret than I even imagined, like something out of science fiction: my mother having triplets by three different men. Maybe there is another Bucharest Philharmonic than the one I know of, a twin of the Bucharest Philharmonic. Maybe the world is all constructed in doubles and twin universes and I am being foolishly tricked by the cruel joke of it all, time and again. *Dimanche, 19 heures.* I must get tickets for the concert, whatever the joke may be. I must get to my class, and I must finish my acrylic painting. I must keep myself in check and not explode in some kind of spring madness.

I almost miss my Métro stop trying to figure out Valentin's surprise visit to Paris, why he didn't give me any warning, whether it's really him: Valentin Teodoru playing the piano in a concert of the Romanian Philharmonic this Sunday. I am irritable and distracted during the acrylics technique class and I actually snap at the teacher, M. Renaud, asking him to stop guiding my hand on the paper, I can do it myself. Only one art teacher has ever been allowed to do that, and that was red-haired fidgety Miss Mantaş. M. Renaud makes a comment about temperamental Romanians and my eyes tear up and I leave the classroom. That's right, when we are not thieves, we are temperamental, and what are we when these two priceless clichés have been exhausted, M. Renaud? We are also Gypsies and that makes us 'bad' because all Gypsies are 'bad' and not even Romanians want to be called Gypsies, they'd rather be called Fascists, they think it's nobler. I am bursting with fury at all the peoples in the world but mostly at these two nations that I am most tied to by birth and by adoption: the Romanians and the French. I hate them both, I love them both. What I once was, what I am, what I could have been, and what I will be is all divided by the blade-sharp red line cutting the waters in the middle and making me quiver and quake at the thought of an encounter with my twin brother.

When I tell Didona about Valentin her eyes fill with tears, but she quickly regains her happy circus face. She isn't going to come to the concert, there is no point, it's all over, and she loves Marcel the actor. I ask Anushka to come with me and she immediately says yes, as she is dying of curiosity to meet my mystery brother. I buy the tickets and at 6.30 we are in front of the theatre. My heart is having its own private revolution that my mind is staring at in astonishment. I have been dividing myself like a mythic creature under parthenogenesis, into many Noras: tearful and agitated, wearing a blue gauzy dress; tough and indifferent, wearing trousers and Agadira's boots; confused and disconcerted, in a yellow cotton dress; cerebral and professional, an artist wearing layers of velvet clothing in mauves and pinks; passionate, sentimental, yearning for my dear brother whom I had last embraced in the blazing sun on the hot sand before diving into the hungry waters towards the Bosphorus. As always, Anushka saves me from my clothing confusion and lends me one of her dresses: a light green chiffon summer dress with a pattern of tiny pink roses and I throw over it a lime sweater I bought at the flea market. Anushka wears a cyclamen silk dress with a black patent belt and black patent shoes. Her shoes are clicking on the Parisian pavement just like I had always thought that Parisian women's shoes clicked before I even came to Paris.

Our seats are in a balcony on the second floor on the left. Anushka is holding my hand. I am sweating and counting minutes in my head. Then I am counting seconds. Then the lights go off, and then they go back on. People applaud, my eyesight goes bleary and when I regain my sight, my brother Valentin Teodoru is standing and bowing at the audience in a white tuxedo with a red carnation at his buttonhole. Before anything else, before Beethoven's Fifth, before an étude by Chopin, he plays the Moonlight Sonata. I know he is playing it for me, as he had played it for me on the evening of our reunion when we were just two rebellious kids. The years had passed with their wrenching separations, their red agonies and pains, with the few rainbow-coloured carnivals of laughter and funny acrobatics, with our strenuous scratching on the walls for survival. A large ship with all my loved ones waving coloured handkerchiefs is floating away into a light blue hazy horizon. The watery notes flowing from Valentin's fingertips bounce and trickle and roll languidly in the eerie light of the theatre. But the luminous string tying our hearts to each other has remained intact and Valentin is bringing it to life in this sumptuous Parisian theatre with red velvet seats and golden balconies, bringing a memory of the grungy basement at number 9 under spider's webs and a cloud of dust, as we are all floating down the creaky staircase in a feathery flight, gathering around the old piano that used to belong to Grandmother Irina in her black taffeta dress with a long string of pearls. My mother with hair like brown sheep pulled back, her angry eyes ready to burn down the world, my father with his melancholy black eyes and an ironic smile, my Uncle Doru with his empty sleeve tucked inside the pocket of his elegant beige blazer and a cigarette in the corner of his mouth, Aunt Tudoriţa holding her baby with a proud smile, and Nora in a yellow dress like Van Gogh's sunflowers with her crooked green smile and her crooked body of Cro-Magnon Venus – we are all floating up to the surface from the wiry, rusting wreck of our ship, we are surviving the wreck, and we are coming up to the surface for a huge gulp of fresh air.

After the concert I run with Anushka through the crowds to the backstage area. A man in a uniform tells me I cannot go backstage. I give him a tip and ask him to take an envelope to Mr Valentin Teodoru backstage. It is Valentin's birth certificate that I had carried tucked inside my mother's plum dumpling box when I crossed over into Turkey. The man comes out after a few minutes and tells me that Mr Teodoru is waiting for us. Anushka doesn't want to come, she says this is family, I should go alone. But I can't face this encounter alone. So she comes behind me in her graceful small-stepped walk.

Valentin is standing in the large hallway behind the stage in his white tuxedo, with his black hair carefully combed back: a handsome man, a piano prodigy, but still my spidery-limbed scrawny brother. Our embrace is long and filled with sobs. Then he smiles, he even laughs, Valentin the ever-unpredictable clown, one eye crying, one eye laughing.

'There you are, Sister, more beautiful than ever!' he says, twirling me round and admiring me. 'I knew we would see each other sooner or later, and I knew you would be here, of course. I knew the easiest way to find you was to give a piano recital.'

'I thought you might be missing your birth certificate by now,' I say, laughing.

'You have no idea of the difficulties its absence has caused me,' he says, laughing as well.

I ask Valentin to come with us for drinks, for dinner, for the next lifetime. He shushes me and says he can't, really. I ask him why didn't he warn me about his visit, what if I hadn't seen the poster? He says then he would have called from Paris, he would have found me somehow and he wanted to surprise me. Didn't I know he was a box of surprises? He also says he couldn't call, the phone was tapped and he didn't want to give them any cause for suspicion. The Philharmonic are on a small European tour and are due back home in a few days. I am convinced that Valentin, once out of the country, will now decide to stay, ask for asylum and never go back to what he calls 'home'. But he is still his old unpredictable self and tells me that no, he won't stay. Romania *is* his home, there is no reason for him to stay in France, he is making it there, dictatorship and all. In Paris he would have to start again. He lets me know also that something is stirring in our country, that there have been riots, manifestoes, demonstrations, dissident activities, and that things are so unimaginably bad that something is bound to change. Soon, he says. Then he notices Anushka, who is standing a little bit to the side and staring at us, mesmerized.

'*Qui est cette magnifique personne?*' Valentin asks in perfect French, gazing at Anushka.

'*C'est Anushka, ma meilleure amie, la fille qu'on a sauvé à la Mer Noire,*' I say, pushing Anushka towards my brother and introducing them to each other.

'And a good thing it is you saved her, Sister. The world would have been a poorer place without her.' Valentin is smiling his most charming smile.

As we spill our stories over *steak frites* and a bottle of red wine in a cheap brasserie near the theatre, my heart is aching for so many reasons on this Parisian night when old wounds are opened by Valentin's rendition of the Moonlight Sonata. I ask the most important question that has stayed glued to my brain all night only at the very end of the evening. The question about Gigi. Valentin tells me what I had found out from my mother's letter: that he was released from prison and is working in the shipyard with his father. He smiles and asks me playfully if I am still so in love with Gigi, haven't I found a nice French man yet? When he sees the globes of tears in my eyes he stops smiling and tells me that Gigi is changed, I might not even recognize him, that he is darker, broken maybe, a shadow of his old self. I am shocked again, the way I used to be after he came to live with us, by Valentin's bald tone about important things, his nonchalant honesty like that of a cruel clown announcing to you with a smile that there is a brick about to fall on your head.

And how about Gigi? I ask myself. 'Did you choose Gigi?' Valentin had asked me that question once on a train, as we were returning from Bucharest after our circus escapade. And now I ask myself: *Are you still choosing Gigi, Nora Teodoru? Changed and darker and broken and a shadow of his old self as Valentin claims that he is? What does that even mean? What does my Pierrot of a brother know about Gigi? Hasn't Gigi always been part of me, my one and incomparable magic fish with whom I was going to build an enchanted red coral castle under the waves of the Black Sea, the Red Sea, the Mediterranean, any sea on this earth? Didn't I once think Gigi was my country, my haven of happiness and of comfort, and that I could face any storms and cataclysms and floods next to him?*

Valentin tells us he is leaving in two days, it was a short tour. I ask Valentin to take something for Gigi from me, can he do that? Will the Romanian police check on him at the border? Valentin mocks me, saying that I seem to have forgotten what I left behind. Of course they will check everything, he says. What am I planning to send, a secret weapon to kill Ceaușescu with? A painting, I tell my brother, he has to take a painting to Gigi. He says of course he will, anything for his sister, a painting is not a big deal.

Valentin has to stay in the hotel with his group of musicians. And besides, the secret police travelling with the Philharmonic to make sure they return with the same number of people they had left with are nearby. I laugh at the idea that the Philharmonic travels with its own private *securitate*, how convenient. I say so what, if he wants to stay he could still do it and send the travelling secret police right to hell, how are they going to stop him in the middle of Paris? I ask him one more time to please stay in Paris and ask for asylum. We could run to the nearest police station right now, I say, my old adventurous spirit rising up in me. Anushka also timidly asks him to stay when we finally part at midnight. Doesn't he want to stay, is he sure? He could become an important pianist in Paris too. Again, he says no, he has to return home, he already *is* an important pianist, not everybody has to leave the country to be fulfilled, and he is sure something will happen soon. And he cannot leave our mother. My heart feels the sharp sting. Our mother has grown older, Valentin had said, she went crazy after my departure. He didn't use the word crazy as a figure of speech. She wouldn't speak for a while. She was a silent storm ravaging everything for weeks. I see my mama going like a hurricane through our house in her green dress, icy, fiery, a burning, chilling phantom wailing for her children.

We tell Valentin to meet us in the Place Alma Marceau the next day for lunch. The musicians are staying one more day, after which they return to Romania. I stay up all night and paint a replica of the painting I am working on in the atelier at school, not in acrylics but in tempera like I used to do in Romania. I place the colours in layers to give the surface more depth and transparency. Many layers of blue and green with a few tinges of red and gold. I make the painting of Gigi and me embracing in a hammock on a ship sailing across the Mediterranean and my three sisters, Agadira, Anushka and Didona, as deities at the helm guiding it through the turquoise waters. I glue Gigi's birth certificate on the back of the painting and then glue another sheet on top of it. Gigi will know to look there for sure, when he feels the thickness of the paper. On the back sheet I paint a self-portrait, just my head, the way I have never painted myself: my round face framed by the mane of brown curls and my green eyes with a special sparkle and a red bow in my hair, like Goya's Marquise de la Solana. Then I paint the small image of Gigi's face in the centre of my forehead, like one of Frida's self-portraits with Diego Rivera in the centre of her forehead. I paint Gigi's face as I remember it from our happiest days: honey-coloured, freckled, with brown shiny eyes like those of Turkish cats, his reddish curls. He is there burning in the centre of my forehead too. And between the two paintings is cradled Gigi's birth certificate, just like I had once deliciously cradled him between my thighs on that low bed of his, or on the sand of our Mangalia beach, under the moon laying its shiny bridge across the waters.

Valentin takes the rolled-up painting and smiles. 'Another one of your bizarre creations, Sister. You've kept true to yourself, haven't you?'

'I should be damned if I couldn't at least keep true to

myself, after this huge escape and immigration mess,' I snap back.

He looks at it again and recognizes Didona in one of the Three Sea Graces, and smiles bitterly. He is not surprised when I tell him she is in Paris, but his face brightens when he sees Anushka a little behind me. I just remembered: Valentin is an unforgiving Pierrot who believes in predestination. Anushka is wearing a bright blue dress like the sea in my painting and looks like Botticelli's Flora in the depiction of spring. Paris is throbbing with whimsical breaths of fresh air and people in love and bold flowers as the two of us take turns embracing Valentin. She tells him that she wants to come to see him in Romania, that for sure they'll see each other soon. Valentin smiles his most ravishing smile and says that yes, she should come to Romania, he'll show her the mountains this time, and show her around Bucharest. Something new, an emerging manliness, seems to have touched Valentin. A spark flickers in his eyes like the one I had caught a glimpse of the afternoon before our departure to the Limanu cave, when he and my father exchanged glances over our kitchen table and a luminous flow seemed to pass between them.

The three of us spend the day walking around Paris, eating sandwiches on park benches and going to the Musée Rodin. Of all the museums in Paris, Valentin wanted to see the one with Rodin's sculptures. Unlike Valentin and Anushka, who are both exclaiming over the hefty bronze and marble nudes, I am angered by them just the way I was when I first went to the Louvre. Something irks me in those overpowering male statues that seem to swallow and dominate the female ones. I am puzzled by the few Camille Claudel statuary groups and the one of the kissing couple that seems to be a reverse replica of the one by Rodin. It's light and slightly bizarre and the woman is not submerged in the man's kiss, but free and nimble though slightly crooked.

Valentin knows what I am thinking, he reads my thoughts, he feels my sudden yearning for Gigi, for our happy threesome on the Sunday afternoons when we met at Mangalia station after my art and his piano lessons in Bucharest, when we would walk back to our homes down the middle of the street whistling one of the newest Romanian pop songs, with the sea always surprising us at the end of the street in a sudden burst of violet blues. As we are rambling through the museum he comes to me and grabs my shoulders in a tight squeeze.

'You'll see him again, Nora, I know it,' he says tenderly. Anushka comes round the other side and confirms Valentin's happy prediction. As I stand cuddled between my brother and my best friend, longing for Gigi in the Musée Rodin, I somehow regain the assurance that I chose Gigi, that I still want Gigi, and that the puzzle pieces are starting to make sense. After being muddled up, in the wrong order, now they are making a recognizable picture. In a quick flicker of my imagination I see the four of us here among these heavy, contorted marble and bronze bodies and shapes, with Gigi right next to me holding me by the waist and saying his favourite is Rodin's hand. I know Gigi would love the sculpture of the hand. As we leave the elegant grounds of the museum, giggling about the contorted nudes like teenagers, I feel particularly happy at the sight of Anushka and Valentin flirting with each other. Maybe my brother is right, there are no chance encounters. As we pass by the formidable statue of the Flame of Liberty in reddish gold at Alma Marceau, a simple and prosaic thought possesses me: I am satisfied that the birth certificates once in my possession are now returning to their rightful owners. To each of us their own birth.

Valentin is leaving the following day and we say our goodbyes in Place de l'Opéra, under a spring rain. Anushka is soaked and her face expresses a strange mixture of joy and sadness simultaneously. I know what it means, she is falling in love with Valentin and she does not want to let him go. I embrace Valentin tightly and, as always, the sharp memory of that last embrace in the August glaze of 1984 on the burning sand makes me lose my balance. The last thing I tell Valentin before we part is to give my mama lots of kisses and tell her that I am doing well, that she would be proud of me. To tell her I devoured every word of the beautiful letter she sent me. At the last second I pull out a letter I have written to my mother the previous night, describing to her my Parisian life, my discoveries and artistic successes. I stick it in his pocket and he taps on it. 'You're always placing me in danger, Sister,' Valentin says, laughing. 'She already is proud of you, Nora!' He turns on his heels like a cabaret dancer. He runs to his Romanian charter bus, packed with instruments, musicians and secret police safeguarding the full formation of artists who have caught a breath of Parisian air and must have wondered in unison about the possibilities of asylum, but were either too scared or too lazy to take the step. Or too stubborn and proud like Valentin.

My twin brother Valentin has passed through Paris for three days like a shiny meteor, leaving a trace of maddeningly palpable music and keening emotion behind him. When he is gone I wonder, just like I used to in the past, whether he actually exists or whether he is a concoction of my turbulent imagination. The smile on Anushka's face, as her small blue eyes filter the sun's rays that have just emerged after the short rain, tells me that he must exist. The smell of lavender from the cologne he was wearing this morning confirms his passage. The deep, controlled moans of the Moonlight Sonata as he played it two nights ago are reverberating inside my head and the image of Valentin's airy ballet at the piano in his white tuxedo is blooming into a new painting against the audacious blue of this morning's Parisian sky. I remember Valentin telling me proudly, soon after our reunion backstage, that he had played in the same theatre where Igor Stravinsky's *Rite of Spring* once caused a scandal. Valentin's passage has marked this Parisian spring and its mysterious rites for Anushka and me with raw yearnings and lunar fantasies.

Ablaze

The eastern skies are aflame. The golden-leafed Flame of Liberty at the Alma Marceau Métro station acquires a new meaning in my jolted consciousness. Wide-eyed and bewildered, I am devouring the French newspapers as they roar about the fall of Communism. First comes Poland in the golden month of September, and Anushka is a riot of emotions. Even though she is only Polish by adoption, the weight of her Polish name and of Natalie's family stories about pre-war Fascism and post-war Communism in Poland is tugging at her conscience. Then comes Hungary in the autumnal chill of October and Anushka is Hungarian in her blood. We are both going through earthquakes of restlessness. All I can think of is: will it happen in Romania any time soon? On the ninth day of cold November, Germans are climbing on the Berlin Wall and hammering it down. On 10 November, Romania's most wretched neighbour, Bulgaria, overthrows its Communist leader. Pushing into the winter of everybody's discontent, on 27 November all of Czechoslovakia is on strike and come December their Communist government is no longer. More frantically than ever I keep asking: will it happen in Romania?

I am spending every spare minute with Agadira, Didona and

Anushka after our work, classes, shows, crowded in front of one of our small TV sets, either in the Lecourbe apartment or in my own miniature apartment on Rochechouart, or in Didona and Marcel's apartment in the Marais. *Le Monde, Le Figaro, Libération, Le Canard enchainé,* left- and right-wing French newspapers are strewn all round our apartments, clippings with images of people celebrating in the streets of Eastern Europe or on top of the Berlin Wall are spread all over our desks and tables. I am drawing on every piece of paper or canvas that I can get my hands on. I draw heads of state, maps of countries, trains, barriers, walls, barns, ships. I draw the map of my own country that I had always refused to draw in school during our art classes. I draw the map in flames, in reds and blues, in rainbow colours, in mourning colours, just like I had once drawn my own body, my black nude, my rainbow self-portraits in Istanbul. Agadira tells me calmly: 'Have a little patience, my dear, it will come any day now.' And the prophetess is right as always. There is no witchcraft, just knowing how to read people and events, I always said. There are riots in Timişoara, which is near Sighetu, near Anushka's birthplace. It all starts with the arrest of a Protestant Hungarian minister. Anushka is proud that the Romanian revolution is started by a Hungarian. We are all seized by nationalistic pride and hatred in our little Parisian apartments.

'The Romanians will start soon, just you wait,' says circus lady prophetess Didona. 'But when they do it's going to be bad,' she says.

'What do you mean, Didona?' I ask, surprised. 'These other countries haven't had much violence; it's all been relatively peaceful, hasn't it?' I say, worrying about new wars and bloody revolutions. I'm worrying about Gigi and about Valentin and my parents. Where are they, what can they be doing, will that long-awaited beast, that shiny freedom, come to their part of the world too? At what price? Anushka also wants to take the next plane to Bucharest. Since May, she has been exchanging with Valentin dozens of poetic letters about all the possible movements of the weather and all the musical forms from the rondo to the quartet to the requiem, in long tear-stained pages.

Didona thinks it will be violent, and that it's coming any day. On 22 December we are gathered in Sally's apartment in Montmartre together with Aleksey the Polish poet, Virgil the Romanian playwright, Roxana the Romanian musician, smoking, drinking cassis and one bottle of Chardonnay after another. We watched Ceauşescu being booed during his speech in the Palace Square in Bucharest on the 21st and now tanks are driving through the capital with crowds of people following them today. By Allah and by the God of France, Didona was right, for the Romanian revolution comes in with shootouts and barricades and street battles, a real war. I recognize the Bucharest streets that I had wandered on with Valentin after my art lessons with Miss Mantaş or during the week of our university exams. People are hiding behind cars and buildings, being shot at and shooting back. I knew then that Romanians could be just as savage as the people in English action movies. Virgil, the tough man and reckless womanizer, breaks into loud sobs. 'Our people are finally awake,' he sobs, 'they have finally picked up their guns.'

I am not in the least moved by his overflow of patriotic sentimentality. 'What guns?' I say. 'It's not like there were barrels of guns at street corners and we just decided not to pick them up and not to use them against our Party leaders while they were forcing us to have children when we didn't want any or to paint portraits of the Party leader until his curly lips seeped into our bloodstream, or when we lost our jobs and faced starvation and persecution at any whim of the secret police. And why do "our people", as you call them, have to be so violent? Where are they getting all those guns from?'

I don't know what to do, what to feel. Is it real, will tomorrow be a brand-new day in my birth country? Will we put together all the broken pieces of ourselves? A red door is opening and closing quickly. Behind the door is a wide, frightening abyss. We all want to open the door, it's irresistible: a glossy, freshly painted crimson door quivering on its hinges and begging to be opened. Behind the door is an infernal world of ghosts, caught in an orgiastic historical carnival: Stalin is dancing with Hitler, two pudgy moustached men swirling in a lascivious tango. Nicolae and Elena Ceauşescu are dancing the cha-cha with big gaping bloody holes in their heads.

I talk to my mother on the phone for the first time in over a year. Her voice is raspy and jerky. She says Mangalia is filled with homeless children, orphans. Where did they all come from? She has no idea, but that's what happened after the revolution, the streets became filled with orphans.

'Will you come home soon, Nora?' she asks, with a sudden softness that I don't remember.

'Not yet, Mama, I'm waiting for things to settle down a little. Besides, I am very busy at the art school, I have to take my exams . . . I'll come, but not just yet, Mama . . .'

'We brought the piano upstairs to the dining room, Nora. You would like to see how we've rearranged the house,' she says as if she hadn't heard what I just said.

'Why did they kill Ceauşescu, Mama?' I ask also as if I hadn't heard her.

'Because we are a savage people, that's why. They wanted revenge for all the years of suffering. He deserved it, the people were starving or dying in prisons while he was building his ruby-studded marble palace. But it was still savage and ugly, the way they did it . . . Nobody died in our town, thank God for that!'

I am happy that, for the first time since I left, my mother is talkative on the phone. We only talked four other times, once a year, either on my birthday or for Christmas. I can never remember what we said to each other when I called her from Istanbul but Lemi and Seda had made me call and tell my parents

I was doing well. That's what I must have told her or my father, who doesn't like talking on the phone; I must have said: *Mama, Tata, I am well, healthy, and everything is fine, Istanbul is beautiful.* My mother has become more political and less aggressive in her old age. She seems unfazed by the revolution, as if she was expecting it and now that it has happened, it isn't any big deal. Then she tells me: 'Take care of yourself, Nora my girl!'

Forget the Romanian revolution, forget the Berlin Wall collapsing, this is my revolution right here in my twenty-square-metre Parisian apartment as I am holding the phone and staring out of the window at the immigrant and French working-class families of my neighbourhood as they swarm home from work into or out of the Métro station. My mother calling me 'my girl' with special warmth in her voice: for the first time ever that I can remember, I feel loved. I can't say anything because of the tears choking me and my mother understands my silence. She is silent too. I hear her breathing, maybe sobbing.

I say without trying to hide my own sobs any longer: 'Goodbye, Mama, I miss you terribly . . . I will come home soon. Kiss Tata for me.'

The New Year descends over Paris with grey drizzle and waves of new refugees from the newly freed East European states. If they are free, why are people leaving in droves, I wonder, instead of staying there to rebuild their disoriented countries?

'They have to test their new freedom, Nora, they have to see that they *can* leave,' says Didona one evening as we enjoy a glass of wine after her new show, a modern rendition of Beaumarchais' *The Marriage of Figaro*, in which she plays Susanna. There are also new waves of Romanian Gypsies playing the accordion or the harmonica in the Métro or outside Parisian cafés, begging for a couple of coins. Didona and I both take out our wallets at the same time to offer a few francs to a young girl standing by our table with her hand stretched out. She is surprised to hear us speak Romanian, and Didona shocks her even more when she starts speaking Romani to her. I had no idea that Didona also spoke Mariţa's language and a penetrating nostalgia for the smell of burnt leaves and enchanting stories about Turkish princesses takes hold of me. The girl, whose name is Corina, tells us that there is chaos and looting and street children sniffing glue and stray dogs, everywhere in Romania. Her family, whom I see waiting at a distance, the father with an accordion, the mother with a harmonica, have come to Paris illegally, hiding on freight and passenger trains, trying to make some money and hoping to go back and start a business: a kiosk selling foreign soaps and chocolates. After the girl leaves with her fist tightly closed over her coins, Didona tells me that she too is thinking of going back soon.

'To visit, right?' I say, sipping my wine and watching the Gypsy family move through the crowd with their instruments, begging for coins.

'No, for good,' she says, leaving me open-mouthed in shock. 'I miss the circus, Nora, this is not enough for me. I love the theatre but the circus is in my blood, I've been doing it for as long as I can remember. I miss the lights, the colours, the din, the thrill of the crowds in the arena; there is nothing like it. My mama and tata are planning to go back first to see if they can get their old jobs back now that the old rats are gone.'

Anushka too keeps telling me she wants to go to Romania to see my brother, maybe something good will come out of it, maybe this time, who knows . . . ? I am surprised by these conflicting journeys of exodus: former immigrants are going back, while Romanian citizens are flooding the Western countries. Why can't everybody stay put for now and see how things go? Strangely, I have no desire to go back, although I told my mother I was coming home soon. I would like to see my mama and Gigi without having to return, meeting somewhere in the stratosphere above post-revolutionary realities and street children and stray dogs. The red line on the black water and the faces of angry naval officers and secret police in raincoats are still crowding my mind and making me tremble with anxiety.

'I am not going back.' I voice my thoughts out loud to Didona. 'Maybe I'll go to Burkina Faso with Agadira, I've always dreamed of going to Africa,' I say glibly.

But Didona understands me and she knows I am not joking about it. She shakes her waves of hair and says: 'I wouldn't go back if I were you either. You are making it here, you will be a famous artist one day, Nora. Just . . .' She is hesitating and I know what she wants to ask.

'You mean Gigi? I don't know. He is also in my blood like your circus is in your blood,' I say, laughing at the analogy. 'Gigi was always my carousel of joys and thrills, but so much time has passed I am scared of what I may find. I feel I need to let more time go by, that he needs to recover, put himself back together, before we can see each other and maybe start over . . .'

'Maybe?' says Didona, surprised.

'Yes, maybe. We have still to pass our big test, Didona. I don't know. I have changed and I have been through so much since I left. And bizarre as it may seem, I still feel complete, making it on my own, devoting all my time to my art . . . I'll have to see what time brings . . .'

Didona smiles and utters Mariţa's kind of lines: 'If he is in your blood, as you say, then blood will return to blood . . .'

'Oh great,' I laugh. 'You and Agadira always speaking in riddles and prophecies!'

We spend the rest of the evening walking arm in arm and talking about our lives and our plans for the future in the delicately ornate Place des Vosges. Didona is gradually transforming herself into a princess, a countess, a Gypsy circus girl, making plans for a bright future as queen of the new Bucharest circus, while I am thinking about what paintings to choose for the students' art show opening in a small gallery in the Marais next month. My first exhibition ever! And what will I call it?

This is a spring like no other. A new decade: the nineties. The eastern walls have collapsed, the skies have been lit up with revolutionary fires, a dictator's blood has soaked Balkan earth. We can't see it from Paris but I feel the path flowing backwards with no red line, just bumpy roads like those Brancusi had paced on with his birch-tree cane at the beginning of the century. I have called my collection of paintings *Looking for the Black Sea in Paris.* The show is set for 1 May and I am shivering with anxiety. Other students from our class will feature. Among them is Sally with collages of photographs and oils entitled *Outbursts.* Anushka is pale with lovesickness and yearning for my brother and whispers to me she wants to visit him soon and see if there is any hope for her. Despite the pallor, I can see she is happy to be suffering from love again. She has to spice her life with a little bit of suffering to know she is really alive. Didona and Agadira are helping out with the refreshments and handing out brochures to people coming in. Their contrasting and exotic beauty makes people stop in their tracks and turn their heads. Agadira wiggles her butt at every step and Didona glides over the shiny floors, barely touching them.

I am tipsy from the two glasses of wine I drank to calm the thumping of my heart and I am surprised at my own paintings. My art technique professors, Duquesne and Renaud, are both here flirting relentlessly with me. I am wearing a colour I hardly ever wear: a crimson knitted dress and a piece of black and gold African jewellery from Agadira. I feel sultry and light, and timidly content with myself. My six years of battles, despair, hope and hopelessness, my journeys and searches, are splattered in raw colours and wicked shapes over the ten paintings I was allowed to include in the show. Corners of the Black Sea and of the other seas and oceans I have appropriated are bursting from almost every painting, and superimposing themselves on Parisian sights, or on portraits of people, from my three sister friends to unknown people in the street, to Mimi Tournelle, and of course to Gigi whose face is hidden like a clue to my heart in at least half of the works. I have used tempera, acrylics and gouache on heavy paper or on canvas board and have even experimented with woodblocks covered in Japanese paper – truly mixed media. For the colour of the sea I have mixed Prussian blue with chrome yellow, the way Van Gogh did to produce his greens when he was really poor. The colour that emerged from his despair and misery, that's the one I use to depict my sea waters. Some works have an eerie transparency, others are severely opaque and the colours strident, almost jungle-like. A little bit of Frida, a little bit of Esma, a little bit of Balchik and Queen Marie's itinerant heart searching for a place to rest. A lot of Nora's searches into her own itinerant heart and frenetic journeys through the world. It's in the acrylics and their dazzling brightness that I have let out my screams of joy, puzzle and sorrow. They are the most unrestrained of all, created against the advice of my teachers and the guidelines of the school. I start hearing compliments and expressions of awe as the evening goes on. '*C'est inoui, vraiment, tout à fait original* . . .' says an older woman with silver-white hair and a face like Egyptian parchment. '*Regarde ça, c'est super, n'est-ce pas?*' says a young man in a grey jacket and dark glasses. There is whispering, voices are crossing each other and getting higher and lower, a lot of laughter, my head is turning on this sparkling Mayday. My professors are patting me on the back proudly. '*Bravo, Nora, tu as de la veine comme je te l'ai dit la première fois* . . .' You have guts, says M. Duquesne.

At some point there is a commotion and loud voices, as if something has changed or intruded into the harmony of the evening. I don't pay any attention. I am talking and giggling with Anushka and Didona, who are relating to me all the gossip they hear around us.

'You are a hit if you managed to impress this tired old

pretentious French crowd. You have a bright future ahead of you, girl!' says Anushka, looking radiant in her silvery silk dress.

'Now you just have to become rich selling your paintings,' says Didona with a twinkle, always thinking of the practical side of things.

'If I do, I'll buy you a circus, your own personal circus,' I say when my eyes stop on the sight at the entrance of the gallery.

The owner, a tall woman with dyed black hair, is raising her voice and telling someone they cannot come in, this is by invitation only. I go towards the entrance and see a shabby man who looks like some pathetic incarnation of Jesus Christ: his hair and beard form an enormous mane around his head while his eyes have a soulful, deep look that I can't resist. I don't want any unpleasantness tonight, so I decide I have to defuse the situation. I quickly go to Mme Rochelle, the owner, and tell her calmly not to worry, that the man is my friend and I had forgotten to give him an invitation. I go to the bearded intruder and look at him more closely. But when I try to say something, my mouth clenches. The eyes, the unmistakable cat eyes, are staring back at me. I tell the owner again, he's all right, an old friend. I take his hand, guide him through the crowd that is staring at me and place him right in front of three of my best paintings: the one with me and Gigi in a hammock on a ship slicing through the Mediterranean, the one of Didona in Place du Tertre standing on her head, with a corner of sea in the distance, and my Frida self-portrait with the face of Gigi imprinted in the centre of my forehead. He whispers my name. That's when it all starts turning: the gallery, the faces of the people, the paintings around me, the street outside the gallery and the people passing by and looking inside. I dare to embrace him and he embraces me back. He is only skin and bones. His body is scrawny but stronger than I ever knew it to be. He lifts me up and I feel his tears on my cheeks, his wet beard. Our childhood, our adolescence, my blood, my flesh, our sea, our love, the red line . . . I hear people whispering, talking, giggling, it all happens in a dream. I am not letting go of my stranger.

'I like best the one of us on the ship,' he whispers. His voice is raspy, tired, sexy.

'Happy birthday, my love,' I whisper back in his ear, still not letting go, remembering the party I once gave for Gigi on his birthday, 1 May. I see my three sisters at the back staring at us with tears in their eyes. Agadira is taking charge and telling everyone that I'm all right, I'll be all right, just enjoy the show. She winks at me and makes a sign with her hand for me to disappear. And disappear we do in the Parisian night.

Stranger Love

I don't remember exactly how we got back to my apartment, except that we took a taxi and did not ease up from our embrace. I remember Gigi carrying me up the staircase all the way to the third floor and us bursting into the apartment and falling on the bed that occupied almost my entire room. He had become stronger and didn't flinch or pant from carrying me up three long flights of stairs in the dark. The chaos of the first minutes . . . the mixture of tears, laughter, words, the night air enveloping us together with the street sounds in French that entered the window. It was Valentin who had arranged and paid for his trip. He had called Anushka to find out the exact day that my show opened and what I would be doing. He wanted the timing to be perfect. So Anushka knew of the impending surprise, apparition, that was why she was so nervous and quivering with emotion at the opening. My brother's bottomless box of surprises and Anushka's newly discovered wicked love of surprises.

It took us a while to recognize and explore each other all over again. Gigi was a new man, yet the man I had always imagined he would become. It was confusing and painful that it took four years of prison hell and almost another two years out of prison, living on the very margins of an already depleted and desperate society, for him to become the man I could fall in love with all over again. I had recognized him by his eyes, his smile and his embrace in the art gallery. He had come to me in unrecognizable shape, a stranger, a man from the street, bearded and dressed like a vagabond, taking refuge inside an art gallery where I happened to be having my first show. But then he unfolded under my very eyes like some enchanted prince from fairy tales who casts off all evil spells and scaly skins upon the kiss of a woman. She recognizes him for what he is: the one next to whom life is a thrill and a carousel, an oasis and a walk through apricot blossoms even in the midst of a dry desert or a dizzying storm.

It was only when the dark reddish Viking beard was off his face that I both recognized the old Gigi, the pretty boy whose smile used to brighten my entire world on even the darkest days throughout our adolescence, and discovered the new man who had survived the unsurvivable. It took him months to tell all the hideous stories of torture, beatings, hunger, cold, being chained standing in the middle of the cell, scratching my name on the walls, the two-by-two prison cell with a small barred window. He talked of the forced labour, the walks in chains in the prison yard, the endless, indeterminate flow of black days. At first he didn't want to talk about it, he just wanted to describe our town in the days and months following the revolution. He talked about his own experience of the revolution more than anything else at first. How he had gone to Timişoara in the days right after it had started, because he wanted to be there, in the middle of the action and of that momentous reversal of order. How he had fought in the streets of that beautiful city next to Hungarians and Romanians, how he had shot at people. How he had been shot at, but somehow never touched, as if his prison past had granted him a magic immunity from bullets.

Three days after his arrival we had our first and last huge fight. We had stayed inside the small apartment rediscovering each other's bodies, talking, making love, sleeping, making love again and surviving on the little food I had in my cupboards and refrigerator. The outside world had ceased to exist and we might as well have been in Istanbul or in Alaska. His body had lost its youthful roundness and was now edgy and bony, with several scars that each told a dark story. His freckled chest was stronger and wider and his face thinner and more angular. He had several greyish hairs in his curls that were still the same beautiful reddish brown as ever. Suddenly, on the third day, Gigi looked at me while still lying in bed and asked me to forgive him.

'What in the world should I forgive you for?' I asked, surprised, thinking some kind of strange joke was coming up.

He looked at me with a frown and almost a shadow of shame and said: 'That summer, I kissed Anushka . . . you know, those days at the beach . . . or she kissed me rather . . . I was a young stupid boy.'

Unfazed, and still reeling from the huge upheaval of the last three days, I replied: 'So did I kiss my art professor . . .' I couldn't believe my own ears, particularly since I had never done anything of the sort.

'So did you what?' he asked.

'So did I kiss my art professor, M. Duquesne, as I was posing for him. In the nude!' I was entirely shocking myself with each word that came out of my mouth, like I had once when I was suffering from amnesia in Istanbul.

'You posed in the nude?' Gigi's face was acquiring a greenish pallor.

'What do you think women do in art school anyway?' I said and jumped off the bed abruptly.

Gigi became furious like I had never seen him throughout all our years of growing up together, since it didn't seem to be in his temperament to get furious, at least not the way everybody in my family always did. Then I became furious too and the sour pain I had suffered more than ten years ago came back with a vengeance. The agony I experienced when I suspected that Anushka was trying to seduce Gigi and how I had some kind of cerebral fever because I had heard them talking in the street at night right by my bedroom window.

We threw recriminations and accusations in each other's face for hours in the small apartment in Boulevard Rochechouart, until the neighbours started banging on the walls and yelling at us to stop making so much noise. I yelled right back at them to leave us alone and go to bloody hell. Cheap Parisian apartments offered you the experience of communal life and of partaking in everybody's misery or ecstasy, whether you cared to or not. How could Gigi be so devious and cheat on me that summer, who else did he sleep with, how could he do such a thing? Who else had I slept with, he asked, how many men, in the six years we'd been separated? Had I posed nude in the centre of Paris? I could have earned more money that way, he said. I replied that I regretted not having been a lot more unfaithful, and that paintings of me nude were displayed all over Paris; he said he regretted just being unfaithful once, though you couldn't really call that unfaithful . . . The recognition that something did go on between Gigi and Anushka sent me into another bout of rage until I finally told him to go right back to the fucking stupid country that he came from. We were panting, red and sweaty from the waves of anger and all the frustrated passion of the last decade. The air in the room was quivering with the words we had thrown at each other like poisoned swords. When I wanted to attack Gigi, he grabbed my hands and immobilized me, stared in my eyes for a few heavy seconds and said:

'Just say the word, Nora, and I'll go away and you'll never see or hear from me again. Just say it! If that's what you want,' he added, looking a little to the side towards the window. 'But if you want me to stay and you have the same love you once had, then we can rebuild everything, we can finally create our magical coral castle, remember?' For the first time since his arrival, his face freshly shaved, I noticed how beautiful his profile had become: statuesque, with the straight yet slightly turned-up nose, the high cheekbones and the smooth forehead on which the same rowdy curls fell in disarray. My true Adonis boy! Maybe a future with Gigi, after all the agonizing experiences we had each gone through, and the huge rift that time had made between us, would be filled with storms and uncertainties, would be rough and disorderly, but the alternative was inconceivable. In that moment, with Gigi's hands forcefully holding my hands in his and as I stared at his elegant profile, the alternative of never seeing that face again was unthinkable. The alternative was an endless reiteration of my black nude in lonely hallways of fogged-up mirrors. It would be blackness like my amnesia period in Istanbul. I had waited for this stranger for years.

'That Anushka . . . she's something, isn't she?' I said and started laughing uncontrollably. 'I never kissed any art professor,' I said, and added wickedly: 'But maybe I should have, my grades might have been better . . .'

My hungry and love-deprived body devoured Gigi's for hours. Gigi was emerging with every new embrace into a smooth and powerful man, a most alluring and irresistible stranger whose skin still smelled and tasted of our beloved salty Black Sea.

An indomitable energy exploded from Gigi in the weeks and months to come, as if part of him had long been asleep. He worked two jobs, one in the hospital where Hajid still worked as a nurse and one at a travel agency on the Champs-Elysées. At night he studied French and repeated complicated sentences from an audio programme of French for foreigners. It took him no effort to obtain those jobs and with the same ease he studied for the naval engineering school of Paris Tech. Whenever he entered an office and smiled one of his colourful smiles, French women woke up from whatever they were doing and listened, enraptured, to his heavily accented French. Secretaries wiggled their bottoms and tilted their heads in some kind of silly flirtatiousness whenever he talked to them or just passed by. His cat eyes sparkled through the Parisian streets and offices with cunning and confidence. I always remembered the evening of his birthday party in our house so many years ago, when I watched him move and dance and smile with such ease, and thought that he had united the sunniest of the sea and the earth where we grew up and that he was going to be every girl's dream. The only thing that betrayed something of his past were his fits while sleeping, which looked like nightmares. He would suddenly choke in his sleep, his breathing became irregular and his hands scratched the air. His nightly struggles were quiet and breathless. I would gently touch his arm and he would go back to sleep. I never mentioned the fits in the morning; something kept me from it, an unexplained embarrassment.

After he passed his entrance exam to Paris Tech and we were both drunk from all the wine with which we had celebrated his results, I said, throwing myself on our bed: 'Don't you think that now, since we are becoming a little bit more respectable among East European refugees in Paris, it's time we moved out of this lousy apartment into a nicer one?'

He smiled happily, threw himself on his stomach next to me and said: 'Absolutely, my love. And how about if we got married too? Will you be my wife, Nora Teodoru?'

Although it shouldn't have, the question took me by surprise. I felt married to Gigi already. I remembered the stupid argument we had had in the street, many years ago, the night after his birthday party, after I suggested marriage and he mentioned converting. *Why get married now?* I thought.

So all I could say to his romantic quest for marriage was: 'Why?'

Unflinching, Gigi rolled one of my brown curls on his finger, with the old gesture he had used since our childhood, and said: 'Because it could be fulfilling to be married to each other. And who knows, at some point we might even want to have a child.'

When he said that, there was a crack in myself. Suddenly I am lying in a pool of blood, with something cold and slimy between my legs. There is no electricity. I am lying on a Turkish bed with unknown faces staring at me. I am lying in my own bed at number 9 with cerebral fever. I am being eaten alive by poisonous jellyfish. In every image, I am lying in some bed and slowly dying. It's not neat and dignified the way I had wanted my death to be, but messy and bloody. I have no parents, I have no country, I have no love. What did Gigi do all these years, what kind of work did he do after he got out of prison, why didn't he mention the painting I sent him with Valentin? Why is Gigi so calm, so unscathed, why does he say so little about what happened? What do we do now that everybody's free? I still haven't had the courage to go back and see my parents. It's been more than a year since the revolution, a year since Gigi appeared in the gallery during my first exhibition. We gobble up time, recklessly thinking we are making it in Paris. But we are strangers to each other and to ourselves, and we have forgotten so much. We just remember little slices of trauma, just enough to make the natives feel sorry for us. And what does 'making it in Paris' really mean?

'No, Gigi, I won't marry you, or anyone. I don't want to get married . . . I don't want to have children. I don't know who I am or who you are. I have to find out first.'

Gigi's arrival and his new refugee status reflected mine like a broken mirror. I saw bits of myself scattered in no coherent order and my own face and heart were unrecognizable. Everything we had lived together before the night of 11 August and the red line of the border patrol seemed irrelevant here in Paris with Gigi reflecting my own confusion and estrangement. When he was away, I could carry everything inside me like a well-packaged pulsing heart. I could idealize my memories and feel superior to all those who hadn't lived what I had lived through. But Gigi had his own frightful packaged pulsing heart and I had no idea what it was saying and what I was supposed to do with it. And I had no idea how to bridge the abyss that stretched between the two points in time: the red line between Romanian and Turkish waters and the moment when Gigi appeared at my exhibition looking like a stranger. I missed that puzzling yet familiar stranger, those electric first minutes when I was falling in love with a delinquent-looking dusty vagabond. And this familiar Gigi seemed more of a stranger every day.

We moved through more weeks of confusion and hesitations until the evening he told me everything, in no particular order other than that of his conscience. Then I started weaving my own avatars until we became each other's Scheherazade in a battle of stories for survival.

'I killed a man during the revolution, Nora!' he announced to me one evening as if he had just won a big prize.

'What man?' I asked in a stupor.

'Nobody knew for sure who was shooting whom, you know; there was such chaos in the streets and yet it was so utterly exciting.' Gigi's eyes were wild and shiny yellow amber like the eyes of the cats on Eminonu Street when he told me that. He scared me and yet I loved the thrill that he gave me.

'I was walking down this street in Timişoara, a hilly street like you see only in that part of the country, and suddenly I hear a conversation between a man dressed in army uniform and a civilian: "Shoot him, shoot the motherfucker!" said the army man.' Gigi was becoming each one of the characters in his story: angry soldier, civilian caught in the fight. "Shoot the guy coming towards us, can't you see the motherfucker, just shoot him, are you deaf?"' Gigi was standing up on our bed in his pyjama bottoms, his torso bare, drops of sweat glistening on his tanned body, his cat eyes fierce and murderous. '"Keep the terrorist thing going, shoot him!"' He was yelling at the top of his lungs, playing the psycho soldier, and our neighbours started knocking on the walls again for us to shut up. 'Shut up yourselves!' I yelled back, caught up entirely in Gigi's revolution. It was only now, seeing him enact what must have been a fiercely chaotic and violent night in the middle of Timişoara, that the famous revolution came alive for me. The terrorists were the old *securitate*, explained Gigi, but those nights in Timişoara, Bucharest, Braşov, it was hard to know who was who. I saw it all in Gigi's eyes and in the quiver of his tight muscles as they strained to enact one shooting after another. One of the scars on his chest became darker, almost bloody with the strain.

'Then I saw the man coming down the street, the one they wanted to shoot to keep the terrorist thing going: he was a young man in a dark blue parka, smiling confidently and carrying an automatic rifle like it was no big deal.' Now Gigi took on the carefree, confident air of the young revolutionary in a blue parka. 'I shot the army man,' he announced proudly. My Gigi turned out to be a bona fide assassin, a murderer, a revolutionary. A hero of sorts? *My kind of man*, I found myself thinking.

'Then the civilian noticed me hiding behind a blue Dacia and pointed his gun at me. I killed him first . . . in self-defence. The army man and the civilian both lay dead next to each other – both killed by me,' he concluded and threw himself exhausted on the bed. Then he stared at the ceiling with two streaks of tears coming down his face. So Gigi killed two men. He had only said one in the beginning, but in fact it was two. Now that made him a hero. He could have been killed but wasn't. That made him a miracle. He killed first, his life hanging on that second: a Russian roulette of life and death. A bullet coming from the other direction shot the young revolutionary in the blue parka anyway. Sometimes Gigi's story told itself and he just kept up with it.

'I can still see the young man in the blue parka coming down the street,' resumed Gigi, his eyes shiny and fixed on a point on the ceiling. 'He had dark, soulful eyes and was scrawny like your brother Valentin. He was breathing in the winter air, bursting with revolutionary excitement. I thought of his life then in those split seconds and imagined it. They say you see your life flash past your eyes in your last seconds of life, but the funny thing was, I saw *his* life in *his* last seconds of life: he had a mother and a girlfriend who were waiting for him anxiously but he wanted to be out in the night to feel this new gust of freedom a bit longer. I had to save him but I couldn't. The hell of a revolution that was, really!'

Gigi knew he had to save the young revolutionary in the blue parka at all cost, so he shot the man who was going to shoot him. I would have shot him too, I tell Gigi. It's in this one piece of Gigi's puzzle that the revolution fully comes to life for me. In the seconds of utmost solidarity between Gigi and an unknown man in the street excited about freedom. And it is only in that piece that I grasp the full absurdity of it as well.

When he goes back to the prison part of his story I become itchy and agitated. I stare at the wall, unmoving, as he tells me about the beatings he received in the middle of the night in his cell and the near-drownings as they stuck his head in a bucket filled with cold water. 'Good thing I was such a good swimmer,' Gigi laughed cynically. The beatings time and again as they tried to get more information about our escape, about Mr Bekta, about other people who might have helped us. Although he was thrown in jail with regular criminals and murderers, there were others in there locked up for political reasons. There were people who died in the neighbouring cells: the professor who had ulcers and received no treatment, the gypsy man who had helped three others escape across the border to Yugoslavia and died from the beatings. And again and again, the scratching on the walls until his fingernails bled and he wrote my name in blood on the cement of his prison cell.

I told Gigi I had amnesia in Istanbul, I could well have killed someone in the streets of Istanbul but I wouldn't remember. I almost died the night of the escape. I had gone into hypothermia and some kind of shock. The captain of the Turkish ship brought me unconscious into Lemi and Seda's house. Several times I had thought of letting myself die. Seda had taught me to cook Turkish desserts and never to think of suicide again. She taught me how to go through a day thinking of all the reasons not to commit suicide. That was why I decided to work in a pastry shop when I came to Paris, to keep myself from committing suicide. No matter how grey those streets and how lonely the life of a poor refugee in Paris, you wanted to put it off, at least for that moment, when you smelled the dough baking or saw the chocolate mousse hardening in the moulds. 'How many bakers in the world have committed suicide?' I ask Gigi.

'How many?' he asks.

'None,' I say proudly. 'Fruit tarts and almond pistachio cakes saved my life. They did, literally!' I insist to a sceptical Gigi.

The torpedo-launching ship that Gigi and I got near to during our big fiasco of an adventure when we swam too close to the port was a guided missile destroyer built by the Romanians following the 1960s Soviet design of torpedo launchers and submarine chasers. It was called a national destroyer. This was supposed to be the biggest ship of its kind built outside the Soviet Union in the Warsaw Pact countries. It wasn't clear why Romania's ambition to build warships was so formidable. Why did my country need a national destroyer, didn't we already have our own national destroyer, that psycho leader of ours? And why was our small city of Mangalia the one graced with such honour? It was in order to fit the size of its Communist dictatorship. It was Gigi's opinion that underneath Ceauşescu's pretence of being more independent from the Soviet Union, we were actually the country most dependent on Russian power. Because of his expert knowledge of naval engineering and of the shipyard, Luca had been asked to join the team of engineers building the ship. But then when the officers found out about Gigi's and my night escapade in the vicinity of the destroyer, they thought Luca was a spy and he was placed under house arrest for a year.

Bugging devices were installed throughout their house. Gigi said that, after the revolution, they found tiny microphones even behind their toilet. In case someone in their family was going to 'leak' something while taking a leak, laughed Gigi, proud of his crude joke. Romanians imported the bugging systems from East Germany, he said.

Luca used every single acquaintance and resource to try to get Gigi out of prison. He petitioned the police authorities in Constanța and Bucharest. Was there going to be a trial? he wanted to know. When were they going to let his son out of prison? Every meeting ended with him being asked to come again, to go to a different office, write a new petition, walk through more dark corridors that led nowhere but to more damp offices with embittered clerks. Finally, after four years, his argument that his son would make a good worker in the shipyard, that he could be rehabilitated by working in the service of the State and the Party, struck a chord with an official. That was how Gigi was released from prison and made to work in the shipyard, finishing the big Soviet torpedo launcher, under oath of secrecy and threat of ending his sorry days back in prison if he told anyone what he was doing at work. And then suddenly all work stopped and the Party no longer wanted to finish the ship. There was no logic to anything the State and the Party did, Gigi concluded.

As he was telling his implausible James Bond version of Romanian spy stories, it appeared to me that Gigi was only now fully becoming himself. It was like a statue receiving the last touch that makes it truly complete: a final indentation in the marble that brings out the expression, or a final polish that gives it its full meaning and beauty. Before, Gigi's contours had always seemed slightly fluid, hard to grasp and to explain. Like a face seen in a watery mirror. He was luminous and charming and I had needed that side of him desperately during my tormented adolescence. He was a tender and a most enthralling lover. His dominant trait had been his smiling. But smiling was not enough. Though I knew it was unfair to think so, I felt that it was the reason why he hadn't made it past the line between Turkish and Romanian waters that night. He wasn't sure; he wasn't sure to the very marrow of his bones and desperate enough to cross it. He was a faster swimmer than I was, he should have been ahead of me.

Gigi had acquired a new gesture that punctuated his speech and his personality and that only became visible to me during his breathless stories that filled the gaping abyss between then and now. It was a gesture of his hand in the air. He would grab the air, close his fist with a quick move and bring his hand back to his chin. He sometimes looked me straight in the eyes, without a smile, with a sharp intensity that gathered in his light brown eyes. Then he smiled. And then his smiles took me by surprise instead of fulfilling an expectation, the way they once used to.

Our little apartment had become a space for exorcism and healing. The walls were filled to the last centimetre with my drawings, watercolours, sketches, acrylics and oils, a true jungle of viscera and emotional explosions. Every piece of furniture was covered in African spreads or in my own strident concoctions that I had created at my sewing machine. There were diagrams and blueprints of ships of all models and sizes on the floor and on the table in the main room. They looked elegant and mysterious in their codified signs and maths. It gave me particular pleasure to see Gigi's mind displayed in complicated geometrical schemes and figures and it gave me a deeper understanding of a part of him I had never understood very well. Gigi's sometimes precise and cutting gestures with his hands, the way he never overused his hands or face in an abundance of gestures and expressions the way most Romanians I knew did, seemed perfectly in tune with the sharply drawn blueprints of mega ships. There were tea and coffee pots and cups on every bit of counter space in the kitchen, red and white wine bottles in wooden crates on the floor, rolling pins and dough recipes spread all over the kitchen table and little tin jars with spices and nuts for all kinds of dessert.

I had stopped seeing all my friends for a while. After work and my art classes I rushed home as if possessed. Gigi entered our room breathlessly from his two jobs and engineering classes. We cooked side by side, mixed condiments and kneaded dough with fury. We went through a bottle of wine every evening and threw ourselves into our stories the way we had once dived into the shimmering emerald surface of the Black Sea. Little by little a timid thread started to stretch across the precipice between 11 August 1984 and 1 May 1990. A shiny path on which we could attempt to take little steps again, like the moon paths that used to stretch across the dark gliding plates of the sea on the nights of our adolescence. Little by little I got to know and irrevocably fall in love with the stranger in my room. Gigi's scars matched my asymmetrical body. He showed me his scars again and again. They were smooth and dark.

I had to find myself in order to fully understand what our pre-11 August life had truly meant and what it could still mean for us now. How we had moulded each other by the shores of that enchantress the Black Sea and how we had to begin again in our new moulds: our post-revolutionary-Romanian-refugees-in-Paris moulds. Then we had to break the moulds once more, crush them to pieces and see what was left. We had to see if it was enough, if we could start again with the bloody pieces of those broken moulds. As a first step, I was incomprehensibly happy that Gigi had killed two men in the revolution. Isn't that what people do in revolutions? He had spent four hellish years in prison. I would have killed someone too. Gigi shot the first man from a noble impulse and the second in self-defence, even if it all turned out to be a mess. They were all on the revolutionary side anyway. Gigi had killed the military man and the civilian who wanted to kill the man in the blue parka. Romanians ran their revolution circus-style too. I was laughing and crying simultaneously at that portion of the show and at Gigi's stark and ironic recounting of it.

We devoured the days through the summer and autumn of that

year with our stories. The night when we felt utterly depleted, I asked Gigi to go for a walk. It was now winter and had started to snow and I had a fierce desire to leave that apartment with all the screaming traces of our exorcisms and to cross as much of Paris as possible on foot in the snow. To take a break from my sea fantasies and test the new earth of this new decade of the post-revolutionary era, arm in arm with my stranger. We walked on the long boulevards in the growing dusk and under the playful snowflakes as all the dirt of the day was mercifully shrouded in the ephemeral white veil.

Slowly I feel us merge into the snowy Parisian landscape. We are part of its watery mirage. Gigi and Nora, two foreigners in Paris, walking arm in arm and giving that impressionist painting by Pissarro or by Monet its final edge, its last touch. There we are on Boulevard Montmartre, on a snowy December evening, two refugees finding refuge in each other.

Just look at those two, the crowds of visitors are saying. Do you see them, over there in the distance? She has curly brown hair and he has curly red hair, they are both wearing old-fashioned green coats. What a funny couple! They seem to melt into each other. His arm is tight around her waist and her head is leaning on his shoulder. They must be in love. They are part of the landscape and yet separate from it. But the landscape would collapse without them in the distance. Despite its melancholy, it is a happy vision. It's the couple in the distance that gives the joyous note to the whole snowy landscape. And the little ballerina in the corner in a pink outfit, I hadn't noticed that. Quite original, isn't it though? The title of the painting is *Carnival in the Snow.* Who's the artist? Oh, it's a Romanian: Nora Teodoru. Haven't heard of her but she has guts. I wonder if that's her in the painting, that brown-haired woman on the arm of the red-haired man. Maybe it's a self-portrait.

Acknowledgements

First and foremost I wish to express my gratitude to my wonderful editor, Jessica Broughton from Transworld Publishers, for her elegant, inspired and precise editorial work. She has offered me invaluable guidance in tightening, polishing and bringing out the best in the writing of *Black Sea Twilight.*

I would like to thank my agent, Jodie Rhodes, for her staunch support of my writing, as well as my foreign rights agents, Vicky Satlow and Jill Hughes. I acknowledge Washington and Lee University for the support with sabbatical leave of absence during the 2009–2010 academic year and for the Lenfest 2009 summer grant, which allowed me to complete my novel and to travel for research needed for its completion.

Finally, I owe a debt of gratitude to my family for their support and appreciation of my creative work.

Bibliography

History and Culture

Braham, Randolph, *The Politics of Genocide: The Holocaust in Hungary*, Wayne State University Press, 2000

The Nazi's Last Victims: The Holocaust in Hungary, Wayne State University Press, 2002

Constante, Lena, *The Silent Escape: Three Thousand Days in Romanian Prisons*, University of California Press, 1995

Dusleag, Dan L. and Stroia, Stanciu, *My Second University: Memories from Romanian Communist Prisons*, iUniverse Inc, 2005

Fonseca, Isabel, *Bury Me Standing: Gypsies and Their Journey*, Vintage, 1996

Franciosi, Robert (ed.), *Elie Wiesel: Conversations*, University Press of Mississippi, 2002

Glajar, Valentina and Radulescu, Domnica (eds.), *"Gypsies" in European Literature and Culture*, Palgrave Macmillian, 2008

Hancock, Ian, *We are the Romani People*, University of Hertfordshire Press, 2002

Hirsch, Marianne and Spitzer, Leo, *Ghosts of Home: The Afterlife of Czernowitz in Jewish Memory*, University of California Press, 2010

Ioanid, Radu, *The Holocaust in Romania*, Ivan R. Dee, the United States Holocaust Memorial Museum, 2000

Kligman, Gail, 'Abortion and International Adoption in Post-Ceaușescu Romania', in *Feminist Studies* 1992, 18(2):405–19

The Politics of Duplicity: Controlling Reproduction in Ceaușescu's Romania, University of California Press, 1998

Liegeois, Jean-Pierre, *Gypsies: An Illustrated History*, Saqi Books, 2005
Mandache, Diana, *Later Chapters of My Life: The Lost Memoir of Queen Marie of Romania*, The History Press, 2004
Marcu, Rozen, *Holocaust Survivors and Remembrance Project*, http://isurvived.org/2Postings/2MarcuRozen-2book/023-Data_Tables.html
Oisteanu, Andrei, *Inventing the Jew: Antisemitic Stereotypes in Romanian and Other Central-East European Cultures*, University of Nebraska Press, 2009
Pakula, Hannah, *The Last Romantic: A Biography of Queen Mary of Romania*, Weidenfeld & Nicolson History, 1996
Stefan, Bruno, *New Europe, Old Jails: The European Integration of the Romanian Penitentiary Culture and Civilization*, Create Space, 2009
Veteranyi, Aglaja, *Warum das Kind in der Polenta kocht*, Dtv, 2001
Wiesel, Elie, *And the Sea is Never Full*, Knopf, 1999
Memoirs: All Rivers Run to the Sea, Schocken, 1996
Night, Bantam Books, 1982
Jew Today, Vintage, 1979

Art and Art History

Adams, Laurie, *A History of Western Art Revised*, McGraw Hill, 2008
Balas, Edith, *Brancusi and His World*, Carnegie-Mellon University Press, 2008
Baldwin, Ann, *Creative Paint Workshop for Mixed-Media Artists: Experimental Techniques for Composition, Layering, Texture, Image and Encaustic*, Quarry Books, 2009
Carp, Gabriela, Covrig, Ana Maria, and Jianou, Lionel Scanteye Ionel (trans. Samuelli, Annie), *Romanian Artists in the West*, American Romanian Academy of Arts and Sciences, 1983
Cole, Bruce, Gealt, Adelheid and Wood, Michael, *Art of the Western World: From Ancient Greece to Post Modernism*, Simon & Schuster, 1991
Drakulic, Slavenka and Pribichevich-Zoric, Christina, *Frida's Bed*, Penguin, 2008
Fernandez, Dominique, *Romanian Rhapsody: An Overlooked Corner of Europe*, Algora Publishing, 2000
Fuentes, Carlos and Lowe, Sarah M., *The Diary of Frida Kahlo: An Intimate Self-Portrait*, Harry N. Abrams, 2006
Janson, Anthony F. and Janson H. W., *History of Art, The Western Tradition, Volume II: Renaissance through Postmodern Art*, Prentice Hall, 2001

Kemp, Martin, *The Oxford History of Western Art*, Oxford University Press, 2002
Manea, Norman, *On Clowns: The Dictator and the Artist*, Grove Press, 1994
Mayer, Ralph, *The Artist's Handbook of Materials and Techniques*, Viking Adult, 1991
Metzger, Rainer and Walther, Ingo, *Van Gogh*, Taschen, 2008
Mujica, Barbara, *Frida*, Plume, 2002
Pearson, James, *Constantin Brancusi: Sculpting Within the Essence of Things*, Crescent Moon Publishing, 2008
Reyner, Nancy, *Acrylic Revolution: New Tricks and Techniques for Working with the World's Most Versatile Medium*, North Light Books, 2007
Roskill, Mark (ed.), *The Letters of Vincent Van Gogh*, Touchstone, 2008
Schaefer, Claudia, *Frida Kahlo: A Biography*, Greenwood Press, 2008
Smith, Ray Campbell, *The Artist's Handbook*, DK Adult, 2009
Varia, Radu, *Brancusi: Revised Edition*, Rizzoli, 2003

Psychology and Philosophy

Baddeley, Alan, *Essentials of Human Memory*, Taylor & Francis, 1999
Courage, Mary and Cowan, Nelson (eds.), *The Development of Memory in Infancy and Childhood*, Psychology Press, 2008
Neiman, Susan, *Evil in Modern Thought*, Princeton University Press, 2004
Ricoeur, Paul, *Memory, History, Forgetting*, University of Chicago Press, 2006
Schacter, Daniel L., *Searching For Memory: The Brain, The Mind And The Past*, Basic Books, 1997
The Seven Sins of Memory: How the Mind Forgets and Remembers, Mariner Books, 2002
Segal, Nancy L., *Entwined Lives: Twins and What They Tell Us About Human Behavior*, Plume, 2000
Terr, Lenore, *Unchained Memories: True Stories of Traumatic Memories Lost and Found*, Basic Books, 1995
Wright, Lawrence, *Twins: And What They Tell Us About Who We Are*, John Wiley & Sons, 1999

Domnica Radulescu won a national prize for a volume of short stories when she was twenty, just before she fled her native Romania during Nicolae Ceauşescu's dictatorship. She settled in the United States as a political refugee in 1983.

She is a Professor of French and Italian Literature and Chair of the Women's and Gender Studies Program at Washington and Lee University in Virginia. She has authored and edited numerous books, collections and articles on Western classical and modern theatre, women and comedy, exile narratives, representations of women in literature and culture, and performance studies. She has worked in the theatre, directed numerous plays and is the founding director of The National Symposium of Theatre in Academe.

Her first novel, *Train to Trieste*, won the Library of Virginia Award for Best Fiction. *Black Sea Twilight* is her second novel. She lives in Lexington, Virginia, with her two sons.